THE MAYAN RED QUEEN

Tz'aakb'u Ahau of Palenque

THE MAYAN RED QUEEN

Tz'aakb'u Ahau of Palenque

Born 610 CE - Married 626 CE - Died 672 CE

Leonide Martin

Mists of Palenque Series Book 3

Made for Wonder PUBLISHING

Made for Success
P.O. Box 1775
Issaquah, WA 98027

The Mayan Red Queen: Tz'aakb'u Ahau of Palenque

Designed by Dee Dee Heathman

Library of Congress Cataloging-in-Publication data

Martin, Leonide
    The Mayan Red Queen: Tz'aakb'u Ahau of Palenque
    The Mists of Palenque Series Book 3

    p. cm.
    ISBN: 978-1-61339-917-0
    LCCN: 2018931255

To contact the publisher,
please email service@MadeforSuccess.net or call +1 425 657 0300.
Made for Wonder is an imprint of Made for Success Publishing.
Printed in the United States of America

CONTENTS

List of Characters and Places

Tz'aakb'u Ahau – Characters

Royal Family of Lakam Ha
Tz'aakb'u Ahau* — wife of Janaab Pakal, called Lalak
K'inich Janaab Pakal* — ruler of Lakam Ha (615-683 CE), husband of Lalak
Sak K'uk* — ruler of Lakam Ha (612-615 CE), mother of Janaab Pakal
Kan Mo' Hix* — husband of Sak K'uk
Kan Bahlam II* — first son of Pakal and Lalak
Waknal Bahlam* — second son of Pakal and Lalak
Kan Joy Chitam* — third son of Pakal and Lalak
Tiwol Chan Mat* — fourth son of Pakal and Lalak
Talol — wife of Kan Bahlam, sister of Chak Chan
Te' Kuy — wife of Kan Joy Chitam, from Chuuah family

Main Courtiers/Warriors of Lakam Ha
K'akmo — Nakom (*Warrior Chief*) of Lakam Ha
Yax Chan* — young architect of Lakam Ha
Oaxac Ok — distant cousin of Sak K'uk
Ch'amak — distant cousin of Sak K'uk
Ch'ok Bahlam* — Ah K'uhun, Lakam Ha noble
Aj Sul* — noble, priest, Ah K'uhun, Ah Yahauk'ak to Pakal, member Chuuah family
Chak Chan* — brother-in-law of Kan Bahlam, astronomer, scientist
Mut* — assistant to Kan Bahlam, painter, stone carver
Yuhk Makab'te* — assistant to Kan Bahlam, Sahal, administrator

Priests/Priestesses
Pasah Chan — High Priest of Lakam Ha
Ib'ach — High Priest successor to Pasah Chan
Utzil — Priestess of Ix Chel, attendant to Lalak

---

* — historical person

Usin Ch'ob — High Priestess of Lakam Ha
Matunha — High Priestess successor of Usin Ch'ob, member Chuuah
    family
Yaxhal — High Priestess successor of Matunha
T'zab Chak — priestess of Ix Zuhuy K'ak, from Ek Bahlam, teacher of
    Lalak
Tz'unun — priestess of Ix Zuhuy K'ak, teacher of Kan Bahlam, in Ek
    Bahlam

Attendants/Tutors
K'anal — scribe of Lakam Ha
Muk Kab — Royal Steward to Sak K'uk and Pakal
Zazil — personal attendant and main courtier to Sak K'uk
Tohom — personal attendant to Pakal
Pomoy — Lalak's Household Steward
Yax Xoc — weaver and wardrobe mistress for Lalak
Tohat — Lalak's tutor
Til'bak — Lalak's scribe
Koyi — boy taken in by Lalak
Popo — Lalak's spider monkey

Other Lakam Ha Nobles
Yonil — young noble woman, in love with Pakal
Tulix — young noble woman
Muyal — young noble woman, wife of Yax Chan
Budz Ek — messenger for royal family
Kab' — wife of Pasah Chan
Ikim — noble artist, stone carver
T'zul — noble widow
Ah Nik — noble brother-in-law of T'zul
Kayum — noble hunter

Kan Characters
Tajoom Uk'ab K'ak* — ruler of Kan (*622-630 CE*)
Yuknoom Ch'een II* "The Great" — ruler of Kan (*630-686 CE*)
Wamaw Took — high ranking noble, Nakom (*Warrior Chief*) of Kan

---

    * — historical person

Usihwitz Characters
Yax Chapat — son of Ek Chuuah
Yahau Chan Muwaan I* — ruler of Usihwitz (603-? CE)

B'aak Characters
Bahlam Ahau* — brother of Lalak, ruler of B'aak (644-679 CE)
Ik' Muuy Muwaan I* — father of Lalak, ruler of B'aak (610?-644 CE)
Mukuy — personal attendant to Lalak in B'aak

Characters from other cities
K'inich Yo'nal Ahk* - ruler of Yokib (603-639 CE)
Aj Tun Bahlam III* - ruler of Pa'chan (629-669 CE)
Itzamnaaj Bahlam II* - ruler of Pa'chan (681-742 CE)
K'ab Chan Te'* - noble warrior of Sak Tz'i, captured during Yokib attack
Nuun Ujol Chaak* - ruler of Mutul (648-679 CE), half-brother Balaj Chan
    K'awiil
Balaj Chan K'awiil* - ruler of Imix-ha (648-692 CE), half-brother Nuun
    Ujol Chaak
K'ak Nab K'awiil* - ruler of Oxwitik (628-695 CE)
Waxaklajuun Ub'aah K'awiil* - ruler of Oxwitik (695-738 CE)
Kaywak - Dzibilchaltún host to Kan Bahlam and Chak Chan on journey

Lakam Ha Visitors
Chit — Macaw trader from Xpuhil
Tezpochtli — wealthy foreign merchant from Chicomoztoc, city in
    Chalchihuitl region of north Mexica

Deceased characters mentioned
Yohl Ik'nal* — grandmother of Pakal, first woman ruler of Lakam Ha
    (583-604 CE)
Kan Bahlam I* — father of Yohl Ik'nal, ruler of Lakam Ha (572-583 CE)
Aj Ne Ohl Mat* — brother of Yohl Ik'nal, ruler of Lakam Ha (605-612 CE)
Ek Chuuah — exiled from Lakam Ha, leader at Usihwitz

---

* — historical person

Cities and Polities

Ancestral Places

Matawiil — mythohistoric B'aakal origin lands at Six Sky Place

Toktan — ancestral city of K'uk Bahlam, founder of Lakam Ha dynasty, "Place of Reeds"

Petén — lowlands area in north Guatemala, densely populated with Maya sites

Nakbe — (*El Mirador*), called Chatan Uinik – Second Center of Humans

Teotihuacan — powerful empire in central Mexica area (*north of Mexico City*), had widespread influences in Maya regions from late Fourth to Seventh Centuries, called a Tulan, "Place of Reeds"

B'aakal Polity and Allies

B'aakal — "Kingdom of the Bone," regional polity governed by Bahlam (*Jaguar*) Dynasty

Lakam Ha — (*Palenque*) "Big Waters," major city of B'aakal polity, May Ku

Anaay Te — (*Anayte*) small polity city

B'aak — (*Tortuguero*) birthplace of Lalak, ally of Lakam Ha

Mutul — (*Tikal*) great city of southern region, ally of Lakam Ha, enemy of Kan

Nab'nahotot — (*Comalcalco*) city on coast of Great North Sea (*Gulf of Mexico*)

Nahokan — (*Quirigua*) southern city, vassal of Oxwitik (*in Honduras*)

Nututun — City on Chakamax River, near Lakam Ha

Oxwitik — (*Copan*) southern city allied with Lakam Ha by marriage (*in Honduras*)

Popo' — (*Tonina*) linked to Lakam Ha by royal marriage

Sak Nikte' — (*La Corona, Site Q*) ally city courted by Kan

Sak Tz'i — (*White Dog*) ally of Lakam Ha

Uxte'kuh — city raided by B'aak, linked later to Lakam Ha by royal marriage

Wa-Mut — (*Wa-Bird, Santa Elena*) later allied with Kan

Yokib — (*Piedras Negras*) switched alliance to Kan

Zopo — small city between Lakam Ha and B'aak

Ka'an Polity and Allies

Ka'an — "Kingdom of the Snake," regional polity governed by Kan

Kan — refers to residence city of Kan (*Snake*) Dynasty

B'uuk — (*Las Alacranes*) city where Kan installed puppet ruler

Dzibanche — home city of Kan dynasty (*circa 400-600 CE*)

Imix-ha — (*Dos Pilas*) southern city, ally of Tan-nal and Kan

Kan Witz-nal — (*Ucanal*) southern city, ally of Kan and Tan-nal, former Mutul ally

Maxam/Saal — (*Naranjo*) southern city, initially offshoot of Mutul, then ally of Kan

Pa'chan — (*Yaxchilan*) Kan ally located on banks of K'umaxha River

Pakab — (*Pia*) joined Usihwitz in raid on Lakam Ha

Pipá — (*Pomona*) contested city on northeast plains near K'umaxha River

Tan-nal — (*Seibal*) southern city, ally of Maxam

Uxte'tun — (*Kalakmul*) early home city of Kan, reclaimed from Zotz (*Bat*) Dynasty

Usihwitz — (*Bonampak*) switched alliance from Lakam Ha, allied with Kan

Uxwitza — (*Caracol*) allied with Mutul, later switched alliance to Kan

Waka' — (*El Peru*) ally of Kan, enemy of Mutul

Coastal, Trading, and Yukatek Cities

Yukatek region — northern Maya region in Yucatan Peninsula

Acanceh — central Yukatek city with zodiac murals, astronomers

Aké — central Yukatek city of tall columns

Altun Ha — trading city near eastern coast (*in Belize*)

Becan — City near Wukhalal Lagoon

Coba — dominant central Yukatek city, near Great East Sea

Cuzamil — (*Cozumel*) sacred island of Ix Chel priestesses

Dzibilchaltún — north Yukatek city near Great North Sea (*near modern Mérida*)

Ek Bahlam — central Yukatek city, home of Ix Zuhuy K'ak priestesses

Ixcan'tiho — central city near Dzibilchaltún (*modern Mérida*)

Kuhunlich — City near Wukhalal Lagoon

K'inich K'akmo pyramids — ancient pyramid structures near Aké (*in modern Izamal*)

Lam'an'ain — (*Lamanai*) trading city on river, near eastern coast (*in Belize*)

Tulan Tzu — (*Kaminaljuyu*) "The Central Tulan," ancient city in southern mountains (*of Guatemala*), with ties to Teotihuacan

Tulum — coastal city on high cliff above Great East Sea

Uuc Yabnal — (*Chichen Itzá*) new city of Chontal Mayas

Xcambo — north coastal city with salt lagoons (*near modern Progreso*)

Xel Ha — port city for Coba

Xpuhil — City near Wukhalal Lagoon
Yalamha — coastal trading city on long peninsula (*Ambergris Caye in Belize*)

Seas and Rivers
B'ub'ulha — western river (*Rio Grijalva*) flowing into Gulf of Mexico near Nab'nahotot
Chakamax — river flowing into K'umaxha, southeast of Lakam Ha
Chih Ha — subsidiary river (*Chinal River*) flows into Tulixha
Chik'in-nab — Great West Sea (*Pacific Ocean*)
K'ak-nab — Great East Sea (*Gulf of Honduras, Caribbean Sea*)
K'uk Lakam Witz — Fiery Water Mountain, sacred mountain of Lakam Ha
K'umaxha — Sacred Monkey River (*Usumacinta River*), largest river in region, crosses plains north of Lakam Ha, empties into Gulf of Mexico
Michol — river on plains northwest of Lakam Ha, flows below city plateau
Nab'nah — Great North Sea (*Gulf of Mexico*)
Nah Ha'al — main tributary (*Pasión River*) of K'umaxha near Imix-ha
Pokolha — southern river (*Rio Motagua*) by Nahokan, near Oxwitik
Tulixha — large river (*Tulija River*) flowing near B'aak
Wukhalal — lagoon of seven colors (*Bacalar Lagoon*)

Small rivers flowing across Lakam Ha ridges
Ach' — Ach' River
Balunte — Balunte River
Bisik — Picota River
Ixha — Motiepa River
Kisiin — Diablo River
Otulum — Otulum River
Sutzha — Murcielagos River
Tun Pitz — Piedras Bolas

Maya Deities
Ahau K'in/K'in Ahau — Lord Sun/Sun Lord
Ahau Kinh — Lord Time

Ahauob (*Lords*) of the First Sky
— B'olon Chan Yoch'ok'in (*Sky That Enters the Sun*) — 9 Sky Place
— Waklahun Ch'ok'in (*Emergent Young Sun*) — 16 Sky Place
— B'olon Tz'ak Ahau (*Conjuring Lord*) — 9 Sky Place
Bacabs — Lords of the Four Directions, Hold up the Sky
Chaak — God of Rain, Storms, Thunder
Hunab K'u (*Hun Ahb K'u*) — Supreme Creator Being, giver of movement
and measure
Hun Ahau (*One Lord*) — First born of Triad, Celestial Realm
Hunahpu — first Hero Twin, also called Hun Ahau
Hun Hunahpu — Maize God, First Father, resurrected by Hero Twins,
ancestor of Mayas
Itzam Kab Ayin — Earth Crocodile-Snake Wizard-Centipede
Itzamna/Itzamnaaj — Paramount Sky God, Sky Bar Deity, Magician of
Water-Sacred Itz, Inventor of Writing and Calendars, First Shaman,
Master Teacher-Builder
Ix Chel — Earth Mother Goddess, Lady Rainbow, healer, midwife, weaver
of life, fertility and abundance, has power over snake energies, waters
and fluids
Ix Ma Uh — Young Moon Goddess
Kalahun Ahau — 12 Lord
K'ukulkan — "Feathered Serpent" God of Transformation
Mah Kinah Ahau (*Underworld Sun Lord*) — Second born of Triad,
Underworld Realm, called Jaguar Sun, Underworld Sun-Moon,
Waterlily Jaguar
Muwaan Mat (*Duck Hawk, Cormorant*) — Primordial Mother Goddess,
mother of B'aakal Triad, named ruler of Lakam Ha 612-615 CE
Oxlahun Ahau — 13 Lord
Unen K'awill (*Infant Powerful One*) — Third born of Triad, Earthly Realm,
Baby Jaguar, patron of royal bloodlines, lightning in forehead, often
has one snake-foot
Wakah Chan Te' — Jeweled Sky Tree, connects the three dimensions
(*roots-Underworld, trunk-Middleworld, branches-Upperworld*)
Witz Monster — Cave openings to Underworld depicted as fanged
monster mask
Wuqub' Kaquix — Seven Macaw, false deity of polestar, defeated by Hero
Twins
Xibalba — Underworld, realm of the Lords of Death
Xmucane — Grandmother Deity of Maya People, Heart of Earth
Xpiyakok — Grandfather Deity of Maya People

Yax Bahlam — (*Xbalanque*), second Hero Twin

Yum K'ax — Young Maize God, foliated God of growing corn, resurrected Hun Hunahpu

Titles

Ah — honorable way to address men

Ahau — Lord

Ah K'in — Solar Priest, plural Ah K'inob

Ah Kuch Kab — head of village (*Kuchte'el*)

Ah K'uhun — warrior-priest, learned member of royal court, worshipper

Ba-ch'ok — heir designate

Batab — town governor, local leader from noble lineage

Chilam — spokesperson, prophet

Halach Uinik — True Human

Ix — honorable way to address women

Ixik — Lady

Ix K'in — Solar Priestess, plural Ix K'inob

Juntan — precious one, signifies relationship between mother and child as well as between deities and ahauob, also translated "beloved of"

Kalomte — K'uhul Ahau ruling several cities, used often at Mutul and Oxwitik

K'uhul Ahau — Divine/Holy Lord

K'uhul Ixik — Divine/Holy Lady

K'uhul Ixik Me' — Holy Lady Mother

May Ku — seat of the may cycle (*260 tuns, 256 solar years*), dominant city of region

Nakom — Warrior Chief

Sahal — ruler of subsidiary city

Yahau — His Lord (*high subordinate noble*)

Yahau K'ak — His Lord of Fire (*high ceremonial-military noble*)

Yum — Master

Maya Regions in Middle Classic Period (500 - 800 CE)

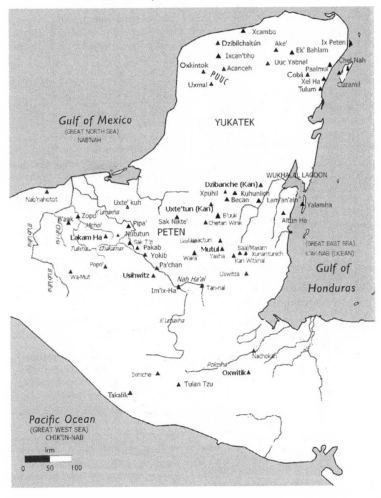

N ames of cities, rivers, and seas are the ones used in this book. Most are known Classic Period names; some have been created for the story. Many other cities existed but are omitted for simplicity.

(Present-day Yucatan Peninsula, Chiapas, and Tabasco, Mexico; Belize, Guatemala, and Honduras.)

Lakam Ha (Palenque) Western and Central Areas Older Sections of City (circa 500 - 600 CE)

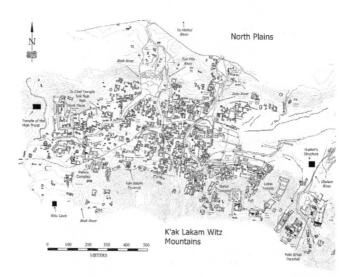

D ark boxes are fictional structures added for the story. Structures important to the story are labeled. This does not signify that these structures were actually used for purposes described in the story. The city extends further east; these sections were built later (see map of Lakam Ha Central and Eastern Areas)

Based upon maps from The Palenque Mapping Project, Edwin Barnhart, 1999.

A FAMSI-sponsored project. Used with permission of Edwin Barnhart.

Lakam Ha (Palenque) Central and Eastern Areas Newer Sections of City (650 - 800 CE)

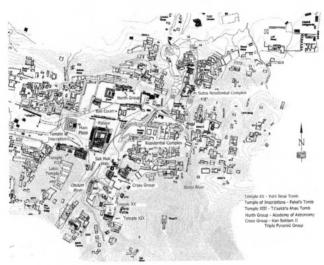

T he most important structures in the story are labeled according to current archeological convention. Their association with characters is indicated in the inset text at right.

Based upon maps from The Palenque Mapping Project, Edwin Barnhart, 1999.

A FAMSI-sponsored project. Used with permission of Edwin Barnhart.

The Rabbit Scribe

"It is his third stone-seating on 10 Ahau 8 Yaxk'in, the twelfth katun. K'inich Janaab Pakal K'uhul B'aakal Ahau oversaw it. Ten becomes ahau. The Jeweled Sky Tree matured. The West ahauob and the East ahauob descend. They seated themselves ... It is Janaab Pakal's second taking of the white paper headband on the altar of the Gods.

"K'inich Janaab Pakal is the beloved of the Gods ... He appeases the heart of the God of the stone seating."

Temple of the Inscriptions, dedicated to K'inich Janaab Pakal
Completed by his son Kan Bahlam II, circa Baktun 9, Katun 12, Tun 11, Uinal 12, Kin 10 (c. 684 CE)
Based on translation of glyphs by Gerardo Aldana, *The Apotheosis of Janaab' Pakal*
University of Colorado Press, 2007

"Red is much more than a color. Red is royalty, blood, passion, life and death.

"No one knows who I am. Maybe they will know me some day as she who made the progression of lords. Perhaps, never... To open the sarcophagus of a queen has unimaginable consequences."

Voice of the Red Queen, Pakal's wife Tz'aakb'u Ahau
Based on interpretation by Adriana Malvido, *La Reina Roja (The Red Queen: The Secret of the Maya in Palenque)*
Conaculta, INAH, Mexico City, 2006.

Tz'aakb'u Ahau—I

Baktun 9 Katun 9 Tun 9
Baktun 9 Katun 9 Tun 12
622 CE - 625 CE

1

The messenger bowed deeply, clasping his shoulder and dropping to his knees. Head bowed, he waited below the raised platform in the reception chamber of the royal couple. All eyes were fixed on him and his sense of importance swelled. The mission entrusted to him was of utmost importance. It concerned nothing less than the future of the Lakam Ha dynasty. Now he brought his report to his patrons and the atmosphere of the palace chamber quivered with anticipation.

"Welcome, Worthy Messenger Budz Ek." Kan Mo' Hix spoke first. "Come forward and sit before us. We are pleased you have returned safely."

"Indeed, your journey has been swift," said Sak K'uk. "You are rightly named, for you travel as quickly as your namesake, Smoking Star-Comet."

Budz Ek smiled at the compliment and edged forward on his knees to take a position on the woven mat set in front of the platform. He was apprehensive, however, because he feared the royal couple would not be pleased with his messages. It was a risk faced by all messengers. Their powerful patrons often unleashed a barrage of fury upon the hapless bringers of bad news, though mostly this was an onslaught of words and not the thrust of a knife. He knew the ruling family of Lakam Ha would not resort to violence, but to be in disfavor would affect his status.

"Speak now of your visit to B'aak. We are ready to hear what you have seen and learned." Sak K'uk waved the hand sign ordering attendants to bring refreshments.

Before speaking, Budz Ek sat up straight and glanced around the reception chamber, his astute eyes taking in every subtlety. In addition to the royal couple, parents of K'inich Janaab Pakal, the youthful ruler of Lakam Ha and the B'aakal Polity, was a small audience including the steward Muk Kab, K'akmo the Nakom-warrior chief, the royal scribe K'anal, and two trusted courtiers who were distant cousins of Sak K'uk, the ruler's mother. The only other woman in the group was Zazil, her primary noble attendant. It was a select group, the messenger observed, so his information was meant for only certain ears.

It struck him as odd that the ruler, the Holy B'aakal Lord—K'uhul B'aakal Ahau—was not there. Surely the report pertained most of all to him. But this was not the messenger's business.

He took note that his report was not being received in high level court protocol. Although the royal couple was dressed in typical Mayan finery, it was modest compared to courtly dress. Sak K'uk wore a white huipil with blue and gold embroidery at the neckline and hem, several strings of alabaster beads, dangling alabaster ear spools, and a small headdress of blue and yellow feathers set in bands of silver disks. Kan Mo' Hix was bare-chested with a short, skirted loincloth of colorful stripes. His small pectoral pendant symbolized the Sun Lord; jade ear spools hung from both ears and worked copper cuffs surrounded his wrists. On his elongated skull perched a tall white cylindrical cap topped with a ceramic macaw-mo, his namesake.

The messenger wore the usual runner attire, a white loincloth with red waistband and short cape loosely tied over his shoulders. A red headband kept his long black hair away from his face. He had arrived at the palace in the early morning, stopping the evening before to rest a short distance from the city. This allowed him to appear refreshed and in clean attire. His years of experience had taught him the wisdom of preparing well for reports to royal patrons. Arriving breathless and sweaty in the heat of midday did not create an advantageous scenario.

Bowing again to the royal couple, he began his report.

"It takes two days of travel, as you know, to journey from Lakam Ha to B'aak. Travel on the Michol River went easily, thanks to our skillful canoe paddlers. More difficulties arose once we left the river and climbed through jungle-covered hills toward our destination. The path is not as well maintained as would be expected, since the river is their main source for trade goods. It is said among traders I encountered along the path that B'aak has declined in prosperity. The ahauob of B'aak buy fewer luxury items such as red spondylus shells, carved jade, quetzal feathers, and fine obsidian for blades. In the city, while mingling among ahauob-nobles and craftsmen in the market, I heard mention of difficult years when crops were less productive. Rumors circulated that B'aak leadership was faltering during this time.

"The B'aak ruler, Ik' Muuy Muwaan, was apparently contending with internal dissension and a plot to overthrow his dynasty. His ambitious younger brother had recruited a cadre of ahauob and warriors, leading to several years of intermittent clashes, often taking place in cornfields and trampling crops. Between skirmishes, the insurgents hid in the jungles, re-grouping for more raids. Only two years ago was the rightful ruler able to suppress this group, when his younger brother was killed in battle. Since then, the ruler has re-established leadership, banished the traitors and is slowly bringing fields back to fertility. This history I confirmed with the calendar priests of the city.

"The day after my arrival, I was received at the ruler's court. There I presented your gifts of cacao, fine woven cloth, and pom, copal incense. These were received with much enthusiasm, and most polite inquiries were made into the health of your royal family and our young K'uhul B'aakal Ahau."

"For the concern of Ik' Muuy Muwaan, we are grateful," interjected Sak K'uk. She was impatient for the messenger to arrive at the purpose of his visit. "What said he to your inquiries about his daughter?"

"Of this, he was most pleased. To have his daughter considered as royal consort for your son was beyond his imagining. He was eager to bring the girl for my viewing, and her mother to extol her virtues. The visit was arranged for that very afternoon."

"Not surprising that Ik' Muuy Muwaan leapt at the chance to wed his daughter to the ruler of Lakam Ha," muttered Kan Mo' Hix under his breath. Only Sak K'uk could hear him. "He is already counting the marriage gifts we will give him."

Budz Ek looked quizzically at the royal couple, observing the murmurings.

"Honored Messenger, do continue," Sak K'uk said, frowning at her husband. "We wish to hear your observations of the girl."

The messenger felt heat rising along his neck and face, and hoped he would not sweat profusely. It was not due to rising morning temperature, for inside the chamber the air was cool and fresh. He knew the flush was caused by worry over what he was about to say. Sucking air in through nearly closed lips, he tried to cool himself and maintain composure as he continued his report.

"Her mother and attendant brought her to the reception chamber. First came lengthy descriptions of her character and abilities. Lady Lalak is, by their words, a young woman of pleasant and quiet character, who treats all kindly and is well loved by her city's people. She is skilled in weaving and makes delicate cloth that has no match. She paints lovely patterns on ceramic bowls with a true artistic flair. Her voice is sweet and clear when she sings, her form graceful and sure-footed when she dances. Children flock to her and she entertains them with clever stories. In conversation, she speaks with a courtly flourish and can address many topics. In particular, she is knowledgeable about the animals and plants of the area. It seems she creates special relationships with animals and has several wild ones as pets."

"Excellent attributes, if these are all to be believed." Sak K'uk doubted everything was true; such praise was only expected when proffering a daughter as a royal bride. Her real interest was revealed by her next question.

"And of her appearance? Tell me not the words of her parents, but your own observations. Is she beautiful?"

Budz Ek hesitated, for this was the exact question he wished to avoid. The intense stare Sak K'uk gave him made it clear that avoidance was impossible.

"Holy Lady, this I must answer honestly, although it pains me. The daughter of Ik' Muuy Muwaan has a sweet and gentle presence, and spoke well when questioned. But she is not a beauty according to standards of our art. She is large-boned and, well, rather rounded of body. Her skin is a deep brown color, her hair thick and lustrous. She has the elongated skull that signifies nobility of the true blood, and her nose line is straight as a blade."

He glanced at the ruler's mother entreatingly, as if beseeching her to forgive him in advance. Only a stern glare was returned to the now copiously sweating messenger.

"Of the face of Lady Lalak, it must be said ... much do I regret to say it, her face is ... homely."

"She is unattractive?" Kan Mo' Hix sounded more curious than displeased.

"You must give more details," Sak K'uk insisted. "Describe her face carefully. You have great powers of observation, you have shown these before."

"As you command, Holy Lady. I wish not to disparage the worthy daughter of our neighbor city and their ruling family. I bring only what my eyes have seen, and it is your prerogative to make your assessment. Now come the details. Her face is wide and square, with a firm chin line. While large noses are common among our people, hers is uncommonly great. The tip is almost bulbous and the nostrils flare out widely. This feature dominates her face. By comparison, her eyes are small and recessed under heavy brows. They do have a nice almond shape and shine with intelligent light. Her lips are thick and down curving, except when she smiles. Her smile is captivating and her teeth straight and white. The ears are also prominent, standing out from her head with long lobes; good for wearing heavy ear spools."

He paused again, pondering whether to impart the next bit of telling information about the girl's appearance. Quickly he gauged it was folly to omit it, for the royal family would see this defect the moment they set eyes on her.

"There is yet one additional observation I made of her features," he continued slowly. "As a young child she contracted an illness that caused a widespread rash over her face and body. Infection set in and she almost died. The healing skills of B'aak priestesses saved her life, but scars were left upon her face from infected bumps. These are most visible upon her cheeks, appearing as dark spots.

"This completes my description." He paused and glanced up expectantly. Did he see a smile curling the chiseled lips of the ruler's mother?

"An excellent description!" she exclaimed. "It is possible to picture the girl clearly. You have done well, Budz Ek, and will be richly rewarded for your work."

Kan Mo' Hix looked appraisingly at his wife. He knew more about her motives than would please her, but his concern was not the girl's appearance. Her bloodlines back to the dynastic founders, the stability of the ruling family, and the political situation of the city were his main interests.

"It is so, Worthy Messenger," he said. "Your report conveys much information about the daughter of Ik' Muuy Muwaan, and we are appreciative. Tell me more about the difficult times and leadership deficits that recently beset B'aak."

Budz Ek launched with considerable relief into details of crop failures and poor decision-making by the ruler and his administrators. This was safer ground, and the men in the chamber listened with avid attention.

B'aak was a small city to the northwest on hilly country not far from Lakam Ha. It did not possess the lofty vista across wide, fertile plains that his home city enjoyed. Lakam Ha, Place of Big Water, sat upon a narrow ridge one-third of the way up a high mountain range, K'uk Lakam Witz. Numerous small rivers coursed through the ridge, tumbling down the steep escarpment in cascades to join the Michol River. The plains below stretched north to the Nab'nah, the Great Northern Sea, transected by the K'umaxha River that served as the major transportation artery for the region. Named for the Sacred Monkeys that lived along its banks, when the K'umaxha River overflowed it deposited rich silt in the fields in which corn, beans, peppers and squash were grown.

Lakam Ha was indeed blessed by its patron deities, the Triad Gods. This favored city abounded in water, flowering and fruiting trees, lush jungle foliage with numerous kinds of animals and birds, and cooling breezes from the soaring mountains to the south. It enjoyed a nonpareil view from its high ridge, and the steep cliffs plunging down to the plains below provided natural defense. The Michol River at the cliff's base offered easy transportation, and the plains rolling gently into the hazy distance supported abundant crops to feed the population.

B'aak had long been in the B'aakal Polity and was an ally of Lakam Ha. The ruling dynasty of Lakam Ha provided oversight for the cities within its polity, acting as *May Ku* or chief ceremonial center and dispensing privileges to rulers and nobles of these cities. This system of cooperation, in which leadership rotated among cities through choices made by a council of ahauob and priests, followed regular cycles of 20 tuns and 260 tuns. The *May* system was ordained by the Gods and kept humans living in peace and harmony. However, recent developments were disrupting this hallowed system, most notably the aggressive actions by Kan rulers in the distant Ka'an Polity. Lakam Ha was still struggling to recover from Kan's devastating attack only twelve years before.

It was important for Lakam Ha to cultivate alliances with its polity cities. Already two cities had switched allegiance to Kan, and had joined in the attack. This was one motive the royal family had for considering marriage ties with B'aak. As Kan Mo' Hix listened to the messenger describing B'aak's troubles, he became even more convinced that the ruling family's daughter was the right choice. This union would guarantee the loyalty of B'aak.

There were other important considerations in selecting a wife for Pakal. However, these were not part of the messenger's report.

"Budz Ek, greatly do we give thanks for your thorough work," Kan Mo' Hix said. "Your report is insightful and provides much information. These things are important and we must consider them carefully."

"Receive also my appreciation for your work," Sak K'uk added. "Our Royal Steward, Muk Kab, will provide your reward to express our deep gratitude. One thing I must stress to you: Do not speak to anyone about this mission. As you see, we consider here things having utmost significance for our city. With this confidence, I charge you."

For moments the eyes of Sak K'uk, recent ruler of Lakam Ha, mother of Pakal the K'uhul B'aakal Ahau, locked with those of the messenger. What he saw in these pools of fathomless blackness made him quiver. She could be ruthless in the service of her son and her dynasty. Any misstep of his, any leaking of secrets, would be fatal.

"It is as you command, Holy Lady," he said, dropping his gaze and bowing.

With hand signs, she dismissed him and ordered the steward to give his recompense. After these two men left, further discussion ensued.

"Pasah Chan, made you study of the bloodlines of the B'aak ruling family?" Kan Mo' Hix addressed the High Priest of Lakam Ha, whose extensive library of codices contained histories of many B'aakal cities and dynasties. A man in his prime, the High Priest was slender with sinewy limbs, a hawk-like face and penetrating half-lidded eyes. From a minor noble family, he had risen to a position of prominence through both brilliant scholarship and shrewd competition.

"So have I done. Our records of the B'aak dynasty are complete." Pasah Chan always enjoyed being in the spotlight. He relished this authority among the highest echelons of Lakam Ha society, especially given his rather humble origins. For a personal reason, he felt sympathy for the "homely" girl under consideration as the ruler's wife. He also had a defect; his skull was not shaped in the fashion of the elite. His parents had failed to apply headboards properly during infancy, a technique used by aspiring nobles to mimic the hereditary elongated skulls of ruling families. Although he now wore headbands to push his hair up from the forehead to resemble this peaking crown, these efforts could not conceal the defect.

"The ruling family of B'aak can justly claim that they are 'of Toktan,' for their ancestors trace back in an unbroken lineage to K'uk Bahlam, founder of the primordial city of Toktan," said Pasah Chan. "These ancestors lived in Lakam Ha for four generations, then left to build their own city a short distance away. They have consistently inhabited B'aak for six generations. According to their traditions, the rulers can rightly call themselves 'K'uhul B'aakal Ahau' because their bloodlines are as pure as your Bahlam family. And, as you well know, their Emblem Glyph bears close resemblance to ours with its use of b'ak-bone and k'uhul-holy symbols."

"Much am I annoyed by this appropriation of our Emblem Glyph," Sak K'uk said, frowning. "Using our Holy B'aakal Lord title is preposterous. Their status in the polity is far less than that of Lakam Ha."

"But their lineage is pristine," observed Kan Mo' Hix. This satisfied his highest priority in selecting his son's wife.

"So have I verified," confirmed Pasah Chan.

"Here is another advantage of this match," Sak K'uk added. "The girl is not of our city."

Pasah Chan shot a quizzical glance toward the ruler's mother, and then recalled their conversation at the celebration of Pakal's Transformation to Adulthood ritual a year earlier. The scene played vividly in his memory. He re-witnessed Sak K'uk's shock upon watching her son dancing sensuously with Yonil, a lissome young woman of minor noble lineage. The strong words of the ruler's mother about preventing this relationship from progressing were clear as on that night; she vowed to find a more suitable match from a neighboring city. Lalak filled those criteria and another one that would remain unspoken. The High Priest surmised that Sak K'uk did not want a beautiful woman as her son's wife.

Kan Mo' Hix had arrived at the same conclusion much earlier. He was fully aware of the special relationship between mother and son, one that Sak K'uk treasured and would strive to preserve. She did not want a beautiful woman replacing her in Pakal's heart.

More discussion ensued about the benefits this alliance would bring. The warrior chief K'akmo commented about strengthening defenses to the west, and the royal cousins speculated about sending expert farmers to help B'aak improve its crops so there could be more tribute and trade opportunities. The group seemed in concordance about this choice for Pakal's wife.

As the session ended and the others departed, Pasah Chan hung back. Sak K'uk alone remained in the chamber; even her husband had left to plan lavish marriage gifts and discuss timing with calendar priests. An event as extraordinary as the marriage of the K'uhul B'aakal Ahau must take place on a very auspicious day, one that promised longevity and fecundity to the royal pair, and abundance and prosperity to the people. Each day of the Mayan calendar held unique qualities based upon positions of stars, sun and moon, and sacred numerology. It took years of study to develop expertise in interpreting calendar auguries, and well-trained calendar priests were required.

Noticing Pasah Chan's continued presence, Sak K'uk walked over so they could speak in low voices. She sensed he desired a private conversation.

"Have you more to say of this matter?"

"A small concern, Holy Lady."

"Then speak, I am listening."

"Your son Pakal is of age, he has undergone adulthood rituals, and he has a strong character as befits a ruler. Think you not that he should be included in selecting his wife?" Pasah Chan was among the few nobles in Lakam Ha who could question the ruling family directly. His status as High Priest put him among the upper elite.

Sak K'uk looked haughtily at the priest.

"Ruler he may be, but he is still my son. Tradition dictates that parents should select their children's spouses. Pakal is well steeped in the protocols of ahauob and ruling dynasties. You, Pasah Chan, also are well aware of this."

"That is so. But has not Pakal shown interest in the young woman of our city, Yonil? Perhaps he desires at least consideration of this possible match."

"Yonil!" Sak K'uk's eyebrows compressed and her eyes glowered. "That young woman is not a proper candidate. You know her family bloodlines. They are marginal at best; she is deficient in lineage. No, it is impossible to even discuss this with him."

"With her deficient lineage I have no argument," the High Priest replied. "It is only to be sensitive to Pakal's feelings that I suggest such a discussion."

Sak K'uk shook her head. Her jaw was set strongly.

"Men cannot make good decisions about their lifelong mate when driven by the passions of youth. If Pakal is continuing to see this woman, I will immediately put this to an end." Sak K'uk paused as a plan formulated in her mind. "Let us quickly arrange a marriage for Yonil to a noble of a distant city, perhaps Nab'nahotot on the shore of Nab'nah, the Great North Sea. Yes, this we must do, to remove any future temptation. Pasah Chan, see to it."

The High Priest clasped his shoulder and bowed. He felt an unexpected twinge of sadness for the lovely young woman Yonil and for

Pakal, who clearly was attracted to her. However, those who served their people as intermediaries to the Gods, who invoked blessings through rituals to guarantee their city's well being, who fulfilled the divine covenant to speak the Gods' names and keep their days properly, could not make purely personal choices. Pakal's destiny would shape his life.

2

Pakal sat cross-legged on the ruler's double-headed jaguar throne, his expression alert and his long body relaxed. Intelligence shone in his tilted almond eyes set above high cheekbones in a slender face. A prominent straight-bridged nose swept in a clean line to an elongated skull, on which perched a headdress of bright feathers and woven bands. Sculpted lips curved sensuously above a strong chin line, framed by large jade earspools. On his well-muscled chest hung a Sun Lord—K'in Ahau pectoral, and his wrists sported copper cuffs with dangling discs. He wore the mat design skirt that signified he was a person of the mat, one who sat upon woven mats to govern and deliberate. Strong and well-shaped legs were left bare and he wore no sandals while sitting.

The overall impression created by his appearance was one of self-assurance without arrogance, incisiveness tempered by kindness. The Sun-Faced Lord of the Shield, as his name K'inich Janaab Pakal meant, was well liked by both nobles and commoners. His mettle as a ruler had not yet been tested, for times were returning to stability at Lakam Ha after the destruction of the Kan attack. The simmering issue remained, however, over the loss of the sacred Sak Nuk Nah—White Skin House that served as a portal to the Upperworld. This portal formed by the Wakah Chan Te'—Jeweled Sky Tree provided the pathway for communication with the Triad Deities, and had been used for generations by B'aakal rulers. In the Kan attack, the shrine had been spiritually defiled and physically demolished; Pakal's mother Sak K'uk performed a ritual termination ceremony to close the structure permanently and remove lingering evil forces.

During the three years of her rulership, Sak K'uk drew upon the Upperworld powers of the Primordial Mother Goddess Muwaan Mat, mother of the Triad Deities, to perform the required rituals. Once Pakal acceded at age twelve, his mother continued to provide leadership until he reached adulthood. During this time, no major calendar periods came to completion, so the truncated rituals she was able to carry out were sufficient. When the next katun ending arrived, however, the ruler would be expected to perform extensive ceremonies that reaffirmed his connection with the Deities and satisfied their requirements for tribute and acknowledgement. Upon this rested the sacred contract between the Triad Deities and people of B'aakal.

Without the portal in the Sak Nuk Nah, it was impossible to imagine how these ceremonies could be properly done. It was an issue that weighed heavily upon Pakal's mind and heart. He had pledged himself to restore the portal to the Gods, but was uncertain how to accomplish it. Thankfully, he had several years to figure this out. The katun ending was eleven tuns (10.8 solar years) in the future. Pakal was considering a smaller ritual when the tuns reached 13, a sacred number of spirit and wholeness. This was over three solar years away; it would be his first significant calendar ritual as ruler.

Pakal's duties today were more mundane. He was adjudicating a quarrel in a noble family over inheritance of a small housing complex in the city. T'zul was a middle-aged woman now living in the main house, the recent widow of the family head with only one living child, a married daughter. By Maya custom, the son-in-law lived for one year with his wife's family, offering his services to the household. After that, he returned with his wife to his own family compound, where they continued to live. In T'zul's situation, the son-in-law had remained in her household, as the family head was ailing and there were no sons to help out. T'zul wanted this arrangement to continue; her in-laws had many other sons and could surely spare one.

The challenge to this arrangement came from Ah Nik, brother of the family head. He argued that the housing complex by right should revert to him, as the second oldest male in the family that built the structures. He was living in a nearby house but considered it too small for his growing family of three sons, all married with children and more on the way. Ah Nik was arguing his position.

"It is only reasonable that my family should move into the complex. It is quite larger than our present house, and has two other buildings that my sons and their families could occupy. T'zul has fewer members in her family and no grandchildren yet, though greatly do I wish her that joyous happening. Do you not confirm the rightness of this, Holy Lord?"

"It was the wish of my esteemed husband, your older brother, that I remain in the house." T'zul broke in, not waiting for Pakal to respond. Her cheeks were flushed and she stared venomously at her brother-in-law. "We have spent many years in this house. It holds our dearest family memories, and under the floor rests the bones of my poor husband, dead before his time. It is heartless to force us to leave. Ever have you been selfish, Ah Nik!"

"I am thinking only of what is best for my family!" he retorted testily. "You are the selfish one, clutching onto the complex that is too large for your needs. Think of your nephews and their children. Open your heart to their needs."

"Every day I pay homage to my husband's spirit at the shrine in my house. Why would you tear me away from what little solace this gives? It is only right that I remain close to my ancestor's bones, to receive their guidance and comfort."

"Forget you that my ancestors too are buried in that house? My own father and mother, and their predecessors also? Be reasonable, T'zul. We can exchange houses; you move your family into my current place, and I move mine into yours. It is all so very reasonable!" Ah Nik was becoming frustrated.

Tears were streaming down T'zul's face as she turned to Pakal and pleaded her case.

"Oh wise and kind Holy Lord, see a widow's grief! Have mercy upon a suffering one and let me have my small comfort. Do not separate me from my husband's bones!"

Pakal raised a hand, commanding silence. Everyone present hung on the moment, wondering how the young ruler could decide this emotional mess equitably. Several courtiers sat on mats lining the walls of the throne room, the royal steward Muk Kab stood attentively nearby, and a handful of other petitioners hovered along the stairs rising to the chamber.

"My heart is pained by the conflict in your family," Pakal said softly. "Yours has long been a kind and loving family, generous to your workers and responsible in tribute. My parents spoke of the assistance you gave as our city began to recover after the villainous attack by Kan. Now remember what has come before. You dishonor your ancestors by such dissension. Take a moment, each of you, and look within your heart and conscience. Ask yourself, T'zul, what would your husband want? And Ah Nik, ask yourself what your brother would say of this argument."

The two petitioners hung their heads, feeling abashed. Until recently, their relations had been congenial and both did regret their current strife.

Neither was yet willing to relinquish the position they had taken, and waited in silence.

"T'zul, it seems the most important consideration for you is your husband's shrine, is this not so?"

Wiping tears from her eyes, T'zul nodded.

"Ah Nik, for you the need of a larger complex for your family is uppermost. You are willing to exchange houses. Would you also be willing to provide labor and materials should T'zul need to enlarge that house in the future?"

"That I would gladly provide," Ah Nik replied, brightening.

"Let me emphasize how important I consider the sacred shrines to our ancestors. These are the very foundations of our culture, for we seek ancestral guidance in every aspect of our lives. This is why we bury their bones in the central chamber of our homes. It is not common, but there are times when ancestral bones must be moved to other locations. This is undertaken with utmost care and all proper ceremonies must be performed."

The young ruler focused his gaze on T'zul and compelled her to look directly into his eyes. Her eyes widened as she was drawn into mesmerizing pools of darkness, from which flowed a force of overwhelming compassion. She felt a pinging sensation in her chest followed by a wave of relief. A sense of deep comfort descended upon her, and the anger she held for her brother-in-law dissipated.

"T'zul, if you will agree to the housing exchange, I will personally conduct the ceremonies to move your husband's bones. You may rest assured this will be done with complete correctness, and his spirit will be satisfied that it is truly honored. He will be happy with his new home, and continue to bless you with his presence."

The widow could not respond for several moments, overcome with gratitude. She had never imagined this solution, and it resonated deeply in her soul. Finally she spoke.

"Blessed are you, K'uhul B'aakal Ahau, that in your wisdom you could see this path to mending the troubles of our family. With much happiness do I accept your suggestions, and with deep appreciation your personal effort on our behalf. No greater honor could be bestowed upon my husband, than the ceremonies for moving his shrine be performed by our Holy Lord."

Fluffy white clouds moved slowly across the blue sky, making a stately procession overhead. Gentle breezes stirred leaves of ramón and pixoy trees, and rippled the summer grasses covering the hillsides. A flock of green parrots darted from one cluster of trees to another, squawking exuberantly. From the distance came the throaty roar of howler monkeys, echoing over forest canopy and resounding from steep mountainsides. Life was everywhere in the tropical jungle, bursting with song and sound. Even the insects added their incessant humming and clacking to the chorus.

A raised and plastered walkway, called a *sakbe,* or white road, left the eastern edge of Lakam Ha and wended between hills, curving as it followed low ground between the temples rising toward the sky. At the summit of the closest hill stood the Temple of Nohol, dedicated to the warming yellow light from the south that brought growth and ripening. A nearby hill served as base for the Temple of Lak'in, facing the eastern sunrise and expressing the awakening powers of red light that brought new beginnings. Swinging around this hill, the sakbe ended and a footpath ascended a steep hillside before dipping toward the Otulum River burbling merrily toward a wide grassy meadow stretching eastward. Across the river was the crest of Yohl Ik'nal's mortuary monument, a temple situated atop a low hill that nestled among others of greater height.

Pakal stood on the hill across from his grandmother's pyramid temple. From this vantage he could see the far edge of the meadow, where the terrain changed suddenly and plunged over a cliff. The Otulum River crashed into tiers of cascades as it plummeted down the precipitous mountainside, joined by its parallel sister, the Sutzha River, in smaller cascades. Breezes ruffled Pakal's hair and cooled his sweaty skin. He wore only a white loincloth with green and yellow waistband, his hair tied into a topknot, for the day was hot. His eyes sought the small stone building situated next to the river, in the center of the meadow. The walls were partially collapsed and the roof had fallen into a pile of rubble. It once was used by hunters, but was long abandoned.

Memories of his previous visits there floated into awareness, and even from this distance he could faintly sense the vortex of energy around the ruined building. His powerful experience of this vortex had convinced him that here was the site to construct a new portal, to build a new Sak Nuk Nah, to re-establish communication with the Triad Deities and divine ancestors.

Standing alone on the hill, Pakal relished his solitude. Rarely did he have an opportunity to be alone, surrounded as he usually was by courtiers, advisors, attendants, administrators, petitioners and countless others who either wanted his assistance or simply wanted to view their ruler. It was no small accomplishment to carve out this time alone. He had used a visit to his grandmother's tomb as the excuse, explaining that he wished to commune with her spirit and bring offerings, and needed privacy to establish these sensitive and subtle connections. His personal attendant Tohom tried to insist that someone was needed to carry water and mats, and his courtiers offered to wait outside, but he had graciously declined.

It had not been easy, but he prevailed. Actually, there was truth in his excuse, for he greatly admired his grandmother Yohl Ik'nal, who had ruled in her own right for twenty-two years and steered the city through several crises. He did want to pay homage at her tomb and renew their spirit connections. His actual motive, however, was a secret meeting with the young woman Yonil.

She would be arriving soon, and he must complete his ritual first. He hurried down the path, splashed across the river and climbed the narrow stairs to the temple on top the pyramid. Sitting before the altar, he recited invocations and placed a round piece of amber over Yohl Ik'nal's name glyph. He had no means of lighting copal incense, and had brought no food offerings. In his heart, he knew simply offering his love was enough. As he concentrated and sensed his grandmother's presence, the amber glowed as if lit from within. He asked for nothing, no guidance or information. He only wanted to experience the deep connectedness between them. Time passed; Pakal kept focus until he heard splashing in the river below. Thanking his grandmother, he bowed and rose to meet the young woman eagerly racing up the pyramid stairs.

The sight of her took his breath away. Her slender form perched on the edge of the temple platform, framed by verdant hills that brought her white huipil to startling clarity. Breezes fluttered the soft fabric so it outlined her thighs and clung to her breasts, where a multicolored band anchored it firmly, leaving her shoulders and arms bare. The shift ended at mid-calf, showing her supple ankles and small feet that slipped into embroidered sandals. Her shining black hair was tied in a topknot, as was his, but hers dangled a long ponytail that swayed sinuously.

She clasped her shoulder and bowed deeply, throwing her ponytail to the floor and exposing the graceful curve of her neck and back. A delicate necklace of copper and white shells clinked softly.

"Greetings, Holy Lord of B'aakal," she murmured without lifting her head.

"Please rise, Yonil," Pakal replied. "And please call me by my name."

He enjoyed watching her form uncurl, movements full of grace and ease. She stood a head shorter, her crown at the level of his shoulders. As their eyes met, he felt an unfamiliar jolt shooting through his body that left his insides humming.

"Did I interrupt you? For this am I sorry," she said, glancing into the temple toward the altar.

"No, no. I had just finished paying homage to my grandmother." Pakal glanced beyond her toward the footpath, relieved to see that no one was in sight. "Let us depart from here; people come often to honor our Holy Ancestor and it is best they do not see us. There is a secluded place I know, and want to show you."

She nodded and followed him down the stairs. At the base, he led her to a faintly visible deer path running alongside the river. The grasses became taller as they entered the large meadow, with an occasional tree casting shadows. Pakal helped Yonil step over some fallen branches and then re-cross the river where it was shallow, hopping on stones when possible but ending up knee deep in clear, cold water. They laughed while splashing onto the bank and Yonil took a moment to wring out the hem of her huipil. Pakal led the way to the partially collapsed building, heading to the far wall that stood highest and blocked them from view. They found some smooth stones and sat, breathless from their efforts, laughing again at nothing in particular.

"Was it difficult for you to get away?" Pakal asked.

"Not so difficult. I am not constantly surrounded by attendants, as must surely be your lot. It is not unusual for me to leave home and visit my girlfriends. My father was away and my mother occupied with weaving, so I just slipped out unnoticed."

"Ah, yes. Much easier for you. I had to make excuses and almost plead to be allowed a visit to my grandmother's tomb alone. This is a rare moment for me."

Yonil lowered her eyes, blushing faintly.

"Truly am I greatly appreciative for this moment that we can share," she said softly.

"Tell me about your life. What do you do all day?" Pakal felt sadly ignorant about details of non-royal lives.

Yonil began an animated description of her daily life, but Pakal found he was not paying attention to her words. Instead, he was fascinated by her movements; the way her arms made delightful arcs, her supple finger signs, how she tilted her head to emphasize a point. The lilt of her voice was intoxicating, and he could almost catch the scent of honey on her breath. His body pulsed with the rhythm of her words.

Pakal felt both elated and disconcerted. Since the moment when his interest in Yonil was ignited by their dancing at his adulthood ceremonies, he had found very few opportunities to speak with her. These few occasions were always in the company of others, and he was aware that his mother disapproved. She gave him a lecture about the importance of not demonstrating interest in the young women of Lakam Ha, not encouraging their aspirations, because the process of selecting his wife was soon to begin. The High Priest, his mentor and spiritual trainer, also took him aside and reminded him about conserving his sexual energies, so vitally important to his ability to carry out demanding and esoteric rituals. Pasah Chan's admonitions were fresh in his mind about the character-sapping dangers faced by rulers—selfishness, greed, pride, sensuality—that would snare their energies and entrap their spirits.

In years of intense training, Pakal had learned how to master the forces of his sexual drive and move them according to intention. He learned these through experience with Lunar Priestesses, specially trained women dedicated to initiating young ahauob into the physical and psychic aspects of using sexual energies, the most powerful creative force in the Middleworld, *cab*, the earth. He knew that combining male and female sexual energies in sacred ways would release immense creative forces. He fully realized how he was expected to channel and to sublimate his sexuality.

However, he had not anticipated his body's reaction to Yonil. Even sitting beside her, his body was vibrating with excitement and desire. He could begin now using breath techniques and meditation to control these sensations, but he did not want to. Instead, when she paused in her recital, he reached an arm toward her and cupped her chin, lifting her face.

"So beautiful!" he whispered, his eyes devouring her features.

Yonil was an exceptionally lovely woman. Her face was oval, with a narrow nose and long straight brow line leading to an elongated skull, the hallmarks of Maya nobility. Tilted almond eyes showed flecks of gold, wide and doe-like, soft as downy feathers. High cheekbones set off smooth cheeks, and her lips were wide and full and voluptuous. Her well-formed chin dipped to a long, graceful neck and softly rounded shoulders. Her skin was the color of light cacao and glowed with health and vitality. In her small ears were tiny amber earspools that reflected the gold in her eyes.

Eyes now wide and mesmerized by Pakal's gaze, Yonil parted her lips as if to catch her breath, her small firm breasts rising and falling rapidly. Pakal's hand dropped to her warm, bare shoulder then moved down, brushing against a breast and wrapping around her waist. She leaned into him, or did he draw her to him? Sparks ignited as their torsos touched; he brought his lips softly against hers then followed her chin to her throat, nuzzling the soft hollow at the base. Her arms wrapped around his neck and she gasped in ecstasy as his arms encircled her waist.

Pakal savored the sensation of her breasts heaving against his chest, aware that he was fully aroused. She was nibbling his ear gently, causing bolts of electricity to shoot through his groin. He could take her now, she would not resist. Her sexuality was exploding through every pore, eager and receptive.

He had to stop it. He could not let this happen. Somewhere, from some depth of determination, he summoned up the willpower to end their embrace. Lifting hands from her waist, he removed her arms from around his neck and gently pushed her body away from his. Still quivering with passion, he turned and walked a short distance away. Now he used the cooling breath technique with vigor, sucking air between nearly closed teeth in deep, steady in-breaths. Simultaneously he chanted a calming incantation until he felt his pulse slowing and the fire in his body retreating.

When he turned back to Yonil, he saw tears glistening in her eyes.

"Yonil, we cannot become lovers," he said with a voice not quite steady.

"Why not? It is what we both want. This passion that I feel, I also feel in you. Why must we deny it?"

"You know why. It is because of who I am. Yonil, as much as I desire you, I am bound by duty to my dynasty and the people of Lakam Ha. I must follow the traditions expected of me, and marry the woman selected by my parents. We both know that will not be you."

"Your mother hates me!" Yonil was crying now, tears streaming down her cheeks. Between sobs, she gasped a few words. "She … always disliked me … from that first time … we danced together."

Her tears tore at his heart, and he grasped her hands in his, pressing strongly.

"It is not you, she does not even know who you really are," he said, trying to sound reassuring. "It is that … that your family lineage is … not suitable for a royal wife. Please do not take offense. You are lovely, so beautiful you cannot imagine. Any man would be fortunate to have you for his wife."

His earnest praise seemed to comfort Yonil, and she stopped crying. Wiping her eyes, she glazed wistfully at Pakal.

"Any man but you," she murmured.

"Not so! I also would be fortunate, but … it cannot be."

"Then take me as your concubine." Her gold-flecked eyes locked onto his with the force of a female jaguar. "You are the ruler. You can have any woman, or all the women, that you desire. Your word is law. Your command is as binding as death. To be with you is all I want … to love you."

"Ah, Yonil ... my heart is aching. There is so much you do not understand, cannot possibly know about me, my destiny. About what I must do and how I must do it. Truly am I sorry ..."

His voice trailed off as her fierce eyes continued to bore into his.

"You can do what you want. You are K'uhul B'aakal Ahau." Her eyes softened into pools of honeyed delight. "All you have to do is command, and I will become yours."

A tiny fount of possibility surged upward from the desolate place within Pakal. What she said was not impossible. He knew of other rulers, not in Lakam Ha but in Pa'chan and Uxwitza, who had married secondary wives, and who kept concubines. He was ruler here, and might he not begin a new practice in his dynasty?

He smiled and she relaxed, breathing out a deep sigh.

"Come," he murmured. "Let us part on a sweet note. As you wisely observe, many things may be possible, even for a ruler."

She melted into his arms, snuggling against his chest, reveling in his masculine scent and hard pectoral muscles. He lightly wrapped one arm around her and stroked her hair with the other, fingers combing through silky tresses, murmuring under his breath "So beautiful, so exquisite."

Neither wanted their embrace to ever end. Long moments passed while the breeze sighed and the river warbled. White puffy clouds bunched over the southern peaks, forming tall thunderheads with gray bellies beginning to fill with rain. The sun was dropping closer to the horizon, sending lengthening shadows across the meadow.

Pakal's lips brushed her crown as he slowly disengaged from their embrace. She did not protest, lifting eyes bright with promise to meet his once again.

"Climb quickly over the hill, there is a deer path through the meadow," he said, pointing the direction. "I will return to my grandmother's temple, so we will seem to come from different places."

She nodded and turned to leave. Suddenly she whirled around, grasped his shoulders and pulled herself up to brush her lips against his.

"Remember that I am waiting, ever waiting, for your command."

3

P akal sat cross-legged on a floor mat in his private reception chamber, staring at a wooden model of a rectangular pyramid. His chief architect Yax Chan had created the model to experiment with new construction techniques. The young ruler envisioned an entirely new area of the city with different building designs that would produce taller temples, airier roofcombs, and administrative and residential structures with higher arches, loftier roofs and wider chambers. The most notable exterior difference between the model and current Lakam Ha architecture was the slope of the temple roof that sat on top of the pyramid. Presently, roofs were square or rectangular with flat sides and tops. The slanting roof edges of the model maintained parallel angles with the slope of the pyramid's sides, creating a pleasing harmony that gave the impression of lightness and elevation. The roofcomb centered upon the flat part of the roof had two parallel, thin honeycombed walls. The double walls braced each other for stability while the large filigreed openings evoked airiness.

Other models of lower buildings lined the walls of the chamber. Most were rectangular with wide stairways leading up three or four platforms to multiple chambers with corbelled arch breezeways. Several of these residential or administrative buildings would be grouped around plazas to create complexes. The roofs of these buildings were also sloped around the edges in angles that reflected stairway and platform angles, and the roofcombs had similar airy styles. The pleasing nature of these models emanated from their grace and lightness, contrasting with the heavy impression given by most contemporary buildings.

Yax Chan had explained to Pakal the key element that made this lightness possible, allowing for thinner walls and higher ceilings. It was the trapezoidal linear truss using high strength timber crossbeams. The trapezoid could resist large gravity loads, supporting high ceilings over wide chambers. This brilliant innovation came from the architect's calculations of horizontal and vertical gravity loading and his profound grasp of the mathematics of gravity resistance by axial forces generated by compression and tension qualities of structural design.

Pakal recalled their conversation clearly.

"What makes trapezoidal linear truss truly revolutionary is combining it with use of pinion stones," Yax Chan had explained. "The truss plus the pinion stones together supporting corbelled arches gives amazing strength and stability. It's a structural spanning system engineered for permanency and inherent strength, and it's capable of resisting large levels of gravity loading."

"Therefore, this system can support a wider span with a higher ceiling than current methods," Pakal had reiterated.

"Exactly! And there are other advantages. It gives both exterior and interior symmetry, harmony, and elegance. The pinion stones allow for a smooth inner vault surface that can be plastered and painted. All the laws of force and mathematics work out perfectly for the design and concept. What remains is to actually build a structure based on these principles."

Pakal's mind glided back and forth between considerations of the new architectural designs and his recent meeting with Yonil. When he thought about the new buildings he intended to create, an image spread before him of numerous structures filling the wide meadow, some tall pyramid temples and others lower complexes around multiple plazas. Among the first he built must be a replacement for the Sak Nuk Nah, a new sacred shrine to honor the Triad Deities. He knew the shrine would be placed in the area of the crumbling hunter's building, but could not yet see its configuration clearly.

Thinking of the hunters' building threw him into remorse. When last there during his covert meeting with Yonil, he had completely forgotten about these plans. Her overwhelming allure distracted him and required him to focus on controlling his strong physical and emotional impulses. The worst thing was that he had not felt the energy vortex surrounding the ruined structure, something he always felt before. This troubled him greatly. Never had he encountered such difficulty being in command of his senses, nor had he become oblivious to subtle emanations from other dimensions.

"Yonil," he anguished, "you make me forget my sacred mission."

His intuition was not lost, however, for he sensed a presence at the doorway. Twisting his head, he saw his personal attendant Tohom enter and bow.

"Yax Chan the architect arrives, Holy Lord," Tohom said.

Pakal signaled to let the architect enter and rose to greet him. After Pakal accepted a bow from Yax Chan, the two men grasped each other's shoulders in a gesture of friendship and sat close together on mats. The young architect had become one of the ruler's closest companions and his most trusted confidant. They shared the same visionary outlook for the future of their city, and both were open to innovation. While respecting tradition and established forms, they were not restricted by these.

"What think you of the pyramid temple model?" asked Yax Chan.

"It is magnificent. Never have I seen such loveliness in a building." Pakal winced as his words evoked a fleeting image of the loveliest woman he had ever seen, Yonil.

"Much is my joy at your praise. I have checked and re-checked calculations. This design should withstand stresses from gravity and natural forces. Correctly built, it will be a monument standing into the indefinite future."

"Conveying to people yet unknown and times yet unpredicted the greatness of our culture and heights of our sciences. Yes, this pyramid model must be used for all the new temples to come when Lakam Ha extends onto the eastern meadow."

"Mean you to shift the city center to this eastern location?"

"Just so. Our city needs to grow, to expand and receive more residents and visitors. We need finer buildings with excellent walls to hold carvings and paintings that express the genius of our artists. A new and much larger palace must be built; one that announces to everyone who looks upon it that Lakam Ha is the most grand of cities, most adept political power and the hub of creativity."

Pakal stopped and laughed, shaking his head.

"Am I not overly ambitious? An unrealistic dreamer?"

"Never say that of yourself!" Yax Chan touched the ruler's arm lightly, another gesture revealing their closeness. "You could not be called unrealistic, for you plan and prepare with precision. Too ambitious? Is that not a young ruler's prerogative?"

Both laughed. Pakal asked Yax Chan to review several details of construction to better commit these to memory. They eagerly conversed about materials, labor and time needed for such a large project.

"When and where will you begin?" asked Yax Chan.

"First must we devote efforts to restoring the damaged structures in our present city center," Pakal responded. "We are much alike, Yax Chan. When we enter our dreams and images of this future building project, we forget time and physical limitations. We put aside the politics of persuasion and the negotiating of resources with ahauob. In our minds, we can begin building tomorrow. Would that it were so!"

"Hmmm, yes, there are such considerations. You are correct, first we must restore and rebuild. Did you say that your grandfather's pyramid temple would be among the earliest to renovate? So much damage was done in the Kan attack; it is a shame to leave that once-grand structure in disrepair."

"Such is my plan. Have you created designs for renovating Kan Bahlam's temple?"

"No, but this will I begin at once. What are your ideas for panels and frescoes?"

Pakal and Yax Chan discussed ideas for restoring the large carved reliefs that adorned the temple's front piers and interior panels. Tohom brought them cool drinks of fruit juices mixed with watered maize, as the day was getting hot. He served inconspicuously and stood nearby, awaiting further signals from the ruler. Pakal nodded in acknowledgement, but soon made the hand signal for his attendant to leave. Tohom raised his eyebrows but quickly turned and left the chamber. He was a noble of good family; it was an honor to serve as the ruler's personal assistant. He enjoyed providing service to the Holy B'aakal Lord, often dismissing the commoner servants on quiet days. This also provided him opportunity to listen, giving an insider's view into royal life. He was disappointed at being sent away.

Conversation paused as the two men sipped the refreshing drink. Pakal startled Yax Chan with his next question.

"Yax Chan, have you ever ... uh, been in love?"

Although they were friends, this topic had not arisen.

"In love?" Yax Chan felt confused and a bit cautious about discussing such personal matters. "Not exactly, that is, I am not certain. There is a young woman here for whom I feel much attraction ... you may know her, she is called Tulix."

"Tulix, of the family of Chakab, our former Nakom who served under my mother?"

"Yes, the very one. Do you recall her?"

"That I do. Much honor to her deceased grandfather Chakab, who was a wise and strong warrior chief."

Pakal omitted the fact that he only remembered Tulix because of his recent meeting with Yonil. Tulix was among Yonil's best girlfriends, and Yonil had talked about the things they did together.

"You ask about love. I am far from sure that I know what love is. But I do have this special feeling about Tulix, and it is more than physical attraction. When I see her, my heart is glad. When we talk, her words are like honey wine and I become intoxicated. When we touch my entire body is on fire. Ah well, that is passion and desire. What I feel for her is beyond that, but includes it too. Is this love?"

Yax Chan smiled and spread his hands, gesturing confusion.

"Do you want to marry her? To be with her the rest of your life?" Pakal queried.

"Hmmm ... perhaps, yes... I think that is what I want. I do yearn to be in her presence, to feel the pleasures she summons in heart and body. Ah, but marriage is a large commitment, one is no longer free to think only of one's interests. Now another must be considered, and then after children... Ha! Am I not confused?"

"No more confused than I am myself," Pakal admitted ruefully.

Yax Chan's eyes enlarged and he stared at Pakal.

"Are you in love?"

Pakal let out a long sigh. His voice dropped to a whisper.

"What I say now you must keep in utmost confidence. No one is to know—agreed?"

Yax Chan nodded, his gaze still riveted on the ruler's face.

"If what you just described is love, then yes, I am afflicted. All the same feelings and doubts and wonderments beset me. But my situation is much worse. The woman who so affects me is Yonil, a friend to Tulix but of lesser family. She would never be acceptable to my parents; it is out of the question that we could wed. She knows and understands this. Here is my dilemma: she wants me to take her as my concubine. She is more than willing; she is eager and in fact almost demanded it. What am I to do?"

The architect could not conceal his shock. Frowning, he lowered his voice even below Pakal's whispers.

"This has never been done in Lakam Ha! There is no precedent and probably good reason why taking concubines by rulers has been avoided. Succession issues become problematic; look at the situation in Pa'chan with so many royal sons as contenders for the throne." He caught himself and laid a sympathetic hand on Pakal's arm. "Truly am I sad that you are in this dilemma. Your feelings for her are very strong, yes? Much more than desire?"

"Ah, if only I knew. My attraction is so intense that I can hardly control myself. She delights me in a multitude of ways. But there is much I do not know about her... only that she is more than willing. Another issue concerns me deeply. When I am with her, I nearly forget my duty. Even more, I lose touch with the unseen forces, the energy vortices and spiritual dimensions that have always guided me. This is deeply disturbing; it is frightening. You know, Yax Chan, there is so much that I must accomplish. I must remain in control of my senses and not deplete my energies."

They sat silently for some moments. Pakal sighed deeply again.

"Although I am no expert, I have heard from more than one older man that the initial passion does not continue," Yax Chan said. "That level of all-consuming intoxication diminishes and the relationship becomes calmer and more balanced. Things normalize with time. And, the Ix Chel priestesses know how to prevent conceptions."

"All you say is true." Pakal brightened and shot a wan smile at his friend. "Things would become more normal. But at this time, before my wife has been selected by my parents, it seems impossible that such an arrangement would be acceptable."

"Tell Yonil to wait, perhaps a year or more. From what you say about her, she would happily wait for you."

Yax Chan shrugged and made hand gestures for the unknown.

"Holy Lord and dear friend, perhaps my advice is not good. We are young and full of passion; we want to follow our hearts. You have immeasurable challenges ahead of you, more than I can imagine. Whether or not a relationship with Yonil would have a negative effect, I cannot say. It would be good to consult one wiser and older than me. Why not talk with Pasah Chan?"

4

The High Priest of Lakam Ha, Pasah Chan, waited impatiently for the messenger he had summoned to arrive. His irritation was greater than the small delay warranted. He searched his mind for the true cause. It did not take long for the reason to be uncovered. He did not like the assignment Sak K'uk, the ruler's mother, had given him. Partly he was upset that she was using him for a task better done by a relative, but more was he disturbed by the unfair nature of his mission. Injustice was not something the High Priest tolerated well.

Rapid footsteps announced the appearance of Budz Ek, the messenger. He bowed to the High Priest and glanced expectantly at the hawk-like face with heavy lids. They were alone in the priest's reception chamber, a fact that did not escape the observant bearer of news.

"It appears you are called once again to bear messages for the royal family," Pasah Chan said abruptly after a slight greeting nod. "Evidently you are highly trusted. I count on your continuing discretion. This is a task that must be done quickly and secretly. Only the involved parties must know, until all is accomplished. You will receive instructions from me and report the replies back to me. What you should know is that our Ixik K'uhul Ahau, the Holy Lady Sak K'uk, is the moving force behind this."

"So shall it be my understanding," replied Budz Ek.

"You are to travel to Nab'nahotot, on the coast of the Great North Sea to convey a marriage proposal to the Sahal of the city. A certain young noble woman of Lakam Ha is to be married to a suitable ahau of their city, who the Sahal will select. Considerable will be his reward for seeing this carried out immediately. You will take to him a rare carved eccentric flint and an amber pendant of exceptional value to signify greater gifts to arrive later. There are similar treasures for the husband's family to demonstrate that the bride gifts will be lavish. It is an offer that cannot be refused; gaining favor of the B'aakal ruling dynasty, strengthening ties between the cities, and many fine and costly luxury items."

"It is an honor to again serve Holy Lady Sak K'uk. What information do I need about the young woman, and when shall I depart?"

"In this scroll I have written her name, description and information about her family. She is called Yonil, and I can personally assure you that she is a lovely young woman. It is essential that she should be relocated to a distant city, for ... ah, personal reasons known to Lady Sak K'uk. There is no blemish upon her reputation; this is to meet certain goals of the ruling family."

Pasah Chan scrutinized the messenger, whose face remained noncommittal.

"Can you convey these messages in a convincing manner?"

"This can I accomplish fully," Budz Ek replied. Knowing the ways of men, he trusted that precious items overcame many moral qualms.

"Leave our city early tomorrow morning. Return here at dawn for the bundles containing the initial gifts and the scroll. How many days will the journey require?"

The messenger made rapid calculations, envisioning the trip along the Michol River to its junction with the B'ub'ulha River that emptied into the Nab'nah-Great North Sea. From there he would take sea-faring canoes along the coast to the city. Travel by water was much faster than over land.

"By my reckoning, the trip to Nab'nahotot should take eight days. Several more days are needed for meetings and negotiations. Then another eight days return. Perhaps in all twenty days, one uinal."

"Excellent! This time frame is acceptable. My steward will provide you with supplies and means of paying the canoe paddlers. As you know well, the Lady Sak K'uk will reward you richly once all is accomplished."

After the messenger left, Pasah Chan walked onto the plaza of his temple complex that perched high along the western border of Lakam Ha. From this lofty vantage point, one of the highest in the city, he looked past a steep cliff and across the wide plains below. The dry season of summer was nearly half over, and bunching clouds hinted of showers to herald the onset of fall rains. Once the rainy season was fully underway, rivers boiled with run-off from the mountains and currents were rapid, making travel by canoe hazardous. There was no time to lose. This mission must be accomplished quickly, including transporting the young woman, her entourage and belongings and the bride gifts, to her home of banishment.

How Sak K'uk would execute the final actions was a mystery to Pasah Chan. He reviewed the difficulties in his mind. The Holy Lady had to convince Yonil's father to acquiesce to the marriage, manage the mother's reaction to having her daughter so far away, and keep the young woman contained as she was taken from her home and torn away from the man she loved. This could produce quite a tense scenario, but no doubt the wily and consummately determined Sak K'uk would see that all was handled. She had, after all, almost single-handedly overwhelmed the Council in the Popol Nah and terrified them into accepting her as ruler until Pakal was of age.

"With the supernatural assistance of the Primordial Mother Goddess Muwaan Mat," he reminded himself.

Pasah Chan's shoulders sagged as he returned to his chamber. He disliked this mission and felt soiled by being a party to it. As Pakal's mentor throughout childhood, the High Priest had developed fondness and great respect for the boy. Now coming into his own as a young man and new ruler, Pakal was more independent. However, they still conferred often. The priest wondered how Pakal would react upon discovering Yonil's banishment and marriage. As much as that loss might pain the ruler, he had things of much greater importance to confront.

Recently they had discussed the upcoming thirteenth-tun ending. Pakal intended to perform ceremony and Pasah Chan could not envision how that would be done without the portal to the Gods. He was reluctant to cast doubt on Pakal's abilities to establish contact with the Triad Deities and invoke their presence, but he felt uneasy. He remembered the most recent katun-end ceremony done on the turning of the ninth katun at 9.9.0.0.0, thirteen years before. Sak K'uk had enacted Middleworld rituals in this very temple as the earthly representative of Muwaan Mat, while the Goddess fulfilled obligations to the Lords of the Upperworld. That arrangement was no longer in place, since rulership had passed to Pakal. The young ruler now bore responsibility to meet the Gods' requirements and provide proper tribute, but the portal for communing with the Gods had collapsed.

Tz'aakb'u Ahau—II

Baktun 9 Katun 9 Tun 12
Baktun 9 Katun 9 Tun 13
625 CE—626 CE

1

Early morning mists hovered over the surface of the small lake, kissed by sunshine into glowing rosy hues. The surface was still until dragonflies dipped to drink or water hoppers skimmed across. In the quiet space between twittering birds and distant screeches, a babbling stream murmured its continuation from the lake's outlet. Rushes grew around low banks, harboring ducks and herons who fished in the abundant waters. One grey heron lifted its stilt legs to prance near the bank, moving noiselessly and sending concentric rings spreading across the water's surface. An occasional frog croaked, still finding time to sing even though its tadpoles had already matured to join it on the bank.

The young woman approached so silently that the restful scene was undisturbed. She had perfected this approach through years of practice and by attuning her senses to the natural world. She quieted her mind and dropped awareness into what she called "the heart place" from which she gently projected feelings of love and acceptance. Nature and all its creatures were her closest friends. She appreciated them in all their aspects, from the nurturing to the fierce. She became one of them, another creature harmonizing with its natural environment. As such, she was accepted by the others.

Lalak came this day to say good-bye. She would soon be leaving this place to start life in another, one that was far away and completely unfamiliar. Before she left, it was of utmost importance to bid farewell to the special places where she had spent so much of her childhood. These special places were in nature, for Lalak felt most at home in the forests, near the lakes and streams, or climbing rocky hills that surrounded her city to marvel at the sky with its ever-changing clouds. Today she would do ritual at each special place to bring closure to this part of her life.

Ducks, herons, insects, birds and frogs hardly noticed as she dropped slowly to her knees on the bank. She scooped water into a half-gourd and said a blessing for its life-sustaining liquid, then sprinkled drops over her head and shoulders. After taking a sip, she trickled the rest over her legs and feet, chanting a sacred water prayer that she had created:

"Liquid of life, receive my love.

From where you come, below and above."

She rose in a smooth movement and spread her arms, palms outward in the blessing gesture, and murmured gratitude to all the creatures and plants of the water. The grey heron eyed her, tilting its head for better views, then nonchalantly continued probing its long beak in shallows, searching for tiny fish. A pair of ducks quacked as if saying good-bye and a sudden frog chorus seemed to wish her well. She brushed tears from her eyes and bowed, clasping hands to both shoulders in the gesture of highest respect.

Turning from the lake, Lalak followed a path into the forest. A mixture of trees thrived in the hills on the western slopes of K'uk Lakam Witz, the Fiery Water Mountain. Just over several more mountain ranges to the east was the lofty city of many waters that was to be her new home. As the path ascended, the dense foliage filtered sunlight to create dappled tapestries of greens and yellows. She inhaled the woody sweetness of cedar and pine, while faint whiffs of intoxicating copal exuded from dried sap of the sacred tree. Tall, straight mahogany and ebony trees reached limbs into the canopy; shorter ramón and oak trees spread limbs around the towering trunks. Lianas draped from branches, tree orchids perched in crooks and low-growing palmettos spread their fans close to the ground.

Lalak veered from the path, taking turns hardly noticeable in the underbrush, until she arrived at a small clearing. She had discovered this place by accident when roaming off established paths. Its ambiance was magical. Perhaps nature spirits used it for their secret purposes. A ring of tall mahogany trees created a circle, and cedars dropped needles to form a soft carpet. She whispered a request for permission to enter, waited until the trees' response came to her inner perception, entered the clearing and settled cross-legged to sit in silence.

Deep stillness enfolded her. A steady hum gradually penetrated into her form and awakened a resonant vibration within her body. In this circle, the hum was loudest although at times she heard it in meadows and on hilltops. She had tried many times to figure it out, to identify where the hum came from. Eventually she concluded that it was not the sound made by insects; those sounds had their particular rhythms and frequencies. This hum came from nowhere and everywhere. It must be the innate vibration of earth, the steady pulse of the very land upon which she sat.

This made Lalak happy. To hear the sound of Mother Earth, to be in resonance with the Giver of Form, gave her immense pleasure. She felt the cushion of cedar and pine needles beneath her and sensed energy flowing from the base of her body deep into the earth. This grounded her, and soon she felt reverse energy flowing upward from inside the earth into her body. The energy flows synchronized and amplified each other until a powerful rush of energy surged up her spine and into her head. When this had first happened, it made her shake violently and caused such pressure she thought her head would explode. After several experiences with these powerful sensations, she learned to focus and direct the energy flow to her forehead, to an area between her eyebrows. From that point she released the energy upward into the cosmos and dissolved into blissful unity with everything.

Lalak did not struggle to understand these strange phenomena; she simply accepted them just as she accepted all the elements and creatures of nature. She was not trained in Maya esoteric sciences; her education was minimal and haphazard. Her parents, the ruling family of B'aak, doted on her younger brother Bahlam Ahau and had left Lalak to grow up on her own. She did not blame them for neglecting to give her preparation that daughters of most elite ahauob received. Her father, Ik' Muuy Muwaan, had his hands full contending with the family feud that had nearly destroyed their city and fractured their kinship network. She could not imagine the pain of having to kill his brother to maintain order and rightful dynastic heritage. Her mother, ever emotionally fragile, was too consumed by these tragedies to think beyond her own troubles.

The trees and forest plants were Lalak's friends and comforters. Mother Earth was her teacher and mentor. For everything they gave her, Lalak was grateful. Now she needed to take leave of this special place and so began her ritual.

She picked up a handful of needles and tossed them over her head. Rising, she placed both hands on each tree in the circle, stroking the bark and pressing her forehead against the trunk. When she completed the circle, she dropped to her knees in the center then stretched out her body, belly against the earth. Arms outspread and fingers caressing the needles, she chanted her tree and earth prayer.

"Tree guardians of my soul, your strength supports me.

Earth Mother of all, in your arms shall everything be."

Reluctantly she separated her body from the engulfing earth energy, stood with arms extended and palms outward, and made a slow circle sending blessings to each tree.

"*In lak'ech*," she whispered. "You are another me."

Although tears stung her eyes, she did not look back as she retraced the hidden trail to the main path and continued climbing the mountain. The forest began to thin out and the path became rocky and steep. Lalak breathed heavily. Grassy hillsides swept upward to a low peak of huge boulders. The path curved around several rock outcroppings where the pale grey limestone was shot with darker veins. Reaching the summit, she scrambled onto bare rock to find an odd assortment of shapes that seemed to form stone benches. She called this her "Popol Nah" where she took council with the rocks.

Intuitively, Lalak knew that rocks and stones were capable of absorbing and holding information. The crystals buried inside had a mysterious force of attraction that captured the essences of things that happened in times past. She did not understand how this process worked, but what she experienced convinced her that the rocks were similar to ancient wisdom keepers. If she attuned to their essence and paid close attention, they would reveal their knowledge. Over years, Lalak had learned to listen to the rocks. They "spoke" in fleeting images racing across her field of awareness. After receiving many images, she began to see patterns that communicated things the rocks had experienced. Much made no sense to her, but she had the impression of immense epics of time through which the rocks underwent changes in form and composition. They experienced extremes of heat and cold, darkness and light. There were periods of great wetness and of intense droughts, and numerous strange creatures clambered over and around the rocks.

What she loved most about the rocks was their equanimity. They were untroubled by the ups and downs of nature, by change or lack of change. They simply existed and persisted through it all. In the rocks, she found ultimate stability.

Sitting upon her favorite rock bench, she closed her eyes and attuned to the ancient wisdom keepers. They knew she was here for perhaps the last time, and that she wanted to honor them in her farewell. She sensed they also wanted to give her something as a parting gift. Rising from the bench, she knelt before a round altar rock upon which she frequently left offerings. On this day, she offered something of herself, something very precious. She took a tiny bundle from her pouch and reverently placed it on the altar. Mentally she communicated to the rock.

"This is a piece of bark paper saturated with drops of my first menstrual blood. You may know, or perhaps not, as my people do not often visit you that a maiden's first menstrual blood is full of special power and magic. It is able to grant wishes and affect things that happen in the Middleworld. You seem to have few wishes, but should one arise, call upon this blood magic and it will be fulfilled."

She bowed her head and placed both hands on the round stone. Moments passed and a light breeze ruffled her hair and swished through the grasses below. Her palms became quite hot, although the day was still pleasant, and she caught a quick image of dancing iridescent butterflies. Perhaps the rocks were requesting the sight of beauty, the feeling of weightless freedom and soaring joy.

"May it be so, may your wish be granted," she murmured.

She buried the bundle in a patch of crumbled pebbles next to the altar stone, and chanted her prayer to the rocks:

"Keepers of wisdom through all the ages,
You are my teachers and beloved sages."

Lalak bowed and gave the blessing gesture to the stone benches. She smiled as she left the rocky peak, because she knew the stones and rocks would speak to her wherever she went. They cheered her on and reminded her that the sources of courage and wisdom were ever within the self.

She descended following a different path, for she would not retrace her steps and enter her special places again. It would be too much to bear, and she had performed the rituals for parting. She did need to acknowledge other things that were special to her, but these had no particular location.

One was the sky that was everywhere above; the other the animals that constantly moved from place to place.

As the downward path wended through grassy fields, she came to a gentle slope with a vista of forests, lakes, streams and her city in the distance. She often came here to appreciate the lush landscape of her home. This was a perfect place to look above at the sky, for it was immensely wide. Impulsively, Lalak grasped the hem of her short huipil and drew it off. With a giggle, she hugged it to her chest and cast quick glances to all sides, making sure no one was present. Assured that she was alone beneath the sky, she laid the white huipil out on the grass and noticed with surprise that its blue borders around the square neck and bottom hem were woven with the geometric sky symbol, a square spiral.

This delighted her into a cascade of laughter as she stretched out her naked body on the huipil, lying on her back with arms and legs spread widely apart. The sun beat warmly on her torso with firm yet ample breasts, rounded belly and long well-muscled limbs. Lalak did not think much about her body, except that it was healthy, strong, gave little discomfort and served her well. She was aware of her unusually tall stature, for she had out-stripped her age-mates at every stage. She was solidly built, a family trait shared with her brother and father. Whether or not she was considered attractive had not concerned her, and she rarely gazed at her face in the mica mirrors used by her mother.

Lalak had no close girlfriends due to her shy and reclusive nature. The nearest to a friend was her personal attendant Mukuy, a noble girl of similar age. They shared interests in singing and story-telling, but rarely delved into such topics as clothing and body adornment, cooking and children, or the young noble men of the city. Lalak showed little appetite for such subjects so Mukuy learned to avoid them. Mukuy also never commented on Lalak's appearance, especially the dark scars on her coarse-featured face, although it puzzled her that her mistress was so oblivious.

The sun brought out bronze gleams from Lalak's brown skin. She relished its vibrant light and soaked sunrays into her body. Lalak loved Ahau K'in and addressed him as Father Sun. Now she felt cradled between Mother Earth and Father Sun, her bare body resonating with both feminine and masculine energies. Opening her eyes, she drank in the vast blueness of the sky. A few thin clouds passed slowly overhead, snaking around in sinuous movements. It comforted her to know the clouds and sun would always be above, no matter where she went. In a lilting voice, she sang the morning greeting to the sun:

"Cut tip il k'ine c'k'amic a than Yum,
Tumel yetel u zazile c'pactic tu lacal baal.
Lebetico cu zaaztale c'k'ubicba tech."

"With the rising of the sun we receive your words, Master,
Because with your light we awaken and contemplate everything.
This is why at dawn we surrender ourselves to you."

The bright light of Father Sun in the sapphire sky made her feel intensely alive. The night sky was another matter. She found it mysterious and unfathomable, with its dark canopy full of distant twinkling stars, always moving and changing configuration. She did not understand the night sky. One of the only resentments Lalak felt was the lack of astronomical teaching. Her brother Bahlam Ahau had studied astronomy from early childhood, something elite nobles and future rulers were required to master. As a woman, even of the ruling family, she was not slated for such training. Her curious mind and love for nature sparked intense wonder about what those celestial denizens were doing and what the ancestors and Gods who were the stars could communicate.

Perhaps in her new home, the central city of the region, she could learn about them. Surely the most advanced astronomers and calendar priests one could find resided there. Thinking about her future city reminded Lalak that she should soon return home to finalize preparations for departure the following morning. Rising to reclaim her huipil and continue down the path, she reflected on the mixed emotions this departure provoked. Partly she was excited to travel and see new places, for she had never left B'aak before. Her new city, Lakam Ha, was the polity's dominant city and had received the high honor of being selected *May Ku* for two cycles. Doing some calculations, she figured that was 260 tuns (256 solar years) per *May* cycle times two cycles, making 520 tuns (512 solar years), a huge time spanning at least ten lifetimes. What great power and influence a city must have to be dominant in the polity for so long!

In this was her contrasting emotion: fear. When she thought of living in Lakam Ha, she was filled with trepidation. It was a large city, much larger than B'aak, so her father said. There were many more people with ideas and experiences she could never imagine. The royal court was splendid and commanding, she felt certain, hosting frequent visitors from widespread cities and receiving tribute from all polity cities. Presiding at court was the K'uhul B'aakal Ahau—the real one—for she knew her father also appropriated that title, though everyone knew he was not Holy Lord of

B'aakal polity. She learned that a new, young ruler had acceded not long ago and she had been selected for his wife.

Wife of the K'uhul B'aakal Ahau! The mere thought made her feel faint. How could she ever fill the role of Ixik Ahau, Holy Lady of this exalted city? And why was she selected, among all the eligible young women in the polity? Her father explained, with obvious pride, that it was because of their family's impeccable bloodlines back to the founder of B'aakal. No purer royal blood could be found, even in the Bahlam family of Lakam Ha. But it seemed no one negotiating this marriage alliance even considered whether she was prepared to be royal wife of K'inich Janaab Pakal. Even his majestic name intimidated her.

More than anything else, however, the previous ruler of Lakam Ha frightened her. Accounts of the incredible feats done by the mother of Pakal, Sak K'uk, were favorites among storytellers. This legendary woman had attained rulership by shape-shifting into the Primordial Mother Goddess Muwaan Mat, mother of the Triad Gods who created the royal lineage of B'aakal. She *became the Goddess;* all present in the Council House that day saw the transformation. Most fell to their knees or cowered on the floor, so overwhelming was the Goddess' presence. After that, none questioned Sak K'uk standing in as Middleworld ruler for Muwaan Mat, who fulfilled ritual obligations to the deities in the Upperworld.

Now that her son Pakal was ruler, they said that Sak K'uk no longer assumed the Goddess' form. But to even have done so, to be capable of such immense shamanic powers, must have left its mark. How could a mere mortal interact with someone who had been a Goddess? Someone who would be her mother-in-law.

Lalak began crying as she followed the path through the forest, beset by anxiety and feeling her losses acutely. No longer could she meet her animal friends and feel their gentle companionship. Since early childhood, animals had come to her without fear. The shy ones such as deer and songbirds did not disappear when she came near, the curious coatimundis and monkeys approached boldly to play, the lizards and frogs sat calmly and eyed her, and bolder birds like hummingbirds and macaws perched on fingers or arms. Predators considered her among their ranks and treated her with respect. She had befriended a mother jaguar to such an extent that she could play with the cubs and share food. Even the foul-tempered wild boar, among the largest animals of the tropical forests, accepted her.

A story was told in B'aak about Lalak and the wild boar. When she had attained seven solar years, she wandered into the forest and got lost. Men were sent to find her after she was gone over a day. They scoured the hills and forests, examined streams and lakes for possible drowning, climbed trees in case she was hiding among branches. One searcher followed footprints of a child mingled with those of a large boar, fearing the worst. These mean beasts had tusks that could disembowel a man. But he found no torn body, only more footprints, side by side. A keen hunter, he smelled the musty odor of the boar and approached a thicket downwind. Carefully parting leaves for a view, he saw the small girl curled up asleep at the boar's side. Afraid to awaken the sleeping boar, he tossed tiny pebbles on the girl until she opened her eyes. He made the hand sign to climb a nearby tree. Once she had stealthily crept away and climbed the tree, he made much noise, banging his shield and shouting, waking the boar, which snorted and quickly crashed away into the underbrush.

No one understood how the child survived and seemed friendly with the wild boar. Everyone knew, however, that Lalak had special and unusual relationships with animals.

Now she sat in a small clearing in the forest, continuing to cry while psychically calling her animal friends. Soon a doe appeared and nuzzled her, and a pair of weasels skittered around her feet. The doe's wet nose and the weasel's antics made her laugh. A large red-crested iguana climbed down a nearby branch to stare with beady eyes, tilting his head to and fro and bobbing it until she hummed with delight. A rabbit, opossum and armadillo joined the medley while birds filtered onto branches: doves, warblers, buntings, azure tanagers, and the laughing chachalaca. Green parrots squawked greetings as they flew in and were joined by a brilliant scarlet macaw and a toucan whose yellow and black beak was as long as its body.

Lalak was overcome with happiness at this show of animal affection, and she thanked each one, making sounds similar to theirs. Soon she heard spider monkeys chattering in the high canopy and the startling roar of a close-by howler monkey. Of all the animals, perhaps she felt closest to the monkeys. Their intelligent eyes spoke to her of kindred spirits, creatures not so different from her own human family. About two years ago she had found a tiny baby spider monkey, alone and trembling high in a tree. She waited and kept vigil, but no monkeys came to take the baby. The monkeys' absence was strange, for there were large groups living around B'aak. When dusk fell, the baby's whimpers compelled Lalak to climb the tree and rescue him. The tiny hands clung to her neck and he cuddled into her shoulder, so she took him home.

The spider monkey baby was so young that it needed to nurse. Lalak found a woman with a suckling baby and arranged to get milk for the monkey. Sometimes the woman suckled the monkey directly, and at other times Lalak fed expressed breast milk to the monkey using a deer udder attached to a small gourd. It was a common practice among Maya people. Women tended to take infant deer and suckle them from their breasts, and then kept them as domestic animals in household pens. Baby coatimundis were raised as pets and ocellated turkeys were bred in captivity.

Lalak named the monkey "Popo." He became her constant companion. Although she took him into the forest from time to time, and he played in trees with other spider monkeys, he always returned to her. Now he would be coming with her to a new home. At least one of her animal friends would stay by her side, she reassured herself, as she said farewell to the others in the clearing.

She sang a song of blessing as she slowly rose and left the forest clearing.

"A uet mucul a xicin; caxtun, caxtun."

"That you live many years; be it so, be it so."

2

66 Lalak! Are you ready to go? The delegates are here and the canoes prepared for departure. Come quickly, do not keep them waiting."

Her mother's shrill voice broke Lalak's reverie as she gazed around her sleeping chamber and wondered if she would ever see it again. She scurried around, gathering her bundles and carrying them to the door of her chamber, where she nearly collided with Mukuy. Her attendant bowed and then dropped to her knees, clasping Lalak's ankles and sobbing. Lalak sank to her knees also and raised Mukuy's tear-stained and puffy face, testimony to much crying.

"What is it? Why are you crying so?" Lalak asked.

"Oh, Lady ... forgive me ... this I cannot do, cannot bear ..." Mukuy choked out between sobs.

"But you are coming with me to Lakam Ha, we are not parting, why do you cry?" Lalak was perplexed, for the plans were that her attendant would accompany her.

"No, no ... oh such a deceitful person I am ... not worthy of your friendship ..." Mukuy kept gasping, making it difficult to catch her words.

"Calm down, come inside my chamber, let not our visitors see this," said Lalak, cradling Mukuy and helping her rise. As she settled her friend on the sleeping pallet, she heard her mother outside instructing servants to carry the bundles to the canoes.

"Mother, I shall be there momentarily," Lalak called out. "I am getting Popo."

The monkey chattered at hearing his name. He sat on his usual perch, a wooden structure with many rungs for climbing. Lalak had put on his collar and leash so he knew he was going somewhere. Going out always excited him.

"Now be of comfort and tell me why you are so upset," said Lalak, sitting beside her friend.

Mukuy swallowed and wiped at her teary eyes. Sniffling, she tried to keep her wavering voice under control.

"Here you see no true friend," she began. "Little do I deserve the love you have given to me. A coward; that is what I am. And dishonest ..."

Tears welled up again. Lalak waited, patting her hand.

"Dearest Lady, please forgive me ... but, but I cannot go with you to Lakam Ha. It fills me with terror, to think of leaving my home. You are strong, courageous ... you can face this strange city and all those exalted nobles and rulers ... I cannot. I am scared. But there is more. Oh, how I regret not speaking to you of this sooner! A vile and cowardly worm, that is what I am!"

Mukuy dissolved into tears and sobs. Lalak felt shaken. She had depended on having at least one person accompany her. Mukuy was her only real friend and she felt close to the young woman.

"Mukuy, this fear can be overcome. You can draw on my strength, you will see that I have enough for us both. You will be protected and cared for, and given much respect. Take heart, we can find ways to make our new home familiar and comfortable."

Lalak spoke with more confidence than she really felt, for her own trepidations were similar to her friend's.

"Oh, Lalak, you are so kind and I am so undeserving of you as a friend!" Mukuy wiped eyes and dripping nose, cleared her throat and squared her shoulders. For the first time she lifted her face to look directly at Lalak.

"Here is my greatest failing, my ultimate cowardice. I have not been honest with you about my plans." Although her voice quavered, she pressed quickly on. "Not long ago a young man began to court me, and we are in love. His father has spoken to mine, and our marriage has been agreed upon. I did not tell you for fear of making you sad, or to avoid upsetting you ... you show so little interest in such things ... I thought there would be time, much time, to slowly break this to you ... oh, I did not foresee these sudden developments, your betrothal to the ruler of Lakam Ha, moving quickly to his city ... oh, forgive me, I am worthless and so sorry!"

Hugging the distraught girl, Lalak felt a cold dread creep through her body. She realized she would travel alone, accompanied only by her monkey. Although as the ruler's daughter she could demand that Mukuy go, she could not inflict the suffering of separation, either from city or beloved, upon her friend. She deliberately numbed her emotions and stilled her mind's wild gyrations; these she would handle later. Now she had to get through the departure with an appearance of equanimity.

"My friend, these things I do understand," she murmured in Mukuy's ear. "Grieve not that you delayed telling me of your betrothal. You meant no harm; none of us could anticipate this offer from the Lords of B'aakal. Do not be troubled that you will not accompany me. The Lakam Ha delegates brought a personal attendant for me, a nice young woman who will see to my needs. For you, I am very happy. Receive now my blessings upon your marriage, and give me your blessings for mine."

They embraced and held each other close for long moments. Mukuy kept whispering her thanks and blessings between sniffles. Lalak's mother called again, even more shrilly.

"I must go. Be of good cheer and may your life be filled with happiness."

She released her friend and took Popo from his perch, turned her back on everything that was familiar and safe and comforting, and walked out of her chamber for the short river trip to a foreign world.

3

The rains had just begun when Lalak arrived at Lakam Ha. The final two days of her river trip were tumultuous, the canoes dipping through swirling currents fed by swelling waters. Their camp on the riverbank was wet and the food soggy, although everyone tried to make Lalak as comfortable as they could. Popo chattered his teeth, a sign of disapproval, as winds whipped stinging rain under open canopies placed on the canoes. Lalak felt bedraggled, exhausted and drenched when the delegation pulled the canoes ashore in the landing area of the Michol River, at the base of a steep escarpment.

She looked with amazement at the city perched high up the mountainside, a curving sakbe ascending from the river. With relief she entered the palanquin sent to carry her up the white plastered road. Her city's palanquin had been destroyed during their internecine battles and she barely remembered riding in it as a young child. She was certain, however, that it had not been near as grand as the palanquin of Lakam Ha. On the swaying ride uphill, her new personal attendant, Muyal, described features of the city while attempting to dry her mistress and the monkey with soft cotton shawls. Muyal was a talkative young woman of good family, close to Lalak's age and unmarried. Lalak found this chatter entertaining and was amused, in spite of her sadness, at the similarity of names: Muyal of Lakam Ha replaced Mukuy of B'aak. The Gods had a sense of humor.

The rain was too heavy to get a good look at buildings through the palanquin drapes. It seemed they traveled a good distance before stopping at a large residential structure that Muyal called the palace. Several women, whom Muyal said were household servants, met them and ushered them into a wing of the complex that was Lalak's residence. She was astounded at the size and elegance of the seven chambers that she was to call home. Seven separate rooms! Her entire home in B'aak had fewer chambers. Mukuy rattled off the purposes of all these rooms: private reception, public reception, dining, bathing and toileting, sleeping, a large chamber for her personal weaving and artwork, and a dressing chamber for clothing and adornments.

Lalak's head was reeling. She had never imagined such luxurious quarters. As Muyal introduced her to six serving women and explained their functions, Lalak felt anxiety rising. Muyal's next words struck near-terror in her gut.

"After you have bathed and rested, later in the day, our K'uhul Ixik Me' the Holy Lady Mother Sak K'uk will call upon you. She is eager to meet you and welcome you to your new home."

"Holy Lady Mother?" Lalak gasped out the title.

"Just so, this is the title we now call Lady Sak K'uk, since you will become K'uhul B'aakal Ixik, the Holy Lady of B'aakal. We must distinguish between our Holy Ladies to keep things clear," said Muyal with a wink.

Lalak felt a cold sweat breaking out on her face and neck. She hoped she could get her emotions under control by the time the legendary Goddess-invoker appeared. A bath and a rest were definitely needed, and some time to center herself.

The bath itself was remarkable. The architects of Lakam Ha had created underground aqueducts that forced water up a narrow channel into a vat built into the floor. She could nearly immerse herself in the square vat as water flowed steadily in, then left through a drain. Muyal explained that when the weather was cold, buckets of heated water were carried in and added for warmth. Even more astonishing was the toilet built into a corner of the room. Its round opening set on a raised stone platform allowed elimination into a flowing current that carried refuse away through separate underground channels. Never had Lalak heard of such a thing, but its obvious convenience was appealing. As a servant washed her with sweet-smelling oils and the soothing water caressed her body, she began to relax.

Muyal left to be with her family and Lalak nibbled at a meal of fruit and nuts, her appetite not very good. She wore her finest huipil, its neck and hem borders woven with yellow and red flowers, and put on jade and pearl jewelry that she never wore in B'aak. Servants seemed to hover everywhere, and she requested to be left alone in the private reception room for a little while. She was given to understand this was the proper chamber in which to receive her royal visitor. Sitting cross-legged on a thick floor mat, she steadied her breathing and worked at calming her mind.

The sounds of raindrops and distant birdcalls soothed her. Memories of walks through the forests of her home and meetings with her animal companions enveloped her in waves of sweet nostalgia. Clucking sounds made by Popo, who sat near her on his perch, were reassuring. She emptied her mind of thoughts and refused to let fear creep in; for these moments she settled into peacefulness.

But peace was short-lived. Excited voices and slapping sandals on plaza stones heralded an approaching contingent that promised to be sizeable. As the noises drew closer, Lalak rose to her feet and stood facing the draped doorway. Uncertainty surged and she dreaded the moment the drape would be pulled aside. Popo chattered his teeth, sensing her distress.

The door drape was flung aside and a finely dressed man entered, holding it open and declaring sonorously,

"Now enters the K'uhul Ixik Me', the Holy Lady Mother Sak K'uk! Honored and blessed are those who receive her Sacred Presence."

A small but undeniably regal figure strode through the doorway, dazzling the eye with her splendid attire. Tall feathers swayed in the headdress, the most precious scarlet macaw and iridescent blue quetzal. Huge necklaces of jade hung over a pristine white huipil with borders sewn in gleaming gold discs; tall-backed sandals were embellished with sparkling beads, and cuffs of jangling seed pods mingling with small white seashells covered wrists and ankles. Every step was a symphony of waving colors and tinkling sounds.

A horde of courtiers and attendants streamed in behind the Holy Lady Mother. They spread across the reception chamber, creating a colorful panorama with their own fine clothing. As their chattering and laughing died down, all eyes fastened upon the lone young woman from B'aak.

Lalak suppressed a gasp, caught herself and bowed deeply to the Holy Lady Mother, clasping her left shoulder. She did not know how long to remain bowed, or what signal would tell her to straighten up. Long moments passed in strained silence. Receiving no cue, she slowly lifted her upper body and released her shoulder clasp. She was startled to find herself looking down at a woman whose head barely reached her shoulder but whose eyes blazed with fierce authority.

Someone tittered in the periphery and Lalak was certain she had violated some important protocol. Should she speak first, or wait for the ruler's mother to break the silence? Tension in the room mounted, suddenly punctuated by Popo's screech. The terrified monkey buried his round eyes in both hands and cowered on his perch. Laughter outbursts rippled through the group, some pointing at the monkey.

The Holy Lady Mother lifted a hand and brought all to silence. She tilted her head to meet Lalak's eyes, but not before the girl caught a furious-appearing glance at Popo. Lalak began to tremble.

"Greetings, Lady Lalak of B'aak. It is our great happiness that you have arrived safely, and we welcome you to our city of Lakam Ha. Let it be said, let it be inscribed, that the future K'uhul Ixik is received into her new home, the mother of our future Holy Rulers is honored. It is a thing of utmost import that the dynasty of B'aakal continues through your pure bloodlines, for which you were searched out and selected. We are honored; you are honored. The Gods and the people are served. Receive now the blessings of our Sacred Triad Gods: Hun Ahauthe First Born of the Celestial Realm, Mah Kinah Ahauthe Second Born of the Underworld Realm, and Unen K'awill the Third Born of the Earthly Realm and Patron of Rulers. These are now your Gods; these are now your people."

The voice of the Holy Lady Mother was rich and melodious, as smooth as unruffled lake water and as opaque as a muddy stream. Despite her severe expression, her tones revealed no emotion. Lalak bowed her head, swallowed hard and replied in what she hoped matched the courtly language of her hostess.

"Much am I honored by this splendid reception. It is my utmost wish to fulfill all my duties as future K'uhul Ixik of this magnificent city of Lakam Ha."

"So shall it be. Much assistance will we provide you in realizing all these duties. There will be time for learning and training. We know that our city is larger and more complex than yours, that there are many customs and ceremonies that will be new and different for you. All will be brought into perfect order, all will be prepared. Now will I introduce you to these nobles who are to be your assistants in various ways."

Sak K'uk, Holy Lady Mother, turned and signaled several nobles to come forward.

"Let me present Til'bak, your personal scribe who will record your deeds and accomplishments. He shall attend you daily with his brushes and books."

A slender young man stepped forward, smiled and bowed to Lalak. She returned his bow and immediately liked his warm, friendly eyes.

"Here is Yax Xoc, who shall tend to your wardrobe and adornments. She is among the most talented of my weavers and artisans of jewelry. You will benefit greatly from her abilities."

The middle-aged woman who stepped forth appeared quite as severe as her mistress, eyes cold and appraising, mouth set with grim lines. She did not smile nor take her gaze off Lalak who felt visually stripped, each body contour noted and evaluated for improvement. Lalak nodded to the aloof weaver, then thought better and bowed too.

"Yax Xoc, you must begin your work on wardrobe and adornments immediately," said Sak K'uk. She gestured toward Lalak with the hand sign for clothing. "Our future K'uhul Ixik requires much finer clothing than this, even for less formal receptions and appearances. See the coarseness of the fabric she wears; we must never allow such in public. Much finer jewelry and sandals are necessary, and be sure to create several spectacular headdresses of the most rare feathers."

"As you command, Holy Lady Mother," replied the weaver. With a disdainful gesture that essentially dismissed Lalak's entire ensemble, she continued. "Indeed we shall dispel the parochial quality of our new Lady's appearance and transform this into the sophistication our great city expects of its royalty."

"Excellent. It is quite certain that your talents can bring elegance even to such a *large* figure." The emphasis on Lalak's size could not be missed.

Lalak's eyes widened and her heart pounded furiously. These two haughty women had virtually ripped off her finest clothing and discarded it in public. Stymied for a fitting response, the young woman kept her counsel and struggled to retain composure.

Moving smoothly on as if nothing were out of the ordinary, Sak K'uk continued introductions. Next was the tutor, Tohat, who would school Lalak in the history, religion and ceremonial practices of her new city. She was assigned her own priestess-healer named Utzil, to attend her hygienic needs and keep her healthy. A musician was assigned to entertain her privately and provide lessons on playing ceramic and wooden flutes. A stout woman was to become her kitchen supervisor and meal planner, responsible for personal meals and for arranging feasts. There was a supple male dance instructor to teach her many complex dances, which she was expected to master for celebrations and feasts where she would be on exhibit. Last introduced was her steward, the man who organized and oversaw her daily activities and managed her appointments and appearances.

"It gives me great pleasure to now introduce Pomoy, your household steward. He has served many years in our palace and knows all you will need about processes of the royal court and household. No finer man can be found for this important position; I am certain you will come to appreciate his abilities as none other."

The square-bodied man who bowed before Lalak conveyed an impression of competent authority. She was not certain that she liked the subtle glint in his eyes, but by this time she felt overwhelmed and questioned her intuition. She smiled and bowed, hoping this ordeal would end soon. But the one person she most wanted to meet was apparently not in this entourage.

Sak K'uk turned away and issued a series of orders to Lalak's newly assigned assistants, sending each off to set up their various duties in the household. The Household Steward remained by her side. Lalak realized the visit was coming to an end, and gathered courage to ask her question.

"Holy Lady Mother, when will I meet your son, the K'uhul B'aakal Ahau, who is to be my husband?"

Sak K'uk turned slowly back, eyes traveling up and down Lalak's long body. With tones as rich and smooth and noncommittal as before, she replied:

"It is natural that you are eager to meet your future husband, my son Pakal. But this you may not know. We are required to follow royal protocol, it is most important that this momentous occasion generates the reverence it rightly deserves, and proceeds with appropriate dignity. After all, this is no village marriage but the merging of two divine and God-imbued bloodlines to continue the grand Bahlam dynasty of B'aakal and satisfy the decrees of the Triad Deities. In deference to these sacred laws, you may not meet privately with Pakal until after the formal court introductions and ceremonious reception has taken place."

With hooded eyes, Sak K'uk curled her lips in what approached a smile, or perhaps a smirk, and made the hand gesture for obedience.

"Naturally you will come to understand the critical importance of royal and courtly protocol. Pomoy, your Household Steward, will instruct you well on the ceremonies and how to comport yourself."

Pomoy nodded and smiled in turn, bowing again toward Lalak.

"We shall begin her training this very day," he said with confidence.

"The Ah K'inob, our Solar Priests and Daykeepers, have determined the time for your meeting with Pakal. It must be a fortuitous time according to placement of the stars and sun, the moon and planets. And it must be within particular calendar cycles of the date your marriage will take place. This date is of utmost importance. The success of your union in producing heirs, and in bringing about abundance and prosperity to our people, depends upon the correct cosmic alignments."

Sak K'uk appeared to have finished her statement and began to turn away. Lalak felt as if she were pleading for information that should rightly be hers. She shifted uneasily on her feet and persisted.

"Might I be told those dates, since they have been set by the Solar Priests?"

Looking annoyed, Sak K'uk whipped her head back full face to Lalak.

"Very well. You are an impatient young woman. You shall meet K'inich Janaab Pakal when the next moon reaches the fullness of her cycle. Your marriage shall take place when the sun attains his perfect balance, the equality of day and night, in the season of new beginnings, in the springtime. That is all. Now shall I depart."

Perhaps it was the sudden clinking and jingling of Sak K'uk's jewelry as she began to walk out, or the murmuring of the group beginning to depart. But most likely it was the sharp burst of painful emotion in Lalak's heart that caused her monkey to react. Popo stretched his full height standing on hind legs, waved his arms wildly and screeched repeatedly at ear-splitting levels.

Everyone froze in their steps, and then almost as one spun around to stare at the monkey. A few clapped hands over their ears. Lalak jumped to Popo's side, grabbed him and cradled him in her arms. Her soothing whispers and strokes reduced his outburst to whimpers. She looked up and saw Sak K'uk glaring with dagger-point eyes. Raising one arm imperiously and pointing at the pair, she hissed,

"Get that filthy creature out of here. It is entirely improper to have such an animal in your reception chamber. Take heed, do not err again."

On her way out, Sak K'uk remarked to the Royal Steward, loudly enough for all present to hear.

"Pomoy, teach her proper manners quickly."

Lalak stood quivering in the deserted reception chamber, holding Popo tightly to her breasts. His small prescient fingers twined her hair as he buried his face into the hollow of her neck. Though her knees felt like soft rubber, she willed them to stay locked and hold her upright. Her breath tried to come out in sobs but she forced steady deep inhalations and fought back tears. Someone might re-enter the chamber at any time, and she was determined not to show weakness. Inside she felt a curious mixture of fury and terror, roiling in her gut and burning in her throat. She walked slowly, stepping with care to be sure her knees would not buckle, from side to side of the chamber. Walking brought some relief and she crooned to Popo, stroking his furry back.

"They will not take you away, dearest Popo," she whispered. "You will always be near me, even if I must keep you only in my sleeping chamber." He clucked and began to relax, loosening his grip on her hair. "It was frightening, this I know. I was frightened too. My little *max* will not suffer this again, be comforted, be calm."

But her mind mocked her back. *You, however, will suffer more and more of it.*

Why did the Holy Lady Mother dislike her so much?

Feeling the need to escape the reception chamber, Lalak slipped out and returned to her sleeping chamber. Popo felt secure enough to leave her arms and settle onto her pallet, curling into a ball and dropping nearly at once into sleep. She removed her jewelry, sandals and huipil, now relegated to "coarse and inelegant." No doubt these would be taken away, given to some servant. It pained her to remember how hard her mother had worked to weave the huipil and select the jewels. This was a world into which her mother would never fit. Would she herself be able to?

Donning a soft cotton shift, she sat beside the small window that looked over an interior courtyard and watched the rain fall. Nature always soothed her, and the pattering of raindrops was almost hypnotic.

Nature has her cycles that are recurrent and inevitable, she thought. *Everything changes and everything returns. All things have their place in nature.*

Surely the patterns among people were also part of nature. She would find her place and learn the patterns of her new home. Somehow, she would do it.

Pakal. When would she meet her future husband? At the time of the next full moon. She was chagrined to realize she had lost track of the moon cycle. The last several nights were cloudy or rainy and she could not see the sky. Where was the moon in her cycle when she last saw the night sky? She seemed to recall a thin crescent hovering on the horizon, but was the moon waxing or waning? Her mind could not recall this information. And her marriage date? Oh, that was so far away! The spring equinox was still nine moons in the future, of that she felt more certain. Wryly, she watched the thought taking form: *They must think that I need a lot of improvement before I am prepared to be Pakal's wife.*

Her reflections were interrupted by Muyal rushing into the chamber, a penitent expression on her face.

"Please forgive me, I should have returned sooner to be with you during the meeting with Lady Sak K'uk," said the breathless attendant.

"Thank you, but I doubt you could have done anything to make it better," said Lalak. She was surprised at how quickly word traveled. It was her first experience of palace gossip, but she was sure it would not be the last.

"Are you ... er, feeling well? Do you need anything?"

Lalak was touched by the young woman's concern and offer of help. At least she seemed to have one friend in the palace.

"Perhaps something to drink, some fruit juice would be good," she replied. As Muyal was leaving to fulfill her request, she made another. "Kindly find out when my Household Steward Pomoy plans to come for my lessons. Then return and help me dress appropriately to receive him."

4

The moon was waning and soon her sliver disappeared, leaving the night sky in utter darkness. As she reappeared and began to swell, life for the new arrival in the palace of Lakam Ha settled into a daily routine. When she awoke, Lalak's personal care was attended to by servants who bathed and dressed her, combing and twining her hair under a simple headband that left two tufts protruding in front and back. She thought it must make her resemble some disoriented bird who could not decide which direction to face. A light meal of fruit and maize porridge was served in her small dining chamber that had an interior doorway into the private reception chamber. In her U-shaped quarters, most chambers had only outward doors facing the patio. At the morning and evening meals she dined alone; at the noon meal one or more of her assistants joined her.

First to appear for the morning's studies in the private reception chamber was her scribe Til'bak. She welcomed him warmly, for his cheerful manner lifted her spirits. He was talkative and never lacked keen observations and amusing stories about life in their city. These snippets began opening a tapestry of its many-layered and elaborate social structure. When her tutor Tohat joined them, she became further immersed in the dynamics of the royal household and the peopling of the royal court. It seemed to Lalak that life in Lakam Ha, and in all of B'aakal polity, was focused around the court. The entire city appeared in some respects to belong to the ruler's extended household.

The people who thronged to the court were such a myriad that it made her head spin. There were the royals and their relatives, upper elite and lesser nobles with their families, advisors and attendants, officials with an array of duties, priests and scribes, guards and warriors, scholars and calendar diviners, healers, artists and artisans, entertainers, visiting dignitaries and ambassadors from other polities, and an assortment of other retainers, servants, guests, dependents and general hangers-on. At times there were political prisoners and hostages of noble lineage who were kept to guarantee their city would not attack. Although none of these had been at court in recent times, stories of famous past hostages revealed that some eventually married into Lakam Ha families. One elite woman who was kept at court with her brother became wife of a Lakam Ha ruler; her brother returned to become ruler of his city.

Lalak was fascinated by the strange people who were present at court for particular purposes. Tohat described a dwarf who always remained close to the ruler, and whose antics caused much laughter. She had never seen a dwarf and marveled that people could be so tiny. What intrigued her more was the dwarf's exceptional privilege to challenge and contradict the ruler with impunity. Tohat explained that since the dwarf could have no ambitions for himself or his family that might threaten the ruler, he could speak more freely than others who had something to lose. The ruler often benefitted from a candid view of situations that nobles might be manipulating to their advantage. Having marginal people at court, such as dwarfs and prisoners, marked it as a liminal place. The royal court hovered between the ordinary world and an extraordinary zone where the exalted and transcendent mingled with the celestial and supernatural.

Courtly protocol demanded a strictly orchestrated set of behaviors. One must wear fine clothing and sport impressive adornments, use formalized courtly language when speaking, follow rules of hierarchical placement in proximity to the throne and ruler, present gifts and tribute to outdo competitors, use gestures and body postures carefully chosen to convey the most subtle communications, and take advantage of opportunities to promote one's goals without causing offense. The favor of the ruler was preeminent. To receive his attention and approval was the utmost accomplishment; to incur his disdain or disapproval the most dismal failure. Provoking his anger could be dangerous to one's fortunes, position, and potentially life itself.

Lalak was terrified by court protocol. She feared she could never master its intricacies and dreaded her upcoming introduction to the ruler and entourage at court. If only she could meet Pakal in private, in a small cozy chamber without hordes of judgmental observers, in particular the Holy Lady Mother. But it was painfully clear that this public spectacle would be required of her. She listened with tense concentration as her tutor explained court organization and protocols, and asked her scribe to write everything down so she could study later. She marveled at his flowing inscription of glyphs on bark-paper pages, using a wooden stylus dipped in plant ink. Tohat was careful to explain that the final authority on court decorum was her Household Steward Pomoy, who would put her through exercises to hone her skills. This frightened her even more, for she sensed that Pomoy was a less forgiving coach than her tutor.

When the morning lessons ended, a midday meal was served in the dining chamber. Her personal attendant Muyal always came and often Til'bak and Tohat joined in a meal of stewed squash, beans and peppers seasoned with epazote leaves and crushed allspice berries. Often small chunks of deer, turkey or tapir meat, and occasionally iguana eggs, were added to the stew. An unheated, thick beverage of ground maize flour and water was served; maize was boiled with *kal* (white lime) to soften the kernels and release essential nutrients, then dried and ground. The drink was flavored with honey or toasted and ground squash seeds. If the day was cool and rainy, cacao and ground chile peppers were preferred seasonings and the drink was warmed.

Pomoy was present at this meal every two or three days, and used the time to critique Lalak's eating manners. She must sip stew delicately from the gourd bowl, and use a smaller gourd or folded avocado leaf as a cup to scoop out remaining chunks of meat or vegetables. Using fingers to remove the last morsels was not acceptable, a hard habit for her to break as she had always eaten this way at home. Drinking the maize beverage required graceful hand and finger movements to grasp, lift and present the ceramic cup to her lips. Every action of eating and drinking must be done with graceful ease. She could not wipe her mouth with hand or fingers, but instead carefully use her tongue to cleanse off drops. She tried but always feared that remnants of stew or maize were drying on her chin. Though meals were more relaxed when Pomoy did not come, Muyal or Tohat kept up the discipline and reminded her when her manners lapsed.

The sessions following the noon meal with Pomoy were hardest for Lalak. He was always impeccably polite and kept an inscrutable face, but she sensed an underlying current of disapproval. His task was to explain her role as wife of the K'uhul B'aakal Ahau, and to train her for every public detail. There were her appearances at court to sit near the ruler, hold regal presence and act with courtly demeanor, while receiving dignitaries with tribute or gifts, greeting visiting ambassadors or nobles, listening to reports by messengers, adjudicating conflicts, considering requests, and dispensing positions or goods to nobles, warriors, or artisans who earned them. The ruler took primary responsibility in these activities, but she would be asked on occasion to comment or give advice. She must be familiar with rules and precedents, and be ready with a flow of courtly language suitable to the occasion. In these things, Pomoy instructed her during long afternoons that left her exhausted.

She welcomed the short rest between the Household Steward and the next assistant, during which she was given another maize beverage, usually laced with cacao and chile for stimulation. Muyal joined her then and often ordered sweet maize cakes made with honey, ground nuts and dried berries. To give her mistress a lift, Muyal told clever stories and made jokes that always drew forth chuckles even on the worst days. When the next session was with the dance or music instructor, Lalak could relax and enjoy these pleasant diversions. Dancing was something she loved, even though her tall and stout body did not move with enviable grace or flexibility. Dance steps at Lakam Ha were more complicated than those at her home, but she was a quick study and reveled in the compliments from her instructor. Even her musician was ready with praise for how rapidly she learned flute melodies, and soon they played lilting duets that caused Muyal to clap her hands with delight.

When the weaver and wardrobe supervisor Yax Xoc came, Lalak felt oppressed and judged once again. Yax Xoc seemed incapable of smiling, her face set in a perpetual frown. She clicked her tongue frequently, apparently frustrated with the challenge of fitting elegant clothing onto Lalak's ungainly frame. At times she muttered under her voice, "How could a woman get so tall?" or "These are limbs for a farmer."

Rarely did Yax Xoc ask for Lalak's opinion about dress and adornments. The weaver selected fabric, colors, patterns for borders, jewelry, sandals, headdresses, waistbands as she saw fit. Lalak did not protest; although she did have preferences, she was loath to provoke the severe woman's criticism. At times other women came to experiment with hair styles according to which headdress Lalak would be wearing. All this attention to appearance was strange and puzzling to her. It made her worry that something was fundamentally wrong with how she looked.

She determined to ask Muyal about this over their evening meal.

It was an especially delicious repast. Maize dough was laid over an avocado leaf, spread with a mixture of mashed beans and cooked chaya leaves seasoned with chile sauce, and wrapped into a tight elongated tube. The stuffed avocado leaves, a form of the tamal, were wrapped in several layers of green banana leaves and put in the *pib* to steam slowly in their residual moisture. The *pib* was an oven pit dug into the ground, lined with stones, and a fire was built inside. When the logs were reduced to hot coals, the banana leaf bundles were placed inside and covered with earth. After a moderate time cooking, the earth was removed, the bundles taken out and carefully opened, and the avocado leaves pulled off to reveal cigar-shaped firm maize tamals that were delectable morsels. Along with fruit stewed in its juices that included mamey, guava, papaya, and nance, and the obligatory maize beverage, it was a completely satisfying meal.

Muyal chattered nonstop, managing to continue her stories even while chewing. How the young woman could talk so much about so little, yet remain entertaining and fresh, continued to amaze Lalak. All the antics of family, animals and weather made for amusing episodes, and descriptions of people's reactions to ludicrous situations were so hilarious that both women often choked with laughter. It soothed Lalak's frayed nerves at the end of a strenuous day expanding her knowledge and abilities. Sipping the last drops of fruit nectar and draining their maize cups, they sat in satiated silence for a few moments.

Lalak determined to seize the opportunity before Muyal started up again.

"There is something that is puzzling me," she said. "It concerns me greatly that my appearance is in some way ... not right. Know you anything of this?"

Muyal looked surprised and hesitated before speaking.

"Er ... your appearance ... what troubles you about it?"

"It is clear that my height is unusual for a woman. That I have known for many years. I am taller than my brother and father. My body is stout, but so are many other women. There must be something else. You must tell me, do not fear to offend me. What is there about my appearance that needs so much improvement?"

"Ah, Lady Lalak, of this it pains me to speak. You are most kind and intelligent and will be a great K'uhul Ixik. See how well you are learning, what skills you have mastered. These are what is important, not appearance."

"Appearance matters greatly to Yax Xoc and Holy Lady Mother Sak K'uk. You cannot deny that. And I do believe my steward Pomoy is displeased with me, not for lack of learning but something else. Perhaps this is my appearance. Muyal, you must speak truthfully to me. It is better that I know, for then I can be prepared. The worst thing is to have an adversary you cannot understand."

Muyal sighed and lowered her eyes, shrugging. Lalak grasped her hand and pressed gently.

"You are forgiven in advance. What you say will never be held against you. You are my closest, indeed my only, friend in this place. Tell me your thoughts and observations, so I may learn and prepare myself."

"With reluctance I will comply with your request," said Muyal in a low voice. She glanced around to be sure no servants were in earshot. "Lady Lalak, have you never seen yourself in a mirror?"

"Not for many years," Lalak replied. She reached back in memory, found images of her mother lifting a mica-coated disk to gaze at a shadowy face. "My mother had a mirror, I remember looking into it when I was quite young, but it made such a poor reflection that I could not really see myself."

"Surely there is a mica disk among your adornments," said Muyal. She clapped her hands sharply and a servant entered the doorway. "Go to Lady Lalak's wardrobe room, find the mica mirror and bring it here. I am certain one is there, go quickly."

Lalak sat in bemused silence, wondering what everyone else saw in her face and annoyed that she was unaware of whatever it was.

"There is a codex that Til'bak was using a few days ago, one with many pictures of noble lineages. Is it still in your audience chamber?" asked Muyal. When Lalak nodded, the young woman went into the adjoining chamber, rummaged around among several codices on a shelf and returned with a folded codex in hand. As she settled down on the floor mat beside Lalak, the servant returned with the mirror. Muyal raised the mirror to her own face, satisfying herself that it provided a true reflection. She handed it to Lalak and gestured her to look.

Lalak held the mirror at face level and examined herself, turning her face from side to side. It was much better than her mother's mirror. She had never seen her own visage and found the contours odd and alien. She stared into eyes too small for the large-jawed head with broad cheeks and forehead. Her nose leapt out like a craggy boulder, broad at nostrils and arched high toward heavy brows, where it dipped downward like a cavern. Her lips seemed huge in comparison to the delicate mouth of Muyal. There were several dark spots on the cheeks and forehead. With the headband holding back hair, her ears protruded widely not unlike wings. She blinked in surprise. An un-summoned "oh" escaped.

Muyal turned the accordion-fold pages of the codex until she found the image she wanted. Making sure the torchlight gave good illumination, she held up a picture for Lalak to see.

"This is the ideal of feminine beauty among nobles of Lakam Ha," she said softly. "Beauty is highly valued here. Women strive to match this appearance as much as possible."

The face gazing serenely from the codex page was the diametric opposite of Lalak's face. Large almond eyes, wide set and fluid, a long slender nose with straight line to an elongated skull, with virtually no dip between thin eyebrows, high cheekbones and small jaw in an oval shaped face, lips full but gracefully sculpted, small ears nearly covered by heavy earspools, and tawny golden skin smooth as fine gauze.

"I do not look anything like that woman," Lalak sighed.

"It is so. With your height and size, and with a face quite different than those admired in Lakam Ha, it is understandable that much concern is given to changing your appearance. Dear Lady Lalak, I am saddened to bring this to your attention. It is only to fulfill your desire that I do so. May I ask another impolite question?"

Lalak could only nod, still shaken by the contrast between what she saw in the mirror and the women in the codex.

"How came those small black spots on your face?"

"Oh ... yes, the spots, let me think." Lalak frowned in concentration. She was hardly aware that there were spots on her face, and had never noticed them before tonight. When was that childhood illness, the one with fever and a rash all over her body? Vaguely she recalled her mother's distress after she recovered, something about scabs, but lost in the overwhelming happiness that she had survived.

"When I was very little, perhaps only two tuns, I was very sick," Lalak said. "An illness swept through my city that killed many children. It caused fever and delirium, and a rash all over. I was fortunate to survive; everyone told me how sick I was. Something happened to the rash on my face, it got infected I think, and caused big scabs. This must have left the dark spots. I never knew what they looked like until now."

"Do not be disheartened, Dear Lady, there are remedies for such things," chirped Muyal, relieved that she could offer something helpful. "I have a facial paste that will cover those spots nicely. It is made from brown clay mixed with avocado oil to keep it moist. We add kal, fine white lime, to lighten the color to match our own skin. I have a good supply at home; I will bring some tomorrow and mix it to your skin tone. It will conceal the spots, you will see. Yes, this is an excellent idea. I will bring other paints and teach you to emphasize the best parts of your face, and diminish the lesser ones."

"Thank you; I appreciate your ideas and help. Please do not fret about revealing these things to me. It is something I must know, and you have done a true service to show me. Yes, tomorrow we shall experiment with your concoction and paints."

5

The swollen moon winked at Lalak through wispy clouds, promising to shine in full glory the following night. A cool breeze rustled leaves of fruit trees in the kitchen garden adjacent to the palace. The leaves whispered of secrets yet unrevealed, of promises yet to be fulfilled. Lalak twirled in dappled moonlight pouring onto the white stucco of her inner patio, relishing the cooling gusts that brushed against her skin. The day had been hot; the stones were finally yielding their warmth to the evening. She savored these moments alone, unattended and without demands, when she could once again connect with nature.

The towering mountains around the city loomed as dark faces swathed in swirls of thin mist. Sounds of the jungle night drifted from their flanks into the city below: chirps and clacks of insects, hoots of owls, and the distant roar of howler monkeys. She longed to walk along liana-draped paths through the jungle, to be immersed in nature, but she was not allowed this pleasure in her new home. Her heart ached for the plants and animals that were her friends in the forests and meadows around B'aak. Only her pet monkey Popo remained beside her; now he was fast asleep curled on her sleeping mat. She wondered how to handle Popo's nightly habit once she married.

That thought halted her moonlight dance in mid-step. Tomorrow, the day heralding the full moon's reign in the night sky, she would meet her future husband in a formal introduction at the royal court of Lakam Ha. This both thrilled and terrified her. Gathering up her gauzy night dress, she sat in the center of the patio, hugging knees to chest. The patio stucco still retained warmth against her bottom. Gazing upward at the moon, a stream of images played through her memory. Much had transpired since she had come to Lakam Ha.

The continuous parade of teachers and assistants charged with preparing her for this new life and her exalted position passed in a jumble. So much to learn and so many personalities to deal with! Sometimes these were gratifying experiences, but frequently they were distressing. The disapproval she felt from her soon-to-be mother-in-law, the Holy Lady Mother Sak K'uk, continued to puzzle her. Something must underlie this coldness, some motive that was yet to be uncovered. The support and friendship given by her personal attendant Muyal warmed her heart and gave solace. Their experiments with various face paints and facial pastes did seem to make improvements.

One memory was so delicious that she replayed it often in her mind. At the end of a long day's study and training, after the last teacher had left, Muyal had rushed into her quarters flushed with excitement and blurted out: "Come quickly! Our ruler Pakal is coming to his mother's chambers to dine. If we hurry we can see him arrive from a nearby corridor. We will stay concealed but should have a good view."

The two young women sped along palace corridors, making turns unfamiliar to Lalak until they were near the Holy Lady Mother's chambers. Crouching behind columns supporting arches of the corbelled ceiling, they looked across an inner patio toward another set of corridors. Muyal signaled that Pakal would pass through the corridor and cross the far end of the patio on his way. The low sun cast golden highlights on the patio corner, while the corridor they occupied was in deep shadow.

Breathless, they waited. Soon they heard sounds of footsteps and men's voices, and three young men walked into the sunlight.

"He is the second one," Muyal whispered in Lalak's ear. She would have known without being told. The second man stood a full head taller than the others, and his regal bearing was unmistakable. Warm sunlight etched the strong lines of his face: tilted almond eyes set above high cheekbones in a long narrow face, prominent straight-bridged nose that swept in a clean line to forehead and elongated skull, sculpted lips curving sensuously above a strong chin line, long slender neck above well-muscled shoulders. He wore a simple white turban headdress and was adorned with gold disc earspools and a single gold pectoral of Ahau K'in, the Lord Sun. His muscular chest was bare and a red sash accented his slim waist, contrasting with the short white skirt and loincloth. Strong and well-shaped legs strode purposefully, and ankle cuffs with tiny shells clinked above woven sandals.

Pakal's body was long limbed and supple, his presence arresting. Lalak felt her breath catch in her throat. She had never felt attraction to a man before, and was shocked at the intensity of her response. It was as if her entire body was suddenly set aflame and her emotions like a volcanic eruption. Heart pounding and palms sweating, she kept her eyes riveted on Pakal until he disappeared from the patio into the corridor. Her ears strained to catch the last few sounds of his footsteps fading away.

Pounding heartbeats nearly muffled Muyal's comments.

"Is he not magnificent? Such an attractive young man. How fortunate you are! Any woman in Lakam Ha would give anything to marry our ruler."

Lalak swallowed hard and rubbed her palms together, trying to get her reactions under control.

"Ummm, yes ... it is so, what you say."

"See how tall he is! He is quite taller than you, and that is excellent. What an impressive pair you two will make, both taller than almost everyone here. Your children will probably be giants!"

That thought sent Lalak into another convulsion of emotions. Thoroughly shaken, she shivered and wrapped her arms around herself.

"My Lady, is something wrong?" Muyal placed a hand on her shoulder.

Lalak burst into a wanton mix of laughter and tears, letting the emotions play out as her friend hugged her.

"Nooo ... no ... nothing is wrong, it is that ... oh, I am overwhelmed at seeing him. He is so ... powerful, yet beautiful. Oh, he is much more than I could have imagined."

Muyal patted her reassuringly, and then led the way back to her chambers while murmuring encouragements that all would be wonderful.

Wonderful was the word. Pakal was himself a wonder, and her feelings for him filled her with wonder. She savored the luscious sensual surges his image sent rushing through her body. The thought of marriage to Pakal took on an unanticipated appeal, although she was uncertain just what that meant.

Squirming as she became aware of discomfort from sitting on hard stone, she rose to return to her sleeping chamber. Unwanted thoughts crept in: worry about her ability to perform court rituals properly tomorrow, uncertainty over how Pakal would respond to her, and confusion about his mother's disapproval. She wished her parents had given her better training in courtly rituals and behavior, and especially in what was expected of a woman in marriage.

The royal court of Lakam Ha began gathering as the sun reached its zenith. Puffy white clouds cast moving shadows across the main plaza, bordered by the palace on the south and the court building with the throne room on the west. Residences of nobles lined the two branches of the Bisik River that framed the royal plaza complex, the streams merging as they flowed north to cascade downward in several tiers to the plains below. Wide stairways descended from the palace and court building to the plaza. Ascending the stairs of the court building were two columns of Ah K'inob (priests) and Ix K'inob (priestesses) wearing brightly feathered capes and headdresses, adorned with jadeite and shells. Beside them were waist-high incense burners decorated with masks of deities pouring out spirals of copal smoke.

The buildings gleamed red-orange in the sunlight, their uppermost chambers bearing roofcombs painted white, yellow and blue. Spreading outward from the main plaza, groupings of stone structures spread over the narrow ridge, residential complexes that clustered on level areas and temples perched on hills. The Temple of the High Priest Pasah Chan crowned a craggy outcropping on the northwest rim of the plateau, hanging onto the mountainside with a breath-taking view of the plains and river below. The temple was visible from almost any location in the city of Lakam Ha, the Place of Big Water.

This venerated city, beloved of the Triad Gods, May Ku and dominant city of the B'aakal polity, was ideally situated on a long narrow ridge of K'uk

Lakam Witz, the Fiery Water Mountain. The fertile plains far below were covered with crops and orchards, bathed regularly by overflow of the Michol River. To the north, the major artery of transportation, the K'umaxha River, crossed the plains as they swept to the shores of the Nab'nah, the Great North Sea.

Ahauob began to gather in the plaza as musicians took their positions. The ceremonial presentation of the ruler's betrothed was an event for elite nobles, a royal court function that was not open to lesser nobles, artisans and commoners. All city residents knew it was happening, and many hovered on the far sides of the Bisik River branches hoping to catch a glimpse. A small contingent of warriors lined the plaza's edges to deter uninvited guests.

The Royal Steward Muk Kab appeared at the entrance to the throne room and signaled musicians to begin. Drums of hollow logs and turtle shells began a stately cadence, joined by the plaintive melodies of clay flutes. Pod rattles and wooden sticks added counter rhythms. The nobles milling in the plaza parted to form a walkway between the palace and court buildings. As long wooden trumpets blared from rooftops and drumming hit rapid rhythms, all gazed up toward the palace platform. In the sudden silence that followed, the K'uhul B'aakal Ahau, Holy B'aakal Lord, K'inich Janaab Pakal, appeared at the top of the stairway.

Tall and stately, attired in formal court regalia with a towering feather headdress and heavy jade and copper jewelry, he wore the green and gold mat skirt of governance. He raised one arm and with an open palm bestowed blessings on the nobles below, while he made the sowing gesture with his other hand, a movement that replicated the motion of sowing corn seeds into the ground. This was the archetypal hand sign of Maya rulers, who were embodiments of the Maize God, First Father, Hun Hunahpu the bringer of life, sustenance and abundance to the people. The nobles raised both open hands to receive the blessing and joined voices in a chant of acceptance that reaffirmed the sacred social contract between ruler and people. They gave their love, support and effort to the works of the ruler in return for his intercessions with Gods to bring beneficence. In this way, Maya society maintained harmony and balance between the natural and spirit worlds.

The drums took up a regular rhythm accompanied by flutes and percussion as Pakal descended the stairs and walked through the aisle of nobles. He stopped several times to exchange words or nods with various men and women. Behind him came his mother, Sak K'uk, the K'uhul Ixik Me', and his father, Kan Mo' Hix, as well as his closest advisors and attendants. This contingent ascended the stairway of the court building, between the rows of priests and priestesses, and entered the throne room where Pakal took his position. The throne was on an elevated platform; no other furnishings diminished its dominance of the room. He sat cross-legged on the woven green and gold mat that was draped over the double-headed jaguar throne. One jaguar head was smaller, indicating a female, while the larger head was that of a male. This symbolized that the ruler seated upon the throne had mastery over both feminine and masculine forces and commanded the powers of the greatest predator of the jungle.

Sak K'uk and Kan Mo' Hix settled onto floor mats next to the throne platform. K'akmo, the warrior chief or Nakom, stood just behind the throne along with several courtiers, including the ruler's relatives Oaxac Ok and Ch'amak and the architect Yax Chan. Behind this select group, the court dwarf squatted on thick thighs and pumped his short arms in excitement. The scribe K'anal took his position below the platform and prepared his wood stylus and paper bark book. Royal Steward Muk Kab stood ready at the entrance to announce visitors. Numerous elite nobles crowded an adjacent chamber, peering as best they could through the side doorway into the throne room.

The High Priestess Usin Ch'ob appeared at the main doorway and the Royal Steward announced her presence while ushering her inside. She formally requested permission to present the esteemed young woman from B'aak, Lady Lalak, the betrothed of the ruler, to the Holy Lord of B'aakal. Face expressionless, he nodded consent.

Lalak and the High Priestess had been carried in the royal palanquin from the palace across the main plaza to the court building. Murmurs and exclamations of nobles jockeying for position to peep inside the swaying curtains accompanied their procession, which was led by several priests. The palanquin bearers lowered their burden at the base of the stairway up to the throne room, and two priests assisted the women inside to step down. Soft drumming accompanied their slow climb between priestly and censor sentinels to the platform above. From the wide doorway of the throne room, Usin Ch'ob signaled the priests to bring Lalak forward.

Silence fell like a heavy curtain as the tall young woman walked slowly through the door. She held herself erect, a headdress of blue and white feathers adding substantially to her height. She wore a magnificent huipil of the finest thin cotton, pure white as the puffy clouds. The neck and hem borders were embellished with complex geometric swirls and squares, embroidered thickly with thread dyed precious Maya blue, an extract of indigo and copal. Sky motifs on the borders brought blue and white together and complemented the headdress feathers. For jewelry she wore a multi-strand necklace of blue-toned jade and gleaming mother-of-pearl shells with matching earspools and wrist cuffs. Her sandals were woven of blue and white cords, decorated with more jade and shells. The simple elegance of her attire was striking, and its expensive quality unmistakable.

Muyal had worked diligently to apply the perfect shade of facial paste to cover the dark spots on Lalak's cheeks and forehead. Artfully applied eyeliner enhanced the small, close-set eyes and made them appear a better match for the protruding nose. Slightly darker facial paste applied below cheekbones and around jaw edges softened the heavy square jaw. The typical forelock style of Lakam Ha, with an arc of hair projecting through the front band of the headdress, further distracted from her coarse facial lines. Lalak knew she had never looked better.

A few half-suppressed gasps escaped the lips of courtiers in the adjacent chamber. Lalak hoped this reaction was stirred by her unusual height and not because her appearance was shocking. She quickly pulled her awareness inward and focused on taking graceful, small steps with inward-tipped toes that made her hips sway; the gait for which she had been coached by her dance teacher. It felt awkward and artificial to her, and she welcomed the moment when she sank to her knees before the Holy Lord of B'aakal, bowing nearly to the floor with both arms folded across her chest.

"Greetings and welcome, Lady Lalak of B'aak," said Pakal. "Immense is our pleasure to have your presence in the Royal Court of Lakam Ha. We greatly hope that your reception to our city was most cordial, and that your stay so far has been full of comfort and ease. We are graced by your appearance here and honored that you are joining our royal family."

The sound of Pakal's clear tenor voice sent thrills through Lalak's heart. She struggled with the urge to glance up and take a full look at him, but restrained herself by remembering that court protocol required her to remain bowed until he asked her to rise.

"Let it be noted, let it be inscribed, on this momentous day when our Lady Moon—Ixik Uc has attained to her fullness in the night sky, in the time of Bahlam, the jaguar star cluster, when the cosmic patterns are most auspicious for our Bahlam dynasty, here has arrived the future K'uhul B'aakal Ixik, our Holy Lady of B'aakal. It happened, it has been recorded, this sacred date."

K'anal the scribe was drawing the complex glyphs that expressed Pakal's words, stylus pen moving meticulously over bark paper. He switched pens to dip in black or red pigment, as the glyph required. The court dwarf rose on tiptoes to peer over the scribe's shoulder, clucking encouragement with each pen stroke.

"It is fitting, and it is our request, that you now may rise, Lady Lalak."

In a well-practiced motion, Lalak pushed backward from her knees to balance carefully on balls of her feet, then smoothly lifted her body and straightened her legs. It required thigh strength and good balance to avoid falling over, especially when one had remained in the kneeling bow for some time. Though she swayed slightly, Lalak managed to extend her long body and settle on both feet. She hoped the blood would drain quickly from her face so its flush would not mar her makeup. As protocol dictated, she unfolded her arms and took her first close look at her future husband.

He was spectacular. As a shaft of sunlight pierced the room and illuminated his copper-lined headdress and pectoral collar, he became a radiant God seated on the double-headed jaguar throne. His long handsome face was solemn, his lithe body erect. The power of his presence almost knocked her over. Their eyes locked, and although it might defy protocol, she could not stop staring. Now her face felt even more flushed, and her heart pounded. Little beads of sweat threatened to begin melting away the facial paste on her upper lip and forehead.

Was she supposed to speak now? Or was it the turn of the royal parents? Suddenly she forgot the sequence in the tense silence of the throne room. Awkward moments passed, and then Pakal dropped his gaze and gave her the hand sign to speak. She blinked, swallowed hard and frantically searched memory for her opening words. She could palpably feel the disapproving glare from the Holy Lady Mother penetrating her back. Sheer determination dredged up the recitation.

"It is well, it is good, that this woman of B'aak has arrived in the exalted city of Lakam Ha," she began, hoping her voice did not sound too tenuous. "For surely this fulfills the mandate of the Holy Triad Gods, our ancestors and founders, the progenitors of the esteemed Bahlam lineage. Long ago must it have been decided, for all that the Gods ordain is written upon the face of the stars, that it should be so.

"Just say it, our ear is listening to every whisper from the Gods. May you talk, may you speak, you are the sculptor, you are the builder.

"This is the way of the provider, the nurturer, when it comes to the planting of the seeds of dawning.

"Your corn kernels, your coral seeds, these that count your days and your lots, these that sow the destiny of your people.

"May you succeed, may you be accurate, may your people follow your divinations."

An out-breath from the observers signaled the release of tension. She had spoken well after a shaky beginning and the court protocol had been fulfilled. Speaking well was critically important in the courtly interactions of the Maya. The words were themselves infused with *itz*, divine life force energy, the sacred current that permeated all things. This sacred *itz* was honored when words were arranged in a sequence that was eloquent and beautiful, that graced the ears of both divine and worldly listeners. The choice of words, the cadences and rhythms of these courtly orations, formed a poetic language that was the basis of the Maya Great Tradition.

The shadow of a smile flitted over Pakal's lips, quickly gone. He nodded gravely for her to continue.

"So it is. Immense is the honor bestowed upon this woman of B'aak. To be selected for such an exalted position, the wife of the K'uhul B'aakal Ahau, is beyond measure. Great you are, great shall your wife be. Her place is higher than all other people, she is the moon to your sun, the days to your years.

"So be it, marvelous is your light. You are the white road and the foothold of your people. Your presence glitters as jewels, shines in the distance, lights up the face of the earth. You are the heartbeat of those who are born in the light, begotten in the light.

"You are the *ch'uh yax kan*, the one who sprinkles offerings with the sacred royal blood, offerings of small things that are green and fresh, offerings of yellow things that are ripe and valuable.

"Through your acts and sacrifice, the Gods will provide an abundance of crops, children and valuable things to the people.

"To you bows this woman of B'aak. For truly you are the Sun-Faced Shield of our people, the inestimable crown of all things: K'inich Janaab Pakal."

Lalak crossed arms over her chest and bowed again. Murmurs of approval rippled through the observers. It was a fine salute to their ruler.

Pakal's eyes sparkled and he nodded, clasping his right hand to left shoulder in a gesture of appreciation. He signaled the Royal Steward to bring a mat for Lalak. Quickly an attendant unfolded a red and yellow woven mat, thick and luxurious, placing it across from the mats of Pakal's parents.

"It gives us pleasure to hear your words, Lady Lalak. Please be seated upon the mat in good comfort and right of place."

Lalak had practiced the art of lowering herself onto floor mats in an elegant flow, one that required thigh strength and used more body muscles than she ever imagined. It must have been the energy drained from her during her recitation, for she could not maintain the slow steady descent and rather plopped down. From the corner of her eye she caught the dwarf imitating her ungainly seating, evoking a few under-breath chuckles from courtiers behind the throne.

Attention shifted to the ruler's parents as Kan Mo' Hix rose to deliver his speech. He recounted the widespread search to find a suitable match, a woman of impeccable bloodlines tracing to the divine founders of their lineage. With a few embellishments it made a good story, spiced up with allusions to the importance of such alliances to the city's defenses and tribute. Lalak had met her future father-in-law in a brief audience in her chambers; he was a distinguished looking man still vigorous in middle age. There was a definite family resemblance in Pakal's facial features.

When he finished, Sak K'uk rose to speak. In her court finery, she indeed embodied the Resplendent White Quetzal for whom she was named. Long, arched white quetzal feathers with their lacy oval tips swayed from her headdress, and white fluffy owl feathers trembled, making tiny blinking eyes with their dark bases. Her huipil was as fine as the most skilled weaver could create, trimmed in yellow and black, and her adornments of gold and obsidian matched perfectly.

Sak K'uk launched into a protracted extolling of the womanly virtues that their future Holy Lady possessed. It was a formulaic declamation, including skills in weaving, music, painting ceramics, dancing, writing poetry, directing households of servants, caring for children, and many admirable traits such as kindness, generosity, and intelligence. Keeping a straight face, she gave not a hint that she might not believe everything she was saying.

Lalak knew better. Although she had a modicum of abilities in all these areas, she actually excelled in none. She found it amusing that the Holy Lady Mother was required to say so many complimentary things about her. But her amusement ended abruptly when Sak K'uk moved to the next topic.

"Now comes something important, most significant," Sak K'uk intoned. "As is our tradition, the long-standing tradition of Maya rulers, we shall bestow a new name upon our ruler's betrothed. This name will become official on the day of their marriage. From this momentous time, she shall be known only by her official name, for indeed her identity is changed and she is a new person, born anew into the light of our royal family. From this time, Lady Lalak no longer exists; she is then fully ensconced as the K'uhul B'aakal Ixik."

Sak K'uk paused for dramatic emphasis, looking around the throne room at all present. For an instant her eyes met those of Lalak, who was staring back in uneasy suspense. The young woman had an instant premonition that Sak K'uk entertained injurious motives in her choice of an official name.

"Much consideration have I given to selection of an appropriate name for our ruler's wife. Such name must embody the essence of her role, convey her sacred purpose and destiny in fulfilling the Gods' will. The name will shape her; she will become the earthly manifestation of its qualities. Now for all to hear, for all to acknowledge, comes this much-regarded and life-shaping name for the Lady:

"Tz'aakb'u Ahau."

A weighty silence followed, for indeed it was a name of substantial potency. In the Mayan language, *tz'aak* was a word that meant to set in order, to make a progression of things. *B'u* was a term that applied the word to whatever followed. *Ahau* was the word for Lord. Taken together, the name meant "to set in order or make a progression of Lords."

The implication was clear: The person who bore this name was "One Who Orders or Produces a Progression of Lords."

Turning in a circle, Sak K'uk repeated the name loudly so all within earshot could hear. Exclamations circulated among the courtiers, while some stomped their feet in acknowledgement. Pakal looked bemused, and the scribe K'anal furrowed his brow while creating the intricate glyphs for the name, and the dwarf executed a gyrating dance in place while making suggestive hand movements near his groin.

Lalak was mortified. It was a public slap from the Holy Lady Mother that made her view of Lalak's position painfully clear. Lalak was to be the producer of heirs for the Bahlam dynasty. She was to set in order, to accumulate a progression of Holy B'aakal Lords to assure the dynasty's future. She was to be a breeder, like a sow bearing litters of piglets for the people's consumption.

There was no beauty of an exotic bird, such as Sak K'uk's name, no vibrant color, no quality of wind or water or flower to conjure lovely images. It was a name fitting a beast that must bear for its masters.

Sak K'uk waved a triumphant arm around the circle, her lips curling in a cruel smirk, her eyes taunting Lalak. She turned to Pakal.

"What think you of this name? Is it not utter perfection?"

"It is a name of utmost descriptive power. It conveys a quite specific image." Pakal was careful to avoid giving complete approval, aware of his mother's underlying motives.

"What say you, my husband?" She turned to Kan Mo' Hix.

"Yet another expression of your unique skills, My Dear Wife," he replied cryptically. All those present living in close contact with the royal family did not miss the sarcasm, being well aware of the often combative relationship between the pair.

She waved her hand toward the courtiers in the throne room, all who obligingly murmured their approval.

"Lady Lalak? We have yet to hear from you. Tz'aakb'u Ahau—does this name not fit exceedingly well?"

Taken by surprise and still immersed in her riotous emotions, Lalak stammered.

"Er ... ah, the name ... ah, yes, the name fits ... fits your purpose ..."

Dead silence filled the chamber. Sak K'uk continued to stare at Lalak as if expecting more. Confusion flooded Lalak's mind, was she now expected to express gratitude for such an insult? She glanced at Pakal, was that a flicker of pity in his expression? Somehow she had to end this excruciatingly painful moment.

"For this powerful name, which I do humbly accept, receive my gratitude," she lied, keeping her voice as steady as she could. She quickly bowed her head.

"Just so!" Sak K'uk seemed satisfied, nodded to Pakal and sat back on her mat.

Hot tears threatened to sting Lalak's eyes, and she struggled to keep her face expressionless, though she could not prevent a flush from darkening her cheeks. She turned her face outward toward the plaza, pretending to gaze over the nobles below while furiously blinking back tears. Deep, steady breaths began to bring her emotions under tenuous control. To herself she repeated her given name, Lalak, over and over as a mantra. She would never give up her name, regardless of what the Holy Lady Mother said. She would require her personal attendants to always use it, not this hideous title. She would somehow convince Pakal to call her Lalak in private.

It was time in the ritual for other nobles to make statements and to acknowledge the ruler's betrothed. Muk Kab the Royal Steward ushered them in, one by one, as they bowed low to Pakal, spoke courtly phrases, bowed to Lalak and Pakal's parents, then returned to the adjacent chamber. Lalak managed to nod courteously to each and keep her face neutral, although she did not really register their words. She refused to look in Sak K'uk's direction for fear of losing control again. The ritual seemed interminable. Her head buzzed and her stomach churned, but she kept her upright seated posture with chin lifted high. Finally she heard Muk Kab summon the High

Priestess to ready the palanquin for her return to the palace. Her parting remarks to Pakal and his parents, the nobles and priestly contingent were a blur.

Sinking gratefully onto the palanquin mats, she used her last bit of energy to maintain composure until she was returned to her chambers. All she wanted was to collapse and cry into her soft blankets, to hug Popo and feel his tiny hands twining into her hair. To find comfort in Muyal's reassurances. Or perhaps return to B'aak. But no, that would bring shame to her family. Running away also meant she would leave Pakal, and that she could not bear. The thought of seeing him again, sitting beside him at the feast this evening in his quarters, was a thread of hope to get her through the ordeal.

In the late afternoon, Muyal came to Lalak's chambers and gently shook her awake from a tear-stained sleep. She had heard a full report of the audience, palace gossip being relentless and instantaneous. Now she raised a cup to her mistress' lips, a soothing brew of coconut water, *Bukut* pulp from bird of paradise flowers, and crushed basil. This combination was a tonic for fatigue and malaise, relieved sadness and grief, and repelled evil magic. Bukut, the Maya name for stinking toe, the pods of a large tree, was especially good for perking up after a strain.

Attendants bathed Lalak in the sunken tub and rubbed her skin with avocado and coconut oils. Muyal reapplied makeup, selected a less formal huipil and colorful headband and dressed her for the feast, all the while murmuring reassurances that things would go more smoothly as time passed. The tonic did help, and Lalak felt that her energy was mostly restored when her Household Steward Pomoy came to escort her to Pakal's chambers for the feast. As Lalak's primary noble attendant, Muyal accompanied them.

The largest interior patio in the palace was surrounded by Pakal's chambers. On all sides were long verandas with narrow columns supporting the corbelled arch roofs that joined with the chambers. A maze of other rooms spread out from this central point to accommodate the numerous relatives, attendants, officials, and servants who lived near the ruler. Many other chambers served administrative, social, and private functions. Someone unfamiliar with this complex could easily get lost, and Lalak was relieved that her steward was guiding her.

Many mats were spread around the patio, most already occupied by nobles sitting in small groups. They wore rich attire but kept headdresses simple and low, as was customary at such social occasions. Servants circulated among the groups offering cool alcoholic beverages made from toasted and fermented maize, called *picul-aqahla*. The name meant "drink in abundance" and it was the mainstay of banquets. This thin drink was lower in alcohol than *balche*, a potent beverage made of the fermented bark of the balche tree that would be served later. Musicians were playing from one veranda, a lyrical melody on wooden flutes accompanied by small drums and shaken gourds. On the largest veranda that flanked Pakal's public reception chamber, several luxurious mats were spread awaiting the arrival of the royal family and closest relatives, courtiers and officials. Servants stood close by waving palm frond fans to circulate the humid, warm air.

Pomoy halted at the entrance into the patio, signaling Lalak and Muyal to wait. In a few moments the musicians switched to a fanfare played on short wooden trumpets to announce the royal entourage. All guests present knelt and bowed. Pakal emerged first from his private chambers, followed by his parents and a small group; most had been at the introduction ritual at court that morning. They proceeded along a lane between mats on the patio, Pakal nodding and welcoming the guests as he passed. He stopped in the center of the patio, his parents on either side, while the remaining entourage went to the royal veranda and stood by the mats.

A sweet melody on a single flute with only gourd rattles behind it signaled Lalak's entrance. Pomoy nodded at her and led the way into the patio. Lalak did her best to use the toed-in steps and sway her hips as she followed with Muyal behind. When they reached Pakal, the steward stepped aside.

Lalak and Pakal bowed to each other, each clasping their own left shoulders with one hand.

"Greetings of the evening and welcome to our banquet," Pakal said. "We are most pleased for your presence, Lady Lalak."

"Much is it my pleasure to attend your banquet, honored Lord Pakal," she replied.

He stretched his hand to her, and she eagerly placed her hand in his palm, fingers tingling with little electric waves when their flesh touched. She looked up into his face, surprised that he stood more than half a head above her. From this vantage his high cheekbones and straight nose were the most striking features of his face. She smiled but he remained impassive. Remembering the protocol, she nodded to acknowledge his parents and avoided Sak K'uk's eyes, then walked beside him to take their places on the veranda mats. For once she did not mind that all eyes were fixed upon her.

They settled onto the largest, thickest mat and the others present both on the veranda and patio floor, also sat to begin the banquet. Lalak was on Pakal's right side and Sak K'uk on his left. Next to Lalak sat the High Priest Pasah Chan and his wife Kab'. Kan Mo' Hix was next to Sak K'uk, then completing the group were Yax Chan, favorite architect of the ruler, K'anal his scribe, and Sak K'uk's two cousins Oaxac Ok and Ch'amak. Muyal sat just behind Lalak. Zazil, primary noble attendant to Sak K'uk, was behind her. On the other mats nearby were important nobles and functionaries, including K'akmo the Nakom, Tohom the personal attendant of Pakal, the stewards of the royals, Ikim an accomplished noble artist, the city's lead stone carver, other royal relatives and their wives and adult children. Tulix, a young noble woman who was the beloved of Yax Chan, was with her family on a peripheral mat.

Pakal introduced Lalak to those at their mat she had not met, and each greeted her with flowery words. Conversation became lively as cups of picul-aqahla were quaffed and the meal served. Large ceramic bowls with geometric patterns were set in the center of each mat, filled with wedges of fruit: papaya, plums, grapes, avocado, guava, nance, mamey and other delicacies. Cashews and cocoyol palm nuts, shelled and boiled, were scattered among the fruit. A stream of servants brought individual ceramic bowls filled with a stew of venison and wild turkey mixed with beans, squash, tomatoes, and sweet potatoes. The pungent seasonings were coriander and oregano in a golden annatto sauce made from ground annatto seeds mixed with starchy yucca root, chile and black pepper. Salt was added liberally, a precious nutrient in the hot tropical climate that caused copious sweating. Salt was brought by traders from the distant seashores where large evaporation ponds were maintained. Flat maize cakes, the ground corn dough mixed with chopped chaya leaves before baking on hot stone hearths, were served in lidded dishes to keep them warm.

Torches placed in niches along the arches and veranda wall were lighted as dusk fell. Changing patterns cast from wavering torchlight added a mysterious quality to the occasion. Lalak was glad for this, sure that she looked better when the lighting was indistinct. She enjoyed how shadows kept changing Pakal's face. When her bowl of stew was served, she quickly took one of the gourd scoops that was placed on the mat and made certain to follow the eating etiquette she had been taught. The food was delicious and she realized that she was hungry, despite all she had been through.

Although she tried to follow the conversation, much of it dealt with things she was not familiar with. She noticed how animated Pakal became when he and the architect Yax Chan discussed points of arch and roofcomb construction. She deduced that they were developing new approaches to a building program that would soon begin. Talk about substantial repairs to important temples reminded her of the serious event in the city's recent past, when an attack by the polity Ka'an caused much destruction.

The High Priest Pasah Chan remarked that the High Priestess Usin Ch'ob was not feeling well enough to attend the feast. Her duties at the introduction ritual that day had exhausted her. This led to a conversation between his wife Kab' and Sak K'uk about the deteriorating health of the High Priestess, who was aging and suffering from aching joints and fevers. Zazil mentioned several remedies for joint aches, including a paste of crushed castor bean leaves, oil, and allspice.

Listening to a discourse by Oaxac Ok about his last hunting trip into the high jungles in search of wild boar, Lalak caught a few words behind her as Muyal visited with Tulix, who had come over to squat beside her and converse. She recalled that Muyal had mentioned a few close women friends, including Tulix. They kept their voices low, but she heard them mention a strange city's name. It would have passed by without making an impression, except that Pakal suddenly turned his head toward the two women and frowned. Their voices stopped immediately, and Tulix quickly returned to her mat.

Sak K'uk turned to Yax Chan and commented that Tulix was a lovely young woman; he was fortunate to be courting her and should not let the opportunity to win her slip by. Yax Chan enthusiastically described his intentions to seek approval of both families very soon, and waxed eloquent in praise of Tulix, loudly enough to carry across the veranda and cause the girl to blush.

"The moon in all her full glory does not shine as brightly as Tulix," he effused, pointing up at the silvery globe hanging among thousands of tiny flickering stars in the indigo night sky. The men around the mat laughed and clapped, except for Pakal.

"Our city is blessed with many beautiful young women," commented Sak K'uk, casting a sly glance toward Lalak.

"Indeed, and I must capture more of their comely faces on my ceramic platters and cups," added Ikim. "But where to begin? Such an abundance of riches. I may not live long enough to paint them all."

"Some leave, and diminish us all by their departures." Pakal's voice carried a tone of anger. "Perhaps your paintings, Ikim, may be done sooner than you think."

"Ah, but more grow into beauties each year," said Sak K'uk.

"Some beauties can never be replaced," Pakal said. His eyes were colder than the most distant star.

"New beauty springs ever forth for those who have eyes to see the truth of things," retorted Sak K'uk.

By now Lalak was at full alert. Her animal instincts, honed by years of subtle interactions with many forest creatures, detected an undercurrent of profound danger. Something was going on between Pakal and his mother, something huge enough to cause icy fury inside him. The tension between them was palpable.

"Loss is ever a part of life," commented Pasah Chan. "All things that come will pass. What we see as beauty now will inevitably deteriorate and decay. Nothing is lasting, except perhaps the ceramics Ikim paints or the panels of our stone carvers."

"And even those fade or erode over time," observed the painter.

"There are more lasting values than beauty," said Sak K'uk forcefully. "Duty or beauty? Which should come first?"

"For the Bahlam family, that is no contest. Duty ever outweighs beauty, and perhaps every other value also." The bitterness in Pakal's voice added to Lalak's concern. Something in the family was terribly wrong.

"Well spoken, Pakal." Pasah Chan's voice carried conciliatory tones. "You of all people understand this, you whose destiny is blazoned in the cosmic pattern. The ultimate expression of beauty is fulfilling one's destiny—doing one's duty—for this most pleases the Gods and brings the cosmos into proper alignment."

"Let us salute our K'uhul B'aakal Ahau," said Ch'amak, raising his cup.

"To K'inich Janaab Pakal!" All around the mat raised cups and joined voices, except Lalak. She sat still and watched a tangle of emotions play across Pakal's face. He glanced at her, eyes deep with anguish, before he dropped the mask of composure over his features. Now he again became inscrutable.

Pakal thanked his companions for their recognition and remarked that dancing should begin. A servant signaled the musicians as others helped move mats to the patio edges and clear the center.

"Shall we begin the dancing, Lady Lalak?"

Pakal rose and offered his hand to help her up. She was so concerned about him that her own self-consciousness disappeared. Sending arcs of loving energy from her heart, she had no space to worry about her dancing. In the patio center, they began a slow and stately dance using a toe-heel step and mirroring each other's arm movements. Palms open and nearly touching, they made circles as they stepped back and forth. He kept his gaze just above her crown, lost in his inner thoughts. At the end of the dance, cheers and stomps rippled through the group.

"You danced most well, Lady Lalak," he murmured, finally giving a small smile and looking into her eyes.

"Dancing with you is effortless and an immense pleasure," she replied. "You inspire me to my best."

"May we all find such inspiration."

They led the next several dances, joined by others until the patio was full of graceful movements, swaying skirts and clinking jewelry. As dancers changed partners in the line dance, Pakal moved away. Lalak had to concentrate with new partners and lost track of his location. After some time she saw he had returned to the mat and was conversing intensely with Pasah Chan. When she approached to sit again, their dialogue stopped. Sak K'uk and Kan Mo' Hix had taken their leave for the night, tired from the day's ritual, she was told.

She spent the remainder of that evening talking with Muyal and Kab' about household things, learning more about Kab's children and daily routine than she ever desired to know. Pakal stayed ever-courteous but remote, finally escorting her to the patio entrance and bidding good night as Pomoy and Muyal accompanied her back to her chambers. Muyal made excuses to hurry home, but Lalak resolved to grill her at the next opportunity.

Tz'aakb'u Ahau—III

Baktun 9 Katun 9 Tun 13
Baktun 9 Katun 9 Tun 15
626 CE—628 CE

1

Sheets of rain plummeted upon the ridges and peaks of the Fiery Water Mountain, called K'ak Lakam Witz. Black clouds obscured the sky, illuminated by repeated flashes of lightning hurling brilliant fingers at mountaintops and scouring hillsides. Thunderous crashes pounded and shook the ground, bursting upon the ears of cowering creatures in both stone structures and jungles. Cascades of water poured over platforms, careened down stairways and rushed through alleys. Thatched palm roofs flapped wildly in the wind that threatened to rip off any layers not well secured. A few inhabitants unfortunate enough to be out in the rainstorm held shawls overhead as they ran to shelter, their feet splashing through puddles and rivulets.

Life in Lakam Ha slowed down during the rainy season. Little could be done outside, and travel between buildings could be hazardous. Torches or lamps were needed inside, even in midday because of heavy clouds and obscuring torrents of rain. Everything felt wet; even bedding and clothing were moist in the oppressive humidity. Between daily deluges, the sun broke through the cloud cover, causing waves of steam to rise from plazas and stairways. The steaming mountainsides wrapped themselves in blankets of mist as the jungle creatures chirped and hummed, pursuing their daily tasks during the short respite.

The rainy season lasted for five moon cycles from the early summer into the fall, though the heaviest rainstorms clustered around the fall equinox. Little interaction with other cities was possible, because the rivers used for travel turned into swollen, boiling cataclysms that smashed canoes into trees and rocks. Overflowing their banks, the rivers swept onto plains and jungles and obscured paths made already dangerous by slippery mud and falling rocks. It was a time to stay put and pursue indoor activities.

During this time, Pakal called several assemblies of the Popol Nah—Council House to review the political landscape and the goals of Lakam Ha for the B'aakal polity. The Popol Nah was a large rectangular structure with stone benches built onto the inner walls on three sides. The benches were covered with mats upon which the council sat. All nobles were automatically members, including women though their attendance was minimal. The ruler sat on a platform that was raised slightly above bench level, but there was not an actual throne. Situated on one narrow end of the building, the platform gave him full view of the nobles seated along the wall benches.

The Mayas had a long tradition of councils giving advice and information to rulers, and sharing decision-making to some degree. When royal succession was challenged, factions formed among council members and they held heated debates about who should ascend to the throne. Royal lineages could be unseated and a new family elevated to rulership through council actions, although at times this required combat between contending forces. Powerful and wealthy nobles wielded considerable influence, controlling human and material resources that could support or undermine a ruler.

Lakam Ha had experienced two contentious royal successions in the last two generations. Many council members remembered from personal experience, or had heard the stories from their families. The first involved Pakal's grandmother, Yohl Ik'nal, who was the only surviving child of ruler Kan Bahlam, in direct lineage from the dynasty founder K'uk Bahlam. Her father trained her for rulership and won over a contingent of nobles to support this departure from the historic pattern of succession. Until that time, rulership had passed only from father to son, or brother to brother.

Male succession was not mandated among the Mayas, nor was continuation of the same ruling family. Elite nobles with the proper bloodlines, those who could trace the most pure lineages back to the founder, were eligible as rulers. In each city, there would be a small number of nobles carrying enough royal blood to be candidates. Sometimes this led to bloody internecine battles, as had recently taken place in Lalak's city of B'aak.

Women had become rulers in some cities before this time, but always in temporary status when they took over for sons too young to rule, or carried on after husbands died until a new ruler was selected. Yohl Ik'nal was the first Mayan woman chosen to rule in her own right. Her father made it clear that she would rule, not her husband, and she served as K'uhul B'aakal Ahau for twenty-two years. He managed to manipulate public attitude and records to accept that her rulership was a continuation of the Bahlam dynasty. Her husband remained her royal consort and loyal supporter.

The second controversial succession followed when Yohl Ik'nal died. She named her son Aj Neh Ohl Mat as ruler, but he proved weak and ineffective. Dissident nobles were forming alliances against the Bahlam family and plans to unseat them were underway. Then the devastating attack from Kan and its allies, Usihwitz and Wa-Mut, destroyed Lakam Ha's most sacred shrine and collapsed the portal to the Gods. Many temples and pyramids were damaged, including Kan Bahlam's mortuary pyramid. Crops were destroyed, the city pillaged, the ruling family humiliated, and the ruler was taken prisoner and later sacrificed by Kan.

Lakam Ha remained in turmoil, without leadership, for over a year. Without access to the Triad Gods, no guidance was available, and without the portal no one could make contact with the Gods. Sak K'uk, the daughter of Yohl Ik'nal, desperately entered a vision quest into the Underworld and braved the Death Lords to gain the assistance of the Primordial Mother Goddess, Muwaan Mat. The Goddess agreed to perform the required rituals in the Upperworld, while Sak K'uk acted as her representative on earth and carried out truncated rituals. Embodying the Goddess in the Popol Nah, Sak K'uk overwhelmed the opposing nobles and won the council's approval of her rulership. She held the throne for three years, until her son K'inich Janaab Pakal was old enough to accede. Sak K'uk was the second woman ruler of Lakam Ha, although the glyphs often depicted Muwaan Mat as actual ruler.

Pakal was twelve years old when he ascended to the throne and his mother acted as regent for several more years. The controversy over her succession gradually receded as Pakal grew into a popular and respected leader. But an undercurrent persisted among some nobles that the Bahlam succession had been improper. To counter this, written accounts and visual depictions of these rulers over the years emphasized the purity of Bahlam family bloodlines, their deep connections to the immortal lineage founders and their ability to embody Triad Deities.

Rain dripped relentlessly off eaves and rivulets trickled down stairways as the Popol Nah sat in council. Discussion focused on suspicious activities taking place in the B'aakal polity city Yokib, located on the banks of the K'umaxha River between two unfriendly cities, Wa-Mut and Pa'chan. There were several large cities and numerous small villages in the B'aakal polity, but the latter two had fallen away and switched allegiance to Kan, the ruling family of Ka'an polity whose dominant city was Dzibanche. Kan was flexing its muscle and expanding its influence from its drier northeast region to the south and west, into the verdant mountains and abundant rivers of B'aakal, even as far south as the venerated city of Mutul. Mutul and Lakam Ha were allies of long standing, but Kan's invasion and defeat of this great city had put it into a hiatus, halting its carving of monuments and interrupting communications.

The respected messenger Budz Ek was sent on an information-gathering visit to Yokib before the onset of the rains. He traveled by canoe eastward on the Michol River, crossing overland to the Chakamax River that flowed into the mighty K'umaxha River, then struggled upstream toward the south. The small party avoided contact with Wa-Mut by carrying their canoe by overland portage on the opposite riverbank. In Yokib they pretended to visit the family of one paddler and spent several days around various hearths, listening to gossip and making discreet inquiries. Since none were nobles, they made no appearance at the ruler's court, but they mingled with the servants of nobles.

"The presence of Kan can be detected in Yokib," reported Budz Ek. "They speak of visits by traders, and coastal trade goods from K'ak-nab, the Great East Sea, were plentiful. They also speak of a high-ranking noble from Dzibanche who is called Wamaw Took. He stayed there more than a moon cycle with his contingent. Many councils were held with Yokib's ruler K'inich Yo'nal Ahk, and rumors circulate that pledges of mutual support were made."

"Wamaw Took, is this not the name of the Nakom of Kan? It is in my memory that he was a leader in their unprincipled attack against our city," said the Lakam Ha Warrior Chief K'akmo.

"Just so, that is his name. This evil event do I remember well," said Kan Mo' Hix.

"Long travel for a man of some age," observed Ch'amak. "This must have been a very important delegation, to send a leader of that status who might prefer the comforts of a warm hearth at home."

"This bodes not well," Pakal said. "Yokib has been delinquent in providing tribute to our city. They have not sent ambassadors to our court for the past katun. Such things point to changing allegiances and Kan has already stolen away Usihwitz and Wa-Mut."

"Faintly do I remember the times when Usihwitz and Wa-Mut were firmly within the B'aakal polity, when their tribute was bountiful and their ambassadors always present at court," offered the oldest ahau present, a stooped elder with knobby joints and few teeth. Respect was always given to elders, especially those who had reached more than three katuns (sixty years). "In those times I was a youth, making my first appearances at court, and this much impressed me. My father named each city and its ruler as they bowed before our revered ancestor Kan Bahlam, now shining among the stars of the night sky. Those were good times. Our city was peaceful and our people were happy. That was when the *May Ku* system was still followed."

"That is so, Honored Grandfather," said Kan Mo' Hix. "These times of peace and prosperity were continued by Kan Bahlam's daughter, the Holy Grandmother of our K'uhul Ahau, during her long rule. The esteemed Yohl Ik'nal protected our city through her visionary abilities. She upheld the tradition of *May Ku* in passing rights of ceremony and tribute among polity cities, a system of shared power given by the Gods to allow people to live in harmony. But this system has deteriorated in recent times, has been violated by such power-hungry polities as Ka'an. Treachery from within our own city set the conditions for Kan to lure away Usihwitz. Never shall we forget how one of our own nobles, the vile Ek Chuuah, corrupted the leaders of his adopted city and fanned the flames of a Kan alliance."

"Cursed be his name and his progeny," said Oaxac Ok. "When he exulted in the defeat of his birth city, seating himself upon the throne and insulting our ruling family, the Gods should have struck him down. Such arrogance, as if it were him and not the Kan ruler Uneh Chan who was the victor."

"That three-day mat person!" Ch'amak spit out the words in disgust. He used this derogatory expression to emphasize that Ek Chuuah had no rightful claim to sit on the mats covering the Lakam Ha throne, despite being placed there temporarily after the shameful defeat by Kan. Ek Chuuah sat on the throne for only three days before returning to his home city.

"It is my understanding, according to coastal traders who visit cities along the K'umaxha River, that Ek Chuuah died not many years ago," said Budz Ek.

"Even so, his son Yax Chapat wields much influence in Usihwitz. This evil whelp was part of the attack and continues to be a dangerous enemy," said K'akmo.

"Ek Chuuah had designs for his son to become ruler of Usihwitz, through marriage to the ruler's daughter, but this did not happen," Pakal observed. "The ways of Kan are not to be trusted, even promises made to form alliances. Around the time of my birth, Kan forces used the city of Pa'chan, long a loyal member of Ka'an polity, to displace that ruling lineage with another family. That is how Yajaw Chan Muwaan came to be ruler of Usihwitz; he was placed there by Pa'chan acting under orders of Kan. This have I learned from my mother, Holy Lady Sak K'uk."

"We must learn more about the status of Yax Chapat in Usihwitz," suggested Pasah Chan.

"Yajaw Chan Muwaan is beholden to Kan for his position, and that makes him our enemy regardless of what influence Yax Chapat has. It appears that the major cities along the K'umaxha River have been falling under the influence of Kan, and if Yokib succumbs then we will have no allies left along that southern route. This concerns me greatly," said Kan Mo' Hix.

Several other nobles exclaimed simultaneously.

"It is a serious situation."

"Lakam Ha is losing power."

"We cannot let such things happen."

"What must we do now?"

"We must take action!" K'akmo the Warrior Chief stood to emphasize his words. He believed that military strategies were urgently needed. "More cities in our polity will fall under Kan's influence if we do not show them the consequences of defying Lakam Ha."

"That we must take a strong stance, with this I do agree," said Pakal. "We must set right the decline in Lakam Ha's influence. But, before committing to use of force, let us apply diplomacy and send an ambassador to the court of Yo'nal Ahk. There has been minimal contact between our cities for too long, we must re-establish relationships. Oaxac Ok, you shall I appoint to head a delegation and make a formal visit to Yokib. Select several nobles and have K'akmo prepare a good-sized group of warriors to accompany you. This will make a statement about our strength. We shall send with you an invitation for Yo'nal Ahk and his family to attend my marriage ceremonies at the spring equinox. Although it shall be phrased in the courtliest language, it is actually a summons and the Yokib ruler will not miss that. We shall see if he dares defy my command."

"With greatest respect to our esteemed K'uhul Ahau, it is my duty to express my concern that waiting for diplomatic results will give Yokib time to prepare their defenses and further solidify their ties to Kan. It is best that we plan and carry out an attack soon to be most effective." Several nobles nodded in agreement with K'akmo.

Pakal surveyed the room; its walls lined with the leading nobles of Lakam Ha, most of whom were many years his senior. He was untried as a leader, had faced few diplomatic challenges and had no battle experience. He was acutely aware that the nobles of Lakam Ha still smarted from their wounds from the Kan attack only fifteen years before. That pernicious event continued to trouble him and had left scars upon his heart. He knew it was his destiny to make retribution, which would require the violence of attack and its inevitable suffering: loss of life, damage to cities, and grief to families. But that time was not yet.

"K'akmo, my honored Nakom, your words come from your love of our city and people and your pride in our history. Know that I take this advice most seriously, and I shall weigh the risks and advantages of pursuing diplomacy first," he said. Waving his hand to include all present, he continued.

"What was done to our city by Kan and its allies Usihwitz and Pa'chan shall not pass without being rectified. It is in divine order that such evil should not be allowed to disrupt the balance and harmony that the Gods have ordained as our birthright. Evil actions unrequited, allowed to hover over our lands, to inject their foul energies into our minds and to poison our souls with hatred, are more destructive than the violent actions required to correct them.

"Hear now and know this truth: This one speaking, who is K'inich Janaab Pakal, vows to make retribution for this attack. Those who perpetrated this immoral and despicable action shall be made to give restitution, to repay for the damage they inflicted. Such is cosmic justice that sets the world in alignment. But you must understand that there is proper timing for all actions, timing that harmonizes with the sacred calendars and follows the patterns the Gods created in the cosmos. To decipher this timing is my holy duty; for this shall I commune with the Triad Deities. This time is not now upon us, and has not yet become clear to me. But know without any doubt, this time shall come."

Murmurs of approval spread through the council. K'akmo and his warriors seemed disappointed, but would not openly oppose their Holy Lord. A few nobles reminded themselves that communing with the Triad Deities would be difficult since the sacred Sak Nuk Nah, the White Skin House, had been destroyed and the portal to the Gods was collapsed. Pasah Chan, the High Priest, worried again about Pakal performing the required rituals at the coming Thirteenth Tun ceremony only a few moons away. It would be a test of his abilities to make contact with the Gods.

A small group of elite nobles gathered in Pakal's private audience chamber. These were his closest advisors and attendants, those he trusted most: his cousins Ch'amak and Oaxac Ok, K'anal the scribe, Yax Chan the architect, Tohom his personal attendant, and his father Kan Mo' Hix. The Royal Steward Muk Kab stood ever ready at the entrance. The purpose of this meeting was to make plans for Pakal and Lalak's marriage. Pakal was in casual attire, wearing a loose tunic and colorful waistband, a simple pectoral collar and a headband with a few feathers. He sat on a slightly raised platform, his long body supported by several large cushions. The courtiers sat on floor mats with cushions around the base of the platform. Servants passed around warm drinks of cacao and maize laced with chiles, for the morning was cool and damp.

Muk Kab announced the arrival of Zazil, personal attendant to Sak K'uk. The woman entered and bowed to Pakal while clasping her left shoulder. He indicated that she could speak.

"Holy Lord, I bring greetings from your Lady Mother. She is most regretful that her presence here is delayed; she is attending to something in need of immediate attention. Soon she will arrive, and she asks your indulgence of this unforeseen happening."

"Such things have their own timing," answered Pakal. "You may convey to my Lady Mother that I accept her regrets for the delay and shall anticipate her presence soon."

Zazil bowed again and left. Pakal exchanged glances with his father, who just shrugged; they knew well that Sak K'uk maintained an imperious attitude and acted at times as if she were still the ruler.

"So it may be that this delay gives an opportunity," Pakal said. "Let us speak about what transpired in the Popol Nah recently. My father, what think you of taking the diplomatic approach to Yokib?"

"It is wisest, that do I believe," replied Kan Mo' Hix. "Our forces are not yet prepared for a significant battle, especially as there is no doubt that warriors from Pa'chan will give support to Yokib. Pa'chan is not far, and the river gives quick access."

"Wa-Mut would also send warriors," said Ch'amak. "We would be trapped in the middle of enemy forces coming from both up and down river. It could be disastrous."

"It seems we must recruit more warriors from our allies," said Oaxac Ok. "Our contingent of warriors still has not been replenished after the losses in the attack from Kan. Many are young and unseasoned, and have never seen battle. They would be overwhelmed by the larger and more experienced forces of our enemies."

"These things you say are true," Pakal said. "We need time. Trying diplomacy first will allow for more training of warriors. It also allows us to negotiate for support from our polity cities, Popo' and B'aak. How stand our alliances with them?"

"Our marriage alliance with Popo' was weakened by the death of Hohmay, sister of the ruler Hix Chapat. It is distressing that she died of suicide after her husband, our ruler during the Kan attack, was killed. Times were so turbulent then that we could not send proper condolences to Hix Chapat, nor invite him for a ceremonial burial of his sister. This have I always regretted." Kan Mo' Hix remembered these painful events clearly, but Pakal was only eight solar years of age at the time.

"Just so, and we have received little tribute from Popo' since then," said Pakal. "Our communications have fallen off. We must re-establish this relationship. K'anal, make note that we will send a delegation to Popo' with invitations to my marriage ceremonies, and with condolence gifts to Hix Chapat for his sister's death. It is late, but gifts are never a bad idea."

The scribe quickly entered these instructions in his folding bark paper book.

"With B'aak we are in better standing," said Kan Mo' Hix. "Naturally we will entertain the parents of Lalak and her brother Bahlam Ahau in the highest of style when they come for the marriage. B'aak is well-seasoned in battle, as they were fighting for over a katun to determine who would retain rulership. That battle between brothers drained resources but honed the skills of their warriors. Ik Muuy Muwaan is no doubt tired of battle and glad to have respite, but Bahlam Ahau, who will be the next ruler, is hot-blooded and ripe for cultivation."

"Well spoken!" said several men present.

"Thus shall we proceed." Pakal looked at all present and then spoke softly, so they had to strain to hear. "Thus shall we begin restitution by punishing those who do the bidding of the wicked snake, humbling them one by one, until we strike into the snake's den and destroy the venom of Kan."

Muk Kab tapped his staff on the floor to signal approach of a visitor, announcing the appearance of the Holy Lady Mother Sak K'uk. As she swept regally into the room followed by a large entourage mostly of women, the men turned their attention to domestic affairs. With weavers and artists and musicians in tow, her own Household Steward and scribe, Sak K'uk launched into planning details of the upcoming marriage of Pakal and Lalak.

Lalak waited impatiently for Muyal to arrive after the morning lessons finished. She had planned carefully about how to extract the information she wanted from her noble attendant. Lalak did not want to offend Muyal, for she valued the young woman's friendship. She had to find out, however, what was causing the undercurrents of tension and anger in the royal family, especially between Pakal and his mother, Sak K'uk.

Muyal breezed in with her usual cheery chatter about happenings in her family household. It was time for the midday meal, and the two women settled onto floor mats to share gourd bowls of stew and maize cakes. Lalak kept the light conversation going for a while, and then began her inquiry.

"You have lived close to the royal family your entire life, is that not so?"

"Reasonably close," replied Muyal. "My father has been an advisor to Kan Mo' Hix for some years and my mother an attendant to Sak K'uk, though not among her closest courtiers. Our family compound borders the east side of the palace complex and my brothers are training as warriors."

"Ah, yes. So you have observed events happening over the past several years, just by being in close proximity and attending royal family functions."

"Many events and functions," laughed Muyal. "Those I really like are feasts and ceremonies, especially with dancing. You did dance very well with Pakal at your introduction celebration."

"Thank you for the compliment," said Lalak, her eyes and voice conveying sincerity. "Your tips about dancing did as much as my dance lessons. You have helped me so much; I cannot express just how grateful I am."

Muyal smiled and patted Lalak's arm. They ate in silence for a few moments.

"When we were seated at the royal family mat before I danced with Pakal, there was a conversation that puzzles me. It was about beauty, and seemed to create intense feelings in Pakal. Then there was some strange talk about duty being more important than beauty. I could sense the tension, especially between Pakal and his mother. What was going on? Can you explain what this was all about?"

Lalak watched as surprise and dismay played across Muyal's features.

"Oh ... uh, that was ... yes, that was unusual," Muyal stammered.

"Please tell me about it. You have been honest with me about my appearance, and that is of great help to me. It allows me to be prepared, to keep my composure. Something must have happened within the royal family before I arrived here. You must help me understand, so I can again prepare for whatever challenges it may bring."

"Dear Lady Lalak, much has happened and much has passed. You need not be troubled about such past events; there are many things that happened in Lakam Ha before you came. We are still trying to recover from the Kan attack. Your tutor has told you of this."

"Yes, I am learning of the Kan attack and its aftermath. What I speak of, I believe, is more personal to Pakal. If you know, I plead to you for the truth. I can bear knowing, but I cannot bear being kept ignorant of things that will affect my future here."

Muyal seemed to weigh these words carefully, sipping her maize drink.

"Of this you will learn at some time or another," she murmured. "If not from me, then from another whose motives may be harmful. But I am most reluctant to speak of things that will give you pain. Truly I believe the issue is passing and will be soon but a faint memory."

"Speak it to me," persisted Lalak. "From what I observed at the ceremony, the issue is very much alive within the royal family. It weighs much upon Pakal's emotions. You must tell me."

Muyal heaved a great sigh, shook her head but gave the hand sign for yielding.

"Now come words that I regret to utter, and beg forgiveness in advance for being the messenger. Give to me your absolution, that you will not reject me for telling you these things."

"Never shall I reject you!" exclaimed Lalak. "You are my true friend and near to my heart. In advance I grant total forgiveness for any pain your words cause me."

"Very well. Now comes the information you seek." Muyal clasped her hands together tightly, not looking directly at Lalak. "As you know, I have two close friends among the young women of Lakam Ha. Tulix you have met, she is now betrothed to the architect Yax Chan. The other is named

Yonil. We are of similar age and have been companions since childhood. Yonil is now married, and lives far away in the coastal city of Nab'nahotot, on the Great North Sea. It is very far away and few people of Lakam Ha have ever been there. But it is one of our allies within the B'aakal polity."

"Of this city I have not heard," said Lalak. "Someday I want to see the Nab'nah. Such a sea is beyond my imaginings. But your friend Yonil, why did she marry into a family from such a distant city?"

"Ah, that is part of the issue. Her husband was deliberately chosen from a far-away city so that she might be removed from contact with Lakam Ha. Visits to Nab'nahotot are difficult and take much time, so are not likely to happen often."

"Why was it desired that she be removed from contact with her home city?"

"Because ... because, oh I dread to say it! Because she is in love with Pakal."

Lalak felt stunned. It had never occurred to her that Pakal might be involved with a woman of his city. She felt stupid and naive. Of course women would pursue him, he was strikingly handsome and the most powerful man of Lakam Ha. Trying to cover up her shock, she sipped the maize drink and mumbled her next inquiry.

"And Pakal? Did he return her feelings?"

"They did not often see each other. All I know is what Yonil told me. She hoped he would love her, even hinted that she believed he had such feelings for her. But the K'uhul Ixik Me' Sak K'uk did everything she could to keep them apart. Yonil knew that Sak K'uk had banned her from attending palace feasts and ceremonies. Then came the process of selecting a wife for Pakal, and while Yonil dreamed of being chosen, she knew that her bloodlines were not pure enough. When it was announced that you had been selected, she was heartbroken. What Pakal felt I cannot say."

"He still feels much for her," said Lalak softly. "That was evident if she represents the beauty that he spoke of at the ceremony, the beauty now lost to his city—and to him."

"Pakal is still a young man, and their hearts can be fickle," Muyal said, brightening a little. "He will get over her, you will see."

"Yonil." Lalak whispered the name, testing its shape and feel. "How looks Yonil? Is she beautiful?"

"Uh ... well, yes I would say so. She is considered to be a beauty."

"Looks she the same as that picture you showed me from the codex? The one that you said represents the ultimate standard of beauty in Lakam Ha?"

"Oh, Lady, much do I regret to say … yes, she looks almost exactly the same as that picture."

"Then she is the ultimate expression of womanly beauty in this city."

That realization hit Lalak like a boulder tumbling from a mountaintop. Now the cryptic discussion about beauty at the mat that evening made perfect sense. Pakal was expressing his pain and loss of the most beautiful woman in the city, a woman who loved him, and who he most probably loved in return. Sak K'uk was admonishing him to put his duty before his valuing of beauty, to give up his passion in order to serve his people and dynasty. The final link fell into place.

"So it was that Sak K'uk arranged for the marriage of Yonil to a man from a very distant city," she said. "She sent away the woman who might cause problems for her dynasty."

"How do you know that?" Muyal's eyes were wide with surprise.

"Is it not obvious? Sak K'uk wields huge power in Lakam Ha. She commanded what she thought best for Pakal's future. He knows she was behind it, and he is angry at her. That was the conflict I sensed between them."

"Oh."

"Yes."

The two young women sat in strained silence. Muyal's eyes flooded with tears of sadness at bringing painful information to her mistress. Lalak felt tears of despair rising; her challenges in creating a relationship with Pakal were much greater than she had thought. Not only was her own unattractive appearance a detriment in its own right, but he was enamored of a stunning beauty. Apparently, beauty held much importance to Pakal, something about which she needed to learn more. This also explained his coolness and distance toward her, though he masked it in courtly politeness. The resentment he felt toward his mother was spilling over onto the homely substitute for Yonil.

2

In the days that followed, Lalak was especially kind to Muyal and never brought up Yonil again. Soon her attendant seemed to have forgotten the painful revelations, or at least made a good pretence of it. Daily life in

Lalak's quarters continued its round of teachers and practice, while Yax Xoc, the gruff weaver, came frequently to take measurements and select fabrics for the wedding garments. Lalak instructed her steward Pomoy to arrange a visit by Pakal's architect Yax Chan. She knew Pakal's building plans were important to him and wanted to learn more. Perhaps by sharing this passion with him she could begin building their relationship.

Yax Chan came several times, surprised by the invitation and quite curious. He explained many aspects of building construction, including his innovations that would create balance and harmony in large buildings. Lalak learned that the young ruler's esthetic sense was strong and a driving force in his visions for a future city of graceful buildings and exquisite panels.

Lalak's intelligence and quickness in learning the principles of architecture impressed Yax Chan. He had never met a woman who cared about building design, even his betrothed Tulix, though she feigned interest. He told Lalak about Pakal's plans for construction and repairs over the coming katuns. First Pakal wanted to restore the mortuary pyramid of his great-grandfather Kan Bahlam, bringing it to even greater elegance and mounting carved panels on the temple pillars that depicted the dynastic lineage. During the same time period, work would begin on a splendid new complex on the eastern meadow. The entire flat grassy meadow would be turned into an immense platform having several levels. The platform would be paved to form the largest plaza ever built in Lakam Ha. The Otulum River that crossed the meadow would be channeled under the plaza and used to bring water into a grand palace complex that would become the seat of governance and court life, and home for the royal family.

The initial structure Pakal wanted to build on the large plaza would be a new Sak Nuk Nah, the White Skin House. This would replace the sacred shrine destroyed in the Kan attack and begin the process of restoring the portal to the Gods. Yax Chan was reluctant to speak more about Pakal's ideas for the Sak Nuk Nah, some of which were radical departures from Lakam Ha traditions. Of these, he told Lalak, she must speak directly to the ruler. Two adjacent buildings would serve as the court seat and formal reception chamber for visiting dignitaries and for receiving tribute. After these were constructed, housing complexes for the royal family and closest attendants would follow. The timeline for this new platform with its plaza and palace complex was rather long, due to the huge amount of stone and plaster needed.

Yax Chan met frequently with Pakal to share their visions of the new face of Lakam Ha. It gave both men great pleasure to dream of their city at its apex, a shining model of innovative architecture and a vortex of creativity for the entire polity, and even beyond. They would make their mark on Mayan civilization, building magnificent monuments that would stand proudly in the jungle for baktuns to come, far into the distant future. Both men realized that many years would be needed to fulfill this dream, and that presently their city's resources were depleted. Immediate concerns about the political situation in the region, re-establishing ties with surrounding cities, and rebuilding a cadre of trained warriors demanded all of the city's material and manpower resources at present.

A few days after visiting Lalak, Yax Chan met with Pakal to discuss some waterway repairs. One of the aqueducts that brought water to the palace complex was collapsing underground and needed its sides reinforced. This was a challenge because the water flow must be diverted temporarily so workers could enter the aqueduct. After some time going over drawings that demonstrated how this process could be carried out, Yax Chan brought up an idea that his visits to Lalak had prompted.

"Know you that your betrothed Lady Lalak has invited me several times to her chambers to learn about our city's architecture and your plans for future building?"

Pakal's eyebrows shot up, and he regarded the architect quizzically.

"This I did not know. She is interested in architecture?"

"So it appears. Although she is untrained in architecture, she quickly understands principles of construction and appreciates how we plan to overcome the limitations of current building techniques. It is quite remarkable. Never have I known a woman's mind to be capable of grasping such concepts."

"Nor a woman's mind to even care to grasp them," Pakal observed sardonically.

"Just so. Lady Lalak is exceptionally intelligent. She seems enthralled with your plans for the new complex in the east meadow. It occurs to me that she would enjoy an excursion to this area, to see the site near the Otulum River where you plan to place the new Sak Nuk Nah."

Pakal's face darkened.

"That will be difficult, it is not a thing that sits well with me," he said.

"She will appreciate why you have selected that site," Yax Chan persisted. "What I have observed is that she is very intuitive. She will sense the energy there."

"Yax Chan, you of all people know why bringing Lady Lalak to the ruins by the river would be difficult for me. That was where I last saw Yonil, before my mother whisked her off to marry in a distant city." Pakal's voice was pained.

"This I know well. And I also know that you must move beyond this. It serves no purpose for you to allow this grief to continue casting shadows over your life. Bring Lady Lalak to this place that is of utmost importance to our future, let her begin replacing your painful memories. She is a woman of much merit and talent. You have not begun to know her. Let this be an opportunity to start that process."

Pakal appeared lost in reflection, eyes downcast.

"We can make a pleasant outing of it," Yax Chan offered. "I will invite Tulix, and we shall bring our attendants and servants to set up a nice meal in the meadow. The weather is improving and the days should soon be blessed again by the Lord Sun. The women will enjoy each other's company, and you can show Lady Lalak other areas of Lakam Ha such as your grandmother's mortuary pyramid. It is my understanding that she does not go out from her quarters much. It would be a kindness to her."

"You speak rightly, I should get to know her," Pakal admitted. "With you and Tulix and our entourage it will be different. Let us proceed. I will instruct Tohom to set things in motion as soon as the weather permits."

Lalak was thrilled at the outing arranged by Pakal. She yearned to be near him, but had not seen him since the introduction ceremony. Muyal fluttered around in excitement, choosing then discarding one huipil after another. Once the right garment was chosen, she dedicated herself to Lalak's facial pastes and paints, spending much time perfecting her appearance. Lalak submitted to her friend's ministrations, but worried that the warm sun would melt the makeup and only cause her to look worse. Garbed in a loose-fitting but gracefully flowing huipil of white with green and blue flowers woven on its borders, wearing small forest-green jade beads for her necklace and earspools, and donning well-made sandals for walking, Lalak regarded herself in the mica mirror and concluded she looked as good as possible.

Tohom came for the two women and their two servants carrying mats and canopies and took them to join the rest of the entourage at Pakal's quarters. Muyal and Tulix embraced and chattered quick updates as servants arrived carrying baskets of food and drink. Yax Chan and Pakal emerged from his chambers and bowed to the noble women, who bowed in return. Both men were dressed in short skirts and loincloths, chests and arms bare except for light pectoral collars. The morning was already warm, the sun bright overhead promising a hot day.

Lalak's heart was thumping as she greeted Pakal, again nearly overwhelmed by his powerful presence. She had not seen him wearing so little and was struck by his long, muscular limbs and torso. Delicious sensations flooded her body. She wondered if she would ever become accustomed enough to him to slow down her physical responses.

When all the servants and attendants were gathered, Pakal took the lead and the group began walking through palace plazas then along white raised walkways through the city. Lalak was happy to be walking instead of riding in a palanquin. Her legs stretched into lengthy strides and she had no trouble matching Pakal's snappy pace, staying a few steps behind him. Yax Chan walked next to Pakal, while Tulix and Muyal accompanied Lalak, followed by the rest of the retinue. People soon gathered along the walkways to see their K'uhul B'aakal Ahau, and the crowd's energy became electric when word spread that his betrothed was walking with him. Pakal waved to the people, making gestures of blessing, which drew waves of "tah," the response for drawing in blessings.

As the buildings became less dense and the walkway wended through hills, Lalak's heart soared. It was the first time she had been close to nature since coming to Lakam Ha. Their path crossed three small rivers, following the low ground and skirting a tall hill with an impressive temple on top. Pakal turned to inform Lalak that this was Nohol, the Temple of the South, built many years earlier and used by priests to conduct rituals for ripening crops and fertility in animals. Ramon trees covered the hillside, their spreading canopy contrasting with stately mahogany and ebony trees. Melodic twitters of tanagers and thrush mingled with squawks of green parrots, and the scarlet and blue flash of macaws shone among the leaves.

Lalak drank in the sounds, sights and smells of the forest and meadow. Her feet itched to detour from the paved walkway and fly across the grass into the forest depths, where she would find her beloved animals. But she kept them firmly upon the path, wanting above all to please Pakal. He turned again to point out the distant Temple of the East, Lak'in, another older structure that honored the direction of new beginnings and fresh possibilities. Soon the path descended steeply toward the Otulum River, running through a gentle gulch. Across the river rose another temple that Pakal identified as the funerary monument of his grandmother, Yohl Ik'nal. The stepped pyramid was built over a natural rock outcropping that was partially hollowed to make the burial chamber. He wanted to pay homage and to show Lalak the beautiful murals painted inside the chamber. A small group of the nobles accompanied him, while the attendants and servants waited beside the river.

A series of stepping stones had been placed to permit crossing the shallow current. Pakal extended a hand to support Lalak, much to her pleasure. They climbed the steps and entered the temple built atop the pyramid, kneeling in front of the altar with Yohl Ik'nal's name glyph. Pakal chanted the ritual greetings for honored ancestors, the others joining in responsively. He next led the group around the pyramid's side to a doorway that opened to steps descending into the bedrock. The narrow passageway was steep but short, going the distance of three tall men, ending at a doorway covered with heavy drapery. Holding the drapery aside, enough light entered the rectangular chamber to see its interior. The walls were coated with plaster painted brilliant red, the color for royal tombs that signified the sacred life force, the *itz*, in the blood of the ruler. In the center of the floor lay the well-wrapped remains of the ruler, covered with several layers of thick woven blankets permeated with red cinnabar. Cinnabar was used to coat the body of rulers, indicative of their *itz*, and acted as a preservative. Adding cinnabar to the mortuary coverings increased this preservative action. The outer layer was covered with hundreds of jade beads, and many fine ceramic vessels were spread around.

Nine life-sized figures were depicted on the walls, outlined in black and painted deeper red with contrasting lighter areas to bring out features and attire. Pakal identified the figures as a progression of ancestors, beginning with Yohl Ik'nal's father Kan Bahlam, his brother Ahkal Mo' Nab, and the next seven rulers going back to lineage founder K'uk Bahlam. All were wearing elaborate headdresses whose feathers reached the ceiling and carried shields. They stood with one arm outstretched; holding serpent-footed K'awiil scepters to indicate their designation by the Triad God Unen K'awiil as divinely ordained rulers. Four figures were on the west wall, four on the east wall and one on the north wall. The figures all faced north and held their scepters so that the God's head also pointed north, the direction of the spirit world.

The talent of the artist who painted the figures was immediately apparent. He used a cursive free-flowing style and showed good knowledge of human anatomy, though all the figures were stylistically slender and supple looking. Small details, such as the God's faces on the scepters, delicate flowers, jewelry, and tiny profile heads on the belts were accurately made with single brush strokes and not corrected. The figures wore elaborate split skirts that swung to the side, decorated loincloths, waistbands with cross-band designs, and diagonally crossed leggings. Their chests were bare except for heavy pendant necklaces. The overall impression was one of power, grace and animation.

Lalak expressed admiration and studied each figure carefully. She could see how such beautiful murals satisfied Pakal's esthetic sense, and he seemed pleased with her praise for the artist. Yax Chan added that this style set an example that would inspire artists to even greater perfection in the panels and murals that would decorate buildings in Pakal's planned constructions. Pakal led the group in chanting to honor the interred ruler, and asked for her guidance and blessings for all. He remarked that this type of interment in which bodies were placed on the floor inside a crypt or submerged chamber had been the standard for many generations of Lakam Ha rulers, but he had ideas about a better form of burial. He thought that carving a large stone box, one with thick walls and a heavy lid that fit snugly, would provide better preservation of bones. It also had several flat surfaces that could be carved with figures and glyphs in relief, adding a historical and decorative feature. This type of royal burial inside a sarcophagus was what he planned for his own interment, and for future rulers. The sarcophagus would still be placed inside a submerged crypt, located deep within the funerary pyramid.

The group began its climb back up the narrow stairs, much to Lalak's relief as the heat and humidity inside the crypt were oppressive. She worried that her makeup was beginning to melt and dabbed a tentative finger at her chin to test. To her relief, the paste was holding, and soon fresh air blowing across the upper platform of the pyramid cooled her skin. From this high vantage, Pakal pointed east toward another even higher ridge. On the other side, he told her, was the large meadow on which his new palace complex would rest. Through the gorge of the river, she could just glimpse part of the meadow.

They followed a footpath by the side of the river toward the meadow. The servants went ahead, crossing at a shallow point and hurrying to the shade of several Pixoy trees with widespread branches. They placed mats on the grass and set up a canopy where the nobles would sit for extra protection from the sun. Baskets were opened and food made ready by the time the ruler and nobles arrived. This group happily settled onto mats, for the hike up from the river in such heat was tiring. They sipped fruit juice mixed with thin maize gruel, and accepted gourd bowls of fresh fruit and nuts, chunks of dried venison and sweet maize cakes. Conversation was chatty; they asked Lalak to describe her home region and her trip down the Michol River, shared anecdotes about trips they had taken, discussed luxury items brought by traders and new fashions.

After the meal was finished, Pakal told Lalak that he wanted to show her a ruined structure by the river that was significant for his future building plans.

"It is much my pleasure, Holy Lord Pakal, to accompany you there," Lalak said.

"Let us drop the use of titles, Lady Lalak," he replied. "You shall I call Lalak, and you shall call me Pakal. We are, after all, becoming one family."

She smiled and nodded, happy that he made this gesture toward being closer. He offered her a hand up, and then said to Yax Chan:

"Come with us to the ruin, you and Tulix."

The four made the short walk to the hunter's structure that lay mostly in crumbling ruins. The Otulum River burbled over rocks nearby. When they stood at fallen stones marking where a wall had been, Pakal turned to Lalak.

"Do you sense anything about this place?"

She closed her eyes and felt into the space of the structure. After a moment, she experienced a magnetic pull, as if the stones wanted to pull her inside. The sensation was one of elation, however, rather than falling into a hole. Releasing her awareness more into the elation, she began swaying as her body responded to a vortex of spiraling energy. It seemed to lift her upward, to project her spirit toward the sky. Something marvelous waited in the sky, but she could not identify it. She opened her eyes to see Pakal watching her intently.

"It is ... some kind of powerful energy," she said. "Similar to a spiral that wants to carry me upward to the sky. It feels very positive, quite wonderful. What was here?"

"Just a simple structure used by hunters in the distant past," he replied with the hint of a smile. "You have detected its secret: here exists a portal. An opening to other worlds, other dimensions."

Yax Chan was smiling broadly and Tulix looked astonished.

"How did you feel that? I did not feel anything," she said.

Lalak shook her head and made the hand sign for not knowing.

"It is spiritual intuition," said Yax Chan. "You either have it or not. Lady Lalak has it; this is a gift of the Gods."

"Yes, so it is," added Pakal. "Lalak, you know that the sacred portal to our Triad Deities was taken down and closed during the Kan attack. Here is where that portal can be opened once again, where the Jeweled Sky Tree can once more rise to connect the Middleworld and Upperworld. This is my sacred mission and obligation as K'uhul B'aakal Ahau. For some years I have known this is the place; what I do not yet know is how to accomplish it."

"My utmost desire is to be of assistance to you in accomplishing this mission," said Lalak, eyes moist. "Whatever I can do, simply command me."

Pakal nodded acknowledgement and without speaking turned and walked into the ruined structure. He went to the far wall that stood highest and blocked the view of the others sitting on the mats. There were some smooth stones beside the wall and he sat on one, looking at the ground. Lalak followed him and stood nearby, while Yax Chan and Tulix went to the river and dipped their feet in its cool water, laughing and talking.

She watched Pakal and knew at once something was wrong. He turned and stood, looking over the wall toward the high mountain ridge at the west end of the meadow. Sighing deeply, he sat again and placed his face in his hands.

"Pakal, are you not well? Is something troubling you?" Lalak sat on a smooth stone next to him, gazing with concern at his bowed head.

"Ummm ... suddenly I am not feeling well," he murmured.

She reached over to touch his shoulder and he winced. He raised his eyes to hers and scanned her face intently. She could not determine what these deep pools of darkness kept hidden. Then he dropped his eyes with a groan.

"Can I do anything? What is hurting you, are you in pain?" she asked.

"I am in terrible pain, but it is nothing you can help," he moaned.

"Then I will seek help, I will go fetch Tohom and send him for help."

"No, no ... go call Yax Chan, send him to me and return with Tulix to the others. Say nothing to them."

She hesitated, but he signaled her to depart. Quickly she covered the distance to the river and told Yax Chan that Pakal was unwell and needed him at once. With Tulix, she reluctantly returned to the mat under the trees, and said only that Pakal and Yax Chan would return shortly.

Yax Chan hurried to find Pakal clasping his temples between both hands.

"What is it? Does your head hurt?"

"Not my head, but my heart. My heart is bursting with pain." Pakal raised tormented eyes to his friend. "This was not a good idea, Yax Chan. All I can feel is her loss; I am aching with yearning for her. This place brings back memories too strong to forget, too wonderful and terrible at the same time. Oh, what am I to do?"

Yax Chan knelt before Pakal and grasped his shoulders.

"Beloved Lord, do not torment yourself. There is nothing you can do but forget her. Did not Lady Lalak show great sensitivity to detect the energy vortex? This is something Yonil could not do; she even distracted you from sensing it."

"Ah, do not chasten me. All of Yonil's deficiencies I know well, and none of them matter. I want her. I cannot live without her."

"You could never marry Yonil, you know this."

"Yes, but I would have taken her as my concubine, even as you suggested. Perhaps later to become a second wife. But my mother made certain that would not happen by banishing her far away, without saying a word to me!"

"Such a thing would not be acceptable to your parents. It breaks with our city's tradition and your family has already pushed beyond expected inheritance patterns. It could threaten the Bahlam dynasty."

"My mother cannot control every aspect of my life!" Pakal's eyes flashed with fury. "Now I am K'uhul B'aakal Ahau, what I want should prevail. She must step back and accept that she is no longer ruler."

"That will happen, give her time. Your mother is a most strong-willed woman. But consider things carefully, Pakal. You have great responsibilities as well as great power. Your very life must be dedicated to serving the wellbeing of your people, your polity. You are the Divine Presence on earth; you are the essence of the Triad Deities. Your mandate is to restore their portal and bring Lakam Ha to glory."

Pakal stared into the distance, body trembling and fists balled. Using steady deep breaths, he slowly decreased his emotions. When his body became more relaxed and he opened his fists, Yax Chan continued softly.

"To marry Lalak is your destiny. You are not giving her a chance by this grasping onto Yonil. You must let go."

Pakal's painful groan startled his companion.

"Lalak ... have you not eyes, Yax Chan? Can you not see how ugly she is? Everything is out of proportion in her face, and her body is large and stout, more fitting for a commoner who works in the fields. When I compare her to Yonil's exquisite, delicate beauty ... ah, it is more than I can bear! How can I become husband to Lalak? She arouses no desire in my body, just the opposite. How far can duty carry a man?"

Yax Chan sat back on his heels, perplexed. He was not blind to Lalak's homeliness, but saw so many admirable qualities in the young woman that he actually found her attractive. That is, her presence and intelligence were attractive.

"She has many things to admire," he offered tentatively. "She is kind and perceptive with a quick and supple mind. Such things may outweigh physical beauty over time. You are in need of a royal consort to rule at your side, bear your children, give sound advice, support you in difficult times. Lalak will fulfill all these duties, of that I am certain. Would you but give her the space in your heart, affection will grow between you."

"At this moment I cannot do anything but grieve," Pakal murmured. "This place where Yonil and I first embraced, where we knew each other's hearts, is full of her presence. We should not have come here."

"Then let us depart," said Yax Chan firmly. "Come, take my hand. We will walk beside the river until you are calm and can return to our group with composure."

3

The Priestess of Ix Chel assigned to personally attend Lalak arrived at the palace with an especially important task to accomplish. Utzil was only a few years older than Lalak, but her life experiences were much broader. The priestess was an accomplished healer and specialized in reproduction. She had mastered the vast array of plant medicine available to tropical Mayas, had been effective in assisting women with problems conceiving, knew the subtleties of preventing pregnancy, tended women with difficult pregnancies and saved many lives during the childbirth process. Many in the city sought her services, and now she had received the highest recognition: the K'uhul Ixik Me' had selected her to attend the young woman who would become the ruler's wife.

On this morning, Utzil would begin Lalak's preparations for her marriage rites. Since the young woman was from another city, Utzil did not expect her to know all the practices in Lakam Ha, but assumed she was given the basic sexual training common for all elite noble girls. She would make an assessment of this knowledge at the outset. Utzil was ushered into the private audience chamber where Lalak waited alone, as the priestess had requested. These intimate details were not for others to hear.

"Lady Lalak, tell me about the training you received in sexuality at B'aak," the priestess began after the greeting protocol.

Lalak had anticipated this question but still felt embarrassed.

"Much do I regret to say, but I received no training in my home city," she murmured.

Utzil could not conceal her surprise. Her eyebrows shot up and her jaw dropped.

"No training? Nothing at all?" she managed to gasp.

"Sadly, no." Lalak blushed and felt ashamed for her parents. "It is unfortunate ... but my parents were preoccupied with internal warfare, a revolt led by my uncle to unseat my father. This went on for most of my childhood. My education was ... ah, it was neglected, and I received very little instruction and nothing on sexuality."

"Oh." The priestess was nonplussed. She could never cover several years of complex instructions in a few moons.

"Utzil, I am a fast learner," Lalak offered. "Although this teaching begins late, surely we can achieve what is needed for my marriage. I am familiar with the reproduction of animals; I observed them for years in the forests around my city. It even happened a few times that I assisted deer and monkeys with births; that is how I came to have Popo. His mother died birthing him and no other females would take him."

Popo chattered happily from his perch at mention of his name.

"Ah, yes ... perhaps ..." The priestess admired Lalak's attitude. "So it is; we must take things as they are. Let us begin."

Utzil's teaching ranged from anatomy to physiological processes of the sexual act through conception, pregnancy and birth. In class after class, she progressed to finer points of satisfying a man sexually, managing conception and its prevention, maintaining health during pregnancy, and handling the challenges of childbirth. Much depended upon proper nutrition, which she would supervise closely after Lalak became pregnant. Utzil stressed the importance of remaining calm and positive while carrying a child, avoiding stresses that might threaten the pregnancy. Exercise was important and she described a gentle walking and stretching regimen. Although she was pleased with how quickly Lalak comprehended these things, Utzil knew there was no substitute for experience. That was something Lalak would not have until the events were actually upon her.

"Lord Pakal is well-trained," Utzil said. "With what you have learned, and his experience, all should go well on your wedding night."

Lalak fervently hoped the priestess was right. It was not the physical techniques that troubled her, but Pakal's emotional state. Since their visit to the ruined structure in the eastern meadow, she had not seen him. She knew something significant had happened for him there, but could not get information about it, even though Yax Chan came several more times for their architectural discussions. Yax Chan remained evasive, saying only that Pakal had felt ill that day, and was recovered now. When Lalak sent her steward to inquire about seeing Pakal, Pomoy returned with excuses. The ruler was busy with diplomatic concerns, meeting with his Nakom and leading warriors, spending long planning sessions with architects and artists. He had petitions to handle and quarrels to mediate.

Utzil's next remarks drew Lalak sharply back from her ruminations.

"Now come specific plans for your conception," the priestess said. "It is to occur immediately, so I will prepare the correct herbs and review the coital positions to conceive a male."

"Did you not recently say that most royal conceptions were delayed for a year or more to allow the woman's body to become prepared?" Lalak asked.

"That is so, but in your situation a rapid conception is desired." Utzil hesitated, but saw no way to avoid giving further reasons for this.

"The Holy Lady Mother, Sak K'uk, has directed me to prepare you to conceive at once," she said. "She wants the Bahlam family to have heirs quickly to consolidate their position in rulership, to guarantee male succession. It is the way to avoid contention over the throne by other elite families."

"Ah, yes ... my tutor explained the history of your ... our city in contended successions." Lalak knew the most contentious succession was that of Sak K'uk. Although she did understand the reasons, it galled her to be treated as a brood sow.

"Just so. Let me show you the herbs that will bring rapid conception." Utzil rummaged among her herbal sacks. "Here is a combination of dried, chopped wild yam and senna root. These are soaked in fermented liquor and a tiny gourd full of the tincture is taken for ten days before onset of menstruation. When you do this for three cycles, fertility is much enhanced. Let me see ... your last menses ended four days ago, correct? You must begin taking this tincture in fourteen days; then again the next two cycles on the eighteenth day after your menses start. Your menses occur every twenty-eight days and have been regular?"

Lalak nodded; she was keeping close track of her cycles.

"Good. Then to ensure ovulation at the time of your marriage, the spring equinox, we will add cedar bark tea. This should be taken before menses at the second cycle before your marriage. Three gourd cups, normal drinking size, are taken for three days before menstruation starts in that cycle."

"Is not cedar bark tea used to prevent conception?" asked Lalak, puzzled.

"Excellent!" Utzil exclaimed. "You remember well. Indeed cedar bark is a short-term contraceptive, but when used during one cycle it stimulates fertility in the next. The womb rebounds with vigor and eagerly awaits its male visitor to create new life. Precise timing is of utmost importance. You must inform me at once if anything changes in your moon cycles."

The birth dates of Maya rulers were carefully calculated to invoke celestial forces having beneficent effects upon the earth. Stellar configurations blazoned in the night sky determined the characteristics of children born under their influences. One's personal qualities, consciousness and destiny were shaped by patterns of stars, planets and constellations. The position of Ahau K'in, the all-potent Lord Sun, was also central in shaping human qualities. The Calendar Priests had determined that Pakal and Lalak should marry on the spring equinox, the time of beginnings and renewals, when the sun stood in perfect balance between darkness and light. A child conceived at this time would be born 260 days later, a number that was the basis for the sacred Tzolk'in calendar.

The Tzolk'in calendar expressed the sacred numerology of 13 x 20. Thirteen was the number for spirit and the celestial realm, and twenty was the number of the human who had twenty digits counting toes and fingers. The average duration of pregnancy was 260 days. This was also the duration of one Tzolk'in cycle. Thus the child would be born at winter solstice nine months later; this was a time of deeply mystical and transformational energies.

A long string of torches lit the sakbe along its route from the palace to the Temple of the East, Lak'in. Soft chants of priests and muffled drumbeats signaled the procession moving solemnly along the paved pathway toward the temple. The night sky was an ebony canopy in which thousands of tiny sparkles danced. Lady Uc, the moon, had already set. No hint of dawn as yet colored the eastern horizon; all was stillness and darkness.

Lalak walked near the end of the royal contingent, Pakal in front, and his family between them. It was the time of commemorating the arrival of the 13th Tun, a minor calendar ceremony in which the count of tuns turned from 12 to 13 with the sunrise. For the Maya, the day was sunrise to sunset, the night sunset to sunrise. The 13th Tun held significance because of its number; 13 was the number of spirit and the infinite, the number of the endless circle. It also represented the 13 main articulations of the human skeletal system, the 13 wandering stars (planets) that were the sun's companions, the 13 constellations of the zodiac, and the 13 annual cycles of the moon. For the Maya, all creation and all calendars could be divided by the number 13. It was the key to understanding how the calendars worked together and synchronized with cosmic laws.

In the great creation of the cosmos, the creator deity Hunab K'u, Giver of Movement and Measure, used the mathematics of 13 x 20 to bring everything into existence. The number 20, represented by the square, symbolized the measurable aspects of the world. The number 13, represented by the circle, stood for the movements of the cosmos that were reflected in the largest to the smallest cycles of earth and sky. Combining movement and measure, placing the square within the circle, communicated their union and was the basis of the sacred Tzolk'in calendar: 13 x 20 = 260, which was used for astrological calculations and divination.

Time itself was divine to the Mayas, eternally flowing without beginning or end. Time expressed itself in recurrent cycles, each having its patron deity who carried the "burdens" of the time period, characteristics that determined the destiny of humans and the universe. The time periods were measured by various calendars through which the Mayas detected the intrinsic order of these cycles, an order that ruled whatever happened. The calendars prescribed formulas for ritual and worship for these God-periods. The larger the calendar count, the more significant was the influence of the time period "burdens" and the more important was the ceremony to commemorate it.

At the completion of each calendar cycle, the Maya performed a *chumtun* or "stone seating." This ritual was also called a *k'altun* or the "binding of the tun" and was required for the beginning of each tun, katun, and baktun. The tun was of lesser importance, for it was a cycle of 360 days, just short of a solar year. Most tun rituals were done by Ah K'inob, the solar priests. The particular significance of the number 13 was what made the 13th Tun worthy of a ceremony by the K'uhul B'aakal Ahau. When the katun cycle of 20 tuns (19.71 solar years) rolled around, a major ceremony was performed by the ruler that involved bloodletting, invoking the vision serpent and receiving predictions for the coming katun. After 20 katuns passed, a large cycle called baktun would be completed. Few rulers saw a baktun ending within their lifetime; baktuns consisted of 400 tuns (394.25 solar years). When a baktun cycle finished, a new era was born, the beginning of a new "Sun" and transformation into a new humanity.

Study of the calendars had become a new fascination for Lalak. Although deprived of basic calendar education during childhood, her diligent efforts brought rapid understanding that impressed her Ah K'in instructor. With her new comprehension of the traditions and philosophy of time that underlay calendar rituals, she was excited to be taking part in the first one of her life, a ritual performed by her betrothed. She realized this was not a grand ritual and knew that only a small number of ahauob were attending. But it was Pakal's first calendar rite, done under inauspicious circumstances due to the collapsed portal to the Gods. She was aware that some would view it as a test of Pakal's abilities, particularly the High Priest Pasah Chan.

The stairs ascending the Lak'in temple were narrow and steep; the wavering torchlight cast moving shadows, making the climb more difficult. Lalak placed her feet carefully, angling them sideways for better balance. The steps were not wide enough to step straight onto them, even for those with smaller feet than hers. Nighttime moisture made the stairs slippery and a few in the procession grunted as they stabilized their progress with their hands. Lalak moved with caution to avoid this awkward maneuver, and successfully reached the top platform without slipping.

The small temple structure on top faced east to receive the first rays of dawn. Pakal entered the single chamber through the middle door, while the lead priests filed in through the two flanking doorways. The group of ahauob spread around the structure, giving the parents of the ruler and his betrothed a central place with a view into the chamber. All turned to face east as chanting and drumming continued. Cool breezes and wisps of mist mixed with copal incense smoke, rustling garments and feathers. The eastern horizon began to lighten, a faint yellow tint outlining distant treetops. The drums increased and reached crescendo, then suddenly stopped.

The High Priest and chief Ah K'in, Pasah Chan, started the dawn incantation. In a chant with responses from other priests, he welcomed the arriving sun. The priests formed a semicircle around Pakal, making an opening so the first shafts of sunlight could enter the middle door of the chamber. Golden hues brought the young ruler's face into strong relief, shadowing his almond eyes and cheeks where they dipped below his prominent cheekbones. Metallic discs on his headdress glowed and red macaw feathers blazed the color of east. He lifted his arms to the sun and chanted.

"Thus it was created, thus it was recorded
Then was its name spoken, when the day had no name.
The k'in was created, the day, as it was called.
The uinal, 20-day cycle, was created and when it was 18,
Came the tun, the year, as it was called.

The Upperworld and Middleworld were created,
The stairway of water descended to the earth;
The things of the sea and the things of the land
Were created.
Every day is set in order according to the count,
Beginning in the east, as it is arranged."

Pakal turned halfway, lowered his arms and accepted a length of white cloth from one priest. Pasah Chan came forward holding an incense burner and spread copal smoke over the cloth, using a small feather fan. He chanted blessings to infuse the cloth with sacred *itz* from copal, sap of the sacred tree that substituted for human blood. Holding the cloth in outstretched arms, Pakal continued the chant.

"All things were created, all things set in order,
By Hunab K'u, Giver of Movement and Measure.
Then he named the 20 days and their creations.
On *1-Chuen* he raised himself to his divinity.
On *2-Eb* he made the first stairway from the sky to the midst of the water,
    when there were neither earth, rocks nor trees.
On *3-Ben* he conceived all things, as many as there are, the things of sky
    and earth and water.
On *4-Ix* sky and earth were tilted.
On *5-Men* he spoke the words that would make everything that was to be made.
On *6-Kib* the first torch was made, it became light from which he fashioned
    the sun and moon.
On *7-Kaban* honey was first created, and fruits and nuts, when there was none.
On *8-Etz'nab* his hand and foot were firmly set on earth, then he placed many
    things on the ground, animals and snakes and plants and birds.
On *9-Kawak* the seven levels of the Underworld were first considered.
On *10-Ahau* the Lords of Death and the nine levels of the Underworld were created.
On *11-Imix* rocks and mountains and rivers were formed, all within the day.
On *12-Ik* the breath of life was created, and it had no death.

On *13-Ak'bal* he took water and watered the ground, and the corn grew, and then

he shaped it into humans.

On *1-Kan* the humans were charged to speak the Gods' names and keep their days.

On *2-Chikchan* the humans discovered evil and forgot their charge.

On *3-Kimi* he invented death, the result of doing evil and forgetting the Gods.

On *4-Manik* he relented and taught humans how to outwit the Death Lords.

On *5-Lamat* was established the thirteen levels of the Upperworld, that the

humans could ascend to become stars.

On *6-Muluk* were the other cycles made, the katun and baktun, the infinite count

of days, the cycles of the ages, that all he created might repeat forever."

When Pakal finished reciting the charge of the days, the priests chanted again as one carried a tun stone to place it atop the one of the previous year. Tun stones were round with two flattened sides, the size of two men's hands in width and one hand in thickness. Each was carved with a cartouche that framed the figure of the tun deity. The deity of the new tun stone was Oxlahun Ahau, Thirteen Lord, since the arriving tun was number 13. The previous tun deity was Kalahun Ahau, Twelve Lord.

The priest placed the Oxlahun Ahau tun stone on top of a stack that balanced against the back wall of the chamber. The stones were joined with quicklime mortar to hold them in place, and a fresh layer was applied for the new stone just before it was seated. Pakal carefully wrapped the white cloth around the new tun stone, the act of binding the tun, called the k'altun or chumtun.

The date was carved on the tun stone.

Baktun 9, Katun 9, Tun 13, Uinal 0, Kin 0, on the date 3 Ahau 3 Uayeb (March 5, 626 CE)

"This binds the tun of Oxlahun Ahau," Pakal announced. "The Moon Goddess is the patroness. The Wind God Ah Yum Ik'ar bears the burden of the baktun. The Sky-Snake Rain God Chikchan bears the katun. The Sky God Oxlahun Ahau carries the weight of the tun. The deity of completion (zero) has the burden of the uinal, and has run his course with the k'in. The God of the Dead rests from carrying the day Kawak, and the Divine

Youth of the Maize likewise has reached the end of his stage with the uinal Kumk'u upon his back."

"Thus has the tun been bound," chanted the priests.

"Thus have the Gods of Time been honored, as it was done by our ancestors, as it shall be done by our descendents," intoned the High Priest.

"Thus is the new tun welcomed," said all present, turning to the rising sun and lifting their arms. All crossed arms over their chests and bowed deeply to Ahau K'in, Lord Sun. Steady drumbeats signaled the ceremony ending, and the entourage descended the pyramid stairs. Lalak stepped down carefully, placing her feet sideways and setting both on each step before moving to the next. This technique gave maximum stability and prevented slipping. After a slow descent, the group returned on the sakbe to their city.

A few days later Pakal came to dine with Lalak after a practice session for their marriage ceremony. The ceremony would be long and complex, with many actors involved, and practice was essential. Pakal had introduced a new element into this ceremony, a ritualized dance that he and Lalak would perform in the costumes of the Young Maize God Yum K'ax and the Young Moon Goddess Ix Ma Uh. They would recreate the union of First Father and First Mother through a snake dance, symbolically joining the primal life force of earth with the life-initiating light of the sun.

"You danced well in the practice," said Pakal as they sat on floor mats, dining on flat maize cakes and a stew of beans, turkey, and squash.

"Much thanks to both my dance teacher and your clear guidance as we did the steps," Lalak responded, pleased by the compliment. "It is a lovely dance; those present will be delighted by it. Has not dancing at rituals been done here before?"

"Not frequently, and not for many years. There were snake dances done by past rulers, but I never observed one. Our ceremonies have been troubled by the difficulties of recent times and much of the beauty was lost."

"It is good, then, that you are bringing back this tradition. All will benefit by enjoying the beauty of this dance." Lalak intended to look as comely as she could and perform the dance with grace and fluidity. She knew that her costume would turn her into a deeply meaningful symbol and hoped observers would envision the lovely young moon Goddess rather than observe her true appearance.

It was a special treat for her to share the evening meal with Pakal. Now that the wedding was near, their paths crossed more of necessity, but his staying to dine was unusual. She watched him as he talked about other aspects of the ceremony, trying to detect the cast of his heart. He seemed calm and composed, untroubled by whatever demons had attacked him at the ruins by the Otulum River. He had not spoken of this, nor had she asked. Perhaps it was better not to know.

"Greatly did I enjoy the calendar ritual for the 13th Tun," she said when the conversation lulled. "This was the first calendar ritual that I have attended. It went very well, such as I could tell, and the sunrise was spectacular."

"So it did go well," Pakal replied. "It was adequate and the requirement to honor the Gods of Time was met. But it was not all that I wished."

"How so? What was missing?"

"For me, it lacked contact with the deities." Pakal appeared pensive, looking away. Then he returned his gaze to meet her eyes. "Perhaps you will not understand, Lalak. It is my impression that you have done very little sacred ritual. When I do these, it is my intention to make connection with the deities, to at least feel their presence and know they are listening. Before the portal collapsed this was easy for me."

He laughed at a sudden recollection and tossed his head, making his forelock and topknot sway.

"Did I ever tell you ... ah, certainly not, as we have talked but little. When I was small, maybe three or four tuns, my mother would take me to the Sak Nuk Nah when she did private devotions there. I often disturbed her prayers by laughing and playing with Unen K'awiil, Baby Jaguar. He is the youngest of our Triad Gods, as you know. Baby Jaguar's presence was tangible; I could see and touch him. Sometimes I felt we were one being sharing two bodies. But I have not experienced this closeness since the portal was destroyed. The Gods seem distant now."

"For this I am much saddened," Lalak said. She was tempted to reach over and touch him, but was unsure her gesture would be accepted.

"Much am I troubled by this. It is a huge problem and I cannot see how to resolve it. You cannot imagine the power of our rituals when we possessed the ability to use the Jeweled Sky Tree to join with the Gods. This is our sacred mandate, and it languishes now. When I saw my mother in the mantle of Muwaan Mat ... more than that, she actually became the Goddess. There was no doubt about the Goddess' presence in her being. I must regain this ability, somehow."

"This you will do, Pakal," said Lalak. "Somehow I am certain that you will find the way. The Gods willing. I will help you restore the portal." She surprised herself at the forwardness of her statement, but knew it was prompted by intuition.

"Would that it were so," he said. "Soon you become Tz'aakb'u Ahau, the One Who Produces a Progression of Lords. With that identity of power, perhaps the Gods will also respond to you."

She winced, but caught herself and realized he was using the odious name as an acknowledgement.

"Just so and let us believe it will be so."

They shared smiles and her heart soared. He was actually looking at her and smiling. She wanted this moment to last forever.

He sighed, whether about the task of restoring contact with the Gods or some other profound difficulty, she could not tell.

"This must I say of you, that your strength and persistence while adjusting to this foreign city are admirable. And, you have mastered much information and gained new skills in not many moons. Hail to you, Lady Lalak." He made the gesture of honoring.

Lalak felt her cheeks color as her heart beat rapidly. She dipped her head and gave the gesture of thanks. This was the time to make a request of him, she decided.

"Pakal, you are most kind and now I have a request of you, to impose on your kindness. After we are married, and my name changes officially, my request is that you always call me 'Lalak' when we are alone."

"That is less a request than a favor," he laughed. "Your own name is much easier to say. So shall it be, between us you are always 'Lalak'."

4

The streets of Lakam Ha were bustling with activity as visitors from across the polity joined with townspeople for the grand marriage ceremony of their K'uhul B'aakal Ahau. The city's population had grown by one-third and many visitors were hosted in housing complexes of nobles. Palace guest chambers were filled with visiting dignitaries, including the family of the bride from B'aak. Noticeably absent was Yokib ruler Yo'nal Ahk and his retinue. Commoners and servants cooked and cleaned ceaselessly, attendants scurried around on various errands, weavers were much in demand for last-minute adjustments to garments, musicians and dancers practiced diligently to bring their art to a fine pitch.

The day of summer solstice broke in a blaze of sunlight as Ahau K'in reached his farthest northern position, flooding the earth with strong energies and rapidly heating the humid air. A cacophony of bird calls heralded sunrise, soon joined by household turkeys celebrating their escape from the stew pot yet another day, and barking dogs excited by the hubbub. Murmurs of multiple voices mingled with strains of flute music and percussion instruments.

Although the sun was just halfway to zenith, crowds began gathering around the main plaza of the palace complex. Those nobles not given places in the elite contingent hastened to secure a good position for viewing the raised platform that had been built in the center of the plaza. The marriage ceremony would take place on this wooden platform with steps on all four sides, built especially for the occasion. It was decorated with colorful banners, trimmed with tassels and strings of beads and shells. Each corner was affixed with green corn plants from the summer crop, a few already sprouting ears. Young corn plants signified the theme of the wedding ceremony, the union of First Father and First Mother, the creator couple of the Mayan people.

At high noon, with the sun flaming overhead in a clear blue sky, the wedding procession began with ranks of musicians filling the air with lively melodies and rhythms. Dancers followed, cavorting in swirling costumes and strewing flowers along the path they took around the plaza. Long wooden trumpets blared from rooftops as the contingent of priests and priestesses entered the plaza, followed by a substantial group of select elite nobles. These found pre-determined positions and stood, forming a maze-like pathway that skirted the edges of the plaza then curved toward the center, ending at the foot of the southern stairs of the wooden platform.

Music and drumming and trumpeting stopped suddenly, and a hush fell over the crowd. Latecomers and commoners climbed the highest structures they could find with views of the plaza, though at a distance. All waited in expectant silence, eyes fixed on the palace doorway from which the wedding party would emerge. A single loud drumbeat from a huge turtle carapace announced the moment.

Through clouds of copal incense emitted by censers lining the palace stairs appeared High Priest Pasah Chan and High Priestess Usin Ch'ob who would officiate at the ceremony. Smaller turtle carapace drums took up a slow, steady beat as the priestly leaders descended the stairs. After them came Sak K'uk and Kan Mo' Hix, parents of the ruler, and Ik' Muuy Muwaan with his wife, parents of the bride. Bahlam Ahau, Lalak's brother, was with them. After this group reached the base of the stairs, several flutes joined the drums playing lilting melodies resembling bird songs. Thirteen youths, a mixture of boys and girls, descended the stairs sprinkling flowers and leaves.

The wedding couple appeared to a barrage of roars and cheers. Pakal raised his hands in the blessing sign, and Lalak followed suit. Wave after wave of accolades swept across the plaza. Side by side, the couple slowly went down the stairs and walked through the maze pathway, following a short distance behind the other wedding contingent. This procession gave everyone in the plaza a good view of the royal pair and their extravagant costumes.

Pakal wore the costume of First Father in the guise of the Young Maize God Yum K'ax. Yum K'ax was the deity of new corn when the ears began showing tassels on tall green plants with spear-like leaves. He represented renewal and rebirth, the eternal sprouting of plants from the seeds of their predecessors. The Maya were the People of Maize, literally formed from corn and earth and blood. It was the most powerful regenerative symbol of the Mayas.

Pakal's chest was bare except for a simple pectoral necklace of purest light green jade. His wide red waistband had a large golden sun God disc in front with tassels hanging on either side. The mat skirt reached mid-thigh, yellow mat patterns over green skirt bordered with a yellow fringe. An elaborate loincloth with geometric designs in multiple colors hung to his calves, where yellow-fringed cuffs repeated the corn silk motif with longer strands dangling corn seeds. High sandals with jaguar spots and flapping front ties covered his feet. On his wrists were long paneled gold cuffs, his huge jade and gold earspools dangled below his shoulders, and his headdress soared in front and back with green leafy elements, red and yellow feathers held by a band with small sun God faces.

Lalak wore the costume of First Mother in her appearance as the Young Moon Goddess Ix Ma Uh, the personification of fertility. She represented the watery elements of conception and birth, the moon just opening to her period of fecundity. The flowing receptivity of this moon deity symbolized readiness for impregnation, openness for the regeneration of life brought by the Young Maize God. It was the most powerful reproductive symbol of the Mayas.

Lalak's costume was dominated by the mat design, its yellow mat pattern over green material appearing in both her shawl and calf-length skirt. Both were fringed with yellow representing corn silk, below a border of round red seeds symbolizing droplets of blood. Her wide waistband was composed of narrow gold panels above red seeds, with front sash having elements of the moon: a stylized mood Goddess face in front and two round white disks decorating the mid-section. Her earspools were of creamy alabaster, matched in her necklace with a moon Goddess face. The feathers of her headdress were white and blue, flaring back from a tall oval hat of green with dense yellow mat patterns. She carried a bundle on her back that represented the many products, from plant and animal to human life, which she had given to the world.

Many "ahs" of admiration escaped the observers' lips as Pakal and Lalak walked through the maze-like pathway to ascend the wooden platform. From the platform, both turned in slow circles, giving the raised hand sign for blessing, evoking more cheers. Usih Ch'ob climbed the steps holding a wooden effigy serpent, and Pasah Chan accompanied her holding a slender stylized ax. Pakal took the ax in his right hand, and grasped the upper part of the serpent with his left hand. Lalak closed both hands around the central portion of the serpent. They performed their snake dance, much rehearsed and perfected, to sounds made by musicians imitating the rattlesnake's rattles and hisses. Slowly, gracefully, they lifted heels and pointed toes, stepping in a circle facing each other. The challenge was to keep grasping the serpent and holding it upright between them as they danced the steps in unison. Around and around they went, slowly at first then faster and faster, until they were nearly spinning.

Shouts of admiration came from the crowd as the pair maintained their mirror imaging without losing their steps. It was no small feat, especially when spinning made them dizzy. Finally the loud turtle carapace signaled the ending, and both stopped moving simultaneously. They stood perfectly still, serpent upright between them, to wild cheers.

After the priest and priestess removed the dance props, the marriage ritual was performed. There were three elements in the ritual: sharing food, binding hands, and having a cloak cover them both. These symbolized the essence of marriage in which each nurtured the other, bound their lives together, and provided care and comfort.

Usin Ch'ob placed the food offerings in the couple's hands. Pakal gave Lalak an ear of corn and a long cacao seed, the raw materials for making food and drink. After accepting these, Lalak offered Pakal a maize cake and cup of cacao, the food fashioned from what he provided. Both nibbled the maize cake and sipped the cacao drink.

"K'inich Janaab Pakal, you have eaten food prepared by Lalak, and by this act your marriage is accomplished," said the High Priestess. Among commoners, this act was enough to seal the marriage. For nobles, additional elements were added for deeper symbolism. The priestess took Pakal's right hand and Lalak's left hand, placing them wrist to wrist, and tied a strand of red agate beads around their wrists. She lifted their bound arms so the crowd could see.

"Their hands are bound together, they are united as one in everything that comes in their lives," she intoned. More cheers sounded among the observers, with stomping of feet for emphasis.

Pasah Chan approached holding a large cloak of fine cotton, dyed the same green tones as young corn plants. It was fringed with yellow tassels below a border of red seeds repeating the blood droplet motif. He swung the cloak out dramaticallyand settled it around the pair's shoulders until they were completely enclosed from neck to feet.

"As this cloak protects you from wind and cold, may the blessings of the Gods surround and enclose you. May your marriage be protected from all forces of negativity, may you be wrapped in the balm of ceaseless love. Keep your hearts open to the truth; listen well and speak with care. Remember your highest loyalty is to each other, even as you are loyal to B'aakal and our Triad Gods. May the deities protect your spirits so that love grows within you as one. May you be blessed with fertility and an abundance of offspring. For you are the source and essence of life for all the people."

The High Priest and Priestess joined voices in a series of chants, with a chorus in response by the priesthood and nobles around the square. The names of the special Maya deities of B'aakal were intoned, and their protection and guidance invoked for the couple's life together and continuing to their progeny.

The wedding ritual completed, a return procession formed, following Pakal and Lalak, wrists still bound and wearing the cloak, as they returned to the palace to a stately drum cadence. The sun had dropped into its afternoon descent and shadows were lengthening across the plaza, though the air was hot and motionless. Most people returned to their homes and sought the coolness retained by thick stone and plaster walls, while the priesthood removed the marriage accoutrements from the plaza and de-sanctified the space. The main plaza would be used for feasting, dancing and celebrating with balche and other alcoholic drinks when dusk fell. A large work crew soon began setting up for the festivities, in which merchants and artisans, commoners and servants would overindulge in rich food and drink that they could enjoy only on such special occasions. To their delight, these festivities would last three days.

Ahauob would feast and drink in other palace courtyards, the elite and visiting dignitaries with the royal family. By custom, the marriage couple were permitted an evening alone before joining the festivities. They were still in sacred space from the ritual and remained so through their first night together as their marriage was consummated.

Each went to their separate chambers first, where attendants ritually removed their marriage costumes and bathed them for purification. A time of rest and reflection followed before they rejoined each other. Pakal would come to Lalak's chambers at dusk, where a light meal was left by discreet servants. Heavy curtains would be pulled tightly across the doorway, and the couple left alone during their first night.

Muyal attended Lalak for the undressing and bathing. It was difficult for the talkative attendant to keep silent, and she murmured little encouragements as she dried her mistress with soft blankets and rubbed her skin with almond oil. Lalak said nothing, lost in wonderment over the perfection of the marriage ritual. It was hard to believe that everything had gone so well; she had worried about losing her balance during the spinning snake dance and falling down ingloriously in front of everyone. The more so, since Pakal told her he planned to have the dance commemorated on a panel for the new palace he would build. The hot sun also worried her, for Muyal had applied even more facial paste and paints than usual, and during the ceremony it seemed to be dripping. However, it was only sweat and the makeup stayed in place. Muyal was a master of this art.

The young woman's eyes sparkled as she helped Lalak into a gauzy white cotton dress, open in front and held in place by a blue waistband. It was an unusual style with obvious functionality, and Muyal patted the thin fabric in place where it draped around breasts and hips. Muyal's own marriage had been postponed until the coming moon cycle, not to detract from the ruler's wedding and to provide a separate time for her preparations. She whispered that Lalak would know the secrets of love-making before she would, making her mistress blush. As final tasks, Muyal applied a light coat of facial paste, just enough to cover the dark spots, and a touch of eye paint to widen Lalak's eyes. She combed Lalak's thick black hair until it fell in silken waves to the mid-back, using water scented with Plumeria flowers. Satisfied that her mistress was as lovely as possible, Muyal parted with a whispered blessing and a kiss on the cheek.

As dusk fell, Lalak's servant brought a meal of fresh fruit, maize cakes, and fruit juice. Without speaking, the servant placed the food on the floor mat, lit two wall torches, bowed low and then departed. This servant, an older woman, would remain in the servants' chamber should anything be needed. Lalak watched the light disappear through the window to her patio, until only torchlight remained. She was nervous, both excited and worried. It seemed Pakal was taking an inordinately long time to appear. A stab of terror shot through her. Would he stay away on their wedding night? She could not bear such humiliation or such heartbreak.

She paced across the room, feeling sorry that Popo had been removed to spend the night with the servant. The little monkey always comforted her. Now she felt utterly alone. Just as she was sinking into despair, she heard footsteps along the corridor. Spinning to face the door, her heart pounded as if to leap from her chest as Pakal pushed aside the drape and entered. She smiled as relief and delight flooded over her.

He bowed and she returned it. With a gesture, she invited him to sit on the mat and partake of the food and drink. They settled on either side of the food bowls, she poured cups of juice, offering one to him. He took it and drank deeply, eyes meeting hers above the rim. How bright were his eyes! They seemed unnaturally shining; making her wonder if he had taken an herbal stimulant, or perhaps had a few too many cups of balche. The torchlight played across his long face, emphasizing high cheekbones and full sensuous mouth. Finally, as if in slow motion, his lips parted in a slight smile.

"It is done," he said. "The marriage is accomplished. It was well done."

"Yes," she murmured. "The ceremony was magnificent, and you were the true embodiment of Yum K'ax. The people adore you; they made that clear."

"You were quite impressive as Ix Ma Uh. Many exclamations were made over your costume, and you danced with the snake perfectly. It was difficult, was it not?"

"Just so!" she exclaimed with a tiny chuckle. "Did you get dizzy? I feared that I might fall."

"Indeed, so did I," he admitted. "The Gods smiled upon us and kept us on our feet."

"Thanks and praise be to the Gods."

He finished his cup of juice. The night was still warm, and he was bare to the waist with a simple white loincloth, hair tied in a single topknot. Her eyes traveled over his well-muscled chest and sensations of desire coursed through her body.

"You must be tired and hungry, do eat. I have little appetite just now."

Pakal took a cut mango and ate slowly, then consumed a few nance plums. He asked for more juice and seemed thirsty. Lalak tried to eat a maize cake, but managed only a few crumbs. The suspense was nearly unbearable and her urge to touch him was hard to control. Why had these fine details been omitted in her marriage training? Who makes the first move, can the woman initiate it, or is that improper? She waited.

He drained his cup and set it down. The brightness of his eyes again struck her. Had he taken a stimulant? From her recent plant medicine classes, she recalled that many plants provided mild stimulation. For some reason, acacia came to mind. She remembered that acacia bark tea was used to stimulate male potency. Before she could pursue those thoughts, Pakal moved to his knees and reached a hand toward her.

"Come, Lalak," he said softly. "Let us proceed. Although your priestess has prepared you, it is my understanding that full training did not take place at your home. It is natural for a woman to be hesitant in this situation. Do not be concerned, we will go slowly."

She quickly moved to place her hand in his, feeling anything but hesitant. Could he not perceive her eagerness? He drew her up and enclosed her in an embrace. A symphony of delight played through her body at the feel of his arms around her, and she leaned into him, slipping her arms around his slender waist. The warmth of their skin touching set her senses afire, as he deftly untied the waistband and slipped off her dress, then let drop his loincloth. Continuing with caresses, he led her to the sleeping bench covered with luxurious soft mats and silken pillows. Without loosening their embrace, they sank onto the mat. His kisses intoxicated her as his experienced hands brought her body to a fevered pitch of desire. Aching and throbbing with readiness, she opened herself to receive him. The slight pain at first was soon lost in waves of ecstasy as they reached a crescendo of release.

He lay beside her quietly for a while, then turned and asked:

"Is it well with you?"

She smiled and snuggled closer, hands caressing his chest.

"It is wonderful beyond description."

"Good," he murmured. "Good. It is done."

He dropped off immediately into sleep. She felt certain he had taken some intoxicant and wondered if this was a custom her teacher failed to mention. For present, she wanted only to drift in the pleasure of his closeness and revisit the joy of their bodies joining. Simply watching torchlight dance across his handsome features made her happy. She could look at him forever without tiring. But the strain of the day and the height of passionate release had tired her, and the soft humming of night insects lulled her into drowsiness. She fought sleep, wanting to imprint this moment indelibly in memory.

She slept. Deep into the night she stirred, reaching for Pakal. But there was no form lying beside her on the sleeping bench. She rolled over but found only emptiness, and sat up suddenly. The wall torches had burned low and the room was mostly in darkness. Pale moonlight streamed in through the window as insects chirped and hummed. She scanned the room but detected no one. Pakal was gone.

Utzil, her priestess, had led her to believe that Pakal would remain beside her through the night, and they would share the morning meal. Then he would leave to attend visitors and ready himself for the feast and dancing that began in the afternoon. For the next two nights, he would return to her chamber to consummate their marriage again. This was planned to maximize the potential for conception, as these nights were during her fertile period of the moon cycle. After that, he would not visit her bedchamber again until the next fertile phase.

But Pakal had not remained with her. For purposes of his own, he must have returned to his own chambers. Distress began tearing away at the edges of Lalak's happiness. Something was missing between them. Her body was satisfied but her heart was empty.

He does not love me, she thought. *He is doing his duty. He performed his duty as husband with outstanding sexual skills. But our hearts are not united. The love I feel for him, he does not return. His heart is still enthralled by the beautiful Yonil.*

Tears flooded her eyes and she threw herself down on the soft mats, cradling plush pillows in her arms. On the night of her marriage, Lalak cried herself back to sleep.

The festivities that afternoon were a blur for Lalak. She talked and danced and ate and drank, and pretended all was well. When Pakal came to her that night, she surrendered again to physical delights and reached ecstatic heights. When he left during the night, she cried again but revealed nothing to him. The same pattern repeated the next afternoon and evening. Then Pakal went to attend political affairs and she received and entertained her family. She kept up appearances, because as the new K'uhul Ixik Tz'aakb'u Ahau, she became a royal icon, a near-deity who must remain a model of strength and serenity.

Her brother Bahlam Ahau visited several times, blustery as usual, and proud of his status as the ruler's brother-in-law. From him she learned that Pakal was planning an attack on Yokib, whose ruler Yo'nal Ahk had spurned the summons to attend the marriage ceremony. This proved that Yokib was in the clutches of Kan, Bahlam Ahau asserted. It pleased him that Pakal courted his assistance and needed him to bring the forces of B'aak into the battle. This was the sort of adventure that Bahlam Ahau lived for. Her parents visited too, dazzled by the pomp and pageantry of the ceremony and impressed with the richness of the feasting. They basked in the honor accorded the bride's parents and praised Lalak more than she had ever received her entire life.

Visitors left and the city on the mountain ridge returned to normal rhythms. By the passing of the next dark moon, Lalak realized that her body rhythms were anything but normal. Her moon flow did not come when it was due. Within a few days, her nipples became extremely tender and her belly felt bloated. She was certain that she had conceived a child by Pakal. Utzil confirmed that these were signs of pregnancy, but advised to wait until the moon neared fullness to announce it. As the full moon approached, Lalak was both elated and disappointed. She was thrilled about conceiving on the first attempt, but saddened that Pakal would not return to her bedchamber. Had she not conceived, they would try again during the next fertile period. But with conception, there would be no sexual contact until after childbirth.

Pakal came to visit her after Utzil announced the pregnancy. He was pleased and tender, but gave her only a brief embrace. She wondered if he was relieved by not having to do his husbandly duty with her again. Many among the elite nobles came to offer congratulations, and Muyal was almost too excited to talk, her laudatory words tumbling over each other. Even the K'uhul Ixik Me' paid a congratulatory visit; Sak K'uk was marginally pleasant and appeared grudgingly pleased.

After Lalak missed her second moon flow, Utzil nodded approvingly and instituted the regimen of diet, exercise, and relaxation that was prescribed during pregnancy. When the next full moon approached, Lalak sensed that all was not well. Her belly began cramping and she felt nauseated. Utzil gave her herbal remedies, but the symptoms increased until she was in severe pain. She began spotting, pale pink at first but soon increasing to bright red blood in a brisk flow. Despite Utzil's ministrations of medicines to prevent miscarriage, the small bloody sac was soon extruded by the womb. The first child of Pakal and Lalak that might have been, was no more.

Lalak recovered quickly from the miscarriage. Her body was young and strong. The comforting hugs of Muyal and the reassurances of Utzil that losing the first child was not unusual bolstered her mood. Pakal was a model of compassion and encouragement, assuring her that they would conceive again soon. The anticipation of evenings with him was the best remedy for recovery. Utzil advised that they wait until Lalak had three normal moon flows before the next conception, and provided brews of the chopped roots of Pu-ja to strengthen the blood and Kaba-yax-nik to return the womb to normal.

The Ah K'inob calculated the winter solstice to be a powerful time for conceiving a son. To Lalak's delight, Utzil prescribed five days of sexual joining to better ensure conception, and Pakal fulfilled his duties impeccably. He even enjoyed their conversations over the evening meal, when he described aspects of his architectural plans that Lalak readily understood. She conceived again without difficulty, followed the regimen for pregnancy to perfection, and the pregnancy passed the second moon cycle successfully. Utzil assured Lalak that if the conception stayed in place beyond the third moon cycle, it was very likely to reach term.

The third moon cycle came and passed. Just as all felt relief, however, the pregnancy became troubled. Lalak started spotting, small drops of bright red blood, with no cramping. Utzil was perplexed; this was not the usual miscarriage pattern. She put Lalak to rest, advised her to minimize walking, and administered hibiscus and wild yam root tea with cinnamon bark to prevent miscarriage. But the bleeding increased and the priestess worried about hemorrhage. Lalak was pale and weak by the time her contractions began. Once it was clear that the womb was trying to expel its contents, Utzil administered repeated doses of strong, hot ginger tea to hasten the process. In the pale dawn approaching spring equinox, less than one solar year after her marriage, Lalak miscarried the second time.

The aftermath was difficult. Lalak had lost a considerable amount of blood and suffered from fatigue and weakness. Sak K'uk sent a messenger to bring her condolences but did not visit her daughter-in-law. Pakal came to sit beside her several times, murmuring words of support and stroking her arms and hands. It was a gesture of kindness, if not affection, that she deeply appreciated. Muyal cried with her, the young women hugging each other. Popo was brought to her side, and he chattered to distract her. Utzil consulted with older Ix Chel priestesses who had seen many difficulties in childbearing, searching for reasons and remedies. The people of Lakam Ha were disappointed that no heir had yet been brought forth for their beloved K'uhul B'aakal Ahau.

The older priestesses advised waiting a full tun, 360 days, before attempting another pregnancy. Lalak needed time to rebuild her blood, cleanse her womb, and strengthen her vital energy. They suggested various regimens, special foods and drinks and herbal tonics, but especially spiritual practices to enlist the aid of the deities of fertility and abundance, those whose special domain was childbearing. Lalak would come to the Ix Chel temple to undergo purification, and visit regularly to give tribute to the Goddess of Healing and Childbearing. Cultivating a relationship with Ix Chel and winning her support was deemed the most critical action.

As soon as she recovered strength, Lalak went religiously to the Ix Chel Temple. While her life focused on spiritual rituals and health regimens, other currents of mobilization were running through Lakam Ha. The Warrior Chief K'akmo instituted an intensive training program for warriors, in preparation for an attack on Yokib. Several mock battles were engaged with seasoned warriors from B'aak, led by Bahlam Ahau. Pakal went on these field excursions and trained for action. Diplomatic visits were made to Sak Tz'i, a small nearby city on the Chakamax River, to recruit forces and garner material support.

On the advice of High Priest Pasah Chan, a new position was created at court to bring spiritual presence into the battle. Titled *Ah K'uhun*, "learned member of the royal court and worshipper," it combined priestly and warrior training. Pakal selected a strong young noble with intelligence and spiritual leanings, Ch'ok Bahlam, to fill the position. With training as both priest and warrior, he would conduct rituals to keep the warriors connected with the deities and read omens in both sky and earth. His warrior skills would protect him in fighting and contribute to Lakam Ha's forces.

K'ab Chan Te', a noble from Sak Tz'i, made several visits with his forces to join in combat practice and develop strategies for the attack. The city of Yokib had been founded earlier than Lakam Ha and was a considerable power along the K'umaxha River. It was a large city that filled hills and valleys set high above the river, making attack from the river side hazardous. Further downstream were steep canyons that made overland travel impossible. The messenger Budz Ek described the path his small group took on their information-gathering trip to Yokib. They made overland portage to avoid detection by warriors of Wa-Mut, the downstream city allied with Kan. He believed the trail continued through the jungles that skirted the steep canyons and permitted access to Yokib from the west.

Scouts were sent to explore that trail and determine whether forces of considerable size could use it for a western approach. They reported that such an approach was feasible but would be difficult; the trail was narrow and would need clearing. It would be an arduous journey of many days after leaving the river near Wa-Mut, but it could be done. The scouts had gone far enough to see Yokib structures perched on high valleys in the distance. Surprise would be a critical element in the attack, because entering the city required a steep uphill climb from the jungle. The planning council called together by Pakal determined to follow this approach to Yokib.

The dry season was preferred for this campaign because travel through the jungle would be easier, but the calendar priests advised the council that the star configurations were not good until dates approaching summer solstice. Although the warriors grumbled, particularly their chief K'akmo, Pakal decided that guidance of the stars was of utmost importance. It would also make their attack less predictable.

The 360-day waiting period for Lalak was completed a moon cycle before the spring equinox. She felt strong and restored in body and spirit, having established a deep connection with the Goddess Ix Chel. When Pakal came to her chambers at the determined fertile time, she received him eagerly. For another five evenings they shared meals and the sleeping bench. Lalak's physical pleasure was as intense as before, but she sensed Pakal was distracted by the pending attack on Yokib. He seemed more distant than usual and left after completing his marital duties. She even risked asking him to stay one evening, but he demurred, claiming need for rest and to prepare for his meetings the next day.

Although Lalak had vowed she would maintain equanimity in whatever situation occurred between them, she could not contain the emotional waves propelling her between elation and despondency. She called upon the Goddess to calm her, to bring blessings upon their conception, to guide her in finding acceptance. But her unhappiness over Pakal's aloofness combined with resentment toward the woman who was damaging her relationship with her husband, causing simmering discontent.

The Goddess' blessings did fall upon at least one part of her prayers. She conceived again and felt healthier than ever during pregnancy. As the spring progressed and the warring forces gathered at Lakam Ha for final preparations before their departure, the pregnancy passed its critical third moon cycle. Utzil was most encouraging although she insisted on strict disciplines of diet, rest, and careful exercise, as well as daily prayers and offerings to Ix Chel. Muyal was bubbling with joy, not only over Lalak's pregnancy, but because of her recent marriage to Yax Chan.

When the forces left Lakam Ha, Lalak struggled against clutching fingers of fear that wrapped around her heart. She felt envious of Muyal, whose husband would not be among the warriors; he was an architect and not trained for battle. Pakal, however, would lead the warring forces against a formidable enemy in the first actual battle in his life.

Tz'aakb'u Ahau—IV

Baktun 9 Katun 9 Tun 15
Baktun 9 Katun 10 Tun 7
628 CE—640 CE

1

Rain dripped from leaves and branches, soaking everything below the jungle canopy, as the combined forces of Lakam Ha, B'aak, and Sak Tz'i slogged over slippery trails and waded through muddy bogs. Their path led up tree-shrouded canyons and down into verdant valleys, winding back and forth as it followed the mountain contours seeking the best passage. Frequently men were sent ahead with long knives to cut back foliage and with axes to hew away fallen tree trunks. In ten days of travel, only three were without rain. Camps were sodden and uncomfortable, fires hard to keep burning. Dried meat and maize cakes sustained the men, with an occasional spit-roasted deer or turkey when hunters were lucky.

K'akmo grumbled about waging battle during the rainy season, Bahlam Ahau complained about camp discomforts, and K'ab Chan Te' questioned the wisdom of the priests' guidance. Pakal walked through camp every evening, bringing encouragement and giving acknowledgement to each warrior. Ch'ok Bahlam sought omens, but rarely could he read the sky due to cloud cover, and many clues the earth might provide were hidden by rain and mud.

Another five days brought the war party just beyond sight of Yokib's western edge. Scouts sent ahead reported no sign of unusual activity in the city, so their approach had not been detected. That evening no fires were allowed, and the men made final preparations of weapons and donned thick cloth armor. The plan was a dawn attack entering Yokib from three paths that led down into the jungle. They would damage temples and monuments, kill as many warriors as possible, and take several captives for display and sacrifice at their home cities. Pakal hoped to do battle with, and perhaps capture, the Yokib ruler Yo'nal Ahk.

The day dawned with sunlight breaking through the clouds. Three warrior contingents climbed the paths to the city as quietly as they could, but distant shouts alerted them that their presence was detected. As the first warriors topped the high valley and entered city roadways, Yokib forces scrambled into action amid blaring trumpets and conches. Pakal and K'akmo led Lakam Ha's forces and raced toward the nearest pyramid-temple, climbed its stairway and began destroying altars, panels, and carved pillars. They encountered Yokib warriors on the way down and battle began, men wielding clubs embedded with obsidian spikes, axes, and long flint knives. Grunts and thuds filled the air, pierced by cries of the wounded.

Pakal fought with double-headed axe in one hand and long knife in the other, slashing and swinging at his enemies. He broke through their ranks and reached the street, seeking a high ranking noble. K'akmo and several experienced Lakam Ha warriors kept close to their ruler, protecting his flanks and back. Pakal was easy to identify by his regal war headdress, cloth jacket and leg padding made of woven multicolored cotton, and his shield lined with bright red macaw feathers. Other warriors wore less colorful attire and simple head protection.

A Yokib noble engaged with Pakal, trading axe blows and parrying knives in a lethal dance. Pakal's height and long arms gave him advantage, and he slashed the noble's neck then delivered a head blow with the axe, knocking the man down in a bloody heap. More Yokib warriors converged upon Pakal as K'akmo and the others took them on, arms swinging and legs stomping, grunting and yelling, as blood splattered onto the white plaza. Battle was primarily one-to-one, and warriors sought enemies of equal rank but needed to defend themselves from any attacker.

The plazas and roadways of Yokib's western section were filled with struggle. In an adjoining plaza, Bahlam Ahau's troops were in fierce combat with swelling ranks of Yokib warriors. The troop from Sak Tz'i had taken a divergent roadway and was out of sight. Pakal moved toward the widest roadway leading east from the plaza, yelling orders.

"This leads to the palace! Follow me!"

His group surged along the roadway as other Lakam Ha warriors moved into the plaza and diverted enemy attack. As Pakal raced ahead, K'akmo cast a worried glance at the one-story rooftops lining the roadway. They were passing through a residential complex, and he sighted men climbing onto the roofs, grasping flint-tipped spears lined with feathers.

"Pakal!" he cried. "Look up! Men with spears, beware!"

Just as Pakal paused to look at the rooftops, the Yokib warriors reached position and started raining down a flurry of spears into his group. One warrior next to Pakal gasped a choked-off cry as a spear entered his throat. Pakal spun around and jumped aside, causing the spear aimed at his chest to graze his upper arm instead. It sliced through his thick cotton armor and slashed a long gash that spouted blood. His warriors closed around him, shielding the ruler with their bodies, and several took wounds.

K'akmo yelled orders to retreat, detecting a wave of warriors racing down the roadway toward them. To his surprise, it was the troop from Sak Tz'i running for their lives. As they surged into the Lakam Ha troops, one noble gasped news.

"They have captured K'ab Chan Te' and killed many of us! We are leaving!"

Battling back through the plaza, they were out of spear reach but faced more Yokib forces that seemed to pour out of every path. Groans, screams, and thuds filled the air as more blood spilled onto the plaza. Slowly Pakal's group edged toward the exit path; he fought as best he could with his good arm. When nearly to the plateau edge, he saw a Yokib noble subdue Ch'ok Bahlam, forcing the Ah K'uhun to kneel with a knife at his throat and grasping his topknot. It was the classic posture of taking noble captives, often portrayed on monuments. Pakal tried to move back into the plaza to help his companion, but K'akmo grasped his shoulder and propelled him onward.

"Ch'ok Bahlam! They have captured him, I must go help!" Pakal cried.

"You cannot help him, it is too late. Their forces are too great; we must escape now and prevent your being captured." K'akmo tightened his grip and nodded to others around Pakal to push him down the path. Half slipping and half running, the Lakam Ha forces followed their allies from

Sak Tz'i down the steep path into the jungle. They could not stop, but kept running desperately through dense foliage when shoved off the narrow path. It seemed they ran for hours, Pakal's wound bleeding and his strength ebbing. By dusk the Sak Tz'i contingent had disappeared into the jungle, seeking their own pathway back to the river.

In the night, a scout from the B'aak forces found them and they planned to reconnoiter in the morning. He reported that Bahlam Ahau had subdued a Yokib noble and taken him prisoner. It was the only successful thing in the attack. Warriors trained in wound care cleaned and bound Pakal's arm wound, which was not deep enough to sever the biceps muscle and had stopped bleeding. The Yokib leaders seemed satisfied with their two captives, as they did not pursue the escaping warriors into the jungle.

Upon return to Lakam Ha, Pakal and his warrior leaders minimized the ineffectiveness of their attack on Yokib. They reported many temples damaged and enemies killed, marched Bahlam Ahau's captive through the streets of Lakam Ha and displayed him in the main plaza. Pakal's wound was promoted as a demonstration of his prowess and stories embellished about how bravely he fought with only one useful arm. Lakam Ha had lost ten warriors in addition to the capture of Ch'ok Bahlam, and B'aak had lost twelve men. Rituals were performed in honor of the fallen, and their families rewarded with gifts and acknowledgement.

In the privacy of his own chambers, Pakal spoke frankly to his closest courtiers about his disappointment. In retrospect, he realized it was an ill-founded action taken at an inauspicious time, despite calendar advice given by the Ah K'inob. He determined to follow his own spiritual divinations in the future, as well as his common-sense knowledge about warfare. And he planned to listen more carefully to the advice of experienced warriors such as K'akmo.

Pakal examined his conscience to further detect reasons underlying his shortcomings in leading the attack. He realized the fallen portal was a major factor, since it prevented communication with the Triad Deities. Now he must put his energies into the lengthy process of rebuilding the portal, beginning with the physical construction that would provide proper foundation for the new Sak Nuk Nah. But he knew another festering problem was stealing his equanimity and draining his spirit.

It was time to come to terms with his anguish over losing Yonil.

He summoned a young trader to his private audience chamber, making certain all servants were out of earshot. Only his steward Muk Kab was to remain, standing outside the door to prevent eavesdropping. He knew the trader and his family well; they were among the most prosperous merchants in the city. Here was a man, he believed, who could be trusted to keep secrets. The young trader agreed to serve his K'uhul Ahau in this manner, and undertook a trading excursion to Nab'nahotot to gather information on the situation with Yonil. The trip required over a moon cycle, for the coastal city lay far north and required voyage by seafaring canoe after completing the trip to the mouth of the K'umaxha River.

The trader returned and gave his report, again in strict privacy. The Lady Yonil was well-accepted in her city, popular among nobles and frequent attendant to the ruler's wife. She had borne two children, the second still an infant, both thriving and the objects of great devotion by their father and grandparents. Upon Pakal's query, the trader observed that the Lady appeared content and happy with her life. He could detect no difficulties in their marital relationship. Pakal thanked and generously rewarded him, filled with a strange mixture of relief and dismay. He resolved to set aside his tortured thoughts about stealing her away from her husband, which would probably require killing him and would create huge turmoil within the polity. The work required for mending his heart would take more time, however.

Lalak was also much relieved for very different reasons. Her pregnancy was now in its sixth moon cycle, progressing without problems. She reveled in the increasing globe of her belly, and delighted in feeling the baby's strong kicks against her abdominal wall. The safe return of her husband from the Yokib attack was another great relief. She had fussed over his wound and attempted to pry out details of the battle, but he would not say much. With her intuition, she sensed that all had not gone well. The pregnancy pleased him greatly, and he enjoyed placing his hands on her abdomen to feel the thumps from tiny feet, declaring that the child was already training as a warrior.

The K'uhul Ixik Me' invited Lalak to join family dinners in her chambers several times. It was always a tense situation for Lalak, who remained guarded against an unexpected verbal assault by Sak K'uk. The evenings went smoothly, however, with Pakal present as diplomat whenever conversation became touchy. Lalak was becoming fond of her father-in-law Kan Mo' Hix, whose acerbic wit put his wife in her place from time to time. Nothing seemed to pass his ever-observant eye. It gratified Lalak that he spoke with genuine kindness to her.

In the time of the fall equinox, when the harvest moon hung like a golden globe over the horizon, Lalak's tenuous happiness was again devastated. One evening as her pregnancy neared the end of its seventh moon cycle, she realized that she was sitting in a large puddle of wetness.

Soon she understood it was not a leaky bladder, but the loss of fluid from the womb. The sac around her baby had broken, and shortly she began feeling labor contractions. Utzil came from her room at once, where she now slept in a chamber next to Lalak. The fluid was clear and appeared normal, but beyond doubt labor was in progress. The priestess summoned other seasoned midwives, well aware that a serious problem was at hand. Few infants born this early survived.

Lalak made light of the early labor, remarking that her son was impatient to enter the world so he could become the warrior his father envisioned. Muyal was informed and rushed to sit in vigil with her friend. Pakal came to confer with the midwives, who were honest with him outside the chamber. His stricken face was enough to tell them that he could not provide much emotional support to his wife. They advised him to return to his quarters after a short visit, and they would keep him informed.

Labor progressed apace and in the early morning, Lalak delivered a son. He was thin and small, with long graceful legs and arms and a face remarkably resembling his father. His reedy wails were encouraging, and Lalak eagerly took him into her arms after the midwives cleaned and wrapped him. She nuzzled and kissed his wispy head, examined his slender fingers and toes, crooned little love songs to him. When Pakal came, she proudly handed the tiny infant to his father. Pakal allowed himself to hope; the baby was pink and wriggling even though so incredibly small.

As the afternoon came, however, it became evident that the baby was having difficulty breathing. His immature lungs were not developed enough to sustain life. He refused to nurse, turning his head aside to gasp for air. Lalak became increasingly desperate, begging the priestesses to help her baby. They made hot herbal potions of calabash leaf and verticilla sprigs and wafted the steam across his face, trying to clear the lungs. They rubbed paste of sweet verbena leaves on his chest to remove mucus. But his breathing became more labored and he turned blue. Pakal came a few times but could not bear the baby's suffering; he turned away from Lalak's pleas, knowing he was helpless, and escaped to his chambers.

During the following night the infant died.

Lalak sat on her sleeping bench propped by pillows, cradling the dead infant to her chest. Her eyes were swollen and red, her face discolored with blotches and hair in a disordered mat around her shoulders. Muyal sat on a mat beside the sleeping bench, red-eyed with head hanging. Utzil stood close by, distraught and ruffling through an herbal collection for some remedy. The other midwives had departed. Servants hovered nervously outside the door, and the steward Pomoy stood by the doorway drape, feeling useless and discomposed. Footsteps sounded in the corridor and he saw the Holy Lady Mother Sak K'uk approaching.

Sak K'uk shoved the steward aside and burst into the chamber like a gale of icy sleet, her face a dark storm cloud.

"So it has been told to me that your child died during the night." Her voice would chill the Death Lords. "You have been such a disappointment to me. You have failed at your sacred duty repeatedly. Now when the pregnancy was nearly at end, you brought forth a perfect son too early into the world. Another heir lost! This is the reason I chose you, and named you as the Producer of the Succession of Lords. You have caused Pakal to fail in his obligation to produce an heir! You have made me a failure for selecting you … you brought nothing but tragedy upon this dynasty!"

The three women stared at Sak K'uk. Muyal and Utzil were frozen in shock and disbelief, but Lalak was jolted into rising fury.

"You— this is beyond belief!" Lalak shouted. "You bring evil and foul intentions. You have always hated me and wished me ill. Now you bring cruel accusations into the depths of my grief! Leave my chambers! Leave at once! I do not want your horrible presence!"

Sak K'uk stepped back as if hit by a blow. Her eyes widened and her lips curled into a snarl.

"You will never be a true K'uhul Ixik here," she hissed. "You are unfit, for you cannot bring forth a child."

She spun on her heel and marched out of the room, head thrown high.

Tense silence settled onto the chamber. Lalak touched her lips to the cold forehead of her baby. Tears started again and she broke into sobs that sounded more like a wild animal wailing its torment. Muyal looked pleadingly at Utzil, who squatted over her herb packets and selected a sedative of dried mimosa leaves, throwing a handful into a gourd of water. She massaged the leaves with fingers to release its substances, and then brought the cup to Lalak.

"Drink," she said. "This will calm you."

"No!" flashed Lalak. She had already refused the sedative several times. "Bring me the poisonous secretions of the toad. That is the only drink I will take."

Muyal stood and put her arm around Lalak's shoulders.

"Let me take the baby," she whispered. "You must rest. Take the drink from Utzil."

"Do not take my baby away! Get away from me, leave me alone!" Lalak shoved Muyal with one arm and the attendant stepped back. Lalak turned her face to Utzil, demanding obedience.

"Give me the poison. This day will I join my son in Xibalba."

Muyal went to the doorway and spoke to Pomoy. "Go, bring Pakal here. Bring him at once."

Pomoy ran down the corridor toward Pakal's chambers. When he returned with Pakal, Muyal whispered to the ruler outside the chamber.

"She is hysterical, out of control completely. She will not let us take the baby away, and she is demanding poison to kill herself."

Pakal walked slowly into the chamber and knelt at Lalak's side. At daybreak he had been informed of the infant's death and felt too wrapped in his own grief to visit Lalak. She did not see him enter, her face buried against the baby's body.

"Lalak." His voice trembled.

She lifted her anguished face to meet his eyes.

"Pakal. Oh, Pakal, I have failed you again."

"It is beyond your doing. It is the will of the Gods."

"Do we not engage with the Gods to make things manifest in the world? All I ever wanted was to be the proper wife for you. To bear your children. To meet your expectations for the K'uhul Ixik. Wherein did I do wrong? Why have the Gods punished me?"

"It is not only you who feels abandoned by the Gods. I too bear their castigation. Together we have lost three children. This one, my son, my firstborn who would be heir to the dynasty ... my heart is breaking too."

"My heart was broken from the day of our marriage!" Lalak could no longer contain the pain and resentment of the past three years. "You kept barriers around your heart; you would not open it to me. In the moments when we should be closest, when we joined our bodies to make our children, you were thinking of her. Do not deny it!"

Pakal sat back on his heels, stunned.

"You know about her ..."

He glanced at Muyal who cowered on her mat, trying to become invisible.

"Yes, the beautiful Yonil, who captured your heart and was banished for doing so, sent away in marriage by ... oh, I cannot even say her evil name!" Lalak's eyes flashed.

"Ah, Lalak ... it is my fault also, that our children would not set foot upon the earth and stay with us. What you say is right. I am sorry, so sorry."

"The Gods knew what you were doing. They saw your duplicity. There was no deep harmony between us because you were not keeping integrity ... this disturbs the balance of male and female energies ... our children could not form rightly or complete their development ... but I am at fault! I did not have courage to face this ... this hard truth that you loved another."

Sobs again wracked Lalak's body as Pakal dropped his face into his hands.

"My only wish now is to die. Command Utzil to give me the poison. Then you will be free to return to her, bring her back to be the wife you wanted."

"No, no ... Lalak, that is not the correct course. That would bring even greater chaos to Lakam Ha. Yonil has her life in Nab'nahotot, her husband and children. Taking her away would violate laws of justice and rightness."

"You are K'uhul B'aakal Ahau, you can bend the laws."

"No, I cannot ... and remain in integrity." He was shaken as Lalak nearly repeated Yonil's words. But from depths of his soul, he knew this would be wrongful action.

"The Gods brought you to me, Lalak," he said softly. "You have been ordained as my wife, my royal consort. It is as it must be. Now I see this clearly."

He rose and sat beside her, putting an arm around her shoulders. She shivered at his touch, tried to shrug him away but he wrapped his other arm around her chest and the dead baby. He held her tightly to his chest, and their tears mingled as their cheeks touched. He stroked her matted hair and whispered into her ear.

"Lalak, hear me. I speak from my heart, now broken open. Much pain have I caused you, and I humbly ask your forgiveness. You are a worthy person, a good person, a woman of many abilities. What has happened to us, we both have helped to create. Why we must suffer so is beyond understanding; the ways of the Gods are not always revealed to us. We must seek to know better their intentions, to restore our relations with them. You must stay with me; you must help in this process. You told me before that it was your greatest desire to help rebuild the portal. For this—for me—you must live."

He felt her rigid body softening in his arms as her head dropped against his shoulder.

"Come, come, let me take the baby," he whispered. "He is my child also, let me hold him."

She lightened her grip on the infant's body, resisted a moment, and then allowed Pakal to lift the tiny cold form from her arms. He gazed upon the tiny face, his tears dropping against its dark skin.

"Ah, my son," he moaned. "So tiny and so perfect. But not yet ready for life. You will be given a name and a royal burial that we may remember and pay homage."

Pakal summoned Pomoy with a hand sign. The steward quickly strode from his post beside the doorway and waited next to Pakal.

"Lalak, I will have Pomoy take our son and have him prepared for burial."

Her eyes became wild for a moment and she leaned forward toward Pakal, reaching for the baby, arms outstretched. Their gaze met and she felt waves of compassion flowing from the black depths of his almond eyes. These waves washed over her like a cleansing torrent, and a tight vise around her heart loosened. She let her arms drop and nodded, holding his gaze until he turned to Pomoy and handed him the baby. With a long sigh, she dropped back onto the pillows.

"Bring the sedative, Utzil," said Pakal.

He sat again beside Lalak while she took the cup and drained it. He helped her settle against the pillows and stroked her tear-stained cheeks tenderly. Leaning toward her, he kissed her forehead.

"This will pass. We must go on; we will find strength to do what we are charged with. Our lives are not our own. Our destiny is written in the stars and directed by the Gods. But we will live from this moment forth in truth and honesty with each other."

2

Swarms of workers scantily clothed in short loincloths labored under the hot sun, sweat dripping from brows despite headbands, and muscled shoulders glistening with moisture. Squatting, kneeling and stooping, they used stone axes and flint knives to chop away brush and fell trees all across the wide eastern meadow. Other crews used digging hoes, flat stone scrapers bound to wooden poles, to remove grass and level the ground. Another group removed the debris, piling it into large cloth sacks that were tied when filled and hauled away on worker's backs using a tumpline across the forehead. At least one-third of the commoner male population of Lakam Ha toiled to prepare the meadow for initial construction of a large platform.

When rulers initiated monumental construction projects, huge investments of manpower were required. Working with stone and flint implements was slow and tedious, but over many generations the Mayas had perfected techniques and manpower needs. They planned these constructions to take advantage of the dry season and used large labor forces and long workdays to make as much progress as possible before rains halted their efforts. Then construction would stop until the rains ended and another dry season began.

While some workers cleared and leveled the meadow, others were sent to nearby quarries to chop limestone into various sized blocks. Lakam Ha was fortunate to have easily available high quality limestone for building blocks and for making cement. For this, limestone was heated to high temperatures and then combined with water to form silica crystals. This cement was used to form cast-in-place concrete that bound stones together, a strong and durable mix that filled voids to produce smooth surfaces. This technique had existed before Lakam Ha was established and gave outstanding strength and lifespan to the Mayas' massive buildings. In addition, the mountains around the city provided a fine-grained limestone that was softer and used for carved panels. Stone carvers used a special tool kit of obsidian, flint, and polished greenstone implements to carve glyphs and figures. They polished their artwork using fine-grained sandstone and other abrasives to produce exceptionally lovely images.

The objective of the workers this season was to create a level surface for the large platform upon which buildings would later rest. They planned to follow natural contours of the plateau, making stepped layers where the land dipped down that would support stacked platforms joined by stairways and roads. The area envisioned for the new center of Lakam Ha was huge, more than doubling the size of the city. It was a major building project that would take many years.

One special consideration in the main platform's initial construction phase was water management. The Otulum River flowed through the meadow and would be used to bring water into the palace and other residential structures. Aqueducts were planned to preserve the river's flow under the palace and channel portions to residences on its eastern side. During the dry season, workers widened and deepened the river's bed and built stone walls to direct the water flows. These aqueducts would be closed on top, forming underground tunnels, when the plaza was paved with stone blocks and stucco. Narrow up-shafts would be placed where chambers for bathing and toileting were to be located; these would force river water upward into receptacles, with discharge flows that deposited used water into underground drains.

Commoners were accustomed to providing labor for building projects of rulers and ahauob. It was part of the religious and social exchange that kept their society in balance, ordained long ago by the Creator Gods. The ruler was their conduit to the Gods; by his rituals he satisfied their needs for recognition and offerings. Through him, the Gods delivered messages to the people, providing guidance for the coming katuns. For the divine beneficence brought into their world by the ruler, the commoners were glad to return the sweat of their labor. In the glory of monuments and the abundance of fields, which the ruler and ahauob shared with the commoners, all lives proceeded in harmony and society carried out its sacred purposes.

Some workers specialized in construction and maintenance of structures; others were farmers or orchard tenders. Agriculture could not be neglected while building projects were underway, and this division of resources contributed to the time it took to build huge palaces and temples. This was the normal pattern, cycles that flowed with seasons and with circumstances. Stone carvers and artisans were always happy when building projects were underway for it provided them with extra work. Only the warriors might be disgruntled, because conducting attacks and producing monuments rarely occurred simultaneously. Few were unhappy in this instance, however, given their recent less than admirable excursion to Yokib.

Pakal and Yax Chan went frequently to observe progress in the eastern meadow. They consulted with overseers and adjusted activities, greeted workers and complimented their efforts. Pakal watched as the crumbling stones of the old hunters' structure were removed, partly relieved and somewhat saddened to see that place of so many memories disappear. He paced off the area where he wanted Yax Chan to construct the new Sak Nuk Nah. Markers were put at the corners. Discussion ensued about an underground passageway that Pakal wanted. It would lead from a set of chambers connecting to the royal residential quarters, where stairs would descend to a tunnel that would emerge via another set of stairs into one end of the Sak Nuk Nah.

The Sak Nuk Nah would be a rectangular structure at slight elevation above platform level, fully visible from the plaza. This was a radical departure from the previous sacred white-skin house, which had been completely underground and accessed by only an elite group of nobles. The sacred shrine's underground location represented the Underworld, where the ruler would journey to access the roots of the Wakah Chan Te', the sacred Jeweled Sky Tree that led through the Middleworld and spread its branches into the Upperworld. Following the tree trunk upward, a portal opened to the sky and gave contact with the deities and ancestors residing there.

Yax Chan understood that having an underground passage into the Sak Nuk Nah, through which the ruler traveled to reach the sacred shrine, was placing it symbolically in the Underworld. He knew about Pakal's intention to make ceremonies in the sacred shrine open to a wider range of the city's nobles, perhaps even the artist and merchant classes. Pakal wanted the city's spiritual life to be more inclusive, to involve a wider range of residents in these highly important rituals.

It was a popularization of religion that did not sit well with the High Priest, Pasah Chan. The power of the priesthood was based on exclusivity and concentration of secret knowledge among a few in the upper ranks. More than anything, Pasah Chan wanted to increase his power; he desired to be a shaping force in Lakam Ha's future. This change that Pakal was bringing about deeply troubled him. Their discussions about it were strained, for the High Priest had taught and mentored Pakal since he was very young. The ruler's independent thinking and strange concepts about religious protocol were beyond the priest's comprehension. It was especially disturbing in light of the collapsed portal; he could not fathom why Pakal would make changes that would further unsettle this situation.

Change was also afoot in Lalak's world. The tragedy of her third lost child had propelled her into a different state of mind. It broke through constraints and fears around her acceptance at Lakam Ha, and taught her the importance of being true to herself. She had spoken her innermost feelings to Pakal, and he respected her more for it. She had lashed back against Sak K'uk's meanness, and the Holy Lady Mother kept a wide distance between them, but acted politely when they were compelled to interact. Lalak resolved to follow her own inclinations now, and to bring back into her life those things she held most important.

Spending time in nature was high on her list. She had Pomoy set up regular excursions into the jungle, although he resisted at first. Lalak exerted authority as K'uhul Ixik and ordered him to proceed, using his wisdom to decide about her entourage but insisting that all members be capable of long and sometimes difficult walks. Pomoy engaged a young noble, Kayum, who was known for hunting skills and had traveled nearly all the jungle paths around the city. With the hunter's guidance, and two women attendants who passed muster as fit for the outdoors, Lalak re-entered the jungle she so loved.

Being swathed in lush greenery, smelling humus and wild flowers, hearing familiar bird songs amid the humming of myriad jungle insects began to restore her soul. She thrilled in catching the flash of scarlet macaws high amid jungle canopy, watching the antics of spider monkeys leaping from branches, discovering a brilliant butterfly with huge wing eyes, uncovering psychedelically patterned frogs beneath drooping pathos leaves, hearing roars of howler monkeys in echoing waves that spoke of primeval worlds. Small whitetail deer sprang across her path, armadillos ambled under low brush, and iguanas rolled their beady eyes at her from safe perches high on tree limbs.

Kayum pointed out tracks of tapir, bobcats, and wild boar. He kept his spear and knives at hand, but she forbade him to kill animals during their walks unless necessary for defense. Sometimes her women attendants squealed at a snake in the path, but Lalak liked snakes and knew their ways. She knew which were dangerous and how to avoid disturbing them. Though she tried to impart this knowledge to her women, they just wanted to stay as far away from snakes as possible.

When the small party paused by streams or ponds, water birds flapped into flight or lifted stalk-like legs to reach positions farther away. Cormorants and pelicans did not often come to jungle streams, preferring open waters, but there were many cranes. Around the shore she might catch glimpse of pheasant, dove, quail, or wood grouse. High in the trees she identified songs of buntings, warblers, tanagers, and the chachalaca's rhythmic call. Seeing a rainbow-billed toucan, pale-billed woodpecker, or rufus-tailed hummingbird was a special treat.

On one trip, Lalak spotted bright red feathers underneath thick brush off the path. She told the rest to move back and stand perfectly still, as she slowly approached to find a young scarlet macaw cowering on the ground. It was wounded, one wing badly askew and unable to fly. She began crooning sounds not used since her days in the forests around B'aak, sounds she used to talk with birds. The macaw shuddered and tried to edge away, but soon responded to her soothing call and allowed her to gently lift it. She wrapped her waistband around the bird to keep it secured while they returned to the palace, then had Utzil bring an animal healer. He found it necessary to remove most of the macaw's wing, for some predator had mangled it and broken several bones. The bird would never be able to fly again, so Lalak tamed it and soon the macaw happily inhabited a perch next to Popo. The two jungle creatures exchanged frequent chattering and clacking dialogue, which Lalak joined, making similar sounds.

As Lalak's strength and confidence grew, she went on excursions farther from the palace. Her curiosity impelled her to begin trips around the eastern meadow, so she could also watch the progress of the new construction. She and Pakal were exploring new patterns in their relationship, and both were hesitant after the intensity of their experience around the baby's death. Utzil and the head priestess of Ix Chel were adamant that there could be no sexual contact between them for several years. Major adjustments were needed and these would take considerable time. Abstaining sexually was common practice among rulers and elite ahauob, who understood the importance of containing sexual energy to build spiritual power. When Pakal and Lalak were together, it usually involved sharing a meal or discussing an issue needing mediation from a woman's perspective. Lalak was pleased when Pakal sought her assistance, and on a few occasions she joined him in the royal reception chamber to adjudicate cases together.

Watching the throng of men working to clear and level the meadow was fascinating to Lalak. With determined hands and well-honed tools, they shaped the face of nature to do their bidding; they molded nature into creations of their minds.

Nature is powerful, she reflected, *but so is the will of humankind.*

When Pakal and Yax Chan were present, she enjoyed their descriptions of the glorious buildings that would rise on the platform, paying special attention to the area marked off for the Sak Nuk Nah. As she walked over the place where the ruined hunters' structure had been, she could still feel the swirling energies of the vortex. Watching Pakal's face, she knew he felt them too.

The aqueduct was a marvel to Lalak. She often watched as workers diverted water flow with sacks of fine gravel so they could dig the riverbed deeper into the limestone bedrock. They deftly raised walls the height of two men, using smoothly cut stone blocks and fastening them tightly together with cast-in-place concrete. The roof was finished with a Maya arch, and then the finished portion was covered with soil. Yax Chan explained that the aqueduct was constructed with a steeper grade as it approached the area where the palace would be built, to increase the speed of the water flow. That would provide greater pressure when water reached the narrow points of the tunnel, forcing water upward through shafts or ceramic pipes. There would be fountains and water flowing into basins for drinking and other domestic needs. Because she showed keen interest, the architect shared his plans for managing water drainage during the rainy season to prevent the flooding of plazas. The aqueduct system would extend upstream to collect water rushing down steep slopes, sending it through a network of tunnels that emptied at the plateau edges. Channeling rivers and springs in this way also provided more building space, as the level areas would not be transected by rivers and ponds and could be paved into platforms.

Lalak drew her small party along the Otulum River to explore the area where it tumbled down a steep escarpment at the eastern end of the meadow. A small deer trail led downhill, following the river. Her women protested that the slope was too steep, but she pressed on, laughing while hanging onto lianas to steady her descent. The women remained at the plateau edge, while Kayum hastened after his royal charge. The crashing of cascades summoned her onward; she slipped on loose pebbles but was determined to find the waterfalls. Pushing through layers of palms, saplings, ferns and shrubs that dripped water on her face and clothes, she entered a small clearing at the edge of a wide pond. Across the pond, a waterfall tumbled over boulders, sending sprays of fine droplets into a misty halo. Dappled sunlight streamed through the high canopy formed by mahogany, cedar, ceiba, and guanacaste trees bound together by twining lianas.

It was a magical place. Lalak caught her breath and stood still, transfixed by its beauty. Sunlight danced on bubbles and glittered on ripples that spread across the pond's surface. Even the jungle birds seemed hushed and only the singing of the waterfall filled the air. Tiger-stripe and iridescent morpho butterflies batted silent wings as they circled around her. The respiration of thousands of dark green plants filled the air with intoxicating energy. Lalak's entire body vibrated; she felt she would burst through her skin any moment. Exquisite chills ran up her spine and neck hairs raised expectantly. Something wonderful hung just beyond the misty veil, something magical that was calling her.

Heavy breathing and thumping footsteps broke her transfixion as Kayum struggled through understory plants and burst into the clearing. He wiped sweat from his forehead and looked extremely relieved to see her. After a preemptory bow, he pleaded with her to take his hand and return to the meadow, warning that it was not safe to venture so far into unexplored jungle. She sighed, reluctant to leave this special place but understanding that the magical moment had passed. Placing her hand in his, she nodded toward the ascending trail and he carefully assisted her in the arduous climb back up.

3

L akam Ha was filled with visitors as the end of Katun 9 approached. Among calendar rituals, the katun ending that initiated the start of the next katun held great importance. The katun was a 20-tun time period, just over nineteen solar years. Not many among the Maya people lived beyond two katuns, except elite nobles and rulers whose nutrition and lifestyle supported better health. For the average commoners, merchants, artisans, and lesser nobles, seeing one katun ending ceremony was all they could expect in a lifetime. Most of them, however, would not actually observe the ritual performed by the ruler. This was reserved for the higher ranking nobles and had always been performed in a sacred shrine not accessible to others.

For the Katun 9 ceremonies, the Sak Nuk Nah where the sacred shrine had resided was not available. It was a difficult situation, because the portal in the sacred shrine used by previous Lakam Ha rulers no longer existed. There was much speculation among the people about how their K'uhul B'aakal Ahau would conduct the expected rituals in the absence of the portal. Visitors from other cities joined the discussions, grasping the ruler's dilemma readily. They came because Lakam Ha was still the May Ku city for B'aakal polity, the designated ceremonial center for the entire region. The ancient *May* system, time-honored and God-gifted to maintain peaceful relations among cities, was gradually falling away, however. The elders who remembered the harmony brought by this system of shared leadership were much dismayed. In recent times certain cities had increased aggression against neighbors, and even beyond their own polities. The Kan dynasty of Ka'an polity was the prime example.

More than anyone, Pakal pondered how he would carry out the katun rituals. He underwent rigorous preparation, including physical austerities and long sessions of meditation and prayer. He engaged in lengthy discussions with Pasah Chan, seeking the High Priest's wisdom and experience. Pasah Chan took this opportunity to chastise Pakal over the ruler's plans to make the new Sak Nuk Nah more accessible. Pakal skirted the issue, re-focusing on present challenges. In a conciliatory move, he agreed to hold the katun ritual at the Temple of the High Priest, although he personally preferred using the Temple of the South, Nohol. Pakal knew this ritual would require bloodletting and seeking the vision serpent, with which he had little experience.

As dusk approached on the day of the ceremony, a select group of elite nobles and high-ranking visitors climbed the long stairway to the lofty Temple of the High Priest. Rosy-hued beams of sunlight threw streamers across thin clouds as the sun dipped below the western mountains. Perched on its outcropping partway up the mountainside, the Temple hung as if suspended in darkening skies. Tall incense burners lined the stairs, spreading plumes of copal smoke over the climbers. Torches lined the platform on which the ceremonial chamber sat. The date of the Katun 9 ending ceremony was inscribed.

Baktun 9, Katun 9, Tun 19, Uinal 18, Kin 19, on the date 13 Kawak 7 Kayab (January 26, 633 CE)

When dawn came, the next day of the Maya calendar started, since days were counted from the first daylight. At dawn, the calendar would roll over into the new katun, the next 20-year period. Katun 10 would be inscribed.

Baktun 9, Katun 10, Tun 0, Uinal 0, Kin 0, on the date 1 Ahau 8 Kayab (January 27, 633 CE)

Inside the ceremonial chamber were the High Priest and Priestess, royal family, and attendant priests. Other nobles and visitors surrounded the chamber, seeking spots on the platform close enough to see inside as they settled onto mats. Drummers at the platform's edges kept up a steady rhythm as a priestly chorus chanted the day-ending prayer.

Lalak sat close to the area where Pakal would perform the ritual. At her left sat the High Priestess, and around her were Utzil, Muyal, and Yax Chan. Kan Mo' Hix and Sak K'uk sat on the opposite side with their closest courtiers. Sak K'uk held the ritual bundle that Pakal would give to the three Sky Gods, consisting of vestments made of finest cotton and jade earspools. It was a meager offering considering the adornments these Gods had been given in the past, but the Gods could not be invoked due to the collapsed portal. In their distant positions in the sky, they would not notice the offering. The offerings would be kept in the High Priest's temple until the portal was rebuilt in the new Sak Nuk Nah. Sak K'uk was in charge of selecting the offerings and deciding upon festivities. From her experience with the Primordial Goddess Muwaan Mat, she understood the appropriate offerings under present circumstances.

Lalak was filled with both anticipation and dread; she had never witnessed a ruler's bloodletting and this was especially significant for her. During her husband's arduous preparations, she had not seen him. She worried about how he was doing, his state of mind and inner preparedness for this important event. To distract herself from anxiety, she looked around the platform to see who was deemed of high enough status to attend. Several leading nobles she knew well, and she recognized most others as Lakam Ha ahauob, but the identities of a group of three people eluded her. Surely they were not from her city, for their dress was different and their faces unfamiliar.

The only woman among the three caught her eye. Of middle years, the woman had a striking appearance and commanding presence. Her muscular body held the energy of a stalking jaguar, her face the sharpness of a hawk. From deep-set eyes came the unblinking stare of a serpent, penetrating the depths of those she viewed with frightening clairvoyance. As the woman sensed Lalak's gaze, their eyes locked and a fierce shockwave coursed through Lalak's body. For a moment, a fiery halo hovered around the stranger's head that glowed red in the dim light. Lalak blinked rapidly to dissipate the energy, then nodded acknowledgement to the woman, who returned the gesture. Deliberately, the mysterious visitor turned away her head.

"Who is that fierce-looking woman?" Lalak whispered to Usin Ch'ob.

The High Priestess discretely looked where Lalak gestured.

"She is a priestess of Ix Zuhuy K'ak. Her name is T'zab Chak. They are from Ek Bahlam," Usin Ch'ob whispered back.

"Ix Zuhuy K'ak, the Goddess of Destruction!"

"Destruction and re-creation, death and birth. Do not overlook the Goddess' powers to bring about radical change and rejuvenation, being born anew in more advanced forms."

"They practice dark magic, do they not?"

"Dark magic contains the alchemy of transformation. More accurately, these priestesses are masters of sex magic. They are a powerful clan, not often seen in our region. Ek Bahlam is far away, in the distant lowlands to the north."

"Ah."

Lalak fell silent, but something had stirred within her. She felt the serpent power coiled at the base of her spine that was nudged by the gaze of the Priestess of Ix Zuhuy K'ak. Instantly she knew that this hint of sexual power was something she wanted to explore. She decided to ask the priestess to stay in Lakam Ha and instruct her in sex magic.

Chanting ceased and the drumbeats rose to a compelling pattern. Priests on all four corners of the temple platform blew conches to the four directions. As the blare of the conches faded and the drums stopped, Pakal entered the chamber. On his chest was a single Ahau K'in pendant, around his waist a short loincloth with a front opening. His headdress soared with scarlet macaw and white quetzal feathers, and his wrists and ankles clanked with shell-draped cuffs.

From the expression of his face and eyes, Lalak knew he had taken plant hallucinogens and pain-numbing herbs. This was standard practice for bloodletting rituals, as it enhanced visionary abilities. The accoutrements for drawing and collecting blood were on an altar beside the low platform where he moved to sit. Pasah Chan chanted the purification prayer while fanning copal smoke from a censer over Pakal's body. Pakal raised his arms and recited a lengthy prayer to the Triad Deities, calling upon their clemency and forgiveness for the imperfect offerings he brought. Sak K'uk handed him the bundle, which he lifted as the High Priest purified it. After the bundle was set aside, he welcomed the new Lord of Time, Hun Ahau, who presided over the coming katun. He ended with a plea for the vision serpent to bring him predictions he could relate to the people about the nature of the coming katun.

Pakal prepared to draw blood from his penis. Blood was the sacred *itz* given by the Gods to sustain human life, and the highest offering a ruler could give was to return that itz from his own body to the Gods. Blood from the penis was especially potent, for it came from the source of male creativity, the origin of bringing new human life into the world. This time-honored ritual of self-offering had been done by Maya rulers since the origins of their people in the misty past.

Although affected by the plant medicine, Pakal felt unusually alert and aware, his senses honed. He took the thin stingray spine from the altar, a needle of great sharpness, and held it up for purification by the High Priest. As Pasah Chan waved incense over the implement and chanted, another priest took a bowl filled with bark paper from the altar and knelt beside Pakal, ready to catch droplets of blood. Pakal tilted his head upward, grasped his penis in one hand and lifted the other holding the spine. Without hesitating, he plunged the spine downward and into the foreskin. While his feathered headdress shuddered, his body remained impassive as he repeated the stabs several times. On his face was an expression of distant calm.

As droplets of blood fell onto bark paper, saturating them bright red, Pakal felt his consciousness drift upward and expand into the night sky. Brilliant stars sparkled and swirled around him, waves of cosmic dust blew over him, and the stillness of outer space surrounded him. With only a tiny part of his awareness, he saw the priest burning the blood-soaked paper in the bowl, setting it on the altar in front of him. Soon a shaft of smoke rose from the bowl, smoke impregnated with his creative itz, smoke that would become the vision serpent if his quest was successful.

He summoned his consciousness from its cosmic journey and focused it on the rising smoke. Inwardly he called to the vision serpent, invoking it to appear. The smoke began to curl and twist, making tantalizing hints at taking serpent form, but it would not coalesce. He focused harder, using willpower to invoke the serpent. It resisted and would not take shape. Pakal began to feel desperation rising; without the vision serpent he would receive no katun predictions. He struggled to remain calm and stay focused, casting about in his mind for sources of help.

The smoke thickened and straightened, pulsating into a shadowy form. It seemed to be a human form, swaying side to side with its back to Pakal. Under nearly closed lids, he gazed at the form, which now appeared to be a woman. He called her gently to turn her face toward him. Slowly, swaying, moving in and out of form, she turned, and Pakal recognized his grandmother, Yohl Ik'nal. A surge of joy filled his heart; he revered his grandmother and often paid homage at her mortuary pyramid. Radiating happiness at seeing her, he mentally sent her welcome.

"Beloved Grandmother, greatly pleased am I to behold you."

"You called for help, I am here."

"Thank you, Grandmother, from my heart's depths. Would you offer me communication from the realm of sky ancestors?"

"What you seek, the vision serpent, is not possible now. You know this, for to raise the vision serpent you must have the Jeweled Sky Tree."

"This I know. Can you advise me how to re-create the Jeweled Sky Tree?"

"For you to raise a new Jeweled Sky Tree, this is what you must do.
Unite the earth and the sky with your body,
That the roots of the Wakah Chan Te' may be planted.
Nourish the roots with the life-creating Liquid of Your Groin,
Received into the Womb of Mother Earth,
That a new Jeweled Sky Tree may be born.
Only with a heart filled with pure love,
Love that encompasses those closest to you and spreads to all your people,
All creatures and things of our sacred B'aakal,
Love that is boundless and unconditional and surpasses human understanding,
Will the Wakah Chan Te' rise again."

Pakal bowed his head and committed his grandmother's words to memory. He did not understand them now, but trusted that with deep contemplation their meanings would unfold.

The swirling smoke of Yohl Ik'nal's form began to loosen and thin. Pakal had one more request of her.

"Honored Ancestor, you who reside among the stars, there is yet another way you can help me. Grant me this great favor, as you know the ways of the Gods, and give to me predictions for the coming katun."

Her words drifted into his inner awareness, faint and becoming garbled.

"Katun 10 will be a time of growth for Lakam Ha. The crops and the structures will all increase; life will expand in many ways. Your heart's desire will be realized. When conflict comes again late in the katun, you will know success. Stand beside your allies, and their strength shall be added to yours."

Though her last words were distorted, with extrasensory astuteness he understood them perfectly. As her form dissipated and the smoke thinned to a tiny string, he made profuse thanks in his heart, bowing low until his head rested on the mat.

All the observers sat in spellbound silence during the ritual, sensing that their ruler was engaged in an intense inner experience.

Lalak's heart pounded as he drew blood, and she showered him with compassion and love, hoping it would provide some support. When he appeared engrossed in watching the smoke, she prayed that he would receive the vision he sought. Reading the subtle changes in his face, which she more than any could detect, her heart soared when she saw the tiny upturn of his lips that signaled he was pleased.

As Pakal bowed low, the observers released pent-up breaths in unison, a sigh of relief.

Pasah Chan and another priest wrapped a cloak around Pakal and helped him rise. He wavered on his feet a moment, and then stood erect without support. In a surprisingly clear and steady voice, he repeated the prediction for Katun 10. Murmurs of delight rippled through the group; it was much more positive than they expected. The Gods had spoken to their ruler, though in what form they knew not, and it was decreed that Lakam Ha was entering good times.

4

T'zab Chak, priestess of Ix Zuhuy K'ak, entered Lalak's private reception chamber and bowed low, clasping her left shoulder. After Lalak's welcome, the priestess straightened and gazed at the K'uhul B'aakal Ixik under half lowered lids.

"Much is my honor to be in the presence of the Holy Lady of B'aakal," she said. "You summoned me, how may I serve you?"

"Of your arts, would I learn," replied Lalak. She sensed that T'zab Chak appreciated directness.

"May I ask, in all humility, for what purpose?"

"For a purpose that is not fully revealed, even to me," said Lalak. "Upon seeing you at the katun ceremony, instantly I knew that your abilities with sex magic would serve a need, not just for me but for my city. This will bring about a great healing, how I cannot understand, but intuitively I know it will happen."

"It is well that you listen so closely to your intuition," the priestess said with a faint smile.

"Perhaps you have heard about my misfortunes bearing children. It is the greatest grief of my life. Before the time comes again to seek conception, some major changes are necessary ... to, ah ... alter the approaches we are using."

"Hmmm." T'zab Chak looked directly into Lalak's eyes, her penetrating serpent gaze stripping away all emotional coverings and laying bare the inner core. "Yes, you have suffered much and your desire to serve your husband and people is clear. That you are sincere, I can see. That you are ready for such arts, I am not certain."

"I will become ready. Among my abilities, rapid learning has often been noted. Now my determination is set. I must follow my own way, the guidance of heart and intuition, rather than rely upon predictions of priests or regimens of healers. These have failed in the past. There must be another approach to using the sexual energies of procreation, one more effective and powerful. This I sense in your abilities."

"Your sensing is quite good," said the priestess, her face softening.

"Will you remain in Lakam Ha and teach me your sexual alchemy? You will be my honored guest, given chambers in the palace near mine, and recompensed however you request."

"Such training requires much time, perhaps a year or more. It is demanding and often difficult. Are you willing to make that commitment?"

"With all my heart and skills do I commit to master the training." Lalak's eyes sparkled and eagerness brightened her face.

"Very well. I shall make arrangements with my companions to find others for my duties in Ek Bahlam, for a solar year. More time I cannot commit."

"Excellent! Honored Priestess, my heart soars in gratitude and I submit myself as your most devoted and industrious student."

The training began the following day, sometimes inside Lalak's quarters and at other times outside in nature. When training took place in the jungle, Kayum accompanied his mistress but was not permitted to observe. He was stationed out of view and hearing, while T'zab Chak took responsibility for Lalak's safety, promising to call loudly should any danger appear. Initially, instruction focused on Lalak becoming familiar with all her senses, learning their most subtle and most intense responses. Sight, sound, smell, taste, tactile sensations, and spatial orientation were stimulated and analyzed. If Lalak did not know intimately her every response, she could not hope to master how she reacted.

It was an amazing experience for Lalak. She plumbed depths of sensations she never knew existed, and reached heights of delight in the ordinary things of the world. Once she lay flat on a grassy field, her bare skin tickled by waving grasses and brushed by light puffs of wind. An ant crawled over her foot but she made no motion, feeling each tiny leg moving against her skin. Her ears were attuned to the faintest birdcall and distant crunch of an animal through the brush. When she gazed at the sky, the clouds were etched against a cobalt blue canvas, every subtle change of shape impressed on her perception. Scents of vervain, hibiscus, and cedar drifted into her awareness mixed with the earthy humus of the forest floor.

Her task was not only to identify these sensations, but to examine the mental and emotional responses they evoked. These responses were not judged as good or bad, pleasant or unpleasant. They were simply to be observed and catalogued. Ultimately, T'zab Chak told her, all experience was neutral. These were merely sensations of the material world, having no absolute value in themselves. They were allowed to pass through the field of perception without altering her internal state.

Some experiences were harder to put in this perspective. Plunging her naked body into cold streams without drawing back, eating nasty tasting skunk root without grimacing, and tolerating the pain of a needle prick without wincing were bigger challenges. Handling fear was the most difficult, for the self-protective instinct set off a wave of physiological responses. T'zab Chak began this training by taking Lalak to a high cliff and having her hover on the edge, then progressed to bringing poisonous snakes and scorpions close. When Lalak could calm her fear responses in these situations, they progressed to psychological ones. Lalak had described her trepidation in the presence of Sak K'uk, with examples of how she had been treated. T'zab Chak would assume the persona of the Holy Lady Mother and play out these scenes, using abusive words and gestures. Finally, Lalak became non-reactive and retained her inner calm.

Lalak's image of herself and sense of self-worth were the next part of her training. Now she must come to grips with her sense of being ugly. T'zab Chak proposed that beauty was not an external quality, but something that radiated from within. Once the knowledge of inner beauty was firmly internalized, then the outer form would communicate this to the world. Others would perceive one as beautiful, even though physical appearance did not meet popular standards.

"Look at me," said T'zab Chak. "Do you consider me beautiful?"

"You are striking, almost beyond beauty," replied Lalak.

"Consider carefully my features, for they do not differ greatly from yours."

Lalak tried to analyze the priestess' face without being influenced by her aura. It was true; this face with its sharp nose, square chin, fierce downturned mouth and deep set eyes was far from the ideal image she had seen in the codex.

"It is so, now I see what you mean," Lalak murmured.

"What people see when they view my visage emanates from the harmony within and its expression in balanced power. This gives my appearance its attractiveness. You also have beauty within, the beauty of compassion and love for creatures. I have seen how you attract beauty to yourself, like a plain trumpet flower, simple and unadorned in its blossom, but filled with heavenly nectar that magnetizes beautiful creatures; the ruby-throated hummingbird, huge morpho butterflies with brilliant jeweled wings. You care for those little ones who are abandoned or injured: your monkey and your macaw. Now you must remove the veil that covers your inner beauty, so it may shine forth for the world to see."

Lalak learned that the veil was self-judgment and self-doubt. She repeated self-assurances to remove her sense of inadequacy and confirm her perfection as a daughter of the Goddess filled with divine itz. Slowly, by disciplining her critical mind and filling it with images of worth, she felt this veil of limitation lifting.

The moon completed six cycles as Lalak perfected her abilities to control physical, mental, and emotional responses. Just when Lalak was wondering if the training would ever take a sexual focus, the priestess launched the next phase.

"You spoke truth about being a quick learner. Few of my acolytes have attained this level of mastery in such short time. You are now ready to work with sexual energies, which is to say, the life force. You are aware of energy channels in the body. Let us proceed with gaining intentional control over these energetic pathways."

T'zab Chak taught her student the locations and movements of energy channels and how life force flowed through them. Energy from the earth entered through soles of the feet, and at times the palms. It could be deliberately drawn into the body, or energy could be discharged from the body into the earth. There were centers within the body that concentrated life force energy into specific expressions, such as love and compassion in the heart center, intuition and clairvoyance in the forehead center, willpower and manifestation in the center near the navel. The crown center was the conduit into the cosmos, through which she could project her consciousness into the sky and also receive divine energies from deities. In the pelvic region was the sexual center, and its powers could be enhanced by certain practices. Lalak's tasks were to develop the ability to move energy through the channels and concentrate it in the centers, using intention. For this, she practiced breathing techniques, body postures and movements that supported her conscious intention.

It was of utmost importance to always remember these were spiritual practices. They required drawing upon the powers of the Gods and Goddesses, in particular Ix Zuhuy K'ak, in a mood of appreciation and gratitude. The deities gave life and all its experiences to humans, shared their powers and vision, for the simple gift of acknowledgement. Deities and humans intertwined their essences; each needed the other to fully become themselves. Before every practice session, Lalak paid homage to the deities and invoked their support of her efforts.

When T'zab Chak was satisfied that Lalak could initiate and move energy within her body, she gave Lalak techniques to magnify her sexual capacities. Breast massage was used to increase female hormones, done by placing the palms over bare nipples and making slow circles with moderate pressure, first in one direction then in the other. These movements were repeated until Lalak felt heat collecting in her breasts. Keeping her palms pressed to nipples, she then inhaled deeply and sucked the energy generated from her breasts into the navel center. Upon exhalation through pursed lips, making "ssss" sounds, she radiated this sexual energy from the navel into her entire body.

Massage of the lower abdomen was used to cleanse the organs and discharge stagnant energy held there. Emotional energy from past traumas was held in these organs, especially the womb, and this decreased free energy flow and affected normal functions. After drawing cleansing energy up from earth through her palms, Lalak placed them over each side of the lower abdomen and used circular motions in both directions as she had before with her breasts. When she felt heat collecting inside, she inhaled deeply and sucked energy from the crown center down through her body, directing it to purify her pelvic organs. Upon exhalation, she discharged the old energies down through her legs to exit from the soles of her feet to be absorbed into the earth.

Toning the pelvic organs was another exercise to increase sexual potency. Lalak started by tightening her anal muscles, then the muscles of the pelvic base, and while still holding these contracted, tightening and lifting upward through the vagina. She inhaled deeply while drawing these muscle sets upward and held her breath and muscles contracted to an increasing count, first five then working up to twenty. Upon exhalation, she relaxed the muscle sets in reverse order. The goal was to do this exercise three times daily, up to fifty sets. This increased tone of the pelvic muscles enhanced the capacity for sexual pleasure of both woman and man, and it also infused the pelvic center with copious itz, sacred life force energy.

These exercises were best done outdoors barefoot on the earth and facing the sun. This gave the best exposure to natural life force energies. Since the weather did not always permit going outdoors, Lalak was instructed to create a space within her chambers dedicated to Ix Zuhuy K'ak with an altar. Consistent use would consecrate this space and it would become charged with itz, containing the vibrations of sun and earth. Once Lalak was proficient in these exercises, T'zab Chak revealed the secrets of sex magic.

"The basic technique of sexual alchemy is the delay or elimination of orgasmic release. Then the sexual energy normally dissipated during physical release is available for spiritual purposes. It can be used to vastly amplify one's spiritual powers, to lift you into higher consciousness, to give access to the intelligence and creative forces of the cosmos. Within those are all sources of Knowledge and Power. It refines and evolves human consciousness and brings union with the deities. An added benefit is increased physical vitality and mental clarity. When sacred itz is not wasted in sexual discharge, the body can rejuvenate itself more readily and heal more quickly. You feel stronger, more youthful, and you vibrate with higher frequencies of energy. You learn to hold a great deal of energy within your body without needing to ground it. This is particularly useful for rulers and elites, priests and priestesses. We must be capable of containing the immense forces that are channeled into us when we embody the deities."

These were novel ideas to Lalak. She could quickly grasp how containing sexual energy would enhance many capacities, but was puzzled about how that affected conceiving a child.

"Honored Priestess, how does this technique affect conception? Surely a child cannot result without the man's release to seed the womb."

"Just so," replied T'zab Chak. "When the goal is conception, there must be sexual release. For successful conception resulting in the greatest empowerment of the child, the technique of delayed release is used. If this is done several times before conception, and by building up of life force energy, the child is permeated with enhanced abilities. I realize you have a great desire to bear Pakal's child, for this is your sacred duty and destiny. It will come to pass, once you have prepared yourself to be a vessel of sexual alchemy. The practices for man and woman together will come later. Now you must learn to control your own sexual release."

The priestess taught techniques for self-stimulation, something Lalak had never done before. Gradually she became skilled in self-arousal to the point of release. Then the priestess had her identify the moment just before orgasm, and with fine timing decrease the surging sexual energy by breathing deeply and relaxing her pelvic muscles. Lalak directed the sexual energy down toward her feet, and then continued with stimulation almost to the point of discharge, controlling the energy again and sending it to the heart center. She repeated the arousal-and-control sequence until she had energized each center. Initially she would complete the sequence by sending sexual energy throughout her body and letting it blossom into her aura as she reached climax. After she became adept at this, the priestess instructed her to radiate the energy into her entire being and hold it there without release. It was uncomfortable and unsettling at first, but Lalak focused on giving gratitude to the Goddess and asking for spiritual growth. This allowed her to contain the immense sexual energy within herself. She felt increasingly invigorated, vibrantly healthy and filled with divine itz.

As the solar year approached conclusion, T'zab Chak finalized her teaching of sex magic and prepared to return to Ek Bahlam. The last set of techniques dealt with the alchemy of sacred sex between woman and man. She could only describe techniques to Lalak, for the prohibition of sexual contact with Pakal had not yet ended. The couple must open their hearts and fully embrace the being of each other, both physical and spiritual. They must focus on the intuitive connection between them that merged their energy fields. Using touch, embraces, and words, they would bring each other to high arousal. Certain sensual channels were most effective, such as those running up the inner thighs and past the ears into the throat. Once they joined sexually, they would follow the pattern of nearly reaching orgasm, then controlling their sexual energy and directing it to their centers. This could end by retaining the immense energy without discharge or by final release if conception was desired.

"Pakal is well-trained in sexual techniques by the Lunar Priestesses," said T'zab Chak. "He may already know how to retain sexual energy; many rulers use this for empowerment. If he needs to learn more, you can quickly teach him. When you perform sexual alchemy together, your energy centers form a circuit that naturally connects to each other and also to the creative force of the cosmos. This forms a conscious connection with your divine selves, and you share your sacred sexual fires to enhance each other. When will you be able to once again join with your husband?"

"According to the priests, yet another solar year. It seems such a long time!"

"Hmmm." The priestess had a distant look in her eyes. "Lady Lalak, you are much empowered through these teachings of sexual alchemy. Seek guidance from your own inner wisdom, for the Ah K'inob are not infallible. You will know when the time is right. Remember that sacred life force passes through your body and spirit. You can now feel that life force, you know that you *are* the force that makes flowers open and close, that makes hummingbirds fly from flower to flower, that makes the jaguar leap and the frog croak. You are in every tree, river, rock, and animal. You are in each one of your people; you are in Pakal. You are the power that moves the wind, that crashes down the cascades, that shines in the sun, that glows in the night. You breathe the world; the entire cosmos is a living being that is moved by the life force, and that is what you are."

As the priestess' words flooded through her, Lalak felt her consciousness soaring into oneness with everything. A profound inner peace settled into her being. She knew beyond any question that she could trust her intuition and follow her own guidance. Her soul blazed with its liberation. Her heart accepted its empowerment.

Lalak was sad to see the Priestess of Ix Zuhuy K'ak leave. She expressed profuse gratitude for the invaluable training and lavished rich gifts of fine cloth and jewels upon her teacher. The striking woman invited her to visit Ek Bahlam, although both knew it was unlikely they would meet again.

5

The plaza being built on the eastern meadow began taking recognizable shape as the dry season drew to a close. Large stones were set on lower levels and stairways marked off. Workers did not have enough time to pave the top level, which was an immense expanse across most of the meadow, before gathering rain clouds began opening soggy underbellies to release their burden. Construction was set aside until the rainy season ended. Before the rains set in, Lalak had her attendant Kayum organize a work group to clear the trail from the meadow's edge down the escarpment to the cascades where she had discovered the magical clearing. She wanted to have easier access to this special place, and visited it several times. She even coaxed her women attendants down the improved path, which now had steps placed where footing was particularly difficult. They spent many delightful moments enjoying the splashing waterfall and lush plants around the clearing.

On one visit, Lalak sat beside the pond dipping her feet into its cool water. The two women were dozing after their midday meal, and the hunter was off exploring adjacent trails. Watching a striped butterfly flutter over the pond, Lalak began to feel vibrations ascending from her feet into her body. Suddenly alert, her senses on edge, she felt a chill up her spine and raised neck hairs. She sensed a presence, something hidden behind the misty veil cast by waterfall spray. A shimmering halo of light settled around the pond and engulfed her, closing off the rest of the clearing and occluding her companions. It was as though she had entered another dimension.

Lalak was not frightened, and she used her new skills to calm her body's reactions. Mentally she reached into the misty waterfall and invited its concealed presence to emerge. Ethereal forms drifted from the mists and hovered over the pond, wavering and swirling. Lalak beckoned them to come forward, radiating loving acceptance. She recalled feeling that something wonderful hung beyond the waterfall's veil, and was eager to learn what had called to her before. Slowly the forms materialized until a woman and two children were splashing through the pond toward her.

The woman's appearance amazed Lalak. Tall and willowy, about Lalak's age, the woman had sky blue eyes and yellow hair the color of new corn silk. Her skin was paler and her nose smaller than any Lalak had seen. Though entirely foreign in appearance, the woman wore a simple villager's huipil, now wet from her swim. Beside her were two children of about eight solar years' age, a boy who looked typically Mayan and a girl with dark hair but the same startling blue eyes.

"Greetings and welcome, people of the waterfall," Lalak said mentally. "You seem to have something to tell me, for I sensed your presence here before."

"Greetings, Lady Lalak of Lakam Ha," replied the woman. They had no difficulty communicating with their consciousness. "This child, this boy, wants to come to you. He has waited a very long time to return to life in your world. He asks permission to enter into your womb and be born as your son, and the son of Pakal."

A rush of joy surged into Lalak's heart. She communicated her acceptance of the child's request. Looking closely at the boy, she detected some resemblance to Pakal. His bright black eyes sparkled into hers and he smiled with supreme confidence. She wanted to reach for him, to gather him into her arms, but could not move a muscle. He threw back his head and laughed, speaking into her mind.

"So shall I be named, for my renowned ancestor, the great-grandfather of my father, the esteemed Holy Lord Kan Bahlam."

"So shall it be," agreed Lalak.

The yellow-haired woman smiled and indicated the girl beside her.

"She is another of your lineage, yet to come in the distant future. She will discover and record much information about your city and your people that was lost. In her will be blended two streams of humanity, that we might know our oneness. In her, the greatness of your lineage will continue. She wished to see you, Tz'aakb'u Ahau, The One Who Produces a Progression of Lords."

"To meet you is my great pleasure," Lalak said to the girl, who tilted her head analytically. The child's intense blue eyes examined Lalak carefully, as if to commit every detail to memory.

"It is my wish to remember you, to be able to see you clearly in my time," the girl said.

"May it be so." Lalak's dark eyes met the woman's blue ones. "May I ask, what are you called? How do you know of me and my city?"

"The name I am called, a strange sound to your ears, is Elie ... El-ee. My people are from a different land, a vast distance from here. But now my family is Mayan, my people are your people. This girl is my daughter, and the daughter of many daughters. In her runs the blood of Pakal's lineage. Speak to him of this. He will remember things."

Lalak pushed the confusion this caused to the back of her mind. She intended to maintain serenity so this vision would not be disturbed. Again she focused on the boy, the child who would come to Pakal and her. From the depths of her heart, she showered love on him that he might know how much he was wanted.

"Kan Bahlam, to you I give my heart; my body is ready to receive you and nurture you into life. Will you come soon? I too have waited so long."

"Soon," the boy answered.

"Before the sun reaches its next time of perfect balance," said the woman. "Do not delay, or the moment will be lost."

Lalak wished to bow in gratitude, but still could not move. As she sent her mental thanks, the forms began dissolving back into wisps and faded into the misty waterfall. The shimmering halo faded and she wiggled her feet in the water, realizing she could move again. Watching ripples playing across the pond, she lifted her face to the sunlight and sent a prayer of gratitude to the deities.

The sun would attain its next perfect balance, when day and night were the same length, at the fall equinox. This was less than two moon cycles away. Lalak realized she could not delay her union with Pakal, and set about planning the occasion. With the help of Ix Chel priestess Utzil, she determined when her next fertile period would be. She took Muyal into her confidence and described the vision by the waterfall. Muyal was more than willing to help. She now had a son of her own and wanted more than anything for her beloved Holy Lady to become a mother. Utzil and Muyal knew this plan went against the advice of the solar priests and other Ix Chel priestesses, but the power of Lalak's conviction swayed them.

Lalak and Muyal planned an excursion with their husbands, Yax Chan and Pakal, to visit the clearing by the waterfall. They would have attendants bring a noon meal and soft mats for an afternoon of relaxation and enjoying the lovely setting. After the meal, Muyal and Yax Chan would make excuses for returning home, leaving the most discrete attendants who would retreat some distance from the clearing. Then Lalak and Pakal would be alone, for her to work some sex magic.

The rainy season was nearing end, but daily showers were still common. Lalak paid homage to the Rain God Chaak, giving him luxurious gifts to keep rain away that day. He must have been pleased, because the day was bright and warm, with a few puffy white clouds drifting overhead. The group set out in good spirits, Pakal relieved to have a day without administrative duties. He and Yax Chan stopped their progress to view the platform and discuss the next building plans when the dry season arrived. It always made them happy to envision the grand complex to be erected there, and the women were caught up in the excitement. Progressing down the improved path, Yax Chan remarked that a secluded housing complex could be built in tiers along the cascading river to take advantage of its copious water. Pakal said he should start drawing plans for one.

Muyal, Yax Chan and Pakal were impressed by the beauty of the clearing. They praised the setting with its wide waterfall and serene pond, wrapped by broad-leafed plants and towering trees. Having developed an appetite from their walk, they sat on mats and enjoyed a meal of dried turkey and venison, maize cakes with nuts and dried fruit, and fresh fruit. For drink, they dipped cups into the pure pond water and remarked on its sweetness. The sun had just passed zenith when they finished the light meal.

Muyal assumed a worried expression and whispered into Yax Chan's ear. He nodded with a serious face, and told Pakal that Muyal just remembered something important they needed to accomplish at home this day. Making profuse apologies, they urged their friends to enjoy the beautiful place without missing them. Pakal looked at his architect friend quizzically, but made no objection. He settled onto cushions and relaxed on the soft mat, gazing up at the sky, hardly noticing when the attendants discreetly disappeared.

Lalak sat nearby, heart fluttering. Simply looking at Pakal's handsome face and lithe body made her begin feeling aroused. It had been nearly five tuns since she had felt his full embrace, anything more than a gentle hug or kiss on the cheek. Could she remember her training in sexual alchemy and use it as the priestess instructed? Or would she dissolve into wild passion at his touch? She did a series of deep breaths and deliberately calmed her heart. Focusing inward, she drew energy from the earth up through her feet and brought it to the pelvic center. When this center felt activated and warm, she moved energy to the heart center and radiated it toward Pakal.

Drawing energy from the sky through her crown center, she filled the forehead center and activated intuition.

Her intuition told her that he was acutely aware of her sitting close to him, although he appeared to be daydreaming. She could feel powerful sexual energy gathering within him, and recalled that he also had been celibate for many tuns. Spontaneously, she placed one hand upon his thigh, close to the inner sensual channel. His skin was hot to touch and the energy fairly burst onto her palm.

"Pakal, let us swim. The day is hot," she said.

He lifted his head from the pillows, eyes wide, and watched her as she rose and walked slowly to the pond's edge. Standing beside the sparkling water, she lifted her huipil over her head and dropped it. Casually she reached for tendrils of hair and tucked them under her headband, swaying her hips and turning her body side to side. Dappled sunlight played over her smooth tan skin and turned the green glow of the glade into an enthralling golden halo around her body.

Pakal sat upright, all attention. He let his eyes travel over her long lithe limbs, voluptuous hips, and rounded abdomen. Moving upward, he admired the firm globes of her breasts and silken shoulders. Her supple neck curved sensuously and her face shone with radiant vitality. Why had he never noticed how lovely she was? Her sensuality evoked powerful surges of desire that coursed through his body. He was intensely aroused.

She turned around and the dappled light played across firm round buttocks and along her shapely back. Swaying and moving arms gracefully, she seemed to dance at the pond's edge, framed by the misty waterfall. Turning again to face him, she smiled and gestured toward the water.

"You ... you plan to seduce me!" Pakal exclaimed.

"Just so. That is my plan. You are very perceptive," she said.

Laughing, she slipped languidly into the pond.

Hot desire flooded his body. He leapt to his feet, threw off his loincloth and plunged into the water after her. With strong strokes he quickly reached her, twining arms and legs around her body. The watery embrace submerged them both and they resurfaced, laughing and spitting water. She swam away toward the shallows, turning to receive him in her arms. He nearly crushed her in a passionate embrace, seeking her lips for a long wet kiss. They remained in watery embraces for some time, relearning the contours of each other's bodies, relishing the delicious sensations of skin against skin.

"Ah, Lalak, I cannot resist this desire, I must have you," he murmured in her ear. "I know it is not time yet ... this goes against the priests' advice ..."

"This is the time," she whispered. "It is a knowing that I have; it goes deeper than any human's advice."

Slipping from his arms, she took his hand and led him from the pond onto their mats. Lowering her body, she drew him down upon her. Through kisses and caresses, he managed to say:

"You know? This is the right time ... for us ...to make a baby?"

"Yes, it is perfect. It is exactly right. A child waits here to come to us, I have seen him. He is ready, I am ready. It is time."

Pakal could question her no longer. Both his intuition and his pulsating groin impelled him to action. Amidst waves of ecstasy, they joined both hearts and bodies in love-making that surpassed any before.

Lalak knew that his heart was open to her now, and he engaged in sexual union with the fullness of his being. She needed little use of technique to bring them both to exquisite release. Lying in tender embrace afterwards, he stroked her back and nuzzled her throat. When he lay back, she traced his strong profile with tingling fingers.

"You perfume my heart," she whispered. "My love spreads like a flower."

"You are the shimmering beauty of my soul," he responded. "Never will I have enough of your kisses. Let me drink again and again the nectar of your lips."

Raising himself on an elbow, he kissed her repeatedly while murmuring endearments. She soaked in every drop of sweetness, reveling in his affection. After some time, Pakal cupped her face in his hands and gazed deeply into her eyes.

"Lalak, I never appreciated you this way before. You are lovely and a consummate sexual partner. You have been hiding your talents."

"In truth, I have developed new talents," she said. "But also in truth, you have opened your heart to me. It makes all the difference in our joining."

"This I understand. It has taken a long time, and I am now entirely glad for it." He rained her face with more kisses. "But tell me more about the child you said waits here for us."

Lalak told him about her vision by the pond. When she described the woman with blue eyes and yellow hair, he immediately remembered her name.

"Elie! I have not thought about her for years. She was connected with my grandmother, Yohl Ik'nal. During a journey I made into the Underworld as part of my shamanic training, I encountered Elie trapped in the domain of the Death Lords. My grandmother had me assist Elie to escape their watery realm and return to the cycles of life in the Middleworld. How fascinating that Elie appeared to you and brought with her the child who will be born to us."

"Kan Bahlam. That is your great-grandfather's name, is it not so?"

"Just so, the father of Yohl Ik'nal. A great ruler who set our city upon the path to growth and influence. This child must be his spirit returning to continue the dynasty. He will be Kan Bahlam II."

Pakal hesitated. He was loath to diminish their exultant mood, but felt compelled to plumb her uncanny knowledge.

"How do you know ... you seem so certain, that this child will be born, and ... and live."

Lalak closed her eyes and summoned memories of her training with the priestess of Ix Zuhuy K'ak. She felt again the profound knowledge and invincible power of the Goddess of Creation and Destruction. There was no place for doubt.

"Much had changed since we lost our last child. From my inner depths, I have changed. I have mastered difficult disciplines and gained cosmic knowledge. Another time, when we have a long evening together, I will tell you about this training. And you, you have also changed. Your heart has been purified and your losses resolved. We come together now as different people, in the fullness of love, our hearts devoted to one another. With all this, our bodies cannot fail in creating a child and bringing him successfully to life."

"May it be so!" Pakal exclaimed, admiring anew her immense life force and self-confidence. "Here, let us anchor this child deeply within your womb. Come to me again, receive my seed again. We shall make certain your womb is filled and refilled."

He drew her into his arms and began a sensuous, leisurely session of love-making. The urgency of their passion now satisfied, they enjoyed pleasuring each other, rising to the edge of release then allowing it to decrease, before again bringing their bodies to the moment of climax. In the long and delicious afternoon, as the sunlight dappled their bodies and the waterfall sang of their consummated love, they joined in sexual union repeatedly. Songbirds chirped sweet melodies and frogs added rhythmic croaks, while soft breezes cooled their fluid-coated bodies.

The sun was low in the western sky and the shaded clearing had fallen into deep shadow before they felt satiated. They bathed in the cool pond water and allowed the waterfall to pour over their heads, hair loosened and fanning down their backs. Using small cloths from their meal, they washed each other gently, and then dried with large cotton blankets. Pakal laughed over the obvious planning that had gone into this occasion, amused at his obliviousness of the set-up. The ever-discreet attendants returned after the couple had put on their clothes, and gathering up mats, blankets and food baskets, they followed their Holy Lord and Lady back up the path to the meadow as dusk fell upon Lakam Ha.

6

W aves of pain crashed like torrents through her body. When the contractions came, Lalak could no longer stand or walk, but had to lie down on the bench in her labor chamber. The spacious room was specially prepared for this momentous event, with a birth platform built in the center. A strong rail between two posts would allow her to grip and support herself, while a carved-out section in the base held the birth basin. Benches lining one wall with sitting mats were filled by the royal family and elite guests. The birth of the Bahlam dynasty heir took ritual form, and would be observed by the principle ahauob of Lakam Ha.

When Lalak learned of these plans, she was initially upset and felt remnants of her former intimidation returning. Pakal allayed her apprehensions, promising to stay beside her throughout the birth process and reminding her of the magic that brought about the child's conception. With such powerful forces summoned through the Goddess' blessings, it was impossible for anything to go wrong. Bringing the image of Ix Zuhuy K'ak to mind and calling upon the training she received, Lalak dispelled all doubt and trusted her body to fulfill its destiny.

Now her body was wracked by pain worse than she had never known. This labor was harder than the first, when she had delivered a child of seven moons who did not live beyond one day. Utzil had advised her that labor would be more intense, especially given the size of the child she now carried. At full term pregnancy, Lalak's belly was enormous, so huge that Utzil secretly worried about twins. However, she could not detect a second heartbeat. Given both parents' unusual height, and Lalak's robust frame, it was likely this was a boy of extreme size. Certainly the baby's kicks against Lalak's abdomen were the strongest the priestess had ever felt.

Utzil coached Lalak to use breathing techniques with contractions, which worked at first but now in the latter part of labor were insufficient to surmount the pain. Attendant priestess-midwives supported Lalak to walk whenever possible and used abdominal stroking to counteract pain during contractions. Overwhelmed by the shattering grip of the womb as it prepared to expel the child, Lalak moaned and at times screamed, indifferent now to the presence of any others except Utzil and Pakal. He stood beside her, touching her face and stroking her hair, murmuring encouragement when she caught her breath between contractions. Utzil offered a strong hand to grip and whispered promises that it would end soon.

Sitting on the bench to observe were Sak K'uk, Kan Mo' Hix, Yax Chan, Muyal, Pasah Chan and his wife Kab' along with the new High Priestess designate, Matunha. Usin Ch'ob the elderly High Priestess was too frail to attend. The plan for a ritual birth had been devised by Sak K'uk and supported by the High Priest and Priestess, who made a convincing case that an event as important as this should be surrounded by ceremony, invoking the support of the deities. The strength of prayers and supplications as labor progressed would help guarantee successful birth, and all would witness and attest to the details. Lalak suspected that the Holy Lady Mother had other motives, though she could not imagine Sak K'uk wishing a negative outcome. Perhaps she wanted to inject her own intentions as early as possible into the B'aakal heir.

The final stage of labor began when Lalak felt an irresistible urge to bear down. The priestesses assisted her onto the birth platform, supporting her on two sides as she gripped the rail. Another midwife encircled her waist with both arms to help push the child downward. Utzil crouched beside her, prepared to guide the child's head out and slide its body into the birthing bowl. Pakal knelt in front, head bowed in profound prayer that the birth would happen quickly and all would be well.

Transposed into a mindless realm of pure physical awareness, Lalak pushed and strained with each contraction. Sweat poured profusely from her brow and face, arms and torso glistening. Utzil waited in hovering suspense, re-calculating in her mind the size of Lalak's pelvic bones and desperately hoping they were large enough for this hefty child. Time seemed to stand still, broken only by Lalak's sustained grunts as she pushed. Finally Utzil saw the dark crown appear, and after several more pushes the baby's head emerged, red and scrunched. Utzil quickly ran a finger around the baby's neck to make certain it was free of the umbilical cord, then grasped the head and turned it slightly to allow first one then the other shoulder to slide out. Another push and the body slid out.

Utzil used soft cloths to remove mucus from the baby's nose and mouth, and to vigorously rub its back and legs. She checked its sex and saw it was a boy as anticipated. Before she had time to flick his feet, the baby took a deep breath and wailed loudly. The chamber echoed with the boy's lusty cries as she held him up for all to see. Pakal's face was filled with relief and amazement, and everyone let out bated breaths in long sighs. The midwives delivered the placenta and cut the umbilical cord. They assisted Lalak back to the bench and cleaned her while Utzil carried the baby around so all could have a good view. He was remarkably large, with long limbs and a chubby round body, his skull even more elongated than usual from molding through the birth canal. She then brought the baby to Lalak, who hungrily swept him into her arms, tears streaming down her face.

His feet touched the earth, the son of Janaab Pakal and Lalak, the Holy Lady Tz'aakb'u Ahau. The long-awaited one, the inheritor of the B'aakal dynasty, the child of magic, whose name as ruler was that of his great-great-grandfather.

K'inich Kan Bahlam II, Sun-Faced Snake Jaguar the Second.

His birth was on Baktun 9, Katun 10, Tun 2, Uinal 6, Kin 6, on the date 2 Kimi 19 Zotz (May 23, 635 CE).

It was not a date the calendar priests would have selected. Pasah Chan had been outraged upon learning of Lalak's pregnancy. It was highly irregular and broke with long-held tradition for planning the birth of future rulers. What ruffled him most was the implied disregard for his priestly powers. Though he was careful not to criticize Pakal openly, his disapproval was apparent when he questioned the ruler about this decision. The High Priest sat through Lalak's labor with mixed emotions; he ardently hoped this child would survive while he resented the affront to his status. Analyzing the auguries for this date, he was concerned about the characteristics the child would exhibit.

The Tzolk'in day was 2 Kimi. Kimi was the day of death, and signified finishing, removing, disappearing. It was a powerful sign for change, even transformation. A ruler born under the Kimi sign would be unpredictable, his motives running deep and unfathomable. He could be a difficult person to control. The number 2 signified duality and polarity, swinging between extremes or taking polarizing positions. Another indication of unpredictability and intensity.

The Haab uinal was Zotz, the bat. This sign was secretive, of the night, and signified qualities of intuition and insight. Those born under the bat were often visionaries with clairvoyant abilities. Such seers were driven by inner forces and tended to follow their own guidance, trusting their intuition and ability to commune with deities. Another signal that the boy would be difficult to influence. The number 6 meant to sprout or hatch, and it was a numeral of balance. The boy was himself a true sprout of the hallowed dynasty, but he might also hatch many plans of his own.

Indeed, the High Priest would have chosen another birth configuration. This new sprout of Pakal's might prove even more impossible to control than his father.

Sak K'uk was swept away by her vigorous, boisterous and chubby grandson. She had not bargained on having such strong feelings for him, or such profound relief when he thrived and grew under Lalak's loving care. Something had changed in her daughter-in-law, and it commanded respect. Tentatively at first, then more openly, Sak K'uk began to make repairs in their conflicted relationship. She wanted to spend time with the child, and Lalak rarely let him out of her sight. So, Sak K'uk requested visits and was always complimentary, though her pride did not yet allow an apology. Lalak seemed agreeable to keeping interactions pleasant though still guarded.

Pakal doted on his son and visited every day. Each progression in Kan Bahlam's development was a source of endless fascination and joy. The bond he felt with Lalak deepened and they spent many evenings together, sharing leisurely meals and talking over many things, including Lalak's training with the priestess from Ek Bahlam, T'zab Chak. Their newly ignited passion drew them into love-making before the prescribed time, while Lalak was still nursing the baby. Though they could prevent conception, both wanted another child, so Lalak reluctantly delegated nursing to a wet nurse. Within two moons, she was pregnant again.

This quick conception surprised everyone except Utzil, who had helped with the preparations, though she had advised waiting. Sak K'uk was delighted and Pasah Chan was incensed. Despite following so closely upon the previous birth, Lalak's pregnancy went well and her next labor at full term was rapid. Again the royal family and elites gathered ceremoniously to witness another royal child's birth.

His feet touched the earth, the next son of Pakal and Lalak.

Waknal Bahlam, Six-Person Jaguar.

His birth was on Baktun 9, Katun 10, Tun 3, Uinal 8, Kin 11, on the date 4 Chuen 19 Xul (July 1, 636 CE).

Waknal Bahlam was smaller than his brother, a delicate and sensitive baby who more closely resembled Pakal. Kan Bahlam had the robust frame of his mother, and also inherited her coarse features, including an excessively large nose and full, protruding lips. His face would be striking and strong, but without the slender handsomeness of his father. He would probably be taller than either parent when mature.

The auguries for Waknal Bahlam's birth date were pleasant. As a child of Chuen, he would watch, guard, and heed other humans, whose number was 4. Xul brought the energies of cycle ends and accomplishing goals, while the number 14 was a doubling of 7 and signified centers of energy in the human body. As he grew, these qualities became evident in his friendliness to everyone and his delightful openness. Waknal Bahlam charmed people; Kan Bahlam mystified them.

Kan Bahlam loved the night sky. He refused to sleep until after the panorama of sparkling lights covered the indigo canopy. The first word he spoke was "*ek*" the Mayan word for star. Babbling and pointing, he danced across the inner patio with long chubby legs prancing. His father fondly observed: "He was born to speak with the stars."

Pakal sensed that his older son was destined to gain profound knowledge of cosmology and become a master astronomer. That the boy would do great works, he had no doubt. Perhaps it would be good to begin training with the Ah K'inob calendar priests at an earlier age than usual.

Lalak wanted to keep her sons close as long as possible, for once they entered training with the priests, she would not see them frequently. At the age of seven solar years, royal and elite boys started a rigorous program to learn the advanced Maya arts and sciences, and the history of their people and polity. From this time until they reached eighteen tuns (17.75 solar years), they resided in temple schools and underwent periodic rituals marking transformations from childhood to adolescence and finally to adulthood. When Pakal suggested early training for Kan Bahlam, she shifted the topic with some non-committal remark. She was not eager to allow Pasah Chan to wrap his tentacles around her son's malleable mind, for she detected his motives to expand his power and influence.

Shortly after Waknal Bahlam's birth, Lalak developed an abscessed upper molar. Utzil prepared a poultice of buttonwood root, a type of elder shrub, and applied it over the swollen gum. The abscess ruptured and drained, but the tooth was left poorly anchored and loose, eventually leading to an extraction. Lalak experienced several other toothaches, prompting Utzil to admonish her that such frequent pregnancies depleted a woman's bones. This made her susceptible to both tooth loss and thinning of skeletal bones, which might result in fractures. Utzil was adamant that Lalak must avoid another pregnancy for a few years.

Pakal and Lalak agreed this was the wisest course, though they wanted more children. Neither was ready to accept abstinence to prevent pregnancy, for they enjoyed the intimacy and fulfillment of their sexual joining. Lalak took a contraceptive made of roasted and ground papaya seeds, a generous pinch of the powder dissolved in warm water and taken daily for three days before menses began. If this preparation was taken monthly for over two and a half years, it could create permanent sterility, but Lalak hoped to have another pregnancy within two years. Its advantage was that it could be discontinued and fertility would return within a moon cycle.

The two royal boys, just a year apart in age, became close playmates, although Kan Bahlam always dominated their games. Waknal Bahlam did not seem to mind his bossy brother, but cheerfully followed orders as they moved from games of chase to hide-and-seek or taking carved toys on imaginary adventures. At times Kan Bahlam teased his mother's spider monkey Popo and the scarlet macaw by pulling their tails or stealing away treats. Then Waknal Bahlam would scold his brother and threaten to tell their mother, for he had inherited her great compassion for animals.

Their grandparents visited often, and at times the boys were taken to stay for a while in the quarters of Sak K'uk or Kan Mo' Hix. Lalak learned to tolerate being away from her children for short periods, though she usually fretted. When Kan Bahlam was almost five solar years old, his grandmother's health began to decline rapidly. Sak K'uk had been losing vigor for the past two years, due to an illness that eluded the healer priestesses' skills. They knew it was a problem with the blood, and tried using various tonics and blood cleansers, but no remedies were effective. The once energetic and forceful Holy Lady Mother became weaker each day. Now in her fifth katun, she was not elderly for Maya elite. Many lived to be "six-katun" people, over sixty solar years. It was apparent, however, that the life force was slipping out of her diminutive body.

In the middle of the rainy season, Lalak received a summons from Sak K'uk. As a heavy downpour pounded the roofs and plazas of the city, sending rivulets across corridors of covered palace archways, Lalak pulled a shawl over her head and ventured through the maze of corridors linking palace chambers. When she arrived outside Sak K'uk's residential chambers, her personal attendant Zazil whispered an update.

"She does not have much longer. She made an urgent request to see you." Zazil's eyes were reddened and puffy.

Lalak nodded and entered through the heavy door drape. The smell of copal incense filled the room, accompanied by soft chanting as priests and priestesses prepared the way for the soul to transition to the Underworld. Kan Mo' Hix and Pakal sat on mats along with their closest courtiers and cousins. Matunha, now High Priestess since the recent death of Usin Ch'ob, sat beside the small form on the sleeping bench, making ritual hand motions. The priestess' cold, aloof eyes met Lalak's as if admonishing her to behave. Matunha gestured to a mat on the other side of the bench, where Lalak dropped to her knees and bent close to her mother-in-law's gaunt face.

It was shocking to gaze into that death mask, skin taut over cheekbones and arched nose as if the skeleton wanted to break through. Deep sockets nearly hid closed eyes, and flaccid lips drooped away from teeth, making the grimace of a fleshless skull. Her breath came in shallow gasps, claw-like fingers clutching blankets over her chest. Although the light was dim, the yellow cast to her skin was unmistakable. The liver and kidneys, or both, had failed. The death paddlers could be sensed hovering in their canoe nearby, waiting to escort her soul across the Xibalba Be, the Road to the Underworld.

"Lady Sak K'uk, you wished to see me?" Lalak whispered.

For a moment she thought Sak K'uk did not hear. The sunken eyelids fluttered, and then yellow-tinged eyes opened and rolled toward her.

"Uhhh ... it is you ... yes ... you came."

"I am here. Much am I saddened to see you so."

Sak K'uk struggled for air, closed her eyes and seemed to drift off. Lalak waited, tentatively covering one thin yellow hand with her own. The touch stirred Sak K'uk.

"This time ... it is late, not much time ... time to say what has been long in coming." Sak K'uk opened her eyes and a spark of energy enlivened them. "It is much my regret ... all these years, not to speak so, not to tell you ... my regrets ..."

"Do not trouble yourself, it is of little importance."

"Not so ... it is of great importance," Sak K'uk said with a tiny flare of her former vivacity. The ghastly lips pulled upward in what was meant as a smile. "You were ever kind ... even to the undeserving. Death peers in my face ... I shall not depart this world without saying ... saying that I am sorry."

Lalak felt the bony fingers curling around her hand, so cold that it seemed the life had already withdrawn from them.

"You ... when you came ... I never treated you rightly. You did not deserve it ... such great unkindness ... the fault is mine. I wanted to keep my son for myself ... to bar other women from his heart ... this only brought injury to others. It was wrong, I was in error, you are worthy of him. Now I ask you to receive ... my deepest apology."

The effort sapped her energy. Sak K'uk's grip loosened and her lids shut, her breath rasping.

Lalak bowed her head, tears streaming down her cheeks. Never had she expected the haughty Holy Lady Mother to acknowledge her mistreatment and apologize. This extreme effort, on her deathbed, touched Lalak's heart. She understood how critical it was to enter the path of the Underworld with a clear conscience. Her greatest desire now was to provide her mother-in-law's spirit with the absolution it needed.

"From the depths of my being, I receive and accept your apology. All is resolved now, my heart harbors no resentment. Receive my love and blessings upon your spirit journey. You will ever be remembered and honored for your great service to our people."

Sak K'uk's eyelids fluttered, her hand trembled then squeezed Lalak's. Momentarily their eyes met in an intense arc of mutual compassion, a moment of soul communion. Then a great sigh escaped Sak K'uk's lips and her body relaxed, hands dropping to her side. She continued with rasping shallow breathing, but appeared to be unconscious.

Lalak sat back on her heels, hands clasped in her lap. She offered silent prayers for the soul's transition and remained beside Sak K'uk until the High Priestess softly informed those in the chamber that the great K'uhul Ixik Me' had released her soul to the Underworld journey.

She entered the road, Ix Sak K'uk, mother of K'inich Janaab Pakal, K'uhul B'aakal Ahau. The date was carved on many monuments.

Baktun 9, Katun 10, Tun 7, Uinal 10, Kin 6, on the date 10 Kimi 14 Yaxk'in (July 15, 640 CE).

Tz'aakb'u Ahau—V

Baktun 9 Katun 10 Tun 8
Baktun 9 Katun 10 Tun 17
641 CE—650 CE

1

Drums and trumpets sounded through the main plaza of Lakam Ha. Ahauob gathered in hazy sunshine breaking through rising mists as the nighttime rainfall evaporated. On this auspicious morning, K'inich Kan Bahlam II would be designated as heir to the Bahlam dynasty of B'aakal. Three important star events marked this as a potent time. In the night sky Yaax Ek, largest of the wandering stars, departed from his second stationary point; the mysterious wandering star Ayin Ek, Yaax Ek's next brother, approached the first stationary point; and fierce Chak Ek, the red wandering star, accompanied Yaax Ek to come into opposition to the Sun. Dynastic ceremonies were especially auspicious when Yaax Ek was resuming his forward motion. As the star of Hun Ahau, Firstborn of the Palenque Triad, Yaax Ek signified positive momentum toward great accomplishments ordained by the Triad.

At the age of six solar years, Kan Bahlam underwent the "deer hoof" ritual to be designated as Ba-ch'ok, young lord, the sprout of the Maize God. The ceremony spanned five days of festivities with lavish performances and feasts. The ritual began in the forest where deer lived, with Kan Bahlam wearing a small set of antlers and enacting the furtive glances and bounding movements of deer. Musicians used wooden sticks to rap on hollow tubes, making the sound of clacking deer hoofs. Proceeding from forest to an open meadow, the ritual symbolized the deer's connections with rain as Kan Bahlam sprinkled water on corn stalks held flat then raised up by attendants. Musicians shook long hollow bamboo tubes filled with seeds to simulate the sound of raindrops. Deer were important to the Maya as a major food source, and as prognosticator of rain, which led to the renewal of crops. Deer were associated with the wandering star Chak Ek, herald of rain. When a deer was depicted suspended from a sky band, it signaled periods of Chak Ek in retrograde, when weather conditions usually led to rainfall.

The five days included a procession to cornfields where the first crops were near maturity, fat cobs sprouting yellow tassels. Kan Bahlam mimicked ripening corn in his Maize God costume, symbolizing his role as young Yum K'ax, bringer of renewal and new life. With his parents, he danced the story of the resurrection of Hun Hunahpu, the First Father through the cleverness of his grandchildren, the Hero Twins, who defeated the Death Lords and won the birthright of the Maya people. Though he was too young to be expected to memorize the B'aakal creation sequence, he was coached to recite his ancestor's names as his parents shared in this recounting of dynastic legitimacy.

On the final day of his heir designation rites, Kan Bahlam stood proud and still while Pakal tied two deer hoofs around his waist with woven cords colored red, yellow, and black. Binding the heir designate with deer hoofs meant that his path was established; the direction where his footsteps would lead was set. It signified that Kan Bahlam was embarking on the path of rulership, assuming deer qualities that brought life-giving rain to the land and sacred itz to sustain his people.

The date of Kan Bahlam's designation as Ba-ch'ok was noted on carved panels.

Baktun 9, Katun 10, Tun 8, Uinal 9, Kin 3, on the day 9 Akbal 6 Xul (June 17, 641 CE).

Lalak watched her stocky son, already taller than most boys his age, with mixed emotions. Her heart swelled with joy at his commanding presence and poise, already showing attributes of a ruler in the making. He showed such abilities playing the Maya ballgame with age mates, using a smaller and lighter rubber ball, that he was nicknamed *Ah Pitz*, He of the Ballgame. Yet sadness also pulled at her heart, because this ceremony meant his training at the High Priest's temple would soon begin. She would miss his noisy presence in her quarters, his tricks on his brother and her pets that both amused and dismayed her. It was clear that Kan Bahlam wanted to move away from the palace women's world, to feel part of the wider world of men. She admired his assertiveness even as she felt him pulling away emotionally. It comforted her to know that Waknal Bahlam would remain by her side for another two years.

Those years flew by too quickly. In that time, as she approached her thirty-third solar year, she experienced the sorrow of her father-in-law Kan Mo' Hix's death, and the happiness of conceiving another child. For this pregnancy, Pakal advised consulting with the Ah K'inob to salve the pride of Pasah Chan and try to remedy their relations with the priesthood. Though she agreed reluctantly, Lalak had to admit their choice of birth date was brilliant. In a session of exquisite love-making amplified by knowledge that they were setting a soul upon a great destiny, they conceived on the date exactly as prescribed. Her pregnancy was easy and a constant pleasure as another boy, she felt certain, grew to swell her womb. Utzil kept her supplied with the most nutritious food, and made brews of blood and bone building herbs to counteract depletion.

The birth ceremony was again enacted when her labor began at full term. Lalak now felt a veteran of this exposed birthing process, and even missed the presence of Sak K'uk. Her mother-in-law would be a more welcome observer than the High Priestess Matunha, who remained an enigma. Matunha fulfilled her duties impeccably but never conveyed any sense of warmth or affection, or revealed her emotions. She was a person one could never fully know.

After a short labor and shorter time of pushing the child down the birth canal, Lalak brought forth her third living son, another large and vigorous baby whose ear-splitting cries filled the room. Pakal was grateful that this birth came so easily, and overjoyed at yet another son to carry forth his dynasty. The naming of their sons followed the dynastic lineage in reverse order, something Pakal wanted for his own reasons. He did not share his childhood vision that prophesied the entire arc of the dynasty, for he judged it best to avoid any focus on future decline and endings. In the coming katuns, the rulers of B'aakal would attain unparalleled heights and bring their city into its apogee; that was his focus.

It was carved, the record of the third living son of Pakal and Lalak, that his feet touched the earth on an auspicious date. His name as ruler was that of the fifth dynastic ancestor.

K'inich Kan Joy Chitam II, Sun-Faced Snake Ties-Headband Peccary II.

His birth was on Baktun 9, Katun 10, Tun 11, Uinal 17, Kin 0, on the day 11 Ahau 8 Mac (November 5, 644 CE).

To be born on the day Ahau, the birth day of Pakal, was to be marked as a leader, a lord who was master of Maya knowledge, an initiate into esoteric arts and guide to others. The number 11 signified entry into the duality of all that is sacred and also what is worldly. It carried the ability to move within and master both domains. The uinal of Mac marked its denizens as full of magnetic personality, dignity and confidence, one who is a gift to all people. The number 8 had cosmologic significance, for it brought one into synchrony with the universal rotation of stars and celestial cycles. This boy was endowed with all the qualities to be a great and mystical ruler.

2

❝ Your brother is stirring up conflict in our polity," Pakal remarked to Lalak as they shared an evening meal.

She glanced up from nursing Kan Joy Chitam, who was pulling hungrily at her breast while she nibbled on maize cakes and strips of spit-roasted turkey. Many noble women preferred to give their babies over to wet nurses immediately, but Lalak relished the close bond of nursing. She would continue until time to wean the baby. An added benefit was that this acted as a natural contraceptive.

"What has Bahlam Ahau embarked upon now?"

"It appears he has started military campaigns against the small city of Zopo, not far from B'aak. He thinks it serves as a stronghold for the remnants of his uncle's followers, those who fought to unseat your father from rulership."

"Oh, this recalls the troubled days of my childhood," said Lalak. "It was my hope that this enmity had been resolved."

"My thought is that Bahlam Ahau is restless and needs battle to provide an outlet. Messengers from B'aak report that his plans will soon extend farther afield, targeting hostile cities along the K'umaxha River." Pakal appeared lost in thought for a moment. "Would that we again join forces against Yokib, to set right that ill-fated attack nearly two katuns ago. Our embarrassment still rankles me."

"Have you communicated with Bahlam Ahau about this possibility?"

"Not yet. It is still a risky venture, given Yokib's easily defensible location and ties to Kan, which guarantees provision of warriors. Our own forces are neither battle-ready nor large enough, for I have diverted many men's efforts into my building projects. The time is not right; I must watch Bahlam Ahau's actions closely and understand better his motives."

"Creating beautiful buildings has much more appeal than fighting battles," said Lalak. "The new central plaza is progressing very well, you must be pleased."

"That is so, I am pleased. Soon we must go there, so I can show you how perfectly the new Sak Nuk Nah is taking shape. Two of the smaller temples bordering the plaza are nearing completion and will be dedicated next year. Work on remodeling the funerary monument of my great-grandfather Kan Bahlam will soon be done. For its re-dedication ceremony, I would greatly desire your participation. Your words at the burial ceremony for my mother were lovely, all present were touched by your eloquence. It would honor my ancestor, the namesake of our oldest son, for you to speak."

Lalak gave her husband a broad smile, lighting up her face and reminding him of her inner beauty. He no longer paid attention to the homely features, but related to the radiance within her being.

"To do so would be my greatest pleasure, you do me honor by this request."

The baby had fallen asleep in Lalak's arms, and she signaled to an attendant to take him to the small sleeping box kept beside her bed. After she finished her meal and servants brought hot cacao laced with chile, the royal pair sat in wavering torchlight, their shoulders touching. Whenever possible, they sought physical contact with each other. Pakal appeared pensive, his handsome features solemn.

"What troubles you, my husband?" Lalak asked softly.

"Some intelligence recently brought to me about the activities of the Kan dynasty," he replied. He did not want to burden her with affairs of state, but her inviting warmth and calm demeanor were more than he could resist. "It appears to be your burden to share such concerns with me," he remarked with a slight smile.

She leaned toward him and kissed his cheek.

"Your burdens are mine also, beloved. If nothing more, I can listen."

"Ah, you are the sweetness of honeysuckle and I am a hummingbird dipping into your deep nectar."

He cupped her chin and kissed her fully on the lips, a long lingering kiss with underlying hints of desire. She leaned into him, marveling at how their bodies touching aroused her, even when both knew they would not pursue it.

"Tell me," she whispered into his ear.

"Ah, yes, since you insist." His eyes twinkled. "Not long ago, hmmm, about one katun past, Yuknoom Ch'een ascended to the throne of Ka'an, the second ruler of that name. Shortly afterwards, Kan forces finally ousted their hereditary enemies, the Zotz dynasty, from the great city of Uxte'tun. It had been their ancestral home, the city created after their lineage left Nakbe, which to them is equivalent to our Toktan. They called Nakbe the 'Chatan Uinik' or the Second Center of Humans. When exactly they moved to Uxte'tun is lost in the mists of ancient history, but for as long as my family has had knowledge of Kan, they have lived in Dzibanche. This city they founded after the Zotz family ousted them. Although Kan tried to retake Uxte'tun, they were never successful until Yuknoom Ch'een became ruler."

"The expansionary policies of Kan have been problematic for some time, is that so?"

"Just so. Going back many katuns, to their defeat of our long-time ally Mutul. This most venerable city, among the earliest built by our people, suffered severe suppression of its political and construction activities. Communication with Mutul leaders has been minimal since then. In more recent katuns, Kan has spread its influence along the K'umaxha River, becoming overlords of cities such as Usihwitz, Yokib and B'uuk that were once in our polity. Now there is more intrigue afoot regarding Mutul. The Mutul ruler K'inich Muwaan Jol has two sons, Nuun Ujol Chaak the heir designate, and Balaj Chan K'awiil, the younger but more ambitious son. It appears that the ruler intends to seat his younger son in a new city he plans to build in the Petexbatun region, encroaching upon the territory of the current dominant family."

"That sounds as if Mutul is making a recovery from its defeat by Kan," Lalak observed.

"Indeed, so it does sound. While this is good, it also creates turmoil in the region. The location of this new city will allow Mutul to control trade routes along the Nah Ha'al River, a main tributary to the K'umaxha.

With regional turmoil and a choice trade route in question, this invites expansionary foreign powers to intervene, such as Kan. It could be a recipe for renewed power struggles in Mutul. One never knows what an ambitious younger son might do."

"This I did not consider, that having several royal sons could pose problems."

"Ah, my sweet flower, you do not think like a man but like a mother," Pakal laughed and brushed her cheek with his lips. "And for this, I am most grateful."

"We must train our sons well," Lalak said seriously. "Now we have three, and most probably all will not become rulers. The younger ones must develop utmost respect and loyalty to their older brother, and always support him."

"Would that the Gods deem it so!" Pakal exclaimed. "We shall do our best. But these sprouts of the sacred royal blood are all born to leadership. It will be challenging."

"Perhaps next we should have a girl," Lalak said pensively. "Yes, a girl would be nice. Do you not think so?"

"Ummm." Pakal declined to comment and instead pulled her to him for another long kiss. He intended for all his children to be sons. He would take no risks with continuing the dynasty. She squirmed and pulled back, putting some distance between their pulsating bodies.

"If you keep kissing me, I shall not be responsible for what I do," she murmured, gazing under lowered lids. "Pakal, we must behave. Tell me, how came you by this information about Mutul?"

"Partly by traders plying their goods along the rivers," he said, sipping his now cool cacao to distract his urges. "But also by carefully selected observers, those nondescript men who can blend into any group and extract information by their apparent friendly interest in the lives of others. A ruler must always keep his antennae up, especially when it relates to our oldest ally and our most dangerous enemy."

"How you manage so many different things does amaze me. It is good to speak of these political concerns; it helps me to understand your challenges better. But even more, I am eager to visit the new plaza and see progress in construction."

"Then we will do so! On the next clear day, we shall take an excursion to the meadow that has now become a wide plaza."

Pasah Chan stood by the window overlooking the main courtyard of the High Priest's temple. Thick mists obscured the vista of the plains below, a breath-taking sight stretching to the far horizon. Drawing his cloak closer around his shoulders, he shivered in the moist coolness seeping inside the reception chamber. The years had not been kind to his thin frame, causing him to stoop with a hunched spine and walk with an arthritic limp. He anticipated the drink of hot maize gruel and cacao that servants would bring when his visitors arrived.

Footsteps sounded in the corridor and his steward announced the High Priestess Matunha's arrival. The priestly leaders bowed to each other, clasping left shoulders and exchanging formal greetings. Once settled onto thick floor mats, with extra shawls for warmth, they were served the hot drink that Pasah Chan eagerly awaited. Warming his hands and sipping the steaming drink carefully, he tilted his sharp-beaked face and contemplated the High Priestess, whose history he knew well. She was chosen for this meeting precisely because of that history. Her path to the ultimate priestess position had parallels to his own; both came from minor noble families and used incisive intelligence and ruthless competition to win over the other contestants. It was his premise that she chose to remain unmarried in order to consolidate her power, not disseminating any energy toward a husband and family. He made the opposite choice, now feeling grateful for the ministrations of his wife during his old age.

Another aspect of her background held greater importance for his current purpose. Her family was linked to that of Ek Chuuah, the traitor who was banished to Usihwitz and spearheaded two attacks against Lakam Ha. Many of the family had been killed in these battles, but several cousins not involved in the plot remained. Ek Chuuah died in his adopted city, and his son Yax Chapat was still influential there. Matunha shared bloodlines with this dishonored family, and Pasah Chan believed she chafed under this shame. He was aware that within her family, resentment still simmered over the reputed improper treatment of Ek Chuuah. Rumor held that he was deliberately given a serious wound in the Flower Wars staged by Kan Bahlam I, violating the rules of this ritualized combat. Ek Chuuah lost the game and was required to serve the conqueror's city, Usihwitz, for over a year. When his service was completed, he married and elected to stay.

Kan Bahlam I was Pakal's great-grandfather, but succession in this lineage had been controversial. Rulership passed to Kan Bahlam I's daughter, Yohl Ik'nal, and through her to her daughter Sak K'uk. Succession through two women was highly unusual among the Maya, even though they did not follow strict patrilineal descent. In the view of lineage purists, Pakal was not of the most pristine Bahlam family line. There were persistent murmurings among certain ahauob that others had better claim to the throne.

Matunha had more than one reason for questionable loyalty to Pakal. For Pasah Chan's purposes, this made her a perfect choice. The High Priest bristled over Pakal's plans to popularize religious traditions, to make elite rituals more accessible to lesser groups that were historically excluded. Where would this go next? It deeply troubled the priest that Pakal's intentions might extend to include commoners. The power of the priesthood rested upon keeping knowledge and rituals secret, on restricting esoteric practices to a small upper echelon. His life had been devoted to increasing and consolidating priestly power, and even his declining years were committed to this. In the High Priestess he saw a potential ally.

"For what purpose, honored High Priest, did you request my presence this day?" Matunha spoke with directness that made Pasah Chan uneasy. She was a challenge to fathom. In her short time in office, she had made a number of changes among the Ix Chel priestesses that were causing upheavals.

"Perhaps we may share common concerns," he replied. "Concerns for the future of our priestly domains. The shadow of change falls over us; change in directions we may not want. Your commitment to serving the Goddess Ix Chel is well-known and admired."

She nodded acknowledgement, eyes cold and calculating.

"Speak of your concerns. We shall see if these are shared between us."

"These things of which we speak must be kept in strict confidence. Have I your pledge to this?"

"My pledge is given."

Pasah Chan described his perceptions of Pakal's plans for popularizing religious rituals. To support this, he noted that the new Sak Nuk Nah was being built upon a broad, open platform on which many thousands could convene. It was not surrounded by other structures that would conceal it, and was above ground in contrast to the subterranean structure of the now-destroyed old sacred shrine. It was not located on top of a high pyramid giving limited access and placing it out of view. It would be exposed and open to the crowds in the plaza.

Matunha appeared to contemplate this information.

"It is so, this approach to construction of the sacred shrine bodes changes. Your thought is that greater inclusion in such rituals will reduce our power?"

"Indeed, you see my concern. It will make Pakal more popular, and push us farther into the background. It will give more people a sense of closer access to the deities, perhaps even a personal connection, and reduce their reliance on the priesthood. This is against long-standing tradition.

Of course, the lineage succession of Pakal goes against tradition, so it is natural for him to see things differently." Pasah Chan put this out as a feeler to gauge her response.

"An interesting observation," she commended without expression. "Pakal is very popular, even now. His ambitious building program keeps workers busy and well-fed, gives a sense of prosperity, a sense of contribution to an emerging greatness. Now with three sons, his dynastic succession seems assured. What have you in mind?"

"Only these concerns," said Pasah Chan carefully. "No definite plans come to mind. What I see is a situation that is troublesome, that poses problems for our future. It was my thought that in sharing our concerns, we might obtain insight into a course of action."

"Perhaps, I must think on it."

"There are some in your family, I believe, who would welcome a change in succession." Pasah Chan risked putting out this treasonous idea.

Matunha's eyebrows twitched, the first sign of reaction. Quickly she composed her expression.

"This is dangerous talk," she murmured, glancing around. No servants or attendants were within earshot.

"Life is dangerous, and unpredictable. Forces set in motion may not exert their impact for long times. Many forces are at play here, which you might wish to influence. We are at a stage of exploration. For this, I have requested your distant kinsman and priest, Aj Sul to join us. He will arrive shortly."

"Aj Sul, he was recently given the title Ah K'uhun, 'One Who Venerates,' by Pakal. He attends court regularly and seems to have close connections with the ruler. Why select him?"

"Because of these court connections. Let us not reveal our underlying concerns, but use him to bring information about Pakal's thinking and intentions. As a dutiful priest, he will follow my instructions. Over time, we can weigh the extent of his loyalty, whether it lies with the ruler or the priesthood."

"A source of inside information is always useful. Why not attend court yourself?"

"Although once I mentored Pakal, he has drawn away from me. Now he follows his own guidance, influenced by his wife. You recall that she took training with a priestess of Ix Zuhuy K'ak."

"The fiery Goddess of Change, Destruction, and Transformation ... I am glad we do not have a temple of these priestesses here."

"Her teacher from Ek Bahlam brought in foreign influences, disturbing occult powers and divergent viewpoints. My informants told me the training focused on sexual alchemy. With this skill she has seduced Pakal from our traditions. It is a dangerous situation, for I know not where her influence may lead."

"It is a serious consideration," Matunha acknowledged. "Much damage can result from improper use of such alchemy, and mastery of its forces is difficult. That is why we have never created a branch of Ix Zuhuy K'ak here. As you say, there is great risk in this situation." She gazed in the distance, as if reading some hidden message. "Yes, let us use Aj Sul to follow developments in the royal court. He was ever a malleable young man. Perhaps we do share more concerns than at first appeared."

Pasah Chan smiled inwardly. The meeting was going as he hoped, and soon the young priest would join them, his naive mind soft clay in their skilled hands to be molded for their purposes. The High Priest had another molding project underway, one that was long-term but held great promise for supporting priestly power. He did not speak of it to Matunha, for strategic reasons. Pakal's oldest son Kan Bahlam II was now in training at the High Priest's temple. The boy would be immersed in learning his people's traditions, and Pasah Chan would see that every teacher emphasized the importance of holding to the old ways. In times of shifting power, a future ruler would find it imperative to maintain control, and could be convinced to follow traditional ways. Exclusivity of religious ritual and esoteric knowledge was the time-honored way to maintain power.

3

A brisk wind fluttered leaves and pushed puffy clouds across the blue sky. Lalak and Pakal finished climbing the hill of the Lak'in Temple, arriving breathless at the summit that provided a vista of the eastern meadow below. Blinding white in the sunlight, a huge plaza set upon several lower platforms stretched across the meadow. At the northern edge, the first few levels of a stepped pyramid were visible, and at the farthest eastern edge other structures were in early construction phases. The foundations for three buildings were marked off near the aqueduct that channeled the Otulum River under the plaza.

"Oh! It is immense!" Lalak gasped in breathless surprise.

Pakal wrapped an arm around her shoulders as the cool breeze whipped their short cloaks.

"We are making good progress," he said. "See there? That is the foundation for the new Sak Nuk Nah." He pointed to the first of the three structures by the aqueduct. "Come; let me show you the subterranean passages that are being constructed."

They descended the hill to the new paved walkway leading past Yohl Ik'nal's temple and along the river, then ascended broad stairs onto the upper plaza level. Two attendants trailed along after them carrying extra shawls and mats. Standing next to the Sak Nuk Nah foundation, Pakal explained the arrangement. It sat on a slightly raised platform, a long rectangular structure that would have three front doorways, two on each short side, and two on the back side. Within would be two long, narrow chambers having two openings between them. The front of the building faced west. Another slightly larger rectangular building adjoined one edge of the north wall, while a smaller one abutted the end of the east wall. The larger building would be the royal court reception and throne room, the smaller one would serve as the Popol Nah, the Council House. To the south of the complex were the subterranean passages, giving underground access into the Sak Nuk Nah and other buildings on the southwest end of the palace.

The subterranean access was through two long corridors built into the lower plaza level that would be framed by arcades with low walls. From inside the arcades, two stairways led down into the tunnels running perpendicular to the corridor. Although these two tunnels were not finished, Pakal wanted to take Lalak into the one connecting to the Sak Nuk Nah. Leading her to the entrance, he used flints to strike a spark and light the wall torch. Carrying the torch, he took mats from the attendants and instructed them to wait in the corridor. Lalak felt a surge of excitement as they began descending down the stairs into subterranean darkness.

The tunnel was low-vaulted, its ceiling just above the top of Pakal's head. The torch he carried colored the fresh-cut white limestone blocks dusky rose. A short walk brought them to the farthest point of construction, where crumbled limestone and several stone-cutting chisels lay on the floor. Pakal looked up and pointed.

"This is nearly halfway to the south end of the Sak Nuk Nah. When completed, stairs will lead up into the southwest chamber, giving direct access to the throne in the next chamber, the main ritual space. The original sacred shrine was entirely underground, with access through a long tunnel running from the Ix Chel temple. Another tunnel ran from the palace, giving rulers a separate entrance. For the most important rituals, the gateway to the Jeweled Sky Tree must be through the Underworld."

"Then these subterranean passages represent the Underworld," said Lalak.

"Just so!" Pakal was pleased that she immediately understood. "The tunnels will be decorated with arches depicting the Maize God being resurrected from the watery Underworld, and the sun passing through the Celestial Caiman's body on its way to sunrise. Other inscriptions on the walls will depict Underworld themes."

"It creates the image of First Father emerging from Xibalba, when you climb the stairs and enter the main chamber."

"And bringing renewed life to his people," Pakal continued. "By building the sacred shrine above ground with a courtyard in front, these most holy rituals become visible to greater numbers of people. Many will be brought into the re-enactment of our people's spiritual history, and partake of the sacramental offerings that sustain and nurture our relationship with the deities."

"It is most generous to include more of our people, for surely they are also loved by the Gods."

"Would that all my advisors saw it the way you do," Pakal smiled. "Not all have hearts as large as yours. Here, let us sit and contemplate these things."

He spread the mats on the floor and placed the torch in a wall sconce. Lalak settled cross-legged and closed her eyes. She had been aware of building energies since they entered the tunnel, and now felt a swirling sensation in her body. She concentrated, trying to understand its meanings. Peering beneath slightly open lids, she saw Pakal's body swaying and knew he also felt the vortex. She heard him murmuring softly.

"It is less than six years until we reach the next katun ending. I plan to conduct katun end rituals in the new Sak Nuk Nah. All must be in readiness; the portal must be opened. It is a crucial time ... a turning point in my reign, for our dynasty. In truth, Lalak, I do not yet see how to open the portal."

She had no reply. This challenge that troubled him deeply was often on her mind. She yearned to offer solutions, to provide wise advice, but felt empty-handed. Re-focusing with eyes closed, she used techniques taught by the Ix Zuhuy K'ak priestess to connect with the earth. She placed both palms on the tunnel floor and intentionally drew energy up from deep within the earth. It entered through palms and soles, filling her with a pulsing rhythm synchronized to Mother Earth's own wave patterns. She directed these waves up through her body's energy centers, moving along the spine to the forehead and crown, and then cascading back into her body through myriads of subtle pathways. When she felt fully activated and surging with energy, she sent a request to the fiery Goddess, asking for guidance about opening the portal.

An intense blast of heat and vibration exploded into her pelvic region, causing her to bounce off the mat slightly. Calming her startled reaction, she invited these sensations into her body and asked their intentions. The heat spread upward into her abdomen and heart, not unpleasant but vivid. Her awareness was pulled toward the center in her forehead where energy concentrated nearly to the point of pain, then suddenly burst into a vision.

She was inside a huge cave, its ceiling soaring high above, walls dripping moisture into an underground river. Mist rose from the water and curled languidly around boulders in a silence broken only by pattering droplets. Her body seemed to have no form, her sight and hearing coming from some disembodied consciousness that hovered inside the cave, waiting. Shivers of anticipation announced something of immense power. She invited it to come forth.

A dark shadow took shape beneath the water, causing surface ripples. In perfect silence the gargantuan head and thick body of an enormous crocodile-snake slipped through the surface and rose before her. Its long snout curled in two directions, and barbels hung from its chin. Its fangs gleamed and its red slit eyes glared. Intricate patterns of iridescent green scales of varying sizes covered its body, shining wetness as fine drops cascaded down its length. The serpent undulated from side to side, dipping its head in a strange dance and waving its forked tongue. As it rose higher from the water, its body became translucent with a moving panorama of life forms: frogs, lizards, and aquatic creatures blurred into trees and bushes, flowers and vines; morphed into birds and animals of every variety; flowed into rivers, lakes, and waterfalls; solidified as rocks and mountains. Every living thing appeared within the endless serpent body looping through the water.

"Itzam Kab Ayin, Crocodile-Serpent of Creation, Who Brings Form to All Life," her consciousness acknowledged.

"You summoned me," the snake hissed.

"In deepest honor and humility, this woman your daughter gives gratitude for your appearance."

"You seek my assistance."

"How might I help Pakal re-open the portal to Gods and ancestors?"

"To do this, you must take me within yourself. You must become the Deep Earth and Source of Life Forms. In your womb must be planted the seeds of the Jeweled Sky Tree. Through your fertile soil the roots will grow so the tree may rise to the sky. You are not yet ready. You must prepare; my Goddess Ix Zuhuy K'ak will show you how."

"To the Goddess shall I turn. I trust her to guide me. What must Pakal do?"

"He must become the Light of the Sun and Stars, to join the Infinite Cosmos with the Deep Earth. He brings the lightning of immortality to strike within the womb of fecundity, to plant the seeds of the Jeweled Sky Tree. He will understand this; he will know to draw upon the Serpent-Footed Lightning-in-Forehead God, Unen K'awill, Third Born of the B'aakal Triad. He must also prepare, he is not ready."

"My eternal gratitude to you, Itzam Kab Ayin, for revealing this to me."

"You love my small relatives who slither upon the earth. Your love opens many portals. May it be so, may you accomplish your goals."

The huge serpent began to submerge into the water, slowly, silently, as mists thickened and the cave became obscured.

Lalak blinked at the bright torchlight, suddenly aware she was inside the tunnel with Pakal. He was watching her with an avid expression. Their eyes met and he smiled but did not move to touch her.

"You were journeying," he said with certainty.

"The Goddess Ix Zuhuy K'ak gave me a vision," she replied softly. "The great serpent Itzam Kab Ayin came to me and explained how we are to give birth to the Jeweled Sky Tree that will re-open the portal."

"Tell me," he murmured, his body tense with anticipation.

She related her vision in minute detail. It was blazoned on her mind, brilliant and irremovable. He hung on every word, drinking eagerly the serpent's prescription.

"Hah!" he breathed when she finished. "Why did I not think of it? We use sex magic to re-create the portal."

"It seems ... so unusual and ... ah, non-traditional."

"But it will work! This approach is capable of creating the vast energies necessary for such a momentous task. There is no power on earth greater than our sexual ability to procreate, to actually bring new life into being. Now we must raise that power into the divine realms, we must perform the acts of creation done by the Gods and Goddesses. Our bodies will be the workshops of the deities, as we merge with them to conceive and birth a new Wakah Chan Te'."

"Ah, Pakal, it sounds overwhelming," Lalak whispered.

"We can do it! You are strong and capable; your Goddess will lead the way. Now we must discover details about how to proceed and how to become prepared. We must commune with our deities and meditate upon their instructions. This will require some time, perhaps over a year. You know much of sexual alchemy, what think you?"

His enthusiasm was contagious. Lalak gazed into his shining eyes and re-grouped herself. To receive such a clear message from the Crocodile-Serpent Wizard was an unbelievable blessing; she must muster her courage and make best use of this guidance.

"Clearly we must follow sexual alchemy techniques to build our internal powers," she said, "through containing the energy dissipated during physical release. But simply abstaining will not amplify creative power enough; we must use the technique of bringing each other to the verge of release, then holding that intense energy within ourselves. Doing this repeatedly over a year will build up a huge reserve of extremely potent creative energy. When the time is right for planting the seeds of the Jeweled Sky Tree, then we enact the procreative act of the deities. It must be done in sacred ceremony, in a state of higher consciousness."

"In the Sak Nuk Nah. This is perfect: we initiate the new sacred shrine with the portal opening and tree birthing ceremony. The potency of the ceremony will be amplified by holding it on an extremely auspicious day. Let me think ... yes, there will be a solar eclipse two tuns before the katun end. Nothing can build an atmosphere so highly charged as a complete eclipse of Ahau K'in. The power will be immense. I must consult with the Ah K'inob to determine the exact date of the eclipse."

Lalak nodded agreement, contemplating the impact of combining their enhanced potency with that of the solar eclipse. It would create forces she could barely imagine, forces that must also contain elements of danger. She was concerned about the aftermath of exposing themselves to such unpredictable elemental powers.

"Pakal, there are other things we must consider. When we open our bodies and minds to become channels for deities, when we offer our sexuality for them to use in this way, we are creating a certain risk to ourselves. This I do not fully understand, but from what I do know, some damage may result from these extremely intense energies flowing through us. What if the tribute such processes extract might prevent us from having more children? It is possible that discharge of the built up sexual alchemy within the extreme forces of a solar eclipse will burn up our procreative abilities."

"That is a serious concern," he replied, frowning. "For we do want another child, at least one more son. That is very important to me."

She chose not to bring up her desire for a daughter. Perhaps this was a sacrifice that would be required of her.

"We have time yet," he reflected. "If we conceive another child soon, he will be born well ahead of the year of preparation. It appears we must join together again without much delay."

Both smiled at the thought, more than ready for the physical intimacy they so enjoyed.

"Kan Joy Chitam is thriving and will soon be attempting his first steps," Lalak said. "It will do him no harm to wean early; he already likes mashed foods as much as milk."

"Good, then proceed with weaning and I will have the Ah Kinob cast auguries for our next son's birth."

Pakal helped her rise, gathered up the mats and took the torch to lead the way out. Lalak hesitated, placing a hand on his arm. She had one more concern to bring up before they returned.

"You said the ceremony will be done in the new Sak Nuk Nah, which I understand and fully support. But, the building will be exposed to anyone in the courtyard, and the solar eclipse will happen during daylight hours. How do you envision keeping privacy for our sexual alchemy during the ceremony?"

"A private ceremony?" Pakal seemed surprised. "The purpose of having the sacred shrine in an exposed setting is to make ceremonies there accessible. Of course, the group attending will be carefully selected, but it cannot be completely private."

He looked deeply into her eyes, dropping the mats to cup her face in one hand.

"Beloved, I see your hesitation about others observing our sexual intimacy. Remember, we will not be our ordinary selves, but the embodiments of Earth Mother and Cosmic Father. We will be fully prepared and fully supported by contingents of the priesthood. Trust in your Goddess, for the Fiery One can overcome all fear. Trust in me, for I am your other self as you are mine. Together we can create a new era for Lakam Ha as we restore the portal."

4

The royal court of Lakam Ha was filled with nobles, several from other polity cities. Pakal sat on the double-headed jaguar throne, legs crossed over the jaguar pelt, wearing Maize God regalia. Near the throne were K'akmo the warrior chief, Yax Chan the head architect, and the ruler's cousins Oaxac Ok and Ch'amak. Several other elite courtiers stood farther back, including the priest and Ah K'uhun, Aj Sul. K'anal the royal scribe sat on his wooden platform beside the throne, poised with bark-paper codex and quill pen for recording happenings in the court session. Tohom, personal attendant to Pakal, and two other attendants hovered behind the throne, ever ready to serve the ruler's needs. The court dwarf squatted in front of the scribe's platform, squinting defiantly at whoever entered the room.

Muk Kab, Royal Steward, stood at the door and intoned names of visitors.

"Now enters Bahlam Ahau, K'uhul B'aak Ahau, brother-in-law of the ruler."

Bahlam Ahau swaggered into the throne room with his head tossed back and chin jutting forward, adorned in splendid costume with tall feathered headdress and heavy jade jewelry. He was full of himself, bolstered by recent victories over Uxte'kuh and Nab'nahotot, both small cities in B'aakal polity. Since becoming ruler of B'aak five solar years before, he had staged attacks on several polity cities, claiming they harbored factions that planned to overthrow him. He was now in Lakam Ha because Pakal had summoned him.

Clasping his left shoulder, Bahlam Ahau bowed just low enough to remain within courtly protocols. The dwarf stuck out a thick tongue and made "pthhhh" sounds. K'akmo bristled, and other nobles in the room tensed as all eyes swung to Pakal.

The Lakam Ha ruler's face remained an impassive mask of royal dignity.

"Greetings, Holy B'aak Lord. It is our pleasure to welcome you to our city. I trust your travels here were easy and your men have found congenial housing for their stay."

Bahlam Ahau had a sizeable contingent in his war party, 200 warriors and another sixty nobles. The common fighters had set up camp on the plains below the escarpment on which Lakam Ha perched; the nobles were hosted by families in the city. Bahlam Ahau and his highest assistants were given quarters in the palace.

"All hail to you, esteemed K'uhul B'aakal Ahau," he responded. "Our journey has been quick and without difficulty, and we are appreciative of your city's excellent hospitality. Indeed, many changes have occurred since I last visited Lakam Ha. May I commend you upon this impressive building program."

"Your commendation is happily accepted. During your stay here, I shall take you upon a tour of the new palace complex and main plaza now being built. You may find the innovations by our architects of interest."

Pakal signaled that Bahlam Ahau could be seated on the mat near the throne. The controlled intensity of this gesture and the flash in Pakal's eyes kept his courtiers on alert. Those who knew him recognized these signs of anger. After the men exchanged a few more niceties, the conversation became serious.

"Of your forays against our polity cities, Uxte'kuh and Nab'nahotot, I have heard much," Pakal said. "These cities have long been loyal; they have given the expected tribute to Lakam Ha and have posed no threats to us. Your raids give me concern; this is unexpected and violates traditional inter-polity relations. For what purpose did you conduct these attacks?"

"Much contention about rulership has troubled my city for years," Bahlam Ahau replied, undaunted. "Of this you are aware, Holy Lord. Even after my father routed his treacherous brother and brought him to the justice of death, followers of the traitor persisted and found harbor in certain cities. When my father passed into the world of ancestors, these followers spread discord within my city and attempted to prevent my succession. To halt their ignominious actions, my forces attacked Zopo where most resided."

"Of this I know; it was several tuns past. Now you have undertaken more attacks. Why is this done if the rebellious group was eliminated in Zopo?"

"All of the rebels were not eliminated. Several escaped and took residence in these other cities. There they drew other men into their cause, claiming great injustices that were false and slanderous. My intelligence reported that plans for an attack against B'aak were formulating. It was necessary to take pre-emptive action. A ruler cannot permit such sources of rebellion to fester and grow into a vile infection."

Bahlam Ahau smiled, bowed his head and spread his hands in a conciliatory gesture.

"Holy Lord, you as ruler of this great city surely understand the need to root out the nucleus of treachery. We who are the chosen of the Triad

Gods, who carry the sacred royal blood of our hallowed ancestors, have the duty to preserve our dynasties. My actions are only what are required to fulfill this sacred charge."

Pakal lowered his eyelids and contemplated Bahlam Ahau with cool aloofness. He knew everything his brother-in-law had said, and he understood taking pre-emptive action to avoid future rebellion. However, he was worried that these attacks would upset the delicate balance of inter-polity loyalties, given his relationship to the B'aak ruler. Another concern pulled upon nearly forgotten feelings, something he preferred to keep submerged in the far recesses of memory. Nab'nahotot was the home of the beautiful woman he once loved, Yonil. Although he had long released his desire for her, he cared about her well-being and that of her family.

"Holy Lord of B'aak, you speak truthfully of our duties as rulers. We have yet other obligations, and these are to act with the greatest possible wisdom. Many factors must be balanced in deciding a course of action; its justice and necessity should be unquestionable. In this lies my hesitance over your recent attacks. How good was your intelligence? How strong was the opposition? How real the threat and how justified the actions taken? Give me an accounting of the men involved in the plots against you, how many were killed or taken prisoner, how much damage done to each city."

Bahlam Ahau began to sweat and feel less confident. He was angered at this public demonstration, disturbed that Pakal was taking him to task over the attacks. At this moment, however, he was sitting before the K'uhul B'aakal Ahau, the highest lord of the polity, who had every right to demand compliance with political processes long-established in the region. The B'aak ruler called his warrior chief and main scribe into the throne room, ordering them to provide the details to Pakal. They gave the accounting and it revealed a small number of men in the two cities involved in the plot, and even fewer rebels killed. No captives had been taken. Damage to city structures was minimal, though some looting had taken place. When Pakal requested names of rebels killed, the scribe dutifully read the list. To Pakal's relief, the name of Yonil's husband was not there.

Pakal did not need to state the obvious: Bahlam Ahau's attacks had insufficient justification.

"We must make reparations to these two cities," Pakal said. "There was a threat to you, this I do see. You acted as you thought best to protect your city and dynasty. Yet it remains that harm was done to innocent people, damage done that cannot be completely justified. Although this is inevitable in warfare, we are not dealing here with enemy cities, but with loyal members of our polity. For future solidarity, it is important to salve the wounds of these cities. I ask you to join me in these reparations, to acknowledge the unintended damage and to reaffirm our alliances."

Bahlam Ahau understood that Pakal was offering a compromise. Although this did not exonerate him, it did provide a way to save face and appear magnanimous. It would cost him some material wealth, but it would preserve relations with Lakam Ha. He swallowed his pride and chose to cooperate.

"Well-spoken, Holy B'aakal Lord," said Bahlam Ahau. "You are ever the dispenser of wisdom. In my assessment, these attacks were necessary, but I can acknowledge the unintended damage and fully support reparations to restore polity harmony. Let us proceed."

The details of reparations were worked out between the two rulers, an exercise in cooperation that impressed the observers from both sides. At the end of this process, Pakal appeared relaxed and Bahlam Ahau was nearly ebullient. Their final exchange in court sealed their newfound amity.

"It would much be my pleasure to have you join my family for our evening meal," Pakal offered. "Your sister, our K'uhul Ixik Tz'aakb'u Ahau, is eager to spend time with you again. She will be delighted to show you our latest son, now more than two tuns old and chattering like a parrot."

"With utmost happiness do I accept your invitation," replied Bahlam Ahau. "You have now four sons, is that so? Much do I admire this production of heirs, for I have only one son. My sister has done well to fulfill her royal name, and set in order a progression of lords for your dynasty."

Lalak's last pregnancy had been more difficult than the previous ones. It had taken them five attempts to conceive, causing the Ah Kinob to recalculate each time her moon flow came. Utzil was troubled, fearing that so many pregnancies had sapped Lalak's reserves and aware of the risks posed by childbearing at the age of thirty-seven. After conception, Utzil kept close watch for any danger signs, constantly admonishing Lalak to follow proper regimes for diet, rest and exercise. The pregnancy progressed well, but Lalak lost another tooth from loosening in the jaw, an upper molar. To Utzil, it pointed toward thinning bones despite her herbal bone-building remedies. Toward the end of pregnancy, Lalak was often fatigued and needed to rest frequently.

Her labor and birth were longer than the last ones. The womb seemed to lack strength, its contractions not very effective, requiring nearly two days completing its expulsion of the infant. Although this caused Utzil extreme worry, the child was born healthy and well-developed, another son.

His feet touched the earth, Tiwol Chan Mat, the fourth living son of Pakal and Lalak, on the date inscribed on monuments.

Baktun 9, Katun 10, Tun 14, Uinal 17, Kin 7, on the day 6 Manik 0 Mac (October 28, 647 CE).

Although Tiwol Chan Mat's birth date was not the original choice of the Ah Kinob, both Pakal and Lalak were pleased with the auguries it brought. Those born on Manik had qualities of continuing, proceeding, and following. The number six meant sprouting or hatching. The uinal sign Mac indicated one who brought gifts, whose personality was dignified and magnetic. Zero was a powerful number for the Mayas; it was round like a circle and signified the endlessness of spirit. It was depicted as a sea shell bearing the vastness and mystery of the oceans.

His name reflected his astrologica characteristics: Tiwol Chan Mat, Spider of the Sky Possessed, the one who proceeded to weave a cosmic web of continuing connections that hatched many gifts; that followed the path of endless spirit. These were qualities holding great promise for continuing the dynasty.

In the year of their fourth son's birth, Pakal dedicated three newly completed temples. The first was the Temple of Kan Bahlam I, renovated and embellished with striking temple façade pillars and interior panels carved in the fine Lakam Ha limestone that allowed intricate details and flowing lines. It was painted vibrant colors and had a roofcomb reflecting the innovative style developed by Yax Chan, two thin facing panels with lacy patterns that allowed airflow and gave the impression of lightness. Lalak participated in the dedication as Pakal had requested, speaking poetic phrases praising his great-grandfather that drew sighs of admiration from observers. It was a special time for Lalak, because she had confirmed her pregnancy just before the dedication.

The Temple of Kan Bahlam I was the first temple dedicated during Pakal's reign. The date of the momentous event was inscribed on the temple panels.

Baktun 9, Katun 10, Tun 14, Uinal 5, Kin 10, on the date 3 Ok 3 Pop (February 23, 647 CE).

The other two temples were dedicated seven moon cycles later. Pakal re-dedicated the mortuary temple of his grandmother, Yohl Ik'nal that was renovated to honor her. On the wide plaza built over the eastern meadow, the first pyramid was completed at the far northern edge, a Temple of the North or Xaman for priests to use when performing calendar rituals honoring the realm of ancestors and occult wisdom. It completed the pattern of temples denoting the four directions of the Maya Middleworld. Lalak did not attend these dedications, because her pregnancy was far advanced and Utzil deemed it too risky.

Having two toddlers in her quarters was a continuous delight to Lalak. She loved children and found endless amusement in their antics, especially since her beloved monkey Popo had passed into the spirit realms. Her scarlet macaw was quite an elderly bird and would also leave her soon. She missed her two older sons, both in training at the High Priest's temple. They had recently completed their transformation rituals into adolescence, at ages fourteen and thirteen solar years. This made them even less accessible to her, for training now expanded into the manly arts of battle and hunting. When they came for infrequent visits, she found Kan Bahlam even more perplexing and inscrutable. While he spoke proudly of his accomplishments, in particular his victories in the ballgame, she was never certain of his inner feelings. There were both domineering and brooding qualities to his personality, and she sensed secrets in his depths that he guarded carefully. Waknal Bahlam was his usual cheerful and easy-going self, only taller and more self-assured. The openness of his personality was a relief after time with his saturnine older brother.

When Bahlam Ahau came to visit his sister after the court session, which Lalak's informants fully described, she was genuinely happy to see him. They had never been close as children, but he was ever part of the nostalgia of childhood memories. They laughed when recalling little spats between them and naughty adventures they had shared. He also loved children, pulling her little ones onto his lap and ruffling their hair, causing some squealing and wiggling. The boys came to enjoy their rough uncle during the moon cycle he stayed in the palace.

Lalak was troubled over conversations Pakal and Bahlam Ahau had during several evening meals in her chambers. She did not show her concern, although the fingers of fear gripped her heart. The two rulers were planning a campaign against Imix-Ha, a city far south along the K'umaxha River. The previous year, this small and insignificant city was overtaken by the brother of the Mutul ruler, initially as an extension of the great southern city but recently his loyalties had changed, much for the worse.

"Know you, it was reported by good sources, that Balaj Chan K'awill now calls himself 'yahau' of Kan?" asked Bahlam Ahau.

"It saddens me greatly that the brother of Nuun Ujol Chaak, heir to Mutul's throne, would make such an ominous switch in allegiance," said Pakal. "The evil snake dynasty has slithered into yet another region. It must serve Balaj's ambitions to become their vassal. Think you he has intentions for the Mutul throne?"

"What else could motivate him? He needs the military might of Kan to overturn succession in his home city, and Kan gains another ally to work its will upon Mutul. This must be stopped; it is dangerous for all along the K'umaxha River if Kan retains power over this critical area for trade."

"Mutul has not yet recovered from the terrible defeat they suffered at Kan's hands, now nearly six katuns ago. Under the leadership of K'inich Muwaan Jol they are making progress, I am told by messengers. Kan must fear that the ruler's heir will continue reviving the city, making it once again a significant rival. Thus they plant seeds of dissention and divide brother from brother."

"Ha! Would that I had those skills of manipulation," chuckled Bahlam Ahau. "Were Kan not such an enemy, we could learn much statesmanship from them."

"It is less statesmanship than coercion," Pakal said dryly. "Winning allies through promises of power and threats of destruction. Lasting alliances are never made this way, and Balaj would be wise not to trust agreements made by the Snake Dynasty."

"In any event, we cannot let this alliance go unchallenged. My men are battle-tested and ready for more. Now they are resting; after the rains stop, time will be right for this excursion. How are your warriors? You have been doing much construction. What is their state of training?"

"Better than it has been for some years," Pakal replied. "I have foreseen the need for military action and asked my Nakom to keep aside a contingent of men, training them for battle instead of wielding axes and hammers against limestone. The manpower of Lakam Ha has been growing. Did you notice how many villages are locating on adjacent hillsides? It seems many people from surrounding regions are being drawn to our city. They can sense the expansion and increased opportunities here. We have recruited many fighters from these villages."

"Excellent! With our combined warriors, we will have formidable forces. Let us call a battle council of our Nakoms and leading warriors, and plan strategies for the campaign. We must strike as quickly as possible." Bahlam Ahau's eyes glowed; he liked nothing better than preparing for battle.

Pakal agreed to schedule the battle council, wryly observing how easily his relationship with Bahlam Ahau had transitioned from animosity to comradeship when they began planning a battle together. He was determined that this attack would go much better than the last one they had shared.

After Bahlam Ahau left, Lalak expressed her concerns to Pakal.

"Time is getting short for our preparations to open the portal," she said. "It troubles me that your campaign with my brother will interfere with this."

"Of this have I also thought," Pakal replied. "It is my intention to defer joining the campaign after assuring that my warriors are well-prepared. I will give utmost support to Bahlam Ahau by providing supplies and auxiliary personnel for the campaign. K'akmo is completely competent to lead our forces. He is a better military strategist than me. Of this, let us not speak to your brother until shortly before our forces depart."

Her relieved expression was all the answer he needed. Leaning close to brush his lips against hers, he whispered: "Beloved, what you and I must accomplish here for our city far outweighs any military campaign against a distant foe. And, I am much anticipating our regimen for building up immense stores of sexual energy."

5

The messenger from Usihwitz left the High Priestess' chambers as stealthily as he had entered. He was certain that few, if any, saw him visit, and those who did would assume he was a supplicant from Lakam Ha seeking spiritual counsel. Upon arriving in the city, he had immediately obtained local clothing and blended into the daily patterns of life. He stayed in the home of Matunha's family, who kept his identity secret. With them he shared news of their relatives in the enemy city, but his message was for Matunha alone.

"Here comes something important." The messenger spoke softly to the High Priestess once assured that no one could overhear their conversation. "Your cousin, the brave and esteemed Yax Chapat, charged me to speak these words only to you. He spoke them on his deathbed, as his final breaths were taken. It is his heart's greatest desire, and you are the one who can fulfill his last wishes. He requests that you avenge his noble father, Ek Chuuah, who was grievously harmed by the Lakam Ha ruler Kan Bahlam I. Their souls will not find rest until this despicable act is righted. In your position, you have the ability to take action against the Bahlam family. Your cousin knows not how, but trusts you will find a way to restore the balance of righteousness. May the Gods guide your course."

Matunha was deeply affected by the dying request of Yax Chapat. As long as she could remember, her family had whispered the story of Ek Chuuah's mistreatment. They displaced blame onto the ambitions of Kan for the attack on Lakam Ha that wrought destruction of temples and collapsed the portal to the Triad Gods. Their stories insinuated that succession through Sak K'uk's family was improper, and that Pakal's rule was not legitimate. Early in childhood, the nucleus of an idea had taken shape in her mind: the image of herself as savior of her family's honor. From this sprang her intense drive to attain a position of power, one in which she might affect her city's destiny. With single-minded dedication, she pursued the path through priesthood and accomplished her goal.

Now time had arrived to take action. It was indeed fortuitous that the High Priest also shared intentions to undermine the Bahlam dynasty. He had no clear plans, however, and she came to view him as ineffective. Pasah Chan was elderly and becoming quite frail, already there was talk about contenders for his replacement. She doubted that he would be a useful ally, and a new High Priest would be too inexperienced to bring into her confidence, even if she could ascertain his true loyalty to the ruler.

A recent meeting with Pasah Chan had planted seeds for her strategy. Shortly before, Pakal had visited the High Priest to discuss his plans for opening the portal, and to enlist the support of the priesthood. Pasah Chan described these plans to her, for he was disturbed that Pakal intended to join with his wife and use sexual alchemy for birthing a new Jeweled Sky Tree. This would be timed for the coming solar eclipse, less than six moon cycles distant. The royal couple was well into preparations for the event, utilizing techniques learned from the Ix Zuhuy K'ak priestess.

Pasah Chan could not openly refuse the priesthood's participation, and had started their instructions for the ritual. He seemed conflicted to Matunha, his intentions wavering. Their use of her kinsman Aj Sul had been nonproductive; the young priest reported little useful information and was now off with the warriors in the attack on Imix-Ha. It was clear that she must take matters into her own hands.

Matunha had elected a life of celibacy and distrusted her own sexuality. These carnal urges appeared to her as distractions from her higher calling. Their sinuous power could pull one into the fetters of relationships and submerge one under householder demands. These bonds she utterly rejected, quelling her body's physical desires through strict austerity that included not just sexuality, but denial of desires for everyday comforts.

Although she could live luxuriously due to her position, she kept her personal chambers minimally furnished and adhered to simple food and drink. Her attempts to apply such disciplines to other Ix Chel priestesses had met considerable resistance.

The use of sexual alchemy was abhorrent to her. Surely it would not be pleasing to the Triad Deities to have their sacred portal opened in this manner. It diminished Pakal's standing in her eyes that he would resort to such methods. Resentment and distrust against Lalak surged; the woman brought the occult skills and cunning of the foreign Goddess to work dark magic upon her husband. This added additional fuel to the fire of anger smoldering within the High Priestess. If use of sex magic was successful, it could lead to establishing a cult of Ix Zuhuy K'ak in Lakam Ha. Every fiber of her being tensed in violent opposition; she would fight to her death such a violation of the sacred energies of Ix Chel.

Gradually a plan took form in her meditations. She could not muster the forces of rebellion, but she could command otherworldly forces even more powerful. She was also trained in dark magic, arts she rarely used because their results could be volatile. If she gained access to Lalak's mind, she could germinate seeds of self-doubt that might undermine the ability to carry out her planned sexual alchemy. Matunha was aware of Lalak's history in Lakam Ha, of how insecure the young woman had been initially, of her conflicted relationship with Sak K'uk. Although the ruler's wife now appeared confident and well-accepted, those residues of doubt and insecurity could be pushed again to the surface. What the royal couple would be attempting was entirely unprecedented; it would be natural to have some uncertainty. Even traces of uncertainty could mushroom into fear, and just a small amount of fear would be disempowering.

The High Priestess planned to inject the poison of uncertainty into Lalak's mind. She would accomplish it with the dark magic of shamanic cursing. To place the curse, she needed something of Lalak's body or essence. Taking aside her most trusted assistant, she instructed the young priestess to obtain some hair left after Lalak used her comb. Such household residues were disposed of in a trash heap hidden behind walls at the edge of the palace complex. The hair must come from trash disposed only by Lalak's servants, and recovered immediately so it did not mix with other debris. It was not necessary to explain her motives; her assistants were trained to obey without question. The purposes of the High Priestess were far beyond their comprehension.

When she had a tiny ball of Lalak's hair, Matunha prepared by fasting, took a drink of a hallucinogenic mushroom brew, sequestered in her chamber shrine, gathered necessary implements, and entered a shamanic trance. She used a stingray needle perforator to let blood from earlobes, that this sacred itz might open her hearing to the voices of Underworld deities. As body awareness slipped away and blood-soaked bark paper burning with copal smoke curled around her, she gazed into a mirror of polished pyrite crystals that helped her see deeply into the spirit world. Her hollow eyes stared back, began wavering and taking frightening shapes, and then suddenly the mirror transported her into the cave of the Death Lords. Chasms of darkness surrounded her, murky waters spread below covered with slime and decaying matter. The stench of death became stronger as a form flitted through shadows, swirled around her and screeched eerie calls in her ears.

Lord Wing, she acknowledged mentally. *Bat God of the Underworld. Hear my supplication and take my blood offering, for the curse to be cast.*

Her consciousness merged with the Bat God, her body became host for him to enter. His powers became her powers, and she conjured a vampire bat whose fangs dripped poisons of self-doubt and uncertainty. She became the vampire bat, flying through jungle foliage in the darkness of night, able to see even without moonlight. Rising above the canopy, the bat soared over the structures of Lakam Ha, locating the palace complex and following its corridors to the targeted chamber. A small window gave access to Lalak's sleeping chamber, and the bat glided through on silent wings. It circled above her head and entered the halo of her dream world, seeking an opening, a moment of distress or sorrow in the dream. A memory flickered, a scene of loss replayed for an instant as the dream re-enacted the death of her firstborn premature son. The bat's radar ticked and it plunged into the sorrowful memory, sinking its fangs into these patterns in Lalak's mind. Like a snake injecting venom, the bat spurted its fearful poisons into the memory pattern.

It was done quickly. The vampire bat returned to its creator, who released her connection with Lord Wing, giving copious thanks for the Death Lord's assistance.

Matunha sat in mindless silence until the hallucinogen softened its grip and her consciousness returned to her body. She must perform one additional act to seal the curse. Taking the hair ball, she wiped it against her ears to pick up bloody residues, spat upon it to infuse her intentions and placed it in the smoldering censer in which she had burned her blood offerings. Chanting the invocation to seal a curse, she watched until the hair ball caught fire. During the momentary flicker of flame, she pronounced the words that would activate the curse in the Middleworld.

"Thus it is done, thus it is accomplished,
The charge is given, the action is taken.
Into your mind, Lady Lalak, is set the fear that you are inadequate to properly enact the portal opening ritual."

Lalak woke in the middle of the night, her head throbbing. Tentatively she rubbed both temples, surprised that her forehead was moist and hair damp. It was not warm enough to cause such sweating, and she felt extremely thirsty. She rose to relieve herself, stumbling in the darkness and using one hand against the wall to guide herself into the adjacent bath chamber, where the stone toilet seat opened to underground drainage. Eyes more adjusted to the dark, she sought the gourd of water her servant always placed near the door. After drinking deeply, she felt better and returned to the sleeping bench. The headache waned and she fell into restless sleep, her dreams a jumble of screeching and flapping night creatures who seemed malevolent, an odd thing for one so attuned to the natural world.

In the days that followed, Lalak felt a building sense of apprehension. The source was unclear, just a vague sense of uneasiness. She did not speak about it to Pakal, hoping it would pass. Their sessions using sexual alchemy to build internal power were so enjoyable that she did not want any negativity to enter. On some days, she felt her usual self and her mood was positive. In the evenings, however, alone in the darkness, the apprehensive feeling returned. She began to sense that it was connected with the ritual for opening the portal, a thought she did not want to harbor. Pakal had allayed her initial concern about their public performance, but now she began to examine whether this was causing her uneasiness.

Shortly after winter solstice, word came from messengers that the forces of B'aak and Lakam Ha would soon return after a successful attack on Imix-Ha. The ruler, Balaj Chan K'awiil, was in flight, seeking refuge in the Kan city Uxte'tun, his warriors routed and the former ruling family reinstated. A delegation from Bahlam Ahau's forces continued on to Mutul to inform their ally of the victory. When the main contingent returned to Lakam Ha, the city celebrated with parades and feasts, and commemorated the *ek'emey* battle in which the warriors "descended upon the enemy," a term that also invoked meteors as arrows of the Gods. Bahlam Ahau's men "mountained" the bones of their victims in a *u-sak ik'il chan* ceremony that sent the defeated warriors' souls to far distant sky places from which it would be difficult to return.

The date of the *ek'emey* battle was inscribed on monuments.

Baktun 9, Katun 10, Tun 17, Uinal 2, Kin 14, on the day 13 Ix 17 Muwaan (December 23, 649 CE).

Bahlam Ahau basked in the accolades he received in Lakam Ha, visited with his sister and young nephews, sat in several war councils to consider future campaigns, and promised to return with his family for the katun end ceremonies in two years. He was eager to return home after over two years of military campaigning. He needed to ascertain that all was well in his city and reunite with his family. While meeting with Pakal, he praised the bravery of the young priest-warrior Aj Sul, whose abilities to strategize and organize attacks were impressive. Pakal heard the same report from his own Nakom, K'akmo. In recognition of Aj Sul's accomplishments, Pakal honored him in a public ceremony and conferred several costly gifts of jade pendants and fine obsidian blades.

Aj Sul was profoundly affected by his experiences in battle and the recognition given by Pakal. The role of warrior-priest brought out unanticipated aspects of his being; he found himself well-suited to fighting alongside the troops then ministering to their souls when they grappled with fears or wounds. He helped them face both death and cowardice, guiding them to find courage and overcome fears, and giving solace when facing their journey into the Underworld. In the process, he had bonded firmly with K'akmo and several leading Lakam Ha warriors, listening around evening campfires to their stories of battle and their affirmations of loyalty to their exceptional ruler. When Pakal acknowledged him, Aj Sul was thoroughly won over.

His conscience troubled him, for he knew that the High Priest and Priestess had charged him to spy on Pakal. He did not understand their motives, but felt their actions should be revealed to the ruler. Requesting a private audience, Aj Sul described to Pakal his meetings with the priestly leaders and the instructions given to obtain and convey information about Pakal's plans. He believed they were especially interested in sacred rituals, such as the pending katun end ceremony. He assured Pakal that he would no longer act as informant, and pledged his loyalty.

Pakal was disturbed by this information. He knew that Pasah Chan disapproved of opening the rituals in the new Sak Nuk Nah to wider groups of nobles, but did not expect secretive scheming from the High Priest. That Matunha was also involved made the situation ominous. The High Priestess remained an enigma to Pakal, for he could not determine either her agenda or her personal commitment to his dynasty. He decided that a visit to the High Priest was in order. This took on a sense of urgency after a conversation with Lalak.

The apprehension building within Lalak found focus on the portal opening ritual. She worried that she would not perform her part successfully. Old anxieties returned, and she experienced self-doubt from which she had long been free. Memories of Sak K'uk's disapproval and Pakal's emotional distance during her early years in Lakam Ha haunted her, causing frequent nightmares. Trying to use reason for reassurance, to remind her self that Sak K'uk had acknowledged her worth in the end and that Pakal truly loved her was not enough to overcome these fears. Applying techniques that she had learned from the Ix Zuhuy K'ak priestess to control her wayward mind was not effective. She felt as though she was slipping into an abyss, being relentlessly pulled into a chasm of darkness by an insurmountable force.

With the portal opening ritual less than a moon cycle away, she was compelled to bring this difficulty to Pakal's attention. In her present state, she knew the internal powers necessary for this vast effort were compromised. When she described to him the dreams, worrisome thoughts and feelings of inadequacy she was having, and gave the time period for their development, he immediately made connections to the schemes of the High Priest and Priestess. Trained as he was in shamanic practices, Pakal saw the hallmarks of dark shamanism in Lalak's experiences.

He visited the High Priest the next day. Pasah Chan was keeping to his residential chambers, his health declining and his arthritic limbs making even short walks difficult. He received Pakal in his private audience chamber, and dismissed attendants when the ruler requested that they speak in complete confidence. Pakal had not seen Pasah Chan for several moons, and was sad to observe such a thin, frail, and shriveled old man bolstered by thick cushions and wrapped in a warm blanket.

"Much is my pleasure to see you again, Pakal," the priest said in a wavering, reedy voice.

"It has been too long," Pakal replied. "It is good to be here, but I am saddened to see your health so frail."

"Ah, one becomes old sooner than one realizes. How the katuns have sped by. It seems only a short while ago that you were a boy studying in my temple."

"This I remember well, and am eternally grateful for your excellent training. We have been close through the years, until recently. Much do I regret our differences; our divergent views about making sacred rituals more open. The future brings change, people and their needs change, and I foresee times when everyone's relationship to the Gods will be more personal."

"Nothing lasts forever, of that we can be certain," chuckled Pasah Chan. "Being old makes one resistant to change. Even now this surprises me. Ever before I thought myself a forward-thinking and flexible person. Ah, the foolishness of aging. Let us go beyond this; my time in the Middleworld is not much longer. You were always a visionary, not only in creating a magnificent new city center, but in the spiritual unfolding of our people."

The old priest hesitated, eyes clouding as he processed some inner experience.

"Initially I was troubled about your plans to use sexual alchemy to open the portal and raise the Jeweled Sky Tree, but after much reflection I am coming to see that ... it is exactly these forces that are necessary for an ultimate act of creation. Perhaps it is the only way to accomplish the goal."

Pakal nodded, using the hand gesture for being in accord.

"Pasah Chan, I am deeply appreciative to hear you express this," the ruler said. "It is exactly the ritual that I have come to discuss with you. Let me be frank, we are bound by duty far greater than our individual fates, and our lives have intertwined to serve our people. The greatest way to serve them now is a successful re-opening of the sacred portal. But I fear you are opposing me in this. Recently have I learned of your meetings with the High Priestess, and use of Aj Sul to convey information he gained as part of my inner circle. This appears to be an action against me. Could you not seek what you want from me directly?"

Pasah Chan drew a breath and sighed deeply.

"It was not correct, and I regret my actions and blame the feebleness of old age that clouded my mind," he said, voice tremulous. "I, too, felt our drawing apart and was too weak to summon strength for a confrontation. Joining with Matunha gave a sense of increased strength, that together we might change your course. There were never any definite plans. I was in error, I ask your forgiveness."

"First I must know more. The situation is serious: someone has taken shamanic action against my wife Lalak. She is beset with fears, nightmares and self-doubt. Such things have not troubled her for many years, and suddenly re-appeared around winter solstice. We are training intensely for the ritual, and these emotions will obstruct the process. What know you of this dark magic?"

"Nothing, I know nothing," said the priest, eyes wide. "This alarms me greatly. In our meetings, Matunha and I never discussed sending a curse. It must be her doing ... something she has done without my knowledge. She is certainly capable of conjuring a shamanic curse; that was included in her priestess training." His sagging eyelids moistened with tears as he bent his head. "Ah, my abilities have faded so much ... when younger I would have sensed such an action ... I am shamed ..."

"It is your deduction that Matunha is the one who has set these fears inside the mind of Lalak," Pakal reiterated.

"Just so, who else is capable? Once I was, but no more. And, I assure you that I did not take this action."

"No one else was involved in your meetings?"

"Only Aj Sul, but his role was to provide information. We did not reveal to him what uses we might make of it. Whether Matunha brought other priestesses into her schemes, I do not know."

Both men sat in silence, each contemplating his concerns.

"Damage has been done to my beloved wife, who is also my irreplaceable partner in re-creating the portal," Pakal murmured. "This is treasonous action; it is an act of violence against our dynasty and our city. The perpetrator will be punished."

"It must be so. All resources of mine are offered in your service. It is my heartfelt desire to again join with you to realize our people's destiny. While breath lasts, I am committed to you and your dynasty."

Pasah Chan bowed, leaning forward until his head nearly touched the floor. The effort caused him to gasp for air. Pakal quickly moved to kneel beside the High Priest, grasping his bony shoulders and helping him sit upright. After being stabilized on his pillows and finishing a coughing spell, Pasah Chan smiled feebly at Pakal.

"So you see. Breath may not last for long."

"Do not strain your self, Holy Father," said Pakal, using a term from his boyhood relationship with the priest. Pakal found a cup with water nearby and assisted his former mentor to drink.

"My heart harbors no grievance against you." Pakal gazed directly into the eyes of Pasah Chan, sending waves of compassion. "The Gods of Time take their toll upon us all. We are rejoined, you and myself. Until your days upon this earth are completed, I shall be ever near to you. And in the afterlife, we will meet in friendship again."

The High Priest crossed both arms over his chest in the Maya gesture of highest respect and bowed, not too deeply this time, in order to preserve his breath.

"What intend you regarding the High Priestess?"

"First I must break the curse placed upon Lalak. Then Matunha will face the consequences of her actions."

A small party of men climbed the steep path to the cave located high up K'uk Lakam Witz, the Fiery Water Mountain south of Lakam Ha. The venerable cave had been used by generations of seekers as a portal into liminal space, that zone between dimensions where the veil was thin. For the Maya, caves were openings to the Underworld that gave access to the mysteries of life and death, from which all things arose and into which they are drawn back, only to be reformed and born to renewed life. The cave was remote and hidden, so far from the city center that it escaped attention during the devastating Kan attack. Not many residents knew of the cave, but Pakal remembered it because of his mother's stories. Sak K'uk had made a vision quest in the cave when the city was in chaos, leaderless with smoldering ruins and desecrated shrines. It was this vision quest that invoked the Primordial Goddess Muwaan Mat, mother of the B'aakal Triad Deities, to become co-ruler of Lakam Ha with Sak K'uk as earthly representative. Manifesting the Goddess' powers on earth, Sak K'uk attained the throne, restored order in the city, and maintained the Bahlam dynasty by holding the throne for her son, Pakal.

There was a clearing in front of the cave, with several large boulders. The cave entrance was tall enough to walk through and the width of four men. Once the cave was kept by a priestly cult who assisted vision seekers, but when the last old priest died, no further attention was given to it. Roots of plants and twining lianas hung across the opening, and the smell of bat guano was strong inside.

Two attendants remained outside, to build a fire and guard the cave entrance in case the visioning of the ruler lasted into the night. The remaining two attendants accompanied Pakal into the cave. They cleared debris and dust from the floor and set up mats and an altar. These two priests were trained to assist at bloodletting and vision quests. They brought ritual implements, including the hallucinogen mushroom brew, stingray spine perforator, bark paper and censer with copal to burn the blood-soaked paper. They had bandaging for wounds and warm cloaks to cover their ruler after his ritual.

Pakal knew that blood offerings were necessary to access the Death Lords of the Underworld. For this ritual, he would draw blood from his inner thighs, another body area infused with creative energy. He could not offer blood from the penis because of the upcoming sexual alchemy for opening the portal.

The priests started a fire to one side of the altar, prepared Pakal's cushions and set the implements in position. When offered the hallucinogen to drink, Pakal sipped only a small amount. He needed to keep his wits for the Death Lord encounters, and had enough visionary experience to proceed with minimal inducement. As the priests chanted and drummed softly, Pakal felt his consciousness shifting into trance. He recited the invocation for visioning and making his self-offering. When he sensed the boundaries of physical and mental identity dissolving, he grasped the perforator and made several rapid stabs into the skin of his inner thighs. His serene expression never changed; indeed, he felt little pain in his altered state.

An attendant placed bark paper against Pakal's thighs to absorb blood, placing the strips into the censor with smoldering copal incense. Soon the paper ignited and thick smoke began curling upward. Pakal joined his consciousness with the smoke and merged with its spirals in the semi-darkness of the high-ceilinged cave. The smoke was sucked into the cave's depths and Pakal felt himself descending, looping and twisting along dank cave walls, deeper and deeper into the earth. He felt a presence, amorphous at first, but soon taking the shape of his animal spirit, his uay, the jaguar. His was a large and muscular male jaguar, body beautifully patterned with dark-eyed spots upon tawny coat. The jaguar silently grunted and he merged into its golden eyes, becoming his uay.

The jaguar bounded effortlessly through labyrinthine tunnels until it entered a huge vaulted cavern above an underground lake. Across the lake was an island with eleven shamans sitting in a circle, each with a fire in front and incense burners emitting copal smoke. As the Pakal-jaguar approached, he saw the shamans were covered by cloaks with hoods concealing their faces. A shimmering veil of dusky energy surrounded the island and prevented entry.

The Pakal-jaguar called out to the Death Lord shamans.

"Here have I come, following the Black Road to your inner sanctum.

Here am I, you know me, I am Janaab Pakal, K'uhul B'aakal Ahau.

To you have I made the blood offerings, given my sacred itz in tribute.

Here are you, and I know you.

Hear as I speak your names,

For I know your names, I can name you and call you.

Come, One Death.

Come, Seven Death.

Come, Scab Stripper.

Come, Blood Gatherer.

Come, Demon of Pus.

Come, Bone Scepter.

Come, Skull Scepter.

Come, Wing.
Come, Packstrap.
Come, Bloody Teeth.
Come, Bloody Claws."

The veil thinned and began dissolving. Pakal had spoken every one of the Death Lords' names rightly. All of their identities were accounted for, there was not a single name missed. He met their requirements to offer proper tribute, traveled the Xibalba road, and named their names. The Lords threw off their cloaks and revealed themselves. An awful stench arose, making the jaguar flare his nostrils. The Lords were a gruesome lot, with protruding eyeballs in open sockets, bony arms and legs, bloated bellies, leering skeletal grimaces, clacking teeth and rattling joints. They emitted putrid belches and vile-smelling farts. Each had a unique appearance or paraphernalia expressing their names.

The Pakal-jaguar alighted in the center of the circle, whipping its tail and dancing lightly on its hind legs. It bowed before One Death.

"Arrgh! Why come you here, Janaab Pakal?" said One Death.

"One among you knows something, a thing that I must learn."

"Why should we tell you this thing?"

"Oh, I know him," said Demon of Pus. "He came here before, and he passed the test of the Dark House. He kept the torch and cigar lit all night, but also kept them from being consumed. He knows some magic."

"This one I know also," said Bloody Claws. "He passed my test on his previous visit, he survived the Jaguar House. The hungry jaguars did not consume him, did not tear his flesh and crunch his bones. He knows magic, all right. He does jaguar magic. He mastered the fear of death."

"Well, then, Janaab Pakal who defeated two Death Lords and conquered fear of death, what will you know?" One Death, leader of the Death Lords, glared with protruding eyeballs and flashed a toothy smile in his fleshless face.

"Which among you placed a curse upon my wife, the K'uhul B'aakal Ixik? Who among you did the bidding of the priestess Matunha?"

Clacking teeth and rattling bones, guffaws and smelly farts were the responses around the circle of Death Lords.

"Hah! You are clever, Janaab Pakal. You know of her workings with us. Who will speak up? Who will admit their handiwork?" One Death glanced around the circle.

Wing rose, supporting his skeletal body on short legs with clawed feet, spreading his winged arms and baring long fangs in a hideous bat face with curled snout and red beady eyes.

"The work was mine," said Wing. "And a good curse it was, a well-placed poison to corrupt the dreams and taint the mind, the most effective entry into a being of immense strength. Only within her sorrowful memories when the guard of intention is slumbering could the vampire bat sink its fangs and place the curse."

"Ah, so I see," said Pakal. "Yes, a most incisive way. You are to be commended, although this work is evil."

"Evil is something with no meaning to us. Only you humans are troubled by such ideas," laughed Blood Gatherer.

"Hear, hear!" The other Death Lords chimed in with more laughing and farting.

"Perhaps that is so, but I live in the Middleworld and this curse is doing great harm. It is damaging an important work that we must accomplish there. Wing, I am here to have you undo the curse," said Pakal.

"Well, that is some request!" Seven Death looked surprised. "You are not a human of timid nature."

"I am also a shaman, I have powers," Pakal replied. "I am the incarnation of the Hero Twins, I am the resurrected Maize God-Hun Hunahpu. You remember what the Hero Twins did to you all, do you not? Shall I also outwit you all and kill you? I have already proven that I am capable."

"He has a point," said Demon of Pus.

"He knows what he is saying," reiterated Bloody Claws.

"Very well," said Wing. "Here is what I will do: I will reverse the curse. But remember this, Janaab Pakal: I will exact payment by taking something that is dear to you. Consider it well."

Pakal did not need to consider it. He knew the curse must be removed, whatever the price.

"I accept your terms. You must do this at once; time in our domain is of the essence, although it is meaningless here."

Wing flashed his fangs, flapped his great wings and rose high above the water, turning somersaults and screeching. Diving down, he disgorged a small hairball covered with foul slime. As it hit the water, flames of cold blue fire burst around it and consumed the hairball in a frothing and sizzling blaze. Wing re-alighted at his place in the circle, bowed mockingly to Pakal and said:

"It is done. The curse is removed. I will have my accounting with you later."

Aj Sul brought the summons to the High Priestess, and escorted her to a reception chamber in the royal residential complex. Upon entering the chamber, her instincts flew into high alert. The ruler was not present, though she had assumed the summons was from him. Instead, in the chamber was K'akmo the Warrior Chief and two burly, well-armed warriors. Aj Sul remained inside, his face noncommittal.

K'akmo was delegated the task of carrying out Pakal's sentence upon the High Priestess. The ruler provided evidence of her treasonous behavior, including his shamanic journey to meet with the Death Lords and Wing's confirmation of placing the curse on Lalak. Within a day of Wing's removal of the curse, Lalak had returned to her normal self, no longer crushed under fear and self-doubt, but readily able to control such thoughts and the emotions they raised. In another day, her confidence in carrying out the ritual surged along with feelings of positive anticipation.

The royal couple needed now to undergo a period of austerities and seclusion, the final building of their inner powers. Pakal perceived the best course was to charge his trusted Nakom with the plan he devised to bring justice with a modicum of compassion. Aj Sul was involved by his own request; he wanted to set right his earlier collusion.

K'akmo got immediately to the point.

"High Priestess Matunha, you are charged with treason against our Holy Lord and Lady. We have uncovered your traitorous actions, learned of the dark shamanic curse you placed upon Lady Lalak, and seen the disastrous effects of this curse. The Holy Lord Pakal himself verified that you did this, taking a perilous journey into the Underworld to meet with the Death Lords. Lord Wing admitted to his cooperation with you. By the Death Lord's own words you are condemned. By the extreme effort of our ruler, the curse has been reversed. For this treachery, you must die."

Matunha stared wide-eyed at the Warrior Chief, too astonished for words. Her mind was reeling: how could this have been discovered? Not even Aj Sul or Pasah Chan knew about her actions. None of her own priestesses had observed her ritual.

"How ... how did Pakal find out?" She gasped out her query.

"Do you forget that he is a shaman-ruler, one who is well-trained and highly skilled? Believe you that only the priesthood possesses such abilities? It appears you have underestimated your adversary."

Matunha admitted to herself that she had discounted Pakal's abilities. She had even underestimated her kinsman Aj Sul, thinking him a pliable simpleton, when it appeared now that he was far more astute and able to navigate court intrigue than she believed. He was obviously in Pakal's innermost circle, participating in her sentencing.

"So it appears," she said coldly. Her eyes lingered on the long knives in the waistbands of the two warriors, and the similar dagger at K'akmo's waist.

"Do you deny this accusation, or wish to say anything for yourself?"

"Have I time to consider?"

"No."

"My only desire is to spare my family. They have experienced enough grief."

"For this, I have something to offer. If you cooperate, we will make your death appear accidental. You will go into the jungle in search of a special herb, one that must be discovered by intuition and must be harvested by you alone. Make your attendant wait some distance from the jungle grove we designate. Enter there by yourself, and my snake-catcher will bring a young fer-de-lance in his basket. One bite of the yellow-jaw snake will bring you a rapid and nearly painless death. This you know, being trained in such arts. Your attendant will come searching after some time, and find your body. Your family can grieve your loss while you still hold an admired position in Lakam Ha. It will spare them the humiliation of an execution for treason."

"Pakal has agreed to this? He would not reveal the incident?"

"It is his own plan. Do not ask me why. His compassion surpasses my understanding." The Warrior Chief stared fiercely at Matunha. "Myself, I would slit your throat with my dagger and announce your treachery. Which I am now prepared to do, should you decline to cooperate."

She returned his stare, her own inner fierceness matching his. For an instant, she held an irreverent thought: They would have made a fine pair. He was as ruthless as was she.

"I accept Pakal's offer." She turned her piercing gaze at the men in the room, locking eyes momentarily with each one. "You stand here as witnesses to my final request. In this chamber, and from beyond the grave, I charge each of you to hold Pakal to his word."

They all nodded and made the hand sign for agreement.

"Is all in readiness?" Matunha asked.

"It is," K'akmo replied.

"Then let us proceed. This very day shall I seek the special herb in your designated jungle grove, and make my journey to Xibalba."

6

T he morning of the solar eclipse opened to clear blue sky once the early mist evaporated. It was the dry season and no clouds were likely to form later in the day. The highly charged and fearful *chi' ibal k'in*, "eating of the sun" would occur in perfect view. While all Mayas knew about solar eclipses, only the Solar Priests and elite ahauob understood why and how this happened, and had the abilities to appease the Lord Sun and Gods of the Night to assure that the sun's bright face would reappear. A subset of Solar Priests specialized in predicting eclipses, a more complicated task than determining times of sunrise and sunset, solstice and equinox. Determining solar eclipses involved correlating synodic lunations with the solar calendar, taking into account the movements of the earth, the sun, and the moon.

Since the orbital plane of the moon follows a five degree incline to the plane of Earth's orbit, eclipses do not happen at each full and new moon, when the moon is between the earth and the sun. The moon's body covers the sun only when it passes into the ecliptic plane at the exact time that it is correctly positioned in line with the sun and earth. Maya astronomer-priests knew this and determined the nodes when paths of moon and sun cross, occurring between every 148 and 177 days. They developed tables with complex calculations to predict solar eclipses far into the future, with remarkable accuracy. With deviations from actual eclipses as small as two to five days, these tables alerted priests when to begin nightly vigils to watch the moon's progress across the sky toward the ecliptic.

With observational fine-tuning, the day of the solar eclipse was determined. On this particular date, a near-total eclipse would be visible over the regions of B'aakal polity. The covering of the sun would begin shortly after it reached apex. The maximum covering would take place by mid-afternoon, and the eclipse would end when the sun was hovering above the western mountains. Residents of the city, nobles and commoners alike, were instructed to remain indoors during the entire eclipse cycle.

They were warned that exposure to such immense forces could damage their bodies and minds. In particular, they were forbidden to look at the sun during this time, for blindness would result. Most people were frightened enough to take heed of these warnings.

The only Lakam Ha residents who ventured out on the day of solar eclipse were the priests and priestesses with responsibilities in the portal opening ritual, the elite nobles attending it, and the warriors assigned to stand guard around the new Sak Nuk Nah to prevent intrusion. Before dawn, the primary performers of the ritual, the K'uhul B'aakal Ahau and the K'uhul Ixik, sequestered themselves in the southern chambers of the new palace complex, built into the platform on which the Sak Nuk Nah sat. From these submerged corridors, they would enter the tunnel leading to the sacred shrine. In different rooms, they kept silence and meditated. When the time drew near, each would perform personal ceremonies to invoke the creator deities.

The new Sak Nuk Nah gleamed brilliant white in the midday sun. It had several characteristics that set it apart from other buildings at Lakam Ha. Its façade was nearly vertical while other structures had a ten-degree incline. The roof had a steeper slope but had no roofcomb; it was the only ceremonial building without one. Most unusual was its white exterior. Nearly all other structures in the city were painted deep red-orange. This white coating reflected its name, White Skin House. Painted on the white exterior walls in long columns were medallions, quatrefoil flowers, eye motifs, and geometric forms colored blue and orange. The images denoted ritual substances, precious itz-infused things that aided the ahau to cross boundaries between dimensions.

Three doors opened along the front façade, with two Ik' windows in a T-shape that denoted wind or breath. In all, there were ten Ik' windows in the sacred shrine, the most of any structure in the city. These windows symbolized the connection between breath and soul, the intentional use of breath techniques to unite physical with divine. Above the eaves were stone slabs carved to resemble thatch, reminiscent of humbler abodes of commoners and linking the sacred shrine to its purpose in fulfilling their needs. A short stairway running the full length of the building led up to the chambers within.

In the primary chamber, the wide flat throne, long as a man's height, had glyphs and images carved along three sides of the seat. These related the story of Pakal's accession, his ancestry and his son's succession. In the front center was a carving of his mother Sak K'uk wearing a cormorant headdress, acknowledging her central role in securing rulership for her son. The throne was supported by thick legs decorated with creator deities holding water lilies containing turtle carapace symbols. These linked Pakal to the Maize God as First Father who was resurrected from the watery Underworld through the turtle's carapace. Fine jaguar pelts and plush pillows covered the seat. On the wall behind the throne were several lines of glyphs depicting Gods and ancestors.

The plaza in front of the Sak Nuk Nah was lined with elite nobles invited to the ceremony. These included the ruler's family and closest courtiers, his warrior chief and primary warriors, and representatives of the High Priest who was too weak to attend. An elder priestess of Ix Chel stood in for the recently deceased High Priestess. At the edge of the upper courtyard, a set of wide stairs descended to the next level platform where a line of guards were posted, their eyes turned outward toward the vast plaza of several levels stretching to the west. Priests and priestesses who served as musicians were stationed on the upper stairway leading to the primary chamber of the sacred shrine.

All was in readiness. All waited in hushed quiet, eyes cast down to avoid looking at the sun. Even the creatures of jungle trees and grassy meadows kept their silence, as if anticipating the momentous event about to transpire. The main Ah K'in gazed through a stone slab with only the thinnest slit at its center; a special viewing device that allowed him to follow the progress of the solar eclipse without permitting destructive light rays to damage his eyes. He detected the early movement of a shadow at the edge of the sun's blazing orb, and signaled to begin the ceremony. Drummers started a slow, stately cadence. A messenger departed around the courtyard edge to inform the royal couple's attendants. The eclipse of the sun was in progress.

Pakal went first through the tunnel that physically connected the Middleworld to the Underworld, passing under archways bearing stucco sculptures of the two halves of the Cosmic Monster, the Celestial Caiman. This primordial being, an immense crocodilian creature with mouths at both ends, had been used to fashion the earth and the sky by creator deities. This great snake-crocodile-monster could be seen in night skies as the Milky Way. At one mouth was the north portal for souls to enter the earth, to be born in the Middleworld, called the Crocodile Tree or Raised-Up-Sky-World-Tree, the place of soul resurrection. This portal appeared when the Milky Way stood upright in its north-south position in the sky. At the other mouth was the south portal, the gate of death and entrance to the Underworld, called the Black Transformer or the White Bone Snake-Centipede; the place of soul pilgrimage through harrowing Xibalba realms, where one's soul could be dissolved and lost or transformed and reborn. This portal appeared when the Milky Way was lying down flat in an east-west position, stretched over the rim of the horizon.

Lalak followed Pakal after a short interval, walking lightly through the cool tunnel, bare feet softly touching the floor. Through the soles of her feet, pulsating energies of the Underworld ascended into her body, the power of the Earth Creator, the Crocodile-Snake-Wizard deity. She gazed upward and paid homage to the Cosmic Monster then climbed the stairs into the southwest chamber where Pakal stood, waiting. Momentarily their eyes met and his lips curved in the slightest smile: a final encouragement before his consciousness was absorbed completely into the Cosmic Creator-First Father-Sun and Lightning-Thunder Deities. Her eyes returned the love emanating from his being. She released herself into the Deep Earth Mother-Crocodile-Serpent of Creation.

In the courtyard, sunlight was beginning to dim slightly. Musicians added the deep thuds of large turtle carapace drums and eerie wooden flute melodies. As several conches were blown, Lalak appeared at the central doorway to begin the dance of re-creation. Tall and stately, her appearance drew awed gasps from observers. Her body was covered by a black cape with blue borders embroidered with water motifs of waterlilies, frogs, fish. A matching waistband with a blue and green beaded fringe held the cape closed. Her bare feet and arms were painted red and decorated with black twisting bands of scales. The red color covered her face and neck where black vines circled up to her cheeks. White fangs hung from the corners of her mouth, and her eyes were painted to resemble the fierce glare of a snake.

Lalak's headdress was small to allow vigorous dancing, and repeated the Earth Crocodile-Snake and water motifs. Above her forehead rested the Waterlily Serpent with its long, down-turned reptilian snout, a bound waterlily pad and blossom on its head, and a tail extending upward. Watery vegetative symbols hung around the side headband with stylized fish and frogs, and more waterlily stems and pods waved above. She wore little jewelry: simple water-drop blue-green jade earspools and a single strand necklace.

She gazed at the group bordering the courtyard, their faces indistinct to her hallucinogen-altered vision. A small part of her awareness was grateful for that. Taking a deep inbreath, she raised her arms and began the sinuous movements of the snake dance. Snakes, crocodiles, and centipedes denoted portals to the Underworld, and also manifested solar fire deep within the earth. These were ancient symbols of resurrection and apotheosis to the

Maya. The color red depicted both their creative fire and ability to draw blood, the itz of all created life. Dance was considered a physical act that put these processes into motion; it expedited the embodiment of the creator deities and brought their actions into manifestation.

With carefully timed steps keeping a drumbeat rhythm, she made toe-heel movements typical of Maya dancing. Her arms followed a series of fluid motions with hand gestures, wrists bent backward and fingers extended into changing configurations. Sometimes above her head, at other times near the waist, her hands moved toward and away from each other and her body. Slowly she danced across the stairs in a snaking pattern, entering the courtyard and dancing into the center. There she held a swaying pose, continuing the toe-heel steps and arm-hand motions.

The drum cadence changed to a quicker pace carried forward by hollow wooden tubes of varying sizes, making high pitched sounds in counterpoint to the turtle carapace drums. Shrill clay flutes joined the softer wooden ones, making sounds resembling bird calls. Multiple rain sticks created the ambiance of a downpour while bone instruments reproduced the sharp cracks of lightning.

Pakal appeared at the central doorway, his appearance also drawing exclamations of awe. His body was covered by a white cloak, its borders decorated with pale blue sky bands representing the moving stars, sun and moon. Golden zigzags of lightning shot down all sides of the cloak. His headdress, also small enough for dancing, brought together motifs of the lineage creator-resurrection deity K'awill, the rain-lightning-thunder God Chaak and the young Maize God Yum K'ax.

A small image of K'awiil rose in the headdress above Pakal's forehead. The long-nosed deity had a cosmic loop in its round eyes, and a smoking celt piercing its forehead that denoted the moment when lightning struck and filled him with divine itz. Long white feathers curled out to represent smoke, and golden tendrils spiked behind for sparks. One leg turned into a serpent whose mouth transmitted lightning to the earth plane along with blood-dotted clouds of itz. It showed the shattering power of a lightning strike to transform matter and consciousness, to bring both death-dealing and life-bearing energies, to rend the portal to the soul.

The headdress also contained a quatrefoil stone representing Chaak that spouted blue feathers for watery outpourings. Elements of the Maize God finished its symbolism with waving green cornstalks and small husks from which corn silk emerged. Pakal held a snake-handled axe in one hand, another Chaak symbol. He wore a small turtle pectoral that represented the Maize God emerging from the cracked turtle carapace into the Middleworld.

The Maya immediately recognized the symbolism of Pakal's attire as central elements of creation mythology, and his dance as one that brought about rebirth and resurrection.

Using the toe-heel step and arm-hand movements that invoked elements of solar fire, lightning, rain, and thunder, Pakal danced across the stairway. Yellow zigzags were painted below his eyes and red solar discs decorated his cheeks. Several lightning streaks went the length of his arms, and his bare feet were covered with white circles signifying stars. Once he completed the dancing descent onto the courtyard, he made several circles around the periphery then moved to face Lalak in the center.

The music stopped and silence hung expectantly over the courtyard. During the royal couple's dances, the moon's shadow gradually crossed over the sun, casting an uncanny orange-hued light that gilded the Sak Nuk Nah with gold. A palpable sense of apprehension mixed with anticipation among the observers. As Pakal and Lalak stood motionless, facing each other, two attendants came forward and loosened their waistbands, slowly slipping off their cloaks and taking Pakal's axe. With sharply drawn in-breaths, observers beheld their Holy Lord and Lady naked before them.

Lalak's body was completely painted red. Climbing up her legs were black bands of serpent scales, which encircled her body and wrapped around her breasts. A serpent head opened its fanged jaws just above her vulva. On Pakal's legs and body were multiple yellow lightning strikes cleaving into white smoke curls. Scattered among these were round red sun discs. Along each side of his erect penis were seven white circles that represented moving stars and the body's energy centers. The circles were called *muluc*, the reunion of everything.

A single drum took up the heartbeat of earth. Slowly, sensuously, Pakal and Lalak danced with their movements and gestures mirroring each other. They danced closer, arms intertwining then releasing, her legs wrapping over his then sliding away, bodies turning to brush together then move apart. As darkness deepened, the drumbeat intensified and the dancers moved energetically, twirling and prancing. Timing was of essence; their sexual joining must occur and complete during maximum eclipse, when the moon's shadow occluded the sun's brilliance. Only their complete absorption into the deities of creation would permit such exact timing.

They were completely possessed by the deities, lost in the overwhelming power of divine communion. She *was* Itzam Cab Ayin, the Earth Creator, Crocodile-Snake-Wizard, the Deep Earth Mother and Former of Life. He *was* K'awill, Lightning-Struck-Serpent-Footed Creator;

Chaak, Bringer of Life-Giving Fluids and Yum K'ax, Young-Maize-Reborn, the Sky Father Creator and Seed of Renewed Life.

Together they danced toward the stairs; Lalak went up first to the throne and lay across the jaguar pelts and pillows. When Pakal reached the top stairs, he turned toward the courtyard and raised both arms toward the darkened sun, now surrounded by a glowing orange-gold halo. Eyes closed, he spread his arms wide and filled his body with the mighty potency of this itz-permeated moment. His fingers were spread like lightning rods to draw down the solar and stellar energy. His body pulsated to the frantic drum rhythm, about to explode.

Sensing the moment of maximum creative potential, Pakal turned to the throne, his eruptive cosmic energy irresistibly drawn to Lalak's waiting cave of deep earth, filled with heat of incubation and liquid of life. The Infinite Cosmos, Light of Sun and Stars, plunged into the Witz Cave-Receptive Earth Darkness. Light joined dark, celestial joined earthly, propulsive release was absorbed into fathomless receptivity. The drums blasted a thrusting rhythm until lightning starbursts completed their celestial seeding into the depths of fertile underground.

In the thunderous drumbeat accompanied by high ululations of priestesses, Pakal collapsed over Lalak and she held him tightly to her. Both sensed the vortex within the Sak Nuk Nah beginning to move deep inside the earth below. This whirlpool gradually increased, rising upward into the chamber, rocking their bodies with its swirling motion, soaring upward through the roof and into the sky above. It was a mighty vortex, ringing in their ears, singing of new life. A thin thread ascended through the vortex, a thread of liminal space that was the newborn opening of the sacred portal to the deities and ancestors.

Pakal lifted his head from Lalak's shoulder to gaze into her eyes. Though still possessed by the creator deities, a small spark of self-awareness returned.

"Do you feel it?" he whispered.

"Yes," she breathed into his ear. "The portal, rising in the vortex. Tiny, but it is there."

He kissed her tenderly, oblivious of everything around them. She smiled back, tears sparkling in her eyes. They had accomplished it. They remembered, and so the Gods remembered and the vortex responded. Their love for each other, for their people, and for the Gods had brought forth a new creation. Together their sexual alchemy had enjoined the tiny intertwined serpents of life, the crystalline double helix of star seed origin, and planted the seed of a new Jeweled Sky Tree. The Wakah Chan Te', a new portal was forming. It was there, deep inside Lalak's body and deep within the cave of Mother Earth; the tree's just-conceived roots already beginning to burrow into nourishing Underworld darkness.

Sunlight slowly brightened the courtyard as the moon shadow moved away. Priests and priestesses, nobles and warriors, exhaled in relief. Once again the *chi' ibal k'in*, "eating of the sun" was passing and light returning to their world. Pakal's attendant appeared at the central doorway, giving the hand signal for "it is accomplished." The Ah K'inob later recorded the momentous solar eclipse at which the Jeweled Sky Tree was re-seeded and the sacred portal re-opened.

Baktun 9, Katun 10, Tun 17, Uinal 4, Kin 19, on the date 6 Kawak 2 Kumk'u (February 6, 650 CE).

Tz'aakb'u Ahau—VI

Baktun 9 Katun 11 Tun 0
Baktun 9 Katun 11 Tun 6
652 CE—659 CE

K an Bahlam perched on the flat roof of the observatory structure in the Temple of the High Priest. His head was thrown back and eyes affixed on the vast canopy of twinkling lights in the blackness overhead. He loved the stars; he was born to study them, to know their secrets, to read their messages. At this time of year, following fall equinox and the rainy season, clouds rarely obscured the sky. Moving stars and constellations were clearly visible in their luminous glory. Even without moonlight, the night was bright enough to easily walk the white roads of Lakam Ha. Viewing the stars was best on nights like this, when the moon hung as a thin crescent on the southern horizon.

The most prominent constellations overhead were Tzek K'anal, with its triangle body and long arched scorpion-tail, and fish-snake Chay Kan forming two half loops from its small triangle body. The great Cosmic Monster stretched its crocodile-centipede form of milky whiteness nearly vertically in mid-sky, forming the Wakah Chan Te' or Upright Sky Tree. As the night progressed it would gradually tilt and dip down toward the horizon, becoming the Black Transformer-White Bone Snake, the canoe of death taking the departed into the Underworld. The young man's favorite wandering star, Yaax Ek (Jupiter) winked saucily at him as it moved slowly south. He also identified the movements of Noh Ek (Venus) and Xux Ek (Mercury). He knew all their names, the wandering stars and constellations, the star clusters that told of his people's origins and destiny.

Although he wanted to stay all night star-watching, Kan Bahlam needed to get some sleep before the morning's important ceremony. His father would perform the katun-end rituals for the ending of Katun 10 and beginning of Katun 11. This was the first major calendar ceremony done in the new Sak Nuk Nah; the first opportunity to use the nascent portal that his parents had re-opened two years earlier. Though Kan Bahlam had not attended the ceremony, for reasons he understood given its sexual nature, he had obtained detailed descriptions from priests who were present. What he heard excited him, kindled the flames of passion that his virile young body found increasingly difficult to contain.

Now at the age of seventeen solar years, he had been training with the Lunar Priestesses for two years. These priestesses devoted their lives to sexual education for young ahauob, providing both skills of sexual performance and an outlet for young men's drives. Already he was tired of these dispassionate women, who approached their work with emotional coolness. The fire in his veins yearned for more intensity, for emotional ecstasy along with physical release. At social events or walking through the city, his eyes wandered to the nubile young women who were around in abundance. He desired them, all of them. The mores of his culture forbade indiscriminate sex and disapproved of premarital affairs, but he was not much troubled by this. His passions were gargantuan, everything from delicious food to exquisite art to yearning for knowledge. The sensuous bodies of young women and their dewy freshness aroused torrents of desire, and he was loath to deny himself.

With a sigh, Kan Bahlam stood up and stretched his long limbs. Not yet fully grown, he was already exceptionally tall with a heavier body than his father. His thighs and torso were thickly muscled, his arms and shoulders bulging. He had inherited his mother's coarse features, sporting a huge arched nose and thick prominent lips. The upper lip curved sensuously while the lower lip protruded out, often hanging slightly open as if waiting to imbibe something delicious. His face was a long oval, resembling his father but with flatter cheekbones, large tilted almond eyes and a strong chin.

While Kan Bahlam would not be called handsome, his was a face of strength and intensity combined with voluptuousness. It was a commanding face that few could forget.

In the morning, he met his brother Waknal Bahlam in the temple dining chamber where they took the early meal with priests, acolytes and other noble youths in training. Over bowls of maize gruel cooked with tomatoes, chiles, and herbs, the brothers discussed events.

"Know you anything of Father's plans for the ceremony today?" asked Waknal Bahlam.

"Not the specifics of his offerings to the Triad Deities," Kan Bahlam answered. "These depend upon what the portal will allow, and he must determine that from his trance meditations beforehand. He has been in seclusion many days, preparing for the ceremony."

"He will do the bloodletting ritual, is that not so?"

"Just so, of that I am certain. Such a momentous calendar date requires no less, and he must seek the Vision Serpent to receive predictions for the coming katun. It is my understanding that Mother will also let blood, to magnify the potency of *itz* for the occasion."

"Ah." Waknal Bahlam thought about his mother drawing blood from her tongue and shuddered. "Fortunate are we to be spared this act."

Kan Bahlam shrugged and kept eating.

"All rulers must do it, and often their consorts. We will be required to perform bloodletting during our transformation to adulthood rites," he added.

"These are yet two years away for me," said Waknal Bahlam, who was a year younger. "Will you take your transformation next year?"

"Perhaps, or perhaps I shall wait so we may do this rite together. There is something I wish to accomplish first. I have been thinking to do the jaguar quest. Even though this manhood rite has been largely abandoned at our city, it calls to me. Why not resurrect it? To hunt a jaguar in the jungle, to kill it and return with its pelt, would be a great adventure. We could do the jaguar quest together."

Waknal Bahlam was not certain this risky adventure held much appeal. But he admired his older brother and wanted his approval.

"Indeed, that would be an adventure and a major accomplishment," he said.

"After the katun end ceremony, I will speak to Father about it. As spring equinox approaches, toward the end of the dry season, jaguars come closer to the rivers. That would be a good time for hunting them."

"So it would. It would give us time to prepare." Waknal Bahlam felt uneasy but saw no way to avoid following his determined brother's wishes.

They finished the meal and returned to their chambers to don ceremonial attire. Joining a stream of priests, they walked along sakbeob from the Temple of the High Priest at the farthest western edge of the ridge to the wide plazas of the new city center at the easternmost end.

Lakam Ha was buzzing with excitement, its population swollen by visitors from near and far who had come for the katun end ceremony. Word of the K'uhul B'aakal Ahau's accomplishment in re-opening the sacred portal had spread, garnering much admiration for both the ruler and his wife. Their use of sexual alchemy added to the innovation for which Lakam Ha was becoming known. Among the visitors were architects and stonemasons, carvers and painters, calendar priests and wizards, scribes and knowledge keepers, musicians and dancers. The new constructions at Lakam Ha with their unusual angles and airy roofcombs, and the use of extensive underground tunnels for water management caught the imagination of many. Exquisite carvings of realistic images and flowing lines of hieroglyphic writing brought Maya art to a new height. The city's archives of bark-paper codices and lengthy well-documented history held treasures for knowledge-seekers. Music, dance, costumes, and culinary arts all bespoke excellence and attracted artisans from great distances.

The large plaza now held several structures in addition to the palace complex, composed of the Sak Nuk Nah and its adjourning Royal Court and Council House buildings. The North Temple was completed and rose in stately tiers to its chamber for priestly rituals. At the northeastern edge, an educational complex contained a smaller pyramid and line of three low-ceilinged buildings with multiple small rooms. These were for study and training, a school of arts and knowledge. A small ball court sat on a lower level between the palace complex and the school. Beginning construction for a large residential complex immediately east of the palace was visible. It was situated next to the eastern end of the underground aqueduct, where the Otulum River resumed its natural flow over a rocky bed before falling in cascades down the steep escarpment.

The city of many waters was growing more impressive each year. Now its spiritual charter was revived as Pakal resumed katun end ceremonies that had been truncated since the collapse of the portal.

The courtyard facing the Sak Nuk Nah was reserved for the royal family, select elite nobles and members of the priesthood. On the plaza below the west stairway, thousands of residents and visitors gathered. Although they could not see into the sacred shrine where the ceremony would be performed, they sensed the energy and attuned their awareness to the momentous event. A line of warriors at the courtyard edge remained inconspicuous in ceremonial clothing but kept weapons handy. Disruption of the ceremony was unlikely, but K'akmo wanted this contingency covered.

Pakal and Lalak remained sequestered in the underground chambers until it was time for the ceremony. He wore the costume of Maize God-First Father-Yum K'ax and she represented Mother Earth Goddess-Ix Chel-Ix Azal Uoh. They passed through the tunnel, beneath the stucco sculptures of the Cosmic Monster, and up the steps to the south chamber of the Sak Nuk Nah. Together they entered the central throne chamber to drumming and music, as dancers whirled on the stairs in front. Behind them followed several attendants carrying bundles, the gifts to the Gods.

The new High Priest Ib'ach, who had succeeded Pasah Chan after his death the prior year, and the new High Priestess Yaxhal, who had replaced Matunha after her unfortunate death by snake bite, stood inside the central chamber. Also within the chamber were the ruler's family, including the four sons, several cousins and his closest courtiers. Lalak's brother Bahlam Ahau and his family were also there.

After the royal couple entered the throne chamber, they appeared at the outside doorway, arms raised and hands upheld in blessing gestures. Cheers of the nobles crowding the courtyard joined conches, whistles and drums.

Pakal recited the tradition-steeped opening words for the katun end ceremony.

"It is the k'altun, the stone seating, the binding of the tun.
It is the tribute, the celestial burden, the earthly burden.
As in times of the ancestors, as in times of the Gods,
The gifts will be given, the names will be called, the days will be kept.
It is the requirement, the penance of the K'uhul Ahau.
Now shall we seat the stones of the katun, the precious k'altun.
It is the k'altun of 12 Ahau 8 Keh.
It is the eleventh katun. Twelve becomes ahau.
The patron of the katun is 12-Ahau, Kalahun Ahau."

The priestly chorus repeated the last three lines that demarcated the presiding lord, specific dates and numeric components of the time period. Pakal's next recitation took a different turn, as he described the events that happened during the re-opening of the portal. He spoke of the "tree births" and referred to them as the *ikatz*, the burden or charge of the earth and sky. He spoke of presenting adornments to dress the three sky Gods, Lords of the First Sky, exactly those Gods whose offerings could not be given when the portal was collapsed, at the katun end ceremony conducted by Sak

K'uk-Muwaan Mat. Then he spoke of giving gifts to the Triad Deities, the B'aakal patron Gods, bundles that contained special hats. In the final line, Pakal informed his people that now he could tie on himself the white paper headband, the ultimate symbol of rulership, as he sat on the throne that was also an altar to the Triad Gods.

"The Jeweled Sky Tree was born of the earth; the Wakah Chan Te' was born of the earth and the sky.
It was their ikatz, the celestial burden, the earthly burden.
There is a necklace; there are earspools.
The 9 Chan Yoch'ok'in, 16 Ch'ok'in, 9 Tz'ak Ahau.
It happens on the 12 Ahau katun.
It is overseen by the katun incense-offerer K'inich Janaab Pakal, K'uhul B'aakal Ahau.
He gives the sacrificial bowl hat; it is the bundle of Hun Ahau, First-Born of the Triad Deities.
He gives the K'ak Chanal Huh Chaak hat; it is the bundle of Mah Kinah Ahau, Second Born of the Triad Deities.
He gives the white paper hat; it is the bundle of Unen K'awill, Third Born of the Triad Deities.
The juntan-beloved of the Gods, K'inich Janaab Pakal, K'uhul B'aakal Ahau takes the white paper headband on the throne of the Triad Deities."

The nobles in the courtyard and inside the chamber joined the priestly chorus in repeating Pakal's titles and names:
"Juntan of the Gods, K'inich Janaab Pakal, K'uhul B'aakal Ahau!"
Pakal lifted his arms in blessing, then turned and repeated the gesture for all present in the chamber. He walked regally to his seat on the dynastic throne, its carvings proclaiming his descent from the Creator Gods and his access to Gods and ancestors through the conduit that the portal provided to the sky realms. Lalak in her persona as Tz'aakb'u Ahau, K'uhul Ixik settled on a mat next to the throne. The others inside the chamber also sat upon their mats. It would be a long ritual.
Ib'ach the High Priest came forward and presented the white headband to Pakal. Attendant priests wafted copal smoke over the headband as Pakal lifted it and then slowly wound it around his head, adding it to his feathered headdress. As he tied it in place, all present chanted his name and title reverently.

Attendants brought forth several bundles wrapped in white cloth, bloodletting implements and copal censers. Lalak received the bundles for the Lords of the First Sky and chanted their gifting invocation.

"Lords of the First Sky, Lords of the Jeweled Tree born of earth and celestial vault, the shining tree of precious gems that reaches from the Middleworld of people to the Upperworld of spirits, it is I your earthly daughter, Tz'aakb'u Ahau, who makes this offering. You are the Jewels of the First Sky, your beauty and radiance is beyond compare, you are perfect. Yet you may enjoy further adornment, so I offer you these beauties of our world, these precious resplendent gems to match your magnificence. Receive, Holy Ones, these offerings."

She opened each bundle carefully and lifted in succession three sets of necklaces and earspools, each selected to match the individual Sky God's qualities.

6 Chan Yoch'ok'in, whose name meant "sky you possess/enter the sun" was offered a necklace of rose-hued spondylus shell and red coral, and earspools of matching red coral carved with the sun glyph.

16 Ch'ok'in, whose name meant "emergent young sun" was offered a necklace of gold beads and amber, with round amber earspools carved with the sun glyph.

9 Tz'ak Ahau, whose name meant "conjuring lord" was offered a necklace of dark green jade and obsidian, with matching jade earspools carved with the glyph for conjuring.

Attendants took the jewelry from Lalak, re-wrapped each set in its white cloth bundle, and put these in front of the altar-throne. Pakal signaled attendants to bring forth his bundles for the Triad Gods. He took each bundle, unwrapped it and lifted the hat it contained, chanting the Triad God's name while making the headdress offering that was renewed each katun by ancient custom.

The sacrificial bowl hat for Hun Ahau was an inverted ceramic bowl painted with exquisite motifs of dancing other-worldly creatures holding implements for bloodletting, including a perforator bone of stingray spine, bark paper burning in censers, and a rope with embedded thorns. Copal smoke curled into Vision Serpents between the dancers.

A Chaak hat was given to Mah Kinah Ahau with a golden, white, and red woven headband supporting flaming scarlet macaw feathers, representing the fire of the sun, mixed with blue feathers for water. White shell discs along the headband symbolized the full moon. These were motifs of the underworld sun-jaguar.

The white paper hat for Unen K'awill had a tall domed shape, white cloth wrapped around artfully with arching feathery white plumes and jaguar skin bands around the base. Ahau face glyphs were attached over the forehead, to symbolize the God's dynastic significance as patron of rulers.

The three hats were taken by attendants and placed in front of the altar-throne. All these offerings would be buried later in a crypt built into the floor of the chamber. Drummers began a solemn cadence as Pakal and Lalak prepared for bloodletting. Attendants positioned ceramic bowls with copal incense at their feet and brought needle-sharp stingray spines. They held strips of bark paper and censers of hot coals ready to set fire to the paper.

The royal pair was already in trance state, having taken hallucinogens and pain-numbing herbs. Pakal proceeded without hesitation, his awareness separated from his body, making several stabs into his penis without any sign of discomfort. His attendant caught dripping blood with paper strips, placed them in the bowl and lit the fire, sending a stream of fragrant copal smoke mixed with the sharp smell of blood into the air.

Lalak waited, concentrating with eyes closed. This was her first bloodletting, and although she was completely trained, she felt hesitant. It was such a crucial act, to be accomplished in full supplication to the deities. Upon it might rest the success of re-establishing communication through the young portal, not yet fully developed. She must keep her self-offering pure, not blemish it with any sign of pain, not minimize it with any holding back. Breathing deeply to focus awareness, she projected her consciousness into the celestial domain. Another part of her mind summoned fierce determination. In the final moment, it was her devotion to Pakal that commanded action.

Gripping the needle tightly, she grasped the tip of her tongue with the other hand and pulled it forward, then quickly stabbed the needle upward from the bottom. A thin thread embedded with thorns was attached to the needle; this would keep blood flowing. Without flinching, she pulled the needle and thread completely through her tongue, and blood fell in rapid droplets onto bark paper her attendant held. Her face remained serene by the grace of the starry Gods, though in recesses of awareness her brain registered pain. It was small and distant pain, fading into the glorious celestial dance surrounding her.

Smoke rose from the ceramic bowl, undulating into the Vision Serpent, whose large jaws gaped wide. Lalak was stunned by its iridescent scaly patterns, glowing slit eyes and elaborate jaw foliations. She watched the serpent sway and curl, morphing back into smoke and then resuming its visionary form. Gratitude swept through her heart, for she knew the Vision Serpent could not appear unless the portal provided by the Jeweled Sky Tree was in place. The portal was there, large enough to sustain the serpent. She knew Pakal must also be seeing his serpent.

Lalak waited for the Vision Serpent's message. Even if it brought none, she would be content. Pakal would receive the katun predictions, as was always the ruler's prerogative and obligation. Her message, if any, was secondary.

The Vision Serpent opened and closed its mouth several times. It seemed to be dissolving, but took shape again and from its gaping jaws a face emerged, the face of Sak K'uk. Lalak gazed into her mother-in-law's eyes, the face now luminescent in its ancestral spirit form. The spirit said no words, but Lalak's awareness received a strong message of approval, even admiration. She bowed her head in gratitude.

The blood-soaked paper in both bowls burned down to ashes and the columns of smoke dissipated. Those present in the chamber felt growing tension as attendants removed the bloodletting paraphernalia and wrapped cloaks around the royal couple's shoulders. Still seated on the throne, Pakal called to the Triad Deities again, performing hand signs that invoked the Gods to accept their hats. All eyes were riveted upon the ruler. It was a moment of truth. Was the portal open enough and sufficiently permeated with itz to give the Gods a pathway into the Middleworld? Had the Vision Serpent appeared and communicated about the coming katun?

In complete silence, the drums stilled, all present waited for a sign. Within moments, a cold breeze swept through the chamber. Even the least intuitive among them could not fail to sense the uncanny chill of other-worldly presences. Hair lifted on necks, gooseflesh rose on arms, chills ran up spines. The eerie energy was palpable, frightening and exhilarating at once. None present doubted that the Triad Gods were within the chamber, claiming their headdresses.

Pakal made hand signs for greeting and homage. Priests chanted softly to welcome the deities. Swirls of cool air ruffled edges of huipils and loincloths, causing feathers in headdresses to flutter. The nobles joined the priests, chanting until the other-worldly presences began to dissipate. After the ambiance in the chamber returned to normal, Pakal stood and walked to the front doorway to deliver the katun predictions that he had received from the Vision Serpent.

Katun 11 would be a time of great expansion for Lakam Ha. The city would take on a new shape, its center relocated to the wide plazas on the eastern meadow. It would present a new face to the polity, the splendid visage of soaring temples and impressive complexes, sparkling waters and graceful panels. As a nucleus of creative arts and intellectual achievements, it would attract visitors from far distant places and spark an exchange of ideas and goods unseen before. People of all station would prosper, the crops and orchards would produce abundantly, life would expand in many ways. Lakam Ha and its allies would be victorious in battle. This katun would see the beloved city of the B'aakal Triad Deities attain the peak of excellence; its date carved on monuments.

Baktun 9, Katun 11, Tun 0, Uinal 0, Kin 0, on the day 12 Ahau 8 Keh (October 14, 652 CE).

The Gods had spoken through the newly opened portal, through the resurrected Wakah Chan Te', through the Vision Serpent sent to the ruler, and they had bestowed largesse upon their people.

Shortly after the katun end ceremonies, Pakal mounted an exquisite oval tablet above the throne in the Sak Nuk Nah. Created by his most talented carvers, the rounded relief depicted a new view of the transfer of rulership. Framed by a carved jaguar skin pattern, the tablet showed Pakal receiving the drum major headdress from his mother, Sak K'uk. This unusual headdress with columns of round discs and soaring feathers symbolized the ruler's power and authority. Pakal was simply dressed, wearing a sun God pectoral medallion, sitting on a double-headed jaguar throne, the traditional symbol of Maya rulership. Sak K'uk wore the traditional mat dress and shawl of rulers. Both were depicted as young adults in their prime, named by nearby glyphs. The intimacy of this accession scene, and its focus on the act of transferring power rather than the actors, was a striking innovation. This famous work captured for eternity the moment of Pakal's inauguration and, when viewed through the doorway of the Sak Nuk Nah, placed him sitting forever on the ruler's throne in front of his people.

2

Late in the dry season following the Katun 11 ceremony, Pakal and Lalak's two older sons ventured forth on their jaguar quest. Both young men had trained with expert spear-throwers, learning the speed and precision required to down a jaguar. Most hunters would have only one chance to throw, for the canny beasts either escaped or attacked if that spear missed its mark. Hunters had little hope of surviving if a wounded jaguar descended upon them; their hand knives were no match for slashing claws and long fangs. Experienced hunters taught methods of finding and stalking the largest jungle predator, secrets of locating their lairs and staying upwind of their acute sense of smell. Few had ever hunted jaguars; one elderly man told frightening tales from childhood memories of the prey becoming the predator.

Kan Bahlam felt exhilarated by the challenge; Waknal Bahlam felt intimidated but kept his fears hidden. As her sons left with their small group of hunter assistants and porters, Lalak felt apprehensive but made no objection, since Pakal had given his approval for the expedition. It was a time-honored tradition of proving one's worth to sit upon the jaguar throne, he reminded her. His great-grandfather, the namesake of their eldest son, had been the last of their dynasty to make the jaguar quest. It was time for this proof of manhood and badge of rulership to be reinstated.

Lalak was not convinced. A deep intuition warned her, one she could not heed, but that proved true. After an agonizing absence of nearly a moon cycle, the hunting party returned. Kan Bahlam strutted into the city proudly, his bearers carrying a magnificent jaguar pelt upon two poles. Waknal Bahlam was carried on a litter into the city, mortally wounded by a jaguar mauling. His spear had not sped to its mark and the wounded jaguar in its fury had pounced upon him before attendants could intervene, covering his body and face with deep gashes. Blood loss and fever drained his body of its resilience and he was comatose upon return. Despite ceaseless ministrations by the city's most skilled healers, who applied remedies continuously day and night, the second son of Pakal and Lalak died after two days.

Lalak's grief knew no bounds. Waknal Bahlam was especially dear to her, his sweet and kind ways in stark contrast to his brother's arrogance. She should never have allowed him to do the jaguar quest. It was not in his nature. Why had she not acted? Her self-blame was a dead weight on her heart. Adding to this agony was the new perception she had of her eldest son. He continued to exult in his victorious jaguar quest even as his brother lay dying. Who was this man? This callous stranger, whom she thought she knew, but now left her dumbfounded.

How could it have happened? This child of her loins, conceived in the most exquisite love-making of her life, during that golden afternoon in the magic glen when she felt Pakal's heart finally open to her. It was the beginning of their true union in precious loving embrace. Kan Bahlam, child of their consummated love. An enigma and unfathomable man of dark appetites and perplexing emotions. She heard things about him, things she did not want to believe—his lust for young women, his multiple liaisons with daughters of nobles and commoners alike, even hints that he was amorous with young men who were "two souls" and crossed the realms of the sexes.

Pakal also grieved for his son, but soon had political conflicts to distract him. Messengers brought news that Sak Nikte', a small city at the edge of the polity situated on a major trade route, was welcoming ambassadors from Kan. The city had been a site of contention between Lakam Ha and Kan for katuns. Pakal was reluctant to allow this city to fall under the influence of the Snake Dynasty, and planned an attack. Trouble was also brewing at Imix-Ha again; its ruler Balaj Chan K'awiil had regrouped after Bahlam Ahau's attack five years earlier and was now undertaking campaigns against Mutul. Bahlam Ahau continued his intermittent battles with Kan ally Yokib, and even made a foray against Uxte'kuh, although Pakal doubted this long-time friendly city had given real provocation. He sent summons to his wife's brother to come for a war council.

Lalak's heart, however, refused to heal. Losing another child, the son closest to her, was an unbearable burden. She fell sick to a malady that Utzil recognized as a spiritual illness, the kind resulting from psychological suffering. The Ix Chel healer gave her mistress brews made of Chink-in, bird of paradise flowers and Pay-Che, skunk root that had powers to dispel sadness and grief, and strengthen spiritual reserves. During several moons Lalak rarely left her quarters and lost weight due to her flagging appetite. Utzil worried that this illness would further drain Lalak's depleted reserves, making her bones more fragile and her blood weaker.

As Lalak's recovery was slowly progressing, Kan Bahlam fell ill to a jungle fever that caused shaking chills and disorientation for many days. Ix Chel healers attended him with herbs and poultices, while priests performed rituals to dispel any spiritual forces present. Despite their ministrations, his fever reached life-threatening levels and his soul hovered between the worlds for much too long, by Utzil's assessment. She worried about permanent effects should he recover. When at last the fever broke, Lalak insisted that her son be brought to his palace chambers, so she could remain at his side and oversee his progress. Stroking his forehead, offering sips of nourishing broth and singing comforting songs from his childhood acted as a salve to her heart. She found her love expansive enough to forgive his shortcomings and move toward accepting his trying personality.

Kan Bahlam's recovery took over four moon cycles. He seemed to appreciate his mother's attention and they shared long conversations. When he had enough strength to be about, they took walks along city streets and remarked on the continuous building underway. Pakal joined them on occasion and pointed out structures where he planned additions or renovations. Building programs struck Kan Bahlam's imagination and he described to his mother some ideas for new complexes he would initiate when he became ruler. As his vigor returned and he regained weight lost during the fevers, Lalak sensed him pulling away emotionally and closing his enigmatic shroud around his inner thoughts. Perhaps it was his way of being his own person, or claiming his manhood in the shadow of his God-like father.

Utzil discussed Kan Bahlam's illness with elder healers and priests, seeking confirmation of what she suspected. If her knowledge held true, this type of jungle fever had a dreaded prognosis. If the sufferer survived, and only the strongest did, there was often permanent damage to the body. The heart, elimination and reproductive systems were most often affected. Early death could result from heart damage or gradual inability to eliminate fluids. If the reproductive system was affected, it could lead to sterility.

She was reluctant to bring this news to Lalak, but did not want her mistress to hear it through gossip. As a priestess healer and long time attendant to the Holy Lady, it was best that she deliver accurate information. Lalak received the news somberly; her immediate concerns were for the dynasty.

"How will this affect his ability to produce heirs?" she asked.

"That is difficult to say at present," Utzil replied. "It could be years before residual damage becomes apparent. But, if the reproductive system is affected, he may never be able to conceive a child."

"Pakal must know. He will be much dismayed. We have been discussing a suitable match for Kan Bahlam, thinking that he should marry soon. Should we proceed?"

"That is not a choice I can advise upon, Holy Lady." Utzil made the hand gesture for disengagement. "It is possible they would remain childless. This we cannot know, until conception has been attempted several times."

"These things I will discuss with Pakal." Lalak added wistfully, "Our children grow up and take their course in life. We observe and rejoice or weep for them, is this not our lot?"

"The ways of the deities are beyond our purview," Utzil murmured. "May Ix Chel comfort your heart."

When Lalak discussed the situation with Pakal, he brooded upon the requital of the deities. The Death Lord Wing was taking more than his fair share of retribution, by Pakal's measure. Surely losing his son Waknal

Bahlam to the Jungle Lord Jaguar was enough payment. Taking away his older son's ability to continue their dynasty by producing heirs would be an excessive toll. He could only hope that one son's life was enough. These dark reflections he hesitated to share with his wife, hoping to avoid greater burden for her troubled heart. But her anguish over not acting to prevent Waknal Bahlam's death prompted him to reveal the deadly bargain.

"If only I had listened to my intuition, which warned me against his jaguar quest," Lalak bemoaned. "Then our son would be with us now."

"You could not have stopped it," Pakal said. "To raise this objection would not stand well in the world of men. He was proving his masculinity, his fitness to be a leader. Unburden your heart, beloved. There is yet other reason for this loss. Of this, I have not spoken before, out of concern for your wellbeing. But recalling our pledge made years ago to be honest with each other, I will tell you now. It bears upon the shaping of our destinies, which lies in the hands of the Gods."

Pakal recounted his journey into the Underworld to undo the shamanic curse placed upon Lalak by the High Priestess Matunha. He repeated the Death Lord Wing's final words, that payment would be exacted by taking something dear.

"It did not seem wise to speak to you about this at the time," Pakal continued. "You were recovering your confidence after the curse was lifted, with only a few days remaining before enacting our ritual to re-open the portal. In the intensity of this process, the agreement with Lord Wing slipped from my mind, or perhaps I wished to forget it. Now I understand the immensity of his recompense."

Lalak allowed this information to settle into her mind. She immediately recognized the grave significance of Pakal's exchange with the Death Lord. Reaching toward him, she laid a hand over his heart.

"You had no choice, Pakal. What else could you do but accept Lord Wing's terms? Your highest obligation was to restore your city's portal to the Triad Deities and Upperworld, regardless of what it cost you and those dear to you."

His eyes were bright with unshed tears as he nodded and signed his appreciation to her. Gathering her in his arms, he whispered into her ear.

"What you give to me passes all praise. You are the perfume of my heart."

After a moment, she murmured back: "The deities have their ways, which are not sensible to us. In a mysterious manner, this gives me relief over Waknal Bahlam's death. But what of Kan Bahlam's situation?"

"Ah, that I believe is beyond the bargain with Lord Wing. But how can I forestay the God? Let us hope that all will be well with our oldest son."

Pakal and Lalak decided it was essential that Kan Bahlam marry. Their best tack was to proceed as if the disease would not have lasting effects. For the heir's consort, they selected the oldest daughter of an elite Lakam Ha family with ambitions for advancement. The family had proper purity of bloodlines but had not distinguished itself through producing notable leaders in the city. They decided against seeking a marriage alliance with a polity city, since a childless royal consort would have political repercussions and bring shame to her family. Such alliances they would seek for their two younger sons.

Talol, oldest daughter in the Chan family of Lakam Ha, was married to Kan Bahlam, Ba-ch'ok of the Bahlam dynasty, with all requisite pomp and ceremony the following year. It was an arrangement agreeable to all, with opulent bride gifts and promises of important court positions. Kan Bahlam was not displeased, for his wife was a lovely young woman, but he had no intentions of restraining his amorous pursuits. An unexpected benefit was the friendship that developed with his wife's younger brother, Chak Chan, who turned out to share Kan Bahlam's fascination with astronomy and mathematics.

Bahlam Ahau arrived in Lakam Ha shortly before Kan Bahlam's marriage ceremony. Lalak's intrepid brother made light of his raid on Uxte'kuh and deftly shifted the war council focus to containing Kan's influence on Sak Nikte'. With K'akmo and the warrior chiefs in agreement, Pakal agreed to an attack on Sak Nikte' undertaken in the middle of the rainy season. Although rivers were difficult to navigate, the site was not far from riverbanks, allowing the combined forces to avoid passing through marshes and wet jungles. Both Pakal and Kan Bahlam joined the warriors to impress upon their enemies the importance that Lakam Ha placed upon keeping trade routes open. Their strike was unexpected, sudden and brutal, the forces descending upon a sleeping city in the misty dawn and slaying most enemy warriors before they could arise and organize a defense. The ruler was subjugated and several elite nobles were captured, and an "axing" performed on city monuments in which they were "chopped down" and destroyed. Pakal left the ruler and his family in the city, with strong admonition to stay away from alliance with the Ka'an polity rulers.

Kan Bahlam reveled in his first battle. At nineteen solar years, his body had matured with bulging muscles, long thick limbs, and a powerful chest. He fought swinging a stone axe to crush heads and break legs of opponents, stabbing with a long obsidian blade in his other hand to finish them off.

The older warriors were impressed by his strength and ferociousness. The victorious forces celebrated with a march through Lakam Ha displaying their nearly-naked and bound captives, and a feast with speeches regaling feats of bravery that especially acknowledged Kan Bahlam. The date of the Sak Nikte' victory was commemorated on glyphs carved on the palace stairway.

Baktun 9, Katun 11, Tun 1, Uinal 16, Kin 3, on the date 6 Akbal 1 Yax (August 26, 654 CE).

3

K an Bahlam bounded effortlessly up the steep stairway rising to dizzying heights as it reached nearly to the crest of the tall hill on which perched the Temple of the East, Lak'in. This hill gave the best vantage point to view the new city center spreading eastward across the white expanse of the great plaza. Standing atop the temple platform with hands on hips, Kan Bahlam grinned at his panting companions as they struggled up the final set of steps.

"Ha!" he exuded. "You all need some warrior training. That will develop your lungs and thighs."

The three young men gasped to recover their breath. Chak Chan, brother-in-law to the heir, was an astronomer and scholar of science with no interest in warrior ways. Mut was a skilled stone carver and painter, and Yuhk Makab'te aspired to prominence in governance. These nobles preferred their intellectual and artistic pursuits to the rigors of warrior training, but admired the heir for his capacity to span both worlds.

"It appears we shall always lag behind you in climbing," said Chak Chan, first to recover his breath.

"Just so, but we are good at going down," said Mut with a smile.

Yuhk Makab'te nodded and wiped perspiration off his forehead.

The day was warm and clear now that the dry season had arrived. Blazing noonday sun brought the white plaza to blinding brilliance, the ruddy buildings standing in etched contrast.

"See, all of this and more yet to be built. All of this will be mine, when I am K'uhul B'aakal Ahau." Kan Bahlam swept his hand to include the entire scene below. "So much more we will build; I can already envision new complexes that will be the crowning jewels of our city. Complexes that will reflect the astronomy of our people's creation, that will encode the history of our dynasty. Perhaps my complex will be built over there."

He turned and pointed southeast to a gently sloped meadow across the Otulum River, located not far from the three buildings of the palace. The striking white walls of the Sak Nuk Nah gleamed, setting off perfectly its delicate blue and red flower symbols arranged in neat rows. His father Pakal had recently dedicated the beautiful White Skin House, now officially the ruler's throne room and sacred shrine of the Triad Deities.

"The residential complex across the river facing the palace is progressing. It will be one of the largest ever, I understand," Mut said. He was meeting with architects and builders, discussing designs for decorating the residences. He saw much opportunity to further his work there.

"Yes, and already there is talk about a more secluded residential complex on the east side of the Sutzha River," added Kan Bahlam.

"That is where I want my residence," Yuhk Makab'te declared. "Such a setting with cascades and ponds, shade trees and multi-level structures will be lovely. There will I be happy to bring my wife, when I have one."

"Is there a candidate?" asked Mut, who was also single.

"Not yet. One can dream, though."

"Ah, my friends, marriage does not make life so different if a man keeps his wits and independence," said Kan Bahlam with a dismissive hand sign. "One still had other pursuits, is that not so?"

The three men laughed.

"For you, that is so. But not all have your dedication to the pleasures of the senses," remarked Chak Chan.

"Your sister is a sensible woman," Kan Bahlam smiled. "All goes well when a woman does not attempt to control her husband. It makes the household compatible."

"Ummm." Chak Chan wondered what his sister thought, although she never gave the family signs that she was discontent.

"Across the plaza, see the group of three low structures with a joined base platform and stairways? These are designated as schools for arts and sciences, and the one farthest right has been given to me by my father. In it will I develop my academy for astronomy and numerology. It will be my temple for study and research, and you are all invited to be part of it. We can delve into the most arcane calculations and discover new patterns within the stars. It shall become my court for esoteric knowledge. What say you?"

Sparked by Kan Bahlam's magnetic enthusiasm, the three men affirmed their interest and commitment to his studies, although they could not quite glean exactly what he meant. They had no doubt that Kan Bahlam's brilliant mind would lead them into exciting discoveries and intriguing theories.

Pakal draped his long body across the raised dais in the new palace reception chamber, one hand casually supporting his chin. Although he appeared relaxed, Lalak, who was seated on a bench beside the dais, picked up subtle signs of tension in her husband. His eyes were intently focused on the messenger standing before him, and his jaw muscles were tight. Several courtiers and warriors were present, including K'akmo, Oaxac Ok, Ch'amak and Yax Chan. The messenger, sent several moons ago to gather information about Bahlam Ahau's latest campaign, was delivering his report.

"It was thus, your honorable relative Bahlam Ahau led his forces into battle against Yokib. For three days the warriors exchanged blows near the city's edge, each retreating into their encampment for the night, then returning to fight again at daybreak. It seemed there would be no clear winner, and each side lost some men each day. In a final push, the forces of Bahlam Ahau broke through Yokib's ranks and entered the city, but continued resistance kept them from doing much destruction. They did take captives, some high-ranking ahauob, but none of the ruling family. They removed some artifacts but were unable to significantly deface monuments. When these warriors were finally forced back outside the city, Bahlam Ahau called for disengagement and sequestered his forces in jungle camps. They are now returning to B'aak."

"Where he will proclaim another great victory," snorted K'akmo.

"Bahlam Ahau is always one to make much of any small success," another warrior added.

"Did you detect any warriors from Kan among the Yokib ranks?" asked Pakal.

"Holy Lord, of this I am uncertain. My view was often obstructed and I found it difficult to question B'aak leaders directly. Campfire rumor held that some Kan warriors were there, but I could not definitely confirm this."

"Whether or not Kan men fought, this will be treated as an assault against the Ka'an polity; of this you can be certain. They will seek retribution." K'akmo added his last observation with darkened brows.

Pakal nodded, thanked and dismissed the messenger. His eyes met Lalak's and she gave a slight shrug. She had long given up attempts to defend her brother's escapades, and knew her husband did not hold her responsible. Bahlam Ahau was unpredictable except in his continuous stirring of waters in the polity.

"K'akmo, did you say earlier that you had recent information about Kan activities?" Pakal looked toward his Nakom, gesturing for him to speak.

"Some information I do have," replied K'akmo. "I cannot vouch for how reliable it is, coming from traders and not our own observers. Balaj Chan K'awiil has been residing in the Kan capitol city Uxte'tun for nearly five years, since his ouster from Imix-ha by Bahlam Ahau and the local ahauob. He still claims rights to the throne of Mutul, claims his half-brother Nuun Ujol Chaak is not rightful heir. There is rumor among Kan allies that Nuun was behind this ouster and lent forces to accomplish it. You can be certain that Balaj Chan K'awiil has spent these years agitating with Kan leaders to restore him to the Mutul throne. The traders said there are war councils happening in Uxte'tun, plans being made for some big campaign. It would not surprise me if this campaign is directed against Mutul, and its purpose is to put Balaj in rulership as a Sahal of Kan to act as their puppet."

"How might this be connected to Yokib and Bahlam Ahau's attack?"

"Bahlam Ahau has attacked two Kan allies in recent years, Yokib and Imix-ha. Kan ruler Yuknoom Ch'een will not take that lightly. He is no doubt eager to join with Balaj to extract revenge against Mutul ... and its allies."

"Let us not forget our role in the Imix-ha attack and ouster of Balaj Chan K'awiil," said Ch'amak. As an elder statesman, he felt it was his job to keep things in long-term perspective.

"Indeed," added another older courtier, Oaxac Ok. "We may expect another *ek'emey* battle from our enemies, in retribution for Bahlam Ahau's mountaining of bones at Imix-ha."

"Kan will not be happy with our neutralizing their overtures at Sak Nikte', either," added Yax Chan.

"Your points are well taken," said Pakal, gesturing appreciation to his older cousins and his architect friend. "We must remain on alert and increase our intelligence about Kan's movements. K'akmo, select some observers and have them join the traders for a trip to Uxte'tun. Also, send a messenger to Nuun Ujol Chaak at Mutul to determine his knowledge and plans in regard to his half-brother's situation. And keep our own forces battle-ready."

Pakal turned to Lalak and gave her a wry smile.

"Let us hope that your brother stays home for a while."

Lalak sat on a thick mat under the shady veranda facing the inner courtyard of her quarters in the old palace. She relished its comfortable familiarity, sighing as she thought of moving from this place that had been her home for over thirty years. The royal residential chambers of the new palace complex were under construction, and Pakal anticipated they would be ready in another four or five moon cycles. She knew the new royal residence would be splendid, much finer and larger than the present one. It would have the latest innovations in inside plumbing and water features, and a pib nah built into the chambers for easy access to the sweat baths that found such favor in Lakam Ha. Still, she felt a tinge of sadness over the move, and wondered if it was a sign of growing older.

Looking across the courtyard, her heart swelled at the sight of her two younger sons playing chase around several large potted plants. They were both wonderful boys, bright and curious and adept learners. Kan Joy Chitam, now thirteen solar years, was more thoughtful and contained, often surprising her with his insightful comments. Tiwol Chan Mat, now nine solar years, was spontaneous and generous, always trying to be helpful even beyond his actual abilities. If she could, she would keep them forever young, protected from the dangers and heartaches of life. A surge of sadness passed through her heart as she thought of Waknal Bahlam's death. What a waste of a promising young life, she thought. What a senseless masculine pursuit, and how Kan Bahlam had flaunted his success. But then, her oldest son was ever self-centered.

She felt sad for his wife Talol, a gentle and compliant young woman who deserved a better husband. It was a good thing that Pakal and the calendar priests decided the couple should postpone having children for several years. Taking herbs to prevent pregnancy would spare Talol the anguish of failure to conceive, if indeed Kan Bahlam's illness led to this.

Her servant announced Pakal's arrival, while another brought a platter of fruit and juice. She smiled at her husband's approach, reaching her hand up toward his as they touched fingers in greeting. The tingle of excitement that coursed through her body at his touch never ceased to amaze her. *Even at this age*, she thought, *his presence delights me.*

Pakal sat beside her and glanced at the boys playing.

"You have stolen them from their studies with the priests," he remarked.

"A mother's prerogative."

"Yes, how quickly they grow."

"Too quickly."

At their father's voice, the boys charged across the courtyard and threw themselves into his arms. After some hugging and wrestling, Pakal told them to sit close by on the mat and have some fruit.

"What would you say, Kan Joy, about a huge body of water, something like a lake, but so immense that you could not see across it?" he asked.

The older boy looked quizzically at his father, thinking about it.

"I would say perhaps that is so, but I should want to verify it with my own eyes," he replied. "My tutors tell of such huge expanses of water, such that many moons travel could not span them. But this is difficult to imagine."

"An excellent reply!" Pakal nodded approval. "It is good to remain open about possibilities you have not encountered, but to seek confirmation of what people claim. You will get your confirmation from your eldest brother after he takes his long journey to explore the lands of the Mayas and visit many cities. Would you accept his word that he saw such vast waters, such seas we call Nab'nah and K'ak-nab?"

"That I would accept, for my brother is smart and would not lie to me."

"How can a sea be so large that you cannot see across it?" asked Tiwol Chan Mat.

"That is a mystery even I do not understand," Pakal replied. "I am told by traders that there are islands in the K'ak-nab that are reached in a day's journey by sea canoe. They speak of other lands that border the Nab'nah far to the north. Although they followed this coast for several moons, they did not reach the ends of these lands."

"Tell me more of the islands, Father," entreated Tiwol.

"They are pieces of land that are completely surrounded by water, and can be very small to quite large. There are many islands off the coast of the K'ak-nab to the east."

"Large enough for villages or cities?" asked Kan Joy.

"Even so. And your brother plans to visit some of these islands in the east sea."

"When does Kan Bahlam intend to leave?" asked Lalak.

"Before the rains start in the spring, so river travel will be less hazardous. He will take Chak Chan as his traveling companion, with several warriors and guides, paddlers and attendants. They will need two large river canoes, and then change to even larger sea-going canoes for the voyage along the coast. I am thinking the excursion should begin by traveling north on the K'umaxha to Nab'nahotot, and follow the coast to the northern cities of the Yukatek Mayas. From there they can travel

overland to such legendary cities as Ek Bahlam and Coba, and then follow
the eastern coast to visit islands and coastal trading cities. They may range
as far as Oxwitik, to cultivate our relations with that powerful city in the
distant south. Their return should take Kan Bahlam to Mutul to consolidate
our alliance and investigate the conditions there. The last portion of the
journey will be re-joining the K'umaxha in the south."

"Where they will need to pass several hostile cities," Lalak observed.
"It could be dangerous."

"Yes, but not as dangerous as beginning the journey going south. The
observer I sent to Uxte'tun reports it is almost certain that Kan is planning
another attack on Mutul. The southern waterways will be full of war parties
and it is possible other cities will be involved in battles. By the time Kan
Bahlam is ready to return from Oxwitik, this situation should be more
settled."

"This will be a very long journey," Lalak reflected.

"It will last several years," Pakal agreed.

"Ah, but it will be so exciting!" said Tiwol. "If only I were old enough
to go with him."

"Our brother will see and learn many things," commented Kan Joy.
"I am envious, such an opportunity is rare. Perhaps when I am older, I can
also take such a journey, might that be so, Father?"

"Perhaps. Do not forget how much there is to learn here. Lakam Ha
has the best astronomers and architects and artisans and calendar priests
in our entire region. Many visitors are coming to study with them, visitors
from faraway cities. Would you like to meet some of them?"

"Oh, yes, Father! When can I see these people from distant places?"

"Soon. I have word there is a delegation coming from far, far in the
north, much farther than Kan Bahlam will travel, from a people we have
never seen among the Maya lands. This I hear from the scarlet macaw
traders. These foreign people highly value the macaw's colorful feathers and
pay great sums to obtain them. Having heard from the macaw traders of
our advances in agriculture and astronomy, these foreigners wish to study
in Lakam Ha."

"See! If you cannot travel to distant places, the people will come to
you. That is the advantage of living in such a remarkable city as Lakam Ha,
in your father's reign," added Lalak.

Pakal's words about Kan attacking Mutul were prophetic. Shortly
after the winter solstice, informants carried the news that Balaj Chan
K'awiil and Kan ruler Yuknoom Ch'een had launched a devastating assault

on Mutul. Balaj carried out an *ek'emey kab'* battle against his half-brother Nuun Ujol Chaak, Ahau of Mutul, resulting in Nuun's banishment and the killing of several elite nobles. Other actions were taken against Mutul leaders, stripping them of wealth, taking several as captives, and leaving Kan warriors to hold Mutul leaders in house arrest until the city settled into the new power structure. Monuments erected by Nuun were destroyed and his palace looted. The ex-Mutul ruler was lucky to escape with his life and a small contingent of followers. They were now hiding out in jungles trying to survive off the land.

Kan Bahlam joined the astronomer-priests to explain the uncanny significance of the date and actions taken at this attack, as the date was noted and analyzed.

Baktun 9, Katun 11, Tun 4, Uinal 5, Kin 14, on the date 6 Ix 2 Kayab (January 15, 657 CE).

In an *ek'emey kab'* battle, meteors of the celestial realm were metaphorically invoked as the arrows of the Gods. Balaj Chan K'awiil used numerological conceptions of significant calendar cycles to tie his revenge against Nuun Ujol Chaak to the allies who had supported him in previous battles: B'aak and Lakam Ha. The date of Balaj's attack on Mutul was 2,578 days after the *ek'emey* battle against Imix-ha headed by Bahlam Ahau of B'aak. This approximated four canonical Noh Ek (Venus) cycles and seven Haab calendar years (tuns) of 360 days. When the great star Noh Ek assumed its Eveningstar position, it was called Chak Ek and was associated with the timing of battles. Balaj chose the Chak Ek anniversary of Bahlam Ahau's attack to conceptually tie together all three cities—Mutul, B'aak and Lakam Ha—as he invoked the star's celestial arrows, combined with the Sun Cycle and the specific Tzolk'in day of Ix.

To Pakal, this was further evidence of consolidating alliances within the two competing power nuclei in the Petén region. Kan at Uxte'tun was the locus of one alliance whose major players were Pa'chan, Yokib, and Usihwitz with Imix-ha and Pakab as peripheral allies. Mutul was the locus of the other, with its major players Lakam Ha, B'aak, and Sak Tz'i, and having Popo', Nab'nahotot, and Uxte'kuh on the periphery. He was certain there would be more conflict to come.

When the next rainy season ended and the fall equinox drew near, Kan Bahlam departed on his journey and Bahlam Ahau arrived with more war council plans. The B'aak ruler was incensed over the ouster of Nuun Ujol Chaak and wanted swift retaliation against Kan and its allies. Pakal agreed that they should search for Nuun's contingent in the jungles and come to their assistance. He would offer them sanctuary in Lakam Ha. The war council argued long and hard, finally concluding that a strike against Kan ally Pa'chan would have more chance of success than assaulting the well-fortified city of Mutul, and would deliver a strong message.

The warriors of Lakam Ha and B'aak would again join forces to foray south along the K'umaxha into the dense jungles between Mutul and Pa'chan where Nuun's group was hiding. Advance scouts were sent to search and report back on the location before the fighting party was sent out. Warriors needed to retrain and re-supply their ranks, and organize both canoe and ground transportation. It would require considerable time to bring all the parts of this expedition together. Bahlam Ahau returned to B'aak to get his forces ready. K'akmo set to preparing Lakam Ha's forces, and Pakal turned to diplomatic affairs.

4

K an Joy Chitam could hardly contain his excitement as he sat in the royal court next to his mother and younger brother. This day his father was receiving delegates and emissaries from other cities and, as promised, among them would be the scarlet macaw trader with those distant foreigners who prized the macaw feathers.

Regally perched on jaguar skins covering the throne on the raised dais, Pakal was attired as Ahau K'in, Lord Sun, in resplendent quetzal feather headdress, copper sun God pectoral, and mat skirt. His scribe K'anal sat just below the platform with stylus and bark paper book ready, the court dwarf squatted in front, and royal attendants stood behind. Royal Steward Muk Kab stood ready at the main doorway to announce visitors. Seated near Lalak and her sons were the leading courtiers and warriors of Lakam Ha. Pakal signaled Muk Kab to begin the court proceedings.

The court building, adjacent to the Sak Nuk Nah, had stairs ascending from the plaza on three sides. Multiple doorways gave access to the long rectangular structure, each flanked by carved and painted piers of ancestral rulers and major deities. These finely etched, life-like figures sculpted on the piers drew admiration from visitors. Roof eaves delineated the gracefully slanted, vaulted roof that sloped parallel with the stairways, giving a pleasing harmony to the building. The eaves were decorated with glyphs and geometric motifs. A delicate double-sided roofcomb, covered with figures and glyphs, crowned the center roof and added height. All the decorative elements were painted bright blue, red, green, and white.

Visitors and city ahauob crowded around the stairs and spread onto the plaza, waiting to be called before the ruler or hovering for a sight into the interior chambers. Mut Kab appeared at the main entrance as musicians blew conches and shook rattles. He called the first visitor, the emissary from the northern Maya city of Coba. As the emissary entered the throne chamber, Pakal's long-ranging scout described this city's location and background. It was a city of antiquity, older than Lakam Ha, and one of the largest and most powerful in the northern Yukatek area. It had some 50,000 residents and thousands of structures, including tall pyramids. From the city a network of sakbeob radiated their raised plaster roadways to numerous smaller sites both toward the coast and into the interior. The longest sakbe ran west to the city of Yaxhuna, a walk of two or three days. Others joined Coba to coastal cities such as Xel-Ha, Tankah, Tulum, and Muyil. Through these port cities, Coba controlled trading routes along the K'ak-nab, the Great East Sea. The city had ample water resources, located as it was between two large lakes and surrounded by marshy regions that provided rich soil for farming. Coba rulers had long been connected with Maya cities in the Petén through arranged marriages among elites, including Mutul and Dzibanche.

"Greetings and welcome to Lakam Ha," Pakal said as the Coba emissary bowed low and clasped his left shoulder. The emissary's attendant brought gift bundles of several varieties of coastal shells, salt and dried fish, which Pakal's scribe recorded. Thanking the visitor, Pakal signed Muk Kab for his attendants to receive the gift bundles.

"All honor to the K'uhul B'aakal Ahau," said the Coba emissary. He spoke the highland Mayan dialect with an accent, his native tongue being Yuketekan. "We have heard much of your city's fame in architecture and astronomy. With me are builders and calendar priests from my city, that we may learn your methods. Already we are much impressed by touring your academies and seeing the many fine structures in your new complex."

"It is my greatest wish that your city should benefit from what you learn here," replied Pakal. "Tell me of your present alliances with cities in our southern regions, and of your trade endeavors."

"Primarily we trade with cities along the K'ak-nab coast, such as those on the lagoon of Wukhalal, and the coastal cities farther south, Altun Ha and Lam'an'ain. Once our ties with Mutul were close, but since that great city's hiatus of many tuns, little interchange has occurred. By marriages, we have connections with Kohunlich and Dzibanche but do not consider these military alliances."

"You are aware of recent contentions between the royal half-brothers of Mutul, and the skirmishes that have resulted?"

"We keep informed. The situation remains unsettled, is that not so? Perhaps new actions are developing."

"That is possible, for many players partake in this game," said Pakal, avoiding mention of the plans his war council made with Bahlam Ahau.

"Coba takes a neutral position in the disputes among Petén cities," the emissary responded smoothly. "Our mission is one of knowledge and skills. Yet another reason impels this visit to Lakam Ha, one our ruler holds dear. You may not know that several royal women have been rulers of Coba, most recently the mother of our current ruler. He is impressed that in your lineage there have been two women rulers, your own mother and grandmother, if I am correct."

"That is so, my holy ancestors Sak K'uk and Yohl Ik'nal. Both led our city through difficult times and brought it to greater stability and abundance."

"While here, I will pay tribute to your ancestors, the K'uhul Ixik rulers as I have been charged. The role of women is central in our society. There is a large island off the coast near Coba called Cuzamil that is a sacred shrine for the Goddess Ix Chel. Her priestesses maintain a large temple and healing complex, where women make annual journeys to worship and pay homage. To be born upon Cuzamil Island is considered a great blessing. Women who can manage the journey there for childbirth believe their children will receive special protection of the Goddess. Women with illnesses may experience miraculous healings through techniques known only to the Ix Chel priestesses on the island. In our regions, every woman, whether noble or commoner, seeks to make the journey to Cuzamil Island at least twice in their lives, at the onset and the cessation of their moon flows. It is an ancient tradition."

"Of this I have not heard," Pakal responded. "It is an admirable tradition. None more than I appreciate the treasures that women bring to our lives and our societies." He glanced toward Lalak and gave the hint of a smile that few but she could recognize. Her eyes glowed back her love in return. "My son Kan Bahlam is now making a lengthy journey around the coast of your northern lands. It is possible that he may visit your city. Should that occur, I would consider it a great favor if you had him instructed in this journey of women to Cuzamil and the Ix Chel shrine. Perhaps women of our city might take this sacred journey in the future."

"As you request, Holy Lord, so shall it be done," replied the emissary with a bow.

After a few more pleasantries, Pakal ended the interview with the Coba representative and signaled for his next visitor.

Mut Kab ushered in the next visitor, a royal son from Altun Ha, as Pakal's scout provided background. Altun Ha was a medium size city with peak population of 10,000 during Baktun 8, now somewhat less. It was located on a coastal plain due east of Lakam Ha, a dry tropical region crossed by a small river with nearby swampland. It was a short half-day walk from the coast of K'ak-nab and conducted significant trade along the protected lagoons between the coast and several large outlying islands. Using various rivers, Altun Ha also traded inland and was known for distributing high quality jade, hematite, and obsidian from the mountains. The city traded unusual artifacts crafted from an alloy of gold and copper; the rare golden metal was found in upland streams of the surrounding countryside. Few Maya artisans knew the alloy technique for crafting metals, so the Altun Ha artists must have learned it from foreign peoples of the narrow isthmus region, far to the south. It was a testimony to Altun Ha's widespread trade networks.

Pakal and the royal visitor from Altun Ha exchanged formal greetings, with gifts presented including lovely pearls, fine jade jewelry, spondylus shell beads, and a stunning pectoral collar of glowing gold-copper medallions interspersed with creamy mother-of-pearl discs and deep blue jadeite beads. Pakal knew at once that this unique collar would find its way to grace Lalak's neck.

The young man from Altun Ha was shorter and more solidly built with a broader face than most highland Mayas, but his bearing was regal and his manner elegant. He spoke excellent highland Ch'olti'an with an exotic trill in pronunciation, admitting that their dialects were not so different. Pakal inquired about the well-being of his royal family and the current conditions of trade, leading to another discussion of the plentiful trading along the K'ak-nab coast. Long reefs lining the coastal islands were a source of copious marine creatures that made up a significant portion of Altun Ha's diet. The diversity of marine life fascinated Pakal, who was unfamiliar with many creatures his visitor named. Pakal was interested in obtaining marine creatures for their shells and dried for consumption, and they agreed to a joint expedition in the near future.

The conversation turned back to family when the young royal mentioned his sister.

"My older sister married some years ago into the ruling family of Uxte'kuh," he said. "She now has children near the age of your two youngest sons. I plan to visit her during this trip, after leaving your splendid city."

"Uxte'kuh, a fortuitous connection," Pakal replied. "Long have we had congenial relations with this city in our polity. I should be pleased for you to convey messages from me to the ruler upon your visit. I shall have them inscribed on a codex for him. We have had little contact the past many years, and I wish to reaffirm our alliance."

"It is my pleasure to convey your messages," said the young royal. "I am eager to see my sister again, and to describe the grand structures and magnificent art of Lakam Ha. Perhaps she will desire to visit here, and your alliances can be further solidified."

Pakal's mind was working on an even better plan for bolstering the alliance. He had been thinking of politically useful marriages for his younger sons, and the idea of marrying one to a royal daughter of Uxte'kuh had much appeal. Now the Altun Ha connection enhanced the political advantage by creating links with this major coastal trading city. Since the raid against Uxte'kuh conducted by Bahlam Ahau, Pakal had been concerned about forging a stronger bond.

"Indeed, make it so. Convey to your sister my deepest regards, and my personal invitation to visit Lakam Ha as my royal guest. It would be my pleasure for you and your entourage to dine with me and my wife, Lady Tz'aakb'u Ahau, in our palace chambers while you are here. Mut Kab, make the arrangements," Pakal said.

Lalak knew Pakal's motives and smiled to herself. It was hard for her to yet imagine her younger sons being married. Kan Joy Chitam squirmed beside her, leaning close to whisper in her ear.

"Mother, when is the scarlet macaw trader going to appear? This is taking so long; Father will be talking to these visitors all day!"

"Shuush," she whispered back. "You know it is your father's obligation to receive visitors and speak pleasantly with them. These courtly procedures cannot be hurried, you must be patient. Listen and you will learn much about the world."

"Be like me," Tiwol whispered behind his mother's back. "Just sit quietly."

Kan Joy gave his brother a nasty look and turned his head away, setting his jaw.

Mut Kab next admitted two delegates from Tulan Tzu. Kan Joy found them interesting because of their strange attire and he perked up. Both men wore multicolored shirts with geometric designs over ankle-length pants with stripes in a mixture of red, yellow, green, blue, and black. Around their waists were striped sashes that dangled long ends with fringes. They wore jade and obsidian jewelry and sported headdresses made mostly of the same colorful cloth with copper medallions around the borders. Unlike the headdresses he was familiar with, these men wore no feathers. Their faces were long and narrow with high cheekbones and small thin noses. From their bearing he could tell they were of high status.

Pakal's scout provided some information about Tulan Tzu, but he had never been there. The city was located in a mountain valley near the great sea to the west, the Chik'in-nab. It was the largest and oldest city in the southern mountains, its history much longer than that of Mutul. The Pokolha River passed nearby, less than a day's walk, and offered easy portage to the K'ak-nab to the east. Other rivers flowed west to the Chik'in-nab. From ports on these two seas, trade routes wrapped around coastlines. This fortuitous location placed Tulan Tzu at the crossroads of major trade routes, and it had long been redistributing goods from both coasts including obsidian, jade, salt, cacao, fruits, and ceramics. The climate was temperate and the soil rich in the valley, providing diverse agriculture including high quality cotton. Textiles of exceptional beauty and strength were made there and exported. The city had long-standing connections with Teotihuacan, the great empire of the far north central region, beyond the lands of the Maya. It was linked to Mutul by ancient lineages, with a nearly mythological story of Mutul's founder, Eb' Xok, invading and overcoming the aboriginal people who founded Tulan Tzu and replacing much of its population. After a period when its former grandeur crumbled, the Mutul infusion brought it to a new florescence within the past Baktun.

Mut Kab presented the Tulan Tzu delegates as a leading warrior-priest and learned courtier, and a solar priest. The men bowed and presented their gift bundles that were wrapped in the fabled brightly colored woven fabrics, and included excellent obsidian blades, beautifully carved jadeite figurines, bags of salt and powdered cacao. It was an expensive offering and Pakal expressed his deepest appreciation. The men spoke the local dialect with clipped phrases but were quite fluent, remarking that their own dialect was similar.

"We are most honored by your visit, Esteemed Delegates from Tulan Tzu. You have traveled long and hazardous routes to arrive here, and I hope your journey was not too difficult. Your visit here is the first from your city, to my knowledge, and it is my greatest desire that future exchanges will occur regularly. Your famous city of unimaginable antiquity has provided much to our Mayan people. It is said that our very language originated in your region, that your people carved the earliest glyphs in the roots of the Cholan language. Many of our religious traditions also sprang from your ancestral culture. For all your gifts, cultural and material, we are most grateful."

The warrior-priest spoke first. "We salute and honor the K'uhul B'aakal Ahau, the renowned K'inich Janaab Pakal. Reports of your accomplishments have traveled widely. Tales of your magnificent structures and innovative building techniques, your effective agricultural methods and your exceptional calendric skills made their way to our ruler's ears. He determined to send a delegation to study with your experts. We are especially interested in your canal system. For Baktuns we have used canals for irrigation, but not to supply our residences. This technique we would learn, among many others."

"Our experts will gladly instruct you," replied Pakal. "We would also gladly learn from you, about your trade routes, your scribal tradition, your exceptional textiles."

"What we know, we will share," said the solar priest. "Perhaps you are aware that we have traded since the times of the Olmecs. Our city's very name, Tulan Tzu means 'The Central Tulan,' pointing to the venerable status of being one of the five original Tulas, or Tollans, sources of the Maya people."

"Of this I was not aware," Pakal answered. "Our tradition relates that the people of B'aakal originated in the lands of Matawiil, the Six Sky Place. But there also are stories of Tulas, places of reeds that figure into our origins. Much distant past is clouded in mystery."

"Just so. We hope to study in your highly-reputed library of codices to further explore these mysteries of origins," said the solar priest.

"So you shall. We will introduce you to our High Priest, Yaxhal, present in court today." Pakal gestured toward his leading priest, who bowed in acknowledgement. "He will make our library available for your study."

"Accept our deepest gratitude. Yet other topics hold interest for us. How go the struggles between Mutul and Kan?" The warrior-priest maintained a neutral tone and expression. "In our journey along the K'umaxha River, we benefitted from the hospitality of several river cities, where we heard much talk about recent conflicts between the half-brothers of Mutul. It seems the ousted brother still wanders in the jungles."

"Things are much unsettled in this situation." Pakal's face was a study in calmness, his expression revealing nothing. "We are seeking more information now. Perhaps you will meet with our Nakom, K'akmo to further examine these things. In addition, we would much desire to know how fares the great empire Teotihuacan, with whom you have long-term relations."

"Ah, our esteemed ally Teotihuacan suffers a serious decline presently." Perhaps it has reached its final days of greatness. There are reports of internal turmoil and assault from enemies. Emissaries have not visited us for many years. Clearly its sphere of influence is waning. We are saddened to see this, after so many Katuns of fruitful exchange."

Pakal expressed his regret to hear this news, and conversation moved to practical matters of housing the Tulan Tzu delegates and connecting them with Lakam Ha experts. The interview drew to an end, and Kan Joy looked hopefully at his mother. She smiled and gave the hand sign for "now it happens." Just then the screech of a macaw penetrated the throne chamber; Kan Joy's eyes widened and he grinned at his brother.

One of the two men that Muk Kab brought in struck Kan Joy as even more exotic than the delegates from Tulan Tzu. He was short, solidly built and very dark skinned with a square face and broad flat cheeks. His eyelids draped over and partly obscured his inner eyes, and his nose was flat and wide. He wore simple clothing, a white shirt embroidered with red step-fret and spiral designs over short pants and plain leather sandals. Only a red headband decorated his dark, shoulder-length hair and he wore no earspools or pectoral jewelry. Kan Joy wondered if he was a commoner, or perhaps very poor. The other man appeared typically Mayan, but on his shoulder perched a large scarlet macaw that cast its round golden eye with white wrinkled skin around it directly at the boy.

The court dwarf jumped up and cavorted around the macaw trader, turning cartwheels and emitting screeches that mimicked the macaw's cry. The bird tilted its head quizzically and eyed the dwarf coldly until he returned to his seat.

Pakal's scout had scant information about the stranger; only that he was of Mexica blood, spoke the Nahuatl language, and came from a city called Chicomoztoc that was so far north few could imagine its location. The macaw trader who accompanied him would serve as translator.

Pakal offered the usual courtly greetings and accepted the foreigner's gift bundle, curious about what it might hold. Inside he found several large blue-green stones traversed by golden and white veins, perhaps the most beautiful stone he had ever seen. There was no color to match it in the Maya lands, and he determined to know what it was. Several small gold nuggets nested among the stones, amazingly pure and bright gold that gleamed even in subdued light. Other sparkling stones colored ruby red, emerald green, and clear crystalline white twinkled in contrast to the gold.

Pakal expressed profuse thanks for the precious stones and gold, and asked the macaw trader to introduce the foreigner.

"Great K'uhul B'aakal Ahau, may I present to you this merchant of Chicomoztoc, who is called Tezpochtli. He is among the leading families of his city, a man of much wealth, one who sits beside the lords and rulers, who has the respect of all." The trader bowed and gestured to his companion. He then translated Pakal's welcome, and the foreigner's words of formal recognition to the ruler.

"What are you called, esteemed trader?" Pakal asked.

"My name is Chit, the rabbit," replied the trader. "My home city is Xpuhil, near the Wukhalal Lagoon. My family has been traders for many generations. I specialize in trade with the far northern Chalchihuitl people. It has been a lucrative business."

"So have I heard," replied Pakal. "Recently I learned that you are trading in scarlet macaws with these northern people, and am much intrigued to know about this."

"Indeed," said Chit, patting the macaw on his shoulder and evoking another screech. "The Chalchihuitl live in a dry, mountainous countryside with no jungles and only pine forests. The birds of their lands are not brightly colored, and few have large feathers. Upon seeing the striking red, blue, and yellow feathers of macaws that we wore in headdresses, these people developed an intense desire to have such feathers for their own decorations. We are now developing methods of bringing live birds to their cities, that they may raise themselves to harvest feathers. It is a challenge, but holds promise for better long-term feather production than just the bundles of feathers we bring."

Pakal noticed that Kan Joy was up on his knees, craning his neck to see better and transfixed by the trader's words.

"Honored Chit, we would hear more details of your care and transport of macaws, but let us arrange this for my personal quarters. It seems my son is fascinated with your macaw trade, and would ply you for information. My steward shall make these arrangements for you and our esteemed guest from Chicomoztoc. Now I have some questions for him. Kindly ask what is the name and nature of the remarkable blue-green stones he has brought."

Chit spoke Nahuatl to the merchant, listened and translated his reply.

"Tezpochtli answers that the stone is called turquoise, and it does not come from his region. His people have contact with other foreign cultures that live in a desert region with many bare mountains; it is very far north of his city and takes two moon cycles to travel there. In these mountains are channels of turquoise that they chip out, shaping it into jewelry that is much valued. It is indeed a rare stone, most precious and costly. The other shining stones are mined from mountains to the west of his city. The stones are very hard and difficult to work, but their brilliance and durability makes them valuable. The gold, a very pure form, also comes from their mountains."

Pakal again expressed appreciation for the rare stones, and inquired how his city might be helpful to the merchant.

Chit translated. "He has made this long trip for several reasons. Having heard about your advanced methods of water management, especially agricultural, his leaders wish to learn about them. Although your terrains are different, many principles will transfer to his region, and perhaps can be disseminated to the turquoise making people in their arid lands. This would enhance his trade relations with them. He also wants to see scarlet macaws in their native habitat and perhaps learn more about their nutrition and health. There is a need in his city for quills, shells, and obsidian that he plans to fulfill during this trip. And, he plans to enjoy a great deal of your delicious cacao, having acquired quite a taste for this beverage."

"All of these things we shall gladly provide," Pakal replied. "See my steward Muk Kab after the court session ends, and he will make arrangements. We shall anticipate receiving you both in my quarters for refreshments this afternoon. My son is most eager for more scarlet macaw talk."

Returning to the palace after the court ended, Kan Joy was nearly dancing with delight and impatient for the macaw trader's arrival. Finally the time came. His parents went through guest hospitality protocols and settled with the visitors onto mats for afternoon maize-cacao drinks and fresh fruit. Chit brought two macaws, one red and the other blue, for the boy's edification. He showed Kan Joy how to feed them chunks of fruit without getting fingers crushed in the birds' strong curved beaks. Lalak remarked that she once had a pet macaw, one she rescued in the jungle after its wing was broken. Both her pet bird and monkey had departed for the spirit realm some time ago.

Kan Joy monopolized Chit and pummeled him with questions.

"How long does the journey take, when you bring the macaws to the city of Tezpochtli? How do you take care of them on the way?"

"From the jungles of the Petén region, where your macaws live, it takes several moon cycles to reach Chicomoztoc. There are two routes, one from your regions and another from the tropical jungles that border the

Nab'nah. Along the Nab'nah coast these regions extend about halfway to the lands of Tezpochtli and his people. That is the shorter route, it requires two moon cycles. The other route from the Petén requires at least three moon cycles, but the macaws are more abundant here. We must capture the birds when they are young. Macaws hatch near spring equinox, and we must wait until they are two uinals old, about forty-five days, before removing them from their nests. We carry them in baskets wrapped in cloth to keep them warm as we journey north. To feed them, we chew softened corn and place it directly into their mouths. They must be fed at short intervals, day and night. Once they fledge, grow up enough to have true feathers, they can eat on their own and like nearly everything a person eats."

"That is giving them much care," Kan Joy observed. "You keep them very close day and night."

"Yes, and because of this close relationship the birds imprint their caretakers as if they were mother birds. They become very attached to their keepers, but can be vicious to strangers. To avoid this problem, we bring people from Chicomoztoc with us to become macaw keepers. Then they manage the birds and harvest feathers carefully over many years. Macaws usually live forty to fifty years, nearly the lifespan of people. Some have lived over seventy years. Being a macaw keeper is a lifetime commitment."

"That is most amazing," said Kan Joy. "Do the macaw keepers breed them also?"

"Ah, that is a problem. The birds do not breed well in captivity. The very attachment to their keepers that nurtures them also causes this problem. The macaws that imprint on humans often do not recognize other macaws as potential mates, they prefer a human."

"Oh, yes, that would be a huge problem!" Kan Joy giggled, turning to his younger brother. "How would you like to mate with a lady macaw? Your children would be strange."

"That I do not believe is possible," Tiwol replied. His expression was serious as he considered the issue. "Is it possible, Mother?"

Lalak, who had been avidly following this exchange, laughed and shook her head, making the "no" hand sign.

"Mother, I want a macaw pet! You had one; cannot I have one also?" Kan Joy rushed up to Lalak and grasped her hand.

"Certainly you can, and Tiwol also. Why not accompany Chit on his next foray into the jungle to capture young birds, and each get one to raise yourself? Then you can each have your macaw mate," she added mischievously.

"Oh, Mother!" said an exasperated Kan Joy. Turning to Chit, he pleaded, "May we come with you? We can climb trees easily, get to the nests and bring down young birds for you."

"Oh yes, we will be good bird catchers!" added Tiwol.

"The next hatching season is still many moons away, but I shall return and take you on a macaw hunt," Chit promised. "After the next spring equinox, we will find your macaw pets and you can feed them day and night from your mouth."

All laughed, including Tezpochtli once Chit had translated.

"Perhaps one of my servants may have that job," Kan Joy retorted. "But I will be close by and make sure the macaw imprints on me."

5

P akal crouched in the underbrush as the setting sun cast long shadows across corn fields. Fat ears hung heavy on tall stalks. Farmers worked quickly to fill their baskets before dark. A steady stream of basket-laden men filed across the long suspension bridge spanning the K'umaxha River, giving passage between the corn fields and the city that perched on a high cliff. Pakal felt increasingly tense. Would those farmers never stop their harvest and return home? He needed the suspension bridge clear to mount his attack on Pa'chan. His forces waited, hidden in the dense jungles beyond the cleared agricultural fields. Timing was everything for this attack; they needed to get into the city before complete darkness.

The campaign against Kan ally Pa'chan had been carefully planned during the past year. No one wanted a repeat of the humiliating defeat their forces had suffered in the first collaborative attack, many years ago. Pakal, K'akmo, and Bahlam Ahau strategized during war councils, using the lessons that bitter experience taught them about assaulting this easily defended city with sheer cliffs rising from the river and steep hills impeding access on the jungle side. It was these lessons that led to their present plan. They would divide forces to distract the Pa'chan warriors: Bahlam Ahau leading his men up the hillside to the rear of the city, K'akmo heading a small contingent to scale the riverside cliffs using stairways built for boat access, and Pakal bringing the main force across the suspension bridge.

The bridge presented a bottleneck and could be lethal to crossing warriors, unless K'akmo was successful in engaging the defenders and keeping the outlet clear. With Bahlam Ahau attacking on the opposite side, they hoped the majority of Pa'chan's forces would converge there, leaving the river side less protected.

Bahlam Ahau was to move first, at an agreed time in the sun's descent. Sunset attacks were uncommon, most battles being staged at dawn. Struggling up a steep hill while fighting was a huge challenge; truly the B'aak ruler had the most difficult task. The next move would be taken by K'akmo, his men quickly scaling the stairs to fight bridge guards. The third wing would be Pakal's forces running across the bridge to gain city access and catch the defenders at their rear. It was a brilliant plan.

If only the farmers would get off the bridge!

Pakal felt a stirring beside him and glanced at Nuun Ujol Chaak, signaling for him to remain still. Scouts had located the ousted Mutul ruler and guided him with his small contingent of nobles and warriors to rendezvous with the Lakam Ha and B'aak forces. Although the Mutul forces were few, they were dead set on revenge, lean and hardened by their years in the jungle. They would be vicious fighters.

The sun slipped closer to the horizon and the clouds took on a rosy hue. Only a few farmers remained in the fields. Pakal regretted the need to kill them but could not risk letting them attack his men from behind. The last group with baskets wasapproaching the far end of the bridge. Pakal gazed at the splendid work of architecture and engineering, marveling at how perfectly placed the support columns were to balance weight and give stability. What a feat to build those pillars of stone and mortar into the riverbed. He regretted that these creative builders were enemies; he should have much preferred to share knowledge and expertise with this admirable city.

A scout moved in behind Pakal and Nuun, breathlessly whispering that K'akmo had begun the ascent up the stairs. It was time to move. Pakal signaled the scout to give word to his waiting warriors, casting a quick supplication to the Triad Gods for their support. The sound of men crashing through underbrush brought Pakal and Nuun to their feet, and they ran to assume leading positions. The few farmers that remained dropped their baskets in alarm but could not move quickly enough to avoid Pakal's warriors, who dispatched them neatly. In moments, a thick stream of warriors surged across the bridge to the sounds of yelling and thudding weapons as K'akmo's men engaged the bridge defenders. Farmers were scattering in panic, some dropping baskets and corn along the road into the city.

Pakal's forces crossed the bridge with minimal fighting. Joining K'akmo and his men, they rushed into the city. The sounds of distant battle alerted them that Bahlam Ahau's group had engaged with the Pa'chan warriors, many of whom were still bounding out of residences with hastily grabbed weapons. Pakal's men assaulted them from behind and fierce fighting filled the streets with screams, thuds and blood. In the dimming light, Pakal could see his forces dominating. He called for a small group to follow him to the royal residence; if he could capture the ruler, the battle would soon end.

The old ruler, Aj Tun Bahlam (Bird Jaguar), remained inside as a group of warriors defended the palace entrance. His son and heir, Itzamnaaj Bahlam, appeared in his war palanquin with numerous warriors and Pakal's forces fell upon them. Some men were lighting torches along the plaza, casting wavering shadows over the writhing, grunting mass of bodies as men slashed with long flint blades, swung battle axes and stabbed with spears, trying to deflect blows with shields. Pakal delivered some wounds with his obsidian sword, but his men surrounded him and warded off attackers. This select group was charged with protecting their ruler, and their honor depended on keeping him safe. Nuun, who was younger and stronger, fought like a demon, relishing every stab and blow, screaming his fury against the despised Kan.

Itzamnaaj Bahlam's men dropped the palanquin to fight off attackers, and the royal heir sprang out, fighting alongside them. He called for more forces, but none appeared as most were engaged battling Bahlam Ahau. After a number of warriors had fallen on both sides, it became clear that Pa'chan was outnumbered and could not prevail; Itzamnaaj Bahlam ordered surrender. Pakal had his warriors bind the heir, remove the warriors' weapons and keep them surrounded, and then went into the palace to subdue the ruler. He sent Nuun's forces to join Bahlam Ahau and finish the battle at the rear of the city.

Torches and a few fires burning in structures cast eerie red light across the routed city. Nuun and Bahlam Ahau subdued the Pa'chan warrior chiefs and accepted their surrender; they brought the leaders to the palace and joined Pakal inside.

The old ruler Aj Tun Bahlam looked dazed, his son dejected, and his warrior chiefs confused. Their city was nearly impregnable, how could this have happened? Yet the victorious triad stood before them and enemy warriors were stationed throughout their city.

"Thus have we avenged the villainous actions of your allies, the ruler of Kan and that upstart Balaj Chan K'awiil of Imix-Ha. Here is the rightful ruler of Mutul, Nuun Ujol Chaak. We will restore him to this throne that justice may be carried out. It would do you well to break your alliances with Kan. The future bodes more conflict." Pakal spoke in clear, ringing tones.

"Here we also set right the ignoble battle that we waged against you many tuns ago," growled Bahlam Ahau. "Here we prove that superior battle strategy can prevail over the best defended cities. Watch and learn. What we did here we can do again."

"Mutul will soon be mine," said Nuun, head thrown high and eyes blazing. "My devious half-brother will sit upon our hallowed throne but a short time. Take this warning and remain out of the struggle."

"We do not intend to loot and damage your city," Pakal said. "We shall remain overnight, rest and feed our warriors, and leave in the morning. We will take some captives from among your ahauob and warriors. But both of you shall remain here and continue your rule. It is not our desire to unseat your dynasty."

Bahlam Ahau shot Pakal a dark scowl, but dared not contradict his words.

"The actions of the Holy B'aakal Lord are indeed wise and compassionate, although I would not be so forgiving." Nuun looked directly at Itzamnaaj Bahlam. "For myself, I claim your war palanquin. It shall be mine to take back to Mutul, to commemorate this victory and remind your city to respect our sovereignty."

"Bahlam Ahau, you may select the captives, and choose which ones to bring back to your city," Pakal said.

"That will be my pleasure." The B'aak ruler felt mollified and was already planning a grand victory procession, captives paraded through the streets at home. He would also sacrifice a few on the next important k'altun celebration.

Tilting his chin upward, Itzamnaaj Bahlam spoke to Pakal.

"Your fame as creator of a magnificent city is only matched by your strategic battle skills," he said, lips curling distastefully. "For your clemency, I express the gratitude of myself and my father. This shall not pass unremembered."

Pakal nodded acknowledgement as the men's eyes met. Again he wished that friendship rather than enmity had prevailed with this city.

As promised, the joint forces left Pa'chan in the morning. They commandeered several canoes to transport the leaders, captives, and many warriors back to Lakam Ha. Among the captives were an ahau from Pipá and

The Mayan Red Queen   267

several from Wa-Mut, confirming the involvement of Kan allies. A smaller group proceeded overland carrying the war palanquin for Nuun. Six days later, they entered the city triumphantly, and Nuun walked before Pakal to emphasize that his restoration to the throne of Mutul was the central purpose of this retaliatory act. Victory marches through the city were held a few days later, with feasting and dancing.

On the stairway of the Royal Court building, the victory over Pa'chan was recorded with hieroglyphs and carved figures of captives. It was a strong statement of Lakam Ha's political authority in the region, and of Pakal's defiance of the spreading Kan influence. This victory was commemorated by Kan Bahlam many years later, when he had the dates and main details carved in glyphs on the panels of Pakal's burial temple.

The date of the great strategic victory over Pa'chan with the taking of captives and the war palanquin of Itzamnaaj Bahlam was inscribed.

Baktun 9, Katun 11, Tun 6, Uinal 16, Kin 11, on the date 7 Chuen 4 Ch'en (August 10, 659 CE).

The procession into the city when Nuun Ujol Chaak "walks before Pakal" was also inscribed on the hieroglyphic stairway and Temple of the Inscriptions West Tablet.

Baktun 9, Katun 11, Tun 6, Uinal 16, Kin 17, on the date 13 Kaban 10 Ch'en (August 16, 659 CE).

Tz'aakb'u Ahau—VII

Baktun 9 Katun 11 Tun 6
Baktun 9 Katun 12 Tun 0
659 CE—672 CE

1

K an Bahlam shivered in the predawn chill, drawing the short cloak closer around his shoulders. Chak Chan stood immobile beside him, eyes fixed on the eastern horizon. The profile of a squat temple with a small square tower gradually took shape at the end of a long walkway as the sky lightened. Although several hundred people were gathered on an immense, low platform at the west end of the walkway, no sounds or movements interrupted the sighing breeze drifting in from the nearby coast. As the gray monochrome sky began to color pale gold, a few birds twittered in the scrubby trees. The ephemeral outlines of numerous structures slowly materialized, long low buildings whose amazing length was matched by endless stairways, pyramids of modest height, ceremonial platforms, and residences.

Dzibilchaltún was a major city of the flat northern lowlands, having 8,500 buildings in the central city and 20,000 in the surrounding area, with a peak population of 100,000 inhabitants. Its history reached into antiquity, much farther back than Lakam Ha. It was known for advanced astronomical features, such as perfectly aligned temples to capture solar and lunar events. An ancient priesthood preserved esoteric calendar knowledge and joined with architects to create structural displays of amazing brilliance. On this morning, the spring equinox, a solar phenomenon would occur. Over the flat landscape when the sun rose in the east, it would ascend exactly through the tower doorways of the squat temple. The tower had two aligned doorways to the east and west, and another two aligned north and south. Every equinox, both spring and fall, the city's residents and visitors gathered to observe this phenomenon and honor solar deities.

Solar priests began chanting prayers to slow drumbeats, and a ripple of anticipation coursed through the crowd. Kan Bahlam and Chak Chan, both taller than the local Mayas, had excellent views. They marveled as the curve of the golden disc appeared exactly inside the east-west doorways, sending brilliant rays streaming upward and forming a red-gold halo around the temple.

"K'uhul Ah K'in, K'in Ahau, we honor your shining face, we draw forth your blessings." The men from Lakam Ha joined thousands of voices to welcome the Sun Lord. Soon the entire globe was glowing within the doorways, filling the temple tower with blazing light that reflected off faces and jewelry. A rectangle of sunlight slowly advanced along the wide walkway inside the temple's shadow. The solar priests headed a procession along the walkway to chanting and drumming, dropping to their knees when they converged with the elongating swatch of sunlight. Leading priests stepped onto a small square platform with a single tall column at its center, where they placed offerings and smoking censers. The priests and column were bathed in golden light, their feather headdresses swaying and sparkling. When the light reached the top of the column, another round of prayers began that continued until the sun's globe ascended to sit atop the square tower of the temple.

It was a magnificent sight. The Sun Lord perched atop his astronomically perfect temple, smiling beneficently upon his people below, pouring blessings that brought warmth and nurtured life, promising renewal and never-ending cycles. Kan Bahlam made a mental note: this was the ultimate expression of Maya cosmology and spiritual beliefs in structures of stone and phenomena of light. He must do something similar at Lakam Ha.

Flutes and rattles joined the drums, taking up lively rhythms, and many people broke into exuberant dance. They cavorted and stomped and twirled, lifting arms and faces to take in sunrays. Chak Chan joined the dancers, while Kan Bahlam stood still, head tilted back and eyes closed, lips parted as he drank in sunlight. His face and body warmed and he loosened his cape, lifting his arms and praying silently. He was of the sun; his title upon becoming ruler would be K'inich Kan Bahlam II, the Sun-Faced Holy Lord of B'aakal. He would honor the sun in his future magnificent creations.

After the ceremony, they joined their local host Kaywak to stroll through the city. He pointed out the impressively long ceremonial structure bordering the central plaza; it had thirty-five doorways along its front that opened into small chambers for rituals. Later that day, dancers arrayed in fantastic costumes would perform on the wide stairway and a feast would be served in the plaza. The entire palace complex nearby had more than one hundred rooms. They walked across the plaza, observing its multiple buildings used mostly for administrative and ceremonial purposes, and reached what appeared to be a pond. Surrounded by an oval of bare rock, the clear blue water bespoke a depth unusual for a pond. Groups of water lilies with pink flowers decorated the surface, and large iguanas stared defiantly at the intruders, creeping under rocky crevasses when approached.

"This is called a d'zonot," said Kaywak. "It is not truly a pond, but an exposed part of underground rivers that network through the limestone plateau of our lands. You may have noticed there are no rivers on the surface here. Our waters are underneath the plateau, forming vast numbers of tunnels, some leading to the sea. Buried springs feed these underground rivers; the water is cold and sweet. When the surface rock wears down, it can collapse and expose the water beneath. Most d'zonotob have small openings and the water level is quite far beneath the surface. We make rope ladders to descend into these. Here we are fortunate, for our d'zonot is nearly at the surface and its opening is very wide."

"Most amazing," said Kan Bahlam. "We have only traversed this region for several days, but I did not see any rivers. In our lands, you cannot go long without finding one."

"Your d'zonot is most lovely," added Chak Chan. "Do you swim there?"

"It is our main water supply, so swimming is only done on special occasions for water ceremonies." Kaywak brought them to one end and told them to look under the ledge overhanging the water. Kneeling at the edge, they leaned over and looked. "See that cave going into the rock wall? That is where the d'zonot flows into the underground river. Our best swimmers go into the tunnel as far as they can, but it is very dangerous. They reach areas where water fills the tunnel and they can go no farther. It is very dark inside."

"Not a feat I should want to undertake!" said Chak Chan.

"There are some fish, I see," commented Kan Bahlam.

"Yes, and they are delicious with sweet white flesh," said Kaywak. "Which reminds me that you are no doubt hungry. Let us return to my chambers for something to eat."

The visitors from Lakam Ha stayed four moon cycles at Dzibilchaltún, studying with astronomers and solar priests, poring over architectural details of buildings that expressed cosmological relationships. They dined with the ruler and elite nobles, learning the history, economy, and political geography of the region. These northern flatland people called themselves Yukatek and their society had many cities covering the flat plateau linked by sakbeob. They relied on coastal waters for a marine-rich diet, since their scrubby forests did not hold abundant animals for food. Using methods of channeling water from the underground rivers, they grew maize, beans, peppers, and squash and their terrain supported many varieties of fruits that tended to be small and seedy, but quite sweet.

Trade was central to their economy, and a major economic activity was making salt. Kan Bahlam and Chak Chan visited the salt flats created along the northern coast of the Nab'nah, especially impressed by those tended by the offshoot city Xcambo. Barriers of stone and driftwood contained seawater that slowly evaporated; leaving a thin crust of salt that was collected, bundled and transported to inland cities. In the marshes surrounding Xcambo, they saw an abundance of riparian wildlife including water birds and small mammals such as weasels, armadillos, and rabbits. Most amazing were the pink flamingos, large crane-like birds with black wing tips and under-curved beaks. Their clacking sounds were heard all day as they fed in the shallows, heads turned upside down seeking tiny red shrimp that gave them their coloring.

A short distance away was the venerable city Ixcan'tiho, reached by an easy half-day walk along the widest sakbe the men had ever seen. This road was constantly traveled by merchants and townspeople moving between the two large cities. Ixcan'tiho had taller pyramids than Dzibilchaltún, elegant elite customs, and smaller population. With several d'zonotob and marshy areas, its water supply was excellent and the land fertile. More centrally located, it was a prime area for settlement and would continue to be sought by future generations.

The entire northern plateau was dotted with cities, and it was difficult to decide where to go next. To the southwest, a low range of mountains called Pu'uk provided higher sites for several important cities. To the southeast, yet more intriguing cities could be found, some of them with roots going into vast antiquity, associated with mythology of the Yukatek peoples' origins. This interested Kan Bahlam, and when he heard that traveling in this direction would bring him to the city of Ek Bahlam, his choice was made. He had been fascinated by the sexual alchemy of Ek Bahlam's priestesses of Ix Zuhuy K'ak ever since his parents had used it to restore the portal to the Triad Gods. This he wanted to experience for himself.

First they traveled two days to the city of Aké, known for its soaring round columns and graceful temples. Aké was a small city, only a Baktun in age, but with mystical traditions. The most impressive building was a long rectangle with wide stairs on its longer two sides. Over thirty-five tall, smoothly plastered round columns held its flat roof aloft and permitted air flow throughout. There were no chambers; the space was left open for ceremonial performances. It was believed that ritual dancing there would connect one with ancient ancestors and bring revelations of their wisdom. Another even longer structure had more typical chambers, with a large pyramid and several modest public buildings and residences.

A sakbe connected Aké to an even more mysterious place, the three huge pyramids of K'inich K'akmo a short distance east. The priests there had knowledge of Yukatek origin myths and would relate these, if they found the visitors worthy. The long strides of Kan Bahlam and Chak Chan covered the distance quickly over the level plaster of the sakbe, and they soon found an elderly priest dozing in a simple hut of wooden poles and thatch roof. No large stone buildings could be found, just a cluster of huts at the foot of a massive pyramid. In the near distance, two more such monstrous pyramids were visible. Although Lakam Ha had taller pyramids, none had such an immense base covering so much ground.

The pyramids had nine tiers leading to a broad platform; on top was a temple structure made of wood posts and thatch roofs. Along the pyramid front, stairways ascended from ground level to the temple platform. Kan Bahlam could not gauge the distance between the pyramids from where he stood, but he immediately guessed their placement represented the three hearthstone stars of Orion. These three bright stars formed an equal triangle; the first symbolic hearth fire set by the Creator Gods was situated in its center. This stellar center of Maya creation was replicated in every Maya home by the three hearthstones inside which burned the cooking fire. It was common practice for cities to have a three-structure complex that also replicated the triangle of Orion stars.

Chak Chan gently shook the old priest awake, making profuse apologies and offering courtly greetings. After blinking away his mid-afternoon sleepiness, the priest accepted the maize cakes and cacao drink they had brought to create a good impression. They conversed politely about his health and the warm weather, then introduced themselves as seekers of truth who came to learn the wisdom of the pyramids. A bit more solicitous chatter and flattery won the old man over, and he offered to take them up the main pyramid and discuss the knowledge it held.

The two visitors were astonished to see how huge the building blocks were. Most of the limestone blocks were half a man's height in all dimensions. How such massive pieces of stone could be moved and raised to ever increasing heights was baffling. The old priest cackled, enjoying their perplexed expressions.

"These stones, it is a mystery how they were put in place," he chortled. "Some say there were giants in those days, men so strong they could individually lift such stones. The height of the steps, which is so great to us, was normal for their size. Come, let us climb. Feel the stones, let your hands linger upon them, receive their messages."

Kan Bahlam took his time, resting hands upon the warm stones with closed eyes. There was something different about touching them, something that felt profoundly ancient and immeasurably deep. He believed that stones held memories within their crystalline quartz elements, as did most Mayas with shamanic training. Through his fingertips and palms, he tried to absorb these memories. No clear images coalesced in his mind, simply the sense of antiquity beyond accounting.

When he reached the top and stood upon the platform, a breath-taking vista stretched below. Never had he seen such flat countryside. He could see clearly horizon to horizon in 360 degrees, unimpeded by mountains or towering rain forest canopies. An absolutely straight line of greenery met sky in the distance. Gleaming white sakbeob traced straight lines through the low scrub forests. To the west he saw the long structures of Aké. Faint white bumps along distant horizons, the tops of high pyramids, marked locations of other cities in every direction. It was vast yet interconnected, this land of the Yukatek.

Entering the temple shade, the priest indicated they should sit as he lighted copal in the small censer and mumbled prayers. The two visitors gladly lowered themselves onto mats, tired and sweaty from the climb. At this height, cooling breezes blew through the temple's open sides and rattled palm fronds on the roof. When the priest finished his rituals, he sat beside them.

"You are men of sincerity and good hearts," he said, squinting through bleary eyes. "Yours is noble, even regal blood. Your quest shall be satisfied. Here it comes, the tale told about my people's origins, the story transmitted from generation to generation, from the times of the First Ones. Thus it was, thus has it been said and told and repeated. There was a time when a people of advanced knowledge lived upon an island surrounded by the rough waters of the Great East Sea, far beyond what we know now as K'ab-nab. They lived so long ago, none can count. The best calendar priests cannot calculate those times long ago. But even so, this people were not the very first, for yet another great island existed before. Maybe it was not this world we see before us, maybe a realm closer to that of the Gods. When this great island broke apart, the people moved to other places. One place was the island of the Great East Sea.

"For many generations these people, who are called in our tradition the Atlantiha, lived and thrived on their island. They developed many sciences and arts, beyond those known to us now. Their powers were such that they could change nature, could regenerate their bodies, could move through water and air in magical boats. They became proud of their knowledge, and some desired to gather that knowledge to themselves and use it to dominate others. Thus came their travails, their troubles. They made experiments using powers over nature, but these things they did went astray. Their errors changed the weather and upset the balance of earth and sky. The mountains surged upward and spouted fuming volcanoes of fire and ashes, the waters lashed and leapt and crashed against their island shores and city walls.

"Their great city crumbled and fell; their island was split by chasms and heaved apart, finally sinking under the turbulent waters. All sign of their world disappeared and waters covered lands near and far. It was the inundation that destroyed the Second Creation of our ancestral people. But some people escaped the destruction of Atlantiha, took sea-faring boats across the waters to faraway places. Among those who escaped was our Creator God Itzamna. He waited for the waters to recede over the lands of Tamuachan. When the carapace of Tamuachan, the Turtle Land, lifted above the waters and the lands dried out, Itzamna and his followers came to begin civilization anew. They brought the new Creation into being, shaping and modeling it after the First Three Stone Place, when the Creator Gods put the first hearthstones into place in the night sky. As each new Creation has been shaped and modeled, including our current Great Sun that began on 4 Ahau 8 Kumk'u.

"Itzamna, First Wizard-Conjurer-Magician was the greatest shaman of all, patron of all shamans since then. He was one who did *itz,* one who knew and used occult powers of enchantment and magic. Perhaps it was he who raised the huge stones to build these pyramids, working his spells to make them float effortlessly upward."

The old priest grinned and winked at his companions, spreading his gnarled fingers in a gesture of "holding secrets."

"In our traditions, Itzamnaaj is a priestly deity of very ancient times who participated in many acts of creation. In the formation of our B'aakal dynasty, it was he who authorized Hun Ahau, first born of the Triad Gods, to accede to rulership during pre-creation times. My family, the Bahlam Dynasty of B'aakal, descended from these Triad Gods," offered Kan Bahlam.

"Ahah!" the old priest exclaimed. "Thus did I sense things rightly, you are of royal blood. Of your quest, I shall not inquire, for young men have their own purposes. Let us return to Itzamna. Although you say his name differently, and he may have other attributes, we are speaking of the same ancestor deity. We are all different faces of the same Maya people. Itzamna was a great teacher; he brought language and all the fields of knowledge to the local people who survived after the inundation. He was *itz'at,* an artist, sage, sculptor, and mason. All that you see here among the Yukatek people resulted from his teachings. These three pyramids are what remain of the original structures built by Itzamna and his followers. They mirror the hearthstones of the First Three Stone Place and hold the vast wisdom that came from that lost civilization, swallowed by the seas."

"May we stay, and learn more from the stones and their keepers, your honored priesthood?" asked Kan Bahlam.

"That you may. The lords of Aké will give you lodging, and my younger priests will share our secrets with more stamina than can this old one. Now let us descend. Perhaps you will kindly assist me, for my steps are not as sure going down."

For another few moon cycles, Kan Bahlam and Chak Chan walked daily from Aké to the K'inich K'akmo pyramids, learning by hours spent meditating upon pyramid stones as well as sessions with the priests of Itzamna. Upon finding about their interest in astronomy, the priests advised them to visit the close by city of Acanceh, where monuments displayed detailed and beautifully painted zodiac symbols. Acanceh astrologers had deep understanding of how stars patterned themselves to communicate the characteristics of each time period during the year; they were master diviners.

Thus the two travelers went with their few attendants along other sakbeob to the city of Acanceh, bearing introductory papers from the old priest. They were warmly welcomed, given lodging with ahauob and assigned a leading astronomer/astrologer to reveal the mysteries of the Acanceh zodiac. The city was small and relatively young, with about 400 buildings. Its main focus was studying and mapping the cosmological patterns that appeared in the night sky. A three-step pyramid dominated the main plaza, its sides bearing huge carved plaster masks of solar deities wearing gigantic circular earspools that resembled the hoops through which players attempted to pass the ball during ballgames. Each mask was tall as a man and wider than an arm span. Additional cosmological motifs included Milky Way spirals, symbols for wandering stars and the moon. Rituals were performed regularly by calendar priests on the pyramid stairs.

Across the plaza ranged a large, low structure of complex design. It had labyrinthine passages connecting numerous small rooms which were used as workshops by the calendar priests and astronomers. Along one wall on the northern side was the zodiac mural, stretching forty paces in an unbroken frieze. The inscription was divided horizontally into three parts. The top band contained a repeating series of figures, composed of inverted conch shells bound to a solar or stellar eye symbol with different geometric borders. Above each symbol two small spirals curled, the cosmic sign. The lower band was wider and held alternating symbols of Noh Ek (Venus) and sections of two intertwined serpents, their jaws appearing on each end. The guide explained that the serpents symbolized the year, marked by the northward and southward course of the sun along the ecliptic. The curves of the serpents' bodies showed the sun's daily course moving above and below the horizon.

In between the bands were carved figures inside individual cartouches. These appeared in two rows; the lower row containing eleven humanoid-animal figures, and the upper composed of twelve figures, ten birds and two humans. Large stylized bird figures sat at each end of the central portion. The interstices between the upper row cartouches held sacrificial cups and feathers. The humanoid, bird, animal, and deity figures inside the cartouches each represented a stellar constellation that was positioned along the serpent year markers at the point they would come into influence as the dominant star configurations in the sky. Astronomer-priests related that these were the constellations visible overhead on the nights during the zodiac period.

Several of these figures were not immediately decipherable to Kan Bahlam, even though he had studied zodiac imagery in Lakam Ha.

Learning their meanings and making connections to cosmologic patterns was the goal of his study, the Acanceh guide assured him. The young royal was immediately captivated and threw himself into intense investigation, spending hours poring over codices and questioning astronomer-priests. Chak Chan applied himself to study, but could not match his companion's passion for the stars. He entertained himself taking walks along shaded paths in the countryside or chatting with priests over cacao-maize drinks. He became impatient and seized an opportunity to urge continuing their travels soon.

One afternoon the two men sat on a breezy veranda of their host's residence, cooling off from the hot day. Three young women crossed the patio, household attendants busy with their duties and oblivious of their observers. Wearing thin white huipils that left brown shoulders bare and revealed shapely calves, the women laughed as their hip-swaying gait took them into the shadows of a corridor. Kan Bahlam's eyes lingered on the women until they disappeared.

"Lovely," Chak Chan commented. "Shorter and darker than our women, but enticing."

"Ummm." Kan Bahlam stroked his chin and fingered his protruding lower lip. "We have been too long without a woman."

"Just so. Let us finish studies here and proceed to Ek Bahlam. You do want to spend time with the priestesses there, do you not?"

"That is certain. There is much to learn from their special talents." Eagerness crept into Kan Bahlam's tone. "Yes, you are correct, Chak Chan. Time has come to divert our studies from calendars, history, and celestial matters to something more human and intimate. We shall find much enjoyment in our studies at Ek Bahlam."

"With this I concur! When shall we depart?"

Only five days later, the two men made their farewells at Acanceh, thanking their teachers and host profusely, and set off with attendants along the sakbe to Ek Bahlam. They sent a messenger in advance, requesting audience with the ruler of the city and the Head Priestess of Ix Zuhuy K'ak. The ruler received them graciously and accepted their gift bundles of coastal salt, flavorful highland cacao pods, and lovely shells, including the prized red spondylus. They were settled into guest chambers in the palace, which was large and impressive. Ek Bahlam itself was a remarkable site with soaring pyramids, administrative buildings and large complexes for the work of the priestesses. Amazing winged deities leaned from upper corners of a majestic pyramid, gazing beneficently at the plaza below.

They each were given separate audiences with the Head Priestess, for she wanted to determine the purposes of each man, and assess suitability for training. Kan Bahlam went into his interview feeling trepidation mixed with excitement. He had offered copal incense and jewels at the Goddess' shrine the night before to request her acceptance. His strategy included describing his mother's training with the priestess who came to Lakam Ha many years ago, and how the abilities she attained in sexual alchemy were critical to reconstructing their city's portal to the Gods.

"T'zab Chak!" exclaimed the Head Priestess. "She was among the most skilled of our priestesses. It does not surprise me that her tutoring your mother led to such success."

"Is she departed to the realm of the deities?" asked Kan Bahlam.

"No, but soon she will sit in the celestial canoe as it dips into the Underworld. She is of advanced age and not well. Perhaps I can arrange a brief visit for you; she would appreciate hearing the fruits of her actions in your city."

Kan Bahlam expressed appreciation for such a visit where he could convey his city's gratitude to the elderly priestess. The Head Priestess grilled him on his interests in sexual alchemy and how he intended to use it. Not all applicants were accepted, she noted. Their motives must serve a greater purpose, as had his mother's. Kan Bahlam was prepared for this question, and eloquently laid out the reasons why sexual alchemy would enhance his creative abilities as he developed plans for major new construction in Lakam Ha that would reflect the celestial and astronomical mainsprings of his people. He focused on the immense creative forces that retaining sexual energies would engender. As heir and future ruler, he needed to augment these forces to raise his city to even loftier heights than his widely-esteemed father, K'inich Janaab Pakal.

The Head Priestess accepted his purposes as worthy. Next she made inquiry into his health. Since he had been without symptoms for years, he knew he could avoid mentioning the life-threatening illness that might have left him sterile. However, he intuited that learning sexual alchemy under any deceptive conditions would not gain the results he wished. It was true that he relished the sensuality of the process; yet more did he intend to gain from it.

"For most of my life, I have been strong and healthy. When nineteen years old, I contracted a jungle fever that nearly caused my death. Our healers were able to save me, and I recovered fully after several moons. No adverse effects have appeared since. It is impossible to know whether there will be later effects which would damage the organs."   "Such   serious jungle fevers we also encounter in our lands," said the Head Priestess. "We know this disease can affect fertility, as well as damage heart and elimination systems. If you survive and recover, it has no communicability. You appear to be in good health; we shall undertake a thorough examination by our healers. All our priestesses take herbs that prevent conception, so that is not a worry, in any case. Your situation is special; you are a future ruler with major works to accomplish. It is clear that you can use the powers gained in learning sexual alchemy to further the wellbeing of your people."

The Ek Bahlam healers could find no sign of disease during their examination. While waiting for formal approval, Kan Bahlam visited the frail elder priestess who had trained his mother before he had been born. T'zab Chak was pleased, her thin claw-like hands reaching to touch his face, for her vision was nearly gone. She croaked her gratitude and repeatedly told him what an exceptional woman his mother was, asking him to bring her last earthly blessings back. It gave the heir pause to reflect; perhaps his mother deserved greater respect than he had awarded her.

Chak Chan had several interviews before the Head Priestess was satisfied. She agreed finally that the young noble would use his training to serve his city through administrative leadership. The two Lakam Ha travelers began training at the same time, each with a priestess specifically selected according to the Head Priestess' assessment.

The priestess selected to train Kan Bahlam was named Tz'unun, which meant hummingbird. She was small and slender, with delicate features, tawny skin, and a flitting manner that evoked her namesake. At their initial meeting, Kan Bahlam asked about her background and why she chose this discipline.

"My mentor was Tzab Chak, and she accepted me into training although many thought I would not be suitable. She gave me the opportunity to realize my dreams of serving the Powerful Fiery One, Zuhuy K'ak. It was something my family never understood, and even now they keep their distance. That is not unusual, however, for once we become initiates, we must forsake family and friends and commit to a life of service. We vow to remain single and forgo the householder life. It is a rigorous discipline."

"Is it something you are glad for having chosen?"

"My work brings me contentment. I am able to serve the needs of others and assist my clients to enhance their creative potential," she replied. "Perhaps I make a meaningful contribution to their lives, assist them in realizing their dreams. Is there any greater gift than being of service to others? This you certainly realize, as your life will be one of dedication to your people and city." She flashed him a smile as she ended.

Kan Bahlam thought he had never seen a more beautiful smile, one that lit up her face and made her dark eyes sparkle. She proved to be intelligent and witty, great fun to be with and capable of discussing philosophy or physiology. As the training progressed to greater intimacy, along with higher demands for control of sexual urges, he realized this was no easy discipline. Containing his sexual release was difficult and something he had not tried before. At first he found it vexing, leaving him highly aroused and much disturbed. She coached him to sublimate this sexual force into the energy channels of his body and release it in expanded consciousness. After some practice, he began noticing increased physical vigor and mental sharpness. He felt fully alive and radiantly healthy, but more than the physical effects, he felt immense wellbeing and flowing happiness.

His heart leapt whenever he saw Tz'unun, and the hours they spent together were the most joyful of his life. He began to wonder if he was in love. Men spoke of love, but Kan Bahlam doubted he had felt anything more than mild affection for a woman. Passion and enchantment, yes, but nothing approaching what he felt now. His wife seemed an afterthought, a person he barely knew thrust into his life by political necessity. A woman for whom he had no strong feelings. With Tz'unun his feelings were exploding, boiling within his heart and body.

As the time of his training drew to a close, Kan Bahlam lay beside Tz'unun after a session of exquisite pleasuring, then holding in titanic sexual forces that left his entire being aflame. He tried to contain this eruptive energy, causing his limbs to tremble and covering his body with sweat. But this time, he could not redirect the burning force into energy channels for sublimation. He traced the straight line of her small nose and ran fingers through her flowing black hair.

"Nectar bird, I am failing. I am a sorry student. This time my body craves release. You said a time would come when that would be acceptable. Surely this is the time."

She laughed at his pleading tone, fingers playing with his large nose and thick lips.

"Ah, great future ruler of Lakam Ha, you must meet your challenges. Just imagine what more you will face on the throne. This is but a small thing."

"Good! Then it will not matter if we continue ... to the natural conclusion," he murmured against her hair.

"You are wrong," she breathed against his bulging shoulder. "You are an excellent student. You have mastered much sexual alchemy, enough to serve your needs. Perhaps I am the one who is failing, for I yearn also for what you desire."

He needed no further encouragement, mouth finding hers as he rejoined their bodies. He felt her eager responsiveness, and then realized her technique had changed and she was bringing him to climax. In a few thundering moments, both found explosive release of long-held sexual forces. Such a volcanic conclusion left them breathless in each other's arms. She surprised him with a soft cascade of laughter.

"Aaaah, I must say that was remarkable," she managed to gasp.

"Ummm." He was not ready to leave the waves of pleasure still reverberating within.

"There is much to be said for the natural outcome," she murmured, stroking his hard chest muscles.

His lips brushed against her ear as he cradled her head in his elbow.

"Come back with me to Lakam Ha," he whispered in her ear. "I am in love with you. I want you beside me the rest of my life. Come, you will live with me in the palace."

She drew back and cupped his face between her hands.

"That cannot be. Your family would never accept me even should I want to come."

"No matter. I shall be ruler, and what I do, they must accept. I can make you a second wife; that is not unknown in our region. I cannot live now without you."

"Dear Jaguar Lord, you are infatuated and lost in your sexual pleasures. You do not know real love. What you ask of me is impossible, it would ruin my life."

"Then you do not love me," he replied, the hurt showing in eyes and tone.

"Perhaps I do, and perhaps I do not. It matters not. My place is here, serving my Goddess. Your place is at your city, serving your people." She gently pulled him toward her and kissed his lips. "You will remain in my heart forever. That is love. You carry it with you wherever you go."

Nothing Kan Bahlam could say deterred her. Their remaining time together was bittersweet, and Tz'unun held firmly to principles of training, never again succumbing to sexual release. He decided it was time to move on to the next phase of the journey that had taken his entourage so far from home.

2

Coba was an immense city, covering more territory than Lakam Ha. The flat terrain encouraged urban spread and the two large lakes provided abundant water for a burgeoning population. Well fed and dressed inhabitants bespoke the city's prosperity and luxury goods were plentiful. Foreigners mingled with natives in the crowded streets and marketplaces, which had an amazing assortment of marine and coastal goods. Towering pyramids outstripped the tallest in Lakam Ha, and multiple sprawling complexes invited one to get lost in labyrinthine passageways. Monuments abounded, particularly the carved stela proclaiming rulers' victories and accomplishments.

Kan Bahlam and Chak Chan were royally received, given quarters in a fine palace and plied with attendants. Their small entourage received choice treatment, lodged at noble houses in plush quarters. There was no doubt that this was the leading city of the region, the hub of multiple spokes whose sakbeob radiated to numerous other cities. They had many receptions and audiences with the ruling family and elite nobles, exchanging courtly flatteries and comparing their lands. The emissary who had visited Lakam Ha met with the men, conveying Pakal's request that Kan Bahlam learn about the sacred women's island, Cuzamil, and their ritual and healing practices. This task, however, Kan Bahlam delegated to Chak Chan, commenting cryptically that he had enough of women's ways at Ek Bahlam.

Chak Chan sensed that something traumatic had taken place during Kan Bahlam's training with the Ix Zuhuy K'ak priestess; although his companion only commented that he had gained much from the training. Chak Chan would not pry; if Kan Bahlam preferred to keep things to himself, so be it. With the assistance of local Ix Chel priestesses, Chak Chan located priestesses from the island and interviewed them, hiring a scribe to record his impressions on a bark paper codex to bring back to Pakal.

At one of many feasts hosted by the Coba ruler, Kan Bahlam heard information that was cause for concern. The ruler described an immigrant group of Chontal-speaking Mayas from coastal regions of the Great North Sea who were building a new city not far inland from Coba.

"They call themselves the Itzá," said the Coba ruler. "Their origin lands may be the central region near Teotihuacan, we are not certain. Clearly they are a Mexica-influenced people and have taken many customs from those militaristic nomadic tribes, including their aggressiveness and expansionary politics."

"They named this new city Uuc Yabnal, the Place of Seven Structures," a courtier added. "It is located between two deep d'zonotob with several others nearby, all connected by underground rivers. Our priests say this area has powerful energies, perhaps the Itzá plan to build structures to take advantage of the potency of the land. A huge cave situated not far away is said to contain the Wakah Chan Te' in stone within its depths. Some priests have done rituals there and report it is infused with itz."

"Some refugees from collapsing Teotihuacan are among the Itzá and bring that empire's expertise," another courtier remarked. "Expertise mainly in domination and tribute extraction."

"This bodes not well for Coba," muttered the ruler, brows darkening. "This incursion by militant foreigners into our regions promises difficulties. Conflict has not marred our lands for generations."

"We have faced similar problems," Kan Bahlam said. "After Baktuns of harmoniously following the *May* system of rotating dominant cities, certain cities in our region became greedy and ambitious. They broke with *May* protocols and instigated raids against neighbor cities, unsettling dynasties and forcing tribute alliances." He glanced around the spacious patio spread with mats and covered with nobles invited to the ruler's feast. "City names I shall not speak, to avoid offending any of your guests."

The ruler eyed Kan Bahlam coldly, lips curling down.

"It does not escape me, of which city you speak," he said. "Even now hostilities persist between your cities. We remain neutral. The Itzá situation is different. With their city so near, and their intentions not known, we observe and wait."

"For my part, the most prudent action is to nip these insurgents in the bud," growled the Coba Nakom. "Eliminate them before a base of power is established and their population grows large."

The ruler shot his warrior chief a warning look.

"We have never attacked without provocation," the ruler said. "Peace has covered our region for many years, leading to widespread trade successes and our present bountiful way of life. The time is not yet to conclude that the Itzá are our enemies. We must remain alert and prepared for action, should it be needed."

Privately Kan Bahlam agreed with the Nakom. Eliminating the threat before it became strong and well-organized seemed the wiser course. His city had learned bitter lessons from Kan and Usihwitz that might have been avoided with pre-emptive action.

The Coba ruler changed the topic by inquiring about Pakal's building plans, giving Kan Bahlam an opening to expound upon their advanced architectural techniques and his own ideas for future expansion. This conversation carried them through the feast, with Chak Chan remarking about the unusual fish and crustaceans in piquant sauces, and all the men imbibing copious amounts of balche.

While in Coba, the Lakam Ha men arranged for large seafaring canoes to take them south along the coast. These canoes were as wide as two men's height and longer than eight men. They needed six paddlers and could hold up to twenty people along with large loads of merchandise. For quicker travel when at sea, a pole was inserted through an opening in the central bench to hold cloth square-rigged sails secured with ropes. When the wind came up, the sails propelled the canoes much faster than the rowers.

Leaving Coba on a sunny morning, the Lakam Ha entourage found seats along the canoe's sides as paddlers sat on front and rear benches. Many bundles of clothes, food and gifts were settled between the seated men. The entourage now included four warriors and five attendants; the initial guides and canoes had been sent back home after arriving at Dzibilchaltún. Heading off shore and clearing the shallow lagoon of the port city Xel Ha, the paddlers raised the square sails, ropes groaning and post creaking as the canoe caught the wind and sprang forward. Salty foam leapt over the prow and moistened the passengers while screeching gulls circled overhead.

Kan Bahlam's ultimate destination was the far southern city Oxwitik, although he wanted to visit some coastal cities along the way. Oxwitik had friendly though distant relations with Lakam Ha, and was reputed to have some of the most ornate and exotic buildings in the Maya world. Making contact with this large and powerful city was important for building an alliance to offset the reach of Kan. The canoe captain, a swarthy coastal Maya whose people had plied these waters for generations, estimated that the sea travel part of this lengthy voyage would take about two moon cycles, if they made no stops to visit cities and only camped along the beach. But, as visiting cities was in the plan, it would take much longer.

Kan Bahlam decided to pass by the port city Tulum, a half-day canoe trip from Xel Ha, to make progress along the coast. From their vantage point well out to sea to avoid shallow reefs, he observed the squared temple towers and massive building complexes of Tulum that lined the cliff. The city had a lovely site, high over white sand beaches with several half-moon coves offering safe harbor. Chak Chan grumbled about missing such an attractive city and having to spend the night camping on a beach.

As sunset approached, the captain put in along an isolated cove with a wide beach and the men set up camp. Mats and blankets were arranged around a fire of driftwood, a party was sent inland to find fresh water and fruit, and others prepared fish caught that day to roast. It was a surprisingly delicious though simple meal, after a great deal of feasting. The captain commented that sea air made men hungry. Being close to the shore, steady breezes kept mosquitoes at bay, and after a round of cigar smoking courtesy of the captain, they all slept well.

The days at sea and nights on the beach repeated themselves over many days. For a long stretch, no coastal cities were visible, though other trading canoes passed from time to time. Kan Bahlam asked if there was any danger from pirates, and the captain said that a few did hover along the coast to steal from traders. As they approached populated islands, the risk was greater and guard shifts were set up during the night. Flat landmasses appeared on the horizon, which the captain described as a series of mostly inhabited islands just landward of an immense barrier reef. Sea canoes avoided this dangerous reef by following a narrow canal that local Mayas had cut through the shortest portion of a long peninsula. The canal gave canoes access from the sea into a lagoon between the islands and the mainland. Not far beyond the canal was the village of Yalamha, home of many canoe crews and traders, one of the largest island towns. They would stay overnight there.

The canal was just wide enough to allow passage of the sea canoe. Over-hanging reeds and mangrove branches brushed against its sides at the tightest curves, and then the canal widened and passed into a calm green-tinged lagoon. Shallow inlets were blocked off to make salt; many white pockets lined the shore. Seabirds stalked the shallows or hovered above an assortment of different size canoes harbored near a small village at the canal outlet, but the captain said it was not their destination. The warm afternoon, lapping sound of waves against the hull, and metered splashes of oars produced a hypnotic effect and most passengers snoozed. They reached Yalamha as the sun dropped, spreading rosy hues across wispy clouds.

The men eagerly disembarked, surprised to find the town still teeming with people, a collage of diverse faces, dress, and dialects. The captain explained these were traders and merchants from many places, including central Mexica regions and inland mountains both north and south. Almost anything could be found here; rare and valuable commodities passed through the town en route to elite markets. Buildings were low structures because of storms that frequently buffeted the island, and many chambers were available to rent in the living complexes. Making some rapid negotiations, the captain obtained quarters for his crew and passengers, including meals cooked by women of the house. The appreciative group relished their evening meal of fish and crustaceans, arguing the merits of nutty spiny lobster, sweet dense flesh of large clams, chewy saltiness of oysters, tender shrimp and rich crab, even the tough tendrils of octopus.

They rested two days in Yalamha, allowing Kan Bahlam and Chak Chan to explore markets of the trading village and obtain impressive gifts for the ruler of Oxwitik. Their supply of cacao beans, the universally accepted currency, was running low and Kan Bahlam wanted to send a messenger to Lakam Ha for more. The captain doubted a messenger could travel to Lakam Ha and rejoin them along the way. Kan Bahlam selected the most resourceful of his warriors, hired local guides to accompany him, and sent off this messenger with plans to meet again in Oxwitik.

Before continuing south, the captain took a detour to show his passengers the Wukhalal Lagoon whose beauty was beyond compare. Wukhalal meant "Lagoon of Seven Colors" and the large body of water lived up to its name. Entering this lagoon near the canal, all watched as the waters changed from deep blue to blue-green then blended into turquoise. Slowly the turquoise faded into creamy blue-green then pale green to milky white closer to shore. It was an astonishing sight with distant shores lined by greenery of marshes blending into low forests. There were many cities not far inland, but these were allies of Kan. The nearest was Dzibanche, recent home city of the Kan dynasty before they re-took their ancestral home of Uxte'tun. With passengers from Lakam Ha, the captain knew a visit to these enemy cities was most inadvisable. After a swing around the lagoon, the canoe returned to its southward direction along the coast.

They stopped to visit two other cities: Lam'an'ain, situated on the banks of a river running into the lagoon, and Altun Ha located a half-day walk from the coast. At Altun Ha, Kan Bahlam was surprised to hear that the ruler's son had visited Lakam Ha nearly two years previously, and grilled him for news of home, even though outdated. The royal heir was impressed by Altun Ha's reputation as a cultural and artistic center. Several days of courtly exchanges, gifting and savory feasting ensued before the travelers pushed on. Their reception in Lam'an'ain was similar, where they took in the graceful buildings overlooking the river and remarked at the abundant wildlife, especially numerous crocodiles and huge aquatic iguanas.

The next phase of their journey went beyond the southernmost islands and into the open sea. They endured many days of rough seas, the canoe tossed by surging waves covering everyone with sea spray. Chak Chan became seasick, retching and groaning over the canoe's sides, much to the crew's amusement. Kan Bahlam felt queasy but managed to keep his food down. One afternoon a squall mounted, dark clouds menacing and winds whipping the sails viciously. Quickly lowering the sails, the captain yelled for paddlers to make for shore. Stinging rain and strong gusts battered the voyagers, and the canoe teetered on boiling wave crests then plunged into chasms deeper than its length. Most of the passengers cowered between bundles, hanging to ribs of the hull or benches to avoid being thrown out.

Kan Bahlam found the storm exhilarating. He wedged his body against a rear bench and grasped the side railing, head thrown back and mouth open to catch rain. His hair and loincloth whipped wildly. The captain, similarly wedged in the prow, grinned and hand signaled his admiration. Everyone else was too preoccupied to notice; the paddlers furiously trying to outstrip the squall and the passengers pressed to the hull, heads down. Kan Bahlam was almost disappointed when they reached shallow waters. He jumped out to assist the paddlers haul the canoe onto the beach, where they all collapsed gasping for breath while exchanging looks of mutual appreciation.

Another long stretch of deserted shore passed, with repetitious routines of nightly beach camping, roasted fish over driftwood fires, shared smokes then sleep to face the next day on the sea. The Lakam Ha travelers were nearly as dark-skinned as the coastal crew, tanned by the relentless sun glinting off steely waters. Only by daily marks scratched on a wood tablet with a stone stylus did Kan Bahlam keep track of time's passage. He watched the moon wax into fullness and wane to a sliver, and calculated that seven moon cycles had passed since leaving the port city near Coba by the time they reached the mouth of the Pokolha River.

A modest village located there provided two river canoes, smaller and lighter than the sea canoe, which could not navigate rocky rapids and shallow passages. A night of rowdy feasting and drinking balche celebrated the long sea journey, and after generous payment, Kan Bahlam and Chak Chan bid reluctant farewell to their sea-going companions.

The Pokolha River was wide and deep near the mouth, spreading across a broad delta. It drained from the high western mountains, and as the river canoes traveled upriver, it became narrower. Terrain changed from flat marshy floodplain to gentle hills that encroached upon the river. In the narrow parts, water became turbulent and frothed over hidden rocks. Occasional golden sand bars formed in bends, making navigation tricky. The seasoned paddlers knew the river's deep channels and carefully steered to avoid rocks and shallows. In rainy seasons, the river swelled with treacherous currents and spilled over its banks in flat areas, enriching the river valley soil that was farmed for maize.

As the valley broadened into a floodplain, the city of Nahokan appeared on the river's north bank. It was positioned at the juncture of several important trade routes and had a modest population of about 1600 of mixed ethnicity, many from the western highlands. Buildings were spread across a large plaza with straggling outlying complexes serving farmers who lived closer to fields. Farming and trading provided its economy, known especially for trade in uncut jade found in the middle reaches of the river valley and obsidian from its upper reaches. Cacao was produced for trade, but the major crop was maize, the central component of the city's tribute payments to its overlords at Oxwitik.

Nahokan was a vassal state of the much larger Oxwitik, located a day's walk overland and less by river though the distance was longer. River travelers had to double back on a tributary from the main flow to reach Oxwitik. Both cities had been founded by elite colonists from the great city Mutul; the first dynastic ruler of Oxwitik installed the first recorded ruler of Nahokan. A devastating flood had hit the city several katuns earlier, covering its surface under a deep layer of silt and changing the landscape. The only usable buildings for many years were on a hilltop. The current ruler, K'awill Yopaat, undertook restoration of the site, cleared silt away, built new monuments, expanded the acropolis, and constructed the first ball court.

The canoe guide pointed out several tall carved stelae that towered on a cliff, visible as travelers approached by river. These unusually large stelae were carved from single blocks of red sandstone brought from nearby quarries. The stone's firm texture allowed carvers to make three-dimensional low relief sculptures, which were shaped into long panels of complex glyphic text, many using full-figure numeric representations instead of the dot and bar system. Painted red, the columns of stelae announced the revival of the city and its newfound importance.

Kan Bahlam and Chak Chan stayed several days in Nahokan, sharing their travels in formal court and at feasts with K'awiil Yopaat and ahauob. They toured the three plazas and admired the altars and sculptures decorating the buildings, although to Kan Bahlam's artistic eye, the formal monumentality was rather stiff compared to the naturalistic, flowing grace of Lakam Ha's carvings. The southern part of the main plaza was close to riverside docking, used as a large marketplace filled with vendors' stalls. An impressive array of goods was offered from mountain, coastal, and marine areas.

They continued by river to Oxwitik, sending a messenger ahead to announce their arrival. A grand reception greeted them as they disembarked from the canoes. Tiers of wide stairs rose from the river dock to the main plaza, lined with warriors and priests burning incense. Standing atop the stairs was the ruler, K'ak Nab K'awiil, an impressive figure regally attired in soaring feather headdress, lavish heavy jewelry and multicolored sash over tan loincloth. Thousands of nobles crowded the plaza edge, musicians drummed and blew conches, and commoners converged along the riverbanks to glimpse their long-distance visitors.

The Lakam Ha travelers had learned about the region's dominant city while en route. On this site, the original inhabitants of the valley had built previous cities since ancient times. Late in Baktun 8, a foreign elite group entered the valley and took over the site, founding a new dynasty with its roots in Mutul. Yax K'uk Mo', the dynastic founder, came from the Maya-Teotihuacan bloodline that mingled at Mutul a generation earlier. The first structures he built, placed over the pre-existing adobe platforms, had elements of central Mexica architecture such as the talud-tablero shape on stepped pyramids, brightly colored wall murals and masks with goggle-eye ornaments of Teotihuacan origin. Subsequent rulers in the new dynasty made major improvements to the site, situated in a fertile valley among moderate height foothills. The valley floor was undulating, swampy and prone to seasonal flooding, so they flattened the valley floor and created raised areas for construction. Their control over the rivers, valleys and surrounding settlements was well established by the time of the second dynastic ruler.

K'ak Chan Yopaat, eleventh in the dynasty, preceded the current ruler. The city underwent an unprecedented rise in population during his reign. Residential land use spread to all available building sites in the entire valley, and cultivation pushed up against the hillsides. In the city center, about 8,000 people resided, with another 17,000 in surrounding areas for a total population of 25,000 in the Oxwitik Valley.

The twelfth and present ruler, K'ak Nab K'awiil, had expanded the city structures and added numerous monuments and a total of sixteen stelae, erecting stelae in the main plaza as well as at prominent positions across the countryside, stamping his authority throughout the whole valley. These monuments expressed quintessentially Maya themes of creation, dynastic history, and deities. Other earlier architecture famous in the region included large Petén Maya style masks of the sun God on the second ruler's tomb, and the ornate red temple symbolically placing the dynastic founder in the center of the sky.

Kan Bahlam, Chak Chan and their group bowed to the ruler as they reached the plaza level, exchanged formal greetings, and then joined in a procession across the longest plaza they had ever seen. The colossal rectangle separated two complexes; the northern one formed of a triple pyramid group, range shaped council house and court, and another large pyramid. A small four-sided platform sat in the plaza center, and the southern end held the ball court and raised royal acropolis, a cluster of multiple structures including palace residences with courts, temples, burial pyramids, and elite quarters. The city center was expansive and elegant, giving a sense of serenity mingled with authority. Sakbeob led to other outlying complexes.

After court formalities, presentation of gifts and flowery welcome speeches, the two ahauob of Lakam Ha joined the Oxwitik ruler and his family for the evening meal. They sat beside K'ak Nab K'awiil, his wife and his young son Waxaklajuun Ub'aah K'awiil.

"How fares your father, esteemed K'inich Janaab Pakal?" inquired the ruler. "There are parallels between us, for we both ascended to the throne at youthful ages. He became ruler at age twelve and me at age fifteen. We are of similar age, he being eight years older. We both made significant changes to the architecture and increased the prominence of our cities, while keeping our regions peaceful and prosperous. A man whom I much admire, a man to emulate."

"So say many," Kan Bahlam replied. "My father has been well, although I have not seen him since traveling more than two years. We have had little communication, but I expect a messenger I sent to Lakam Ha to arrive while I am here. Then we shall have more information. I will convey to him your admiration, which I feel confident he returns."

"You are fortunate to travel so widely, few except traders can do this. We shall have a court session in which you both may relate stories of your travels. I understand you went along the coast by sea canoe much of the way. How do you plan to return from here?"

"We thought to go by river to the middle Petén region then overland to Mutul, to assess the situation with Nuun Ujol Chaak and renew our friendship. Though he was forced to leave by Kan's attack, this sibling battling between the Mutul ruler and his brother goes back and forth and he may be reestablished by now."

"You might reconsider those plans," said K'ak Nab K'awiil. "You must not know of recent developments at Mutul, but then you have been in far northern lands. The rightful ruler of Mutul has not returned to his throne, wandering for some time in the jungles. Not long ago he arrived at your city. His traitorous brother sits now upon Mutul's throne, but I doubt that will hold up for long. It is my hunch that your father and Nuun will plan retaliation soon."

"Ah, we have indeed been out of touch since traveling," Chak Chan observed.

"The situation is most unsettled," added K'ak Nab K'awiil. "Kan's ally Yokib has been skirmishing against its neighbors and Imix-Ha is smarting under its defeat by your father and uncle, Bahlam Ahau. This humiliation will not remain unanswered. And the evil instigator of such aggressions, Kan, will lend forces in support."

"Of this I did not know!" Kan Bahlam narrowed his eyes. "Tell us more details of my father and uncle's attack."

The Oxwitik ruler described what he knew of the strategies that overcame the best-defended city along the K'umaxha River. Kan Bahlam's eyes sparkled at his father's cleverness and he expressed regret that he was not there.

"The fate of Mutul is close to my heart, you know that our dynasty came from there," said the ruler. "We should be delighted to see your father help Nuun reclaim his throne and repulse the tendrils of Kan. I am thankful the despicable city is far away, may the distance ever keep them from our lands."

"May it be so." Kan Bahlam and Chak Chan raised hands in saluting this sentiment.

"For your return journey, my advice is to travel as traders," said K'ak Nab K'awiil. "You have too many enemies along the K'umaxha, who would love nothing better than to capture the heir of Lakam Ha. We can make arrangements for your group to join one of our trading expeditions and get you safely home. You would be wise to avoid larger cities and stop only at villages."

They agreed this was a good plan, and conversation drifted to other topics. As the evening ended, Kan Bahlam spoke softly to the ruler.

"My city values our friendship with yours," he said. "It is my thought to make our relations closer with a marriage between our families. We would be honored to send a royal daughter of Lakam Ha to wed one of your successors, though that might be far in the future."

"This we shall see accomplished," the ruler replied. "It would be an enhancement to our lineage to join with your hallowed family."

The travelers lingered several moons in the hospitable city, waiting on the arrival of Kan Bahlam's messenger. They toured farmlands to admire the space-efficient terracing used to exploit every tillable location. They explored the large city and marveled at the unique red temple. This small, two-tiered temple was a tribute to the founder, Yax K'uk Mo' and was striking in its ebullient imagery. The lower walls with one doorway on each side had huge sculptures of the great sky deity Itzamnaaj in his avian aspect, with yellow talon feet and widely spread green wings around his beaked face. The dominant color was red with motifs in white, green, and yellow that expressed personalized mountains, skeletons, and crocodiles. Geometric patterns and masks adorned the roof eaves and upper temple, all beautifully modeled in thick stucco. Vents in the façade permitted incense and smoke from fires lit inside to billow out as swirling clouds that interacted with the sculptures in an animated tableau. The face of Yax K'uk Mo' was placed at the center of this mythological tableau, merging him with Itzamnaaj as the center of the sky. Hieroglyphic stone steps carried a dedicatory inscription, built by the ruler's grandfather. This was the last building to use stucco on such a lavish scale, since population pressure had deforested the valley and the vast quantities of firewood needed to reduce limestone to plaster were no longer available.

When the messenger from Lakam Ha arrived, he brought a written codex from Pakal confirming the assessment of K'ak Nab K'awiil. Pakal warned Kan Bahlam to avoid Mutul and return by river straight to Lakam Ha. The cacao beans he provided permitted his son to arrange disguise as traders, give further gifts to the ruler, and obtain quantities of excellent uncut jade for his parents.

3

The rainy season delayed the departure of Kan Bahlam and his contingent. Their journey with the traders would primarily follow river routes, and both the Pokolha and K'umaxha Rivers turned into raging torrents as turbulent storm clouds released a deluge upon the shuddering jungles. A long stretch of overland portage was necessary between the rivers, surmounting steep mountain passages that became treacherous when drenched. Mudslides and falling rocks had ended many a life and seen precious cargo lost. The traders had learned the wisdom of patience and caution. They would not depart from Oxwitik until conditions were favorable for travel.

Kan Bahlam resigned himself to study with the city's architects and archivists. He became fascinated with the ruling dynasty's ties to Teotihuacan. Pouring over old codices and plying elder priests with questions, he pieced together a story of international intrigue.

The ruling dynasty at Oxwitik traced its origins to a time of upheaval at Mutul. Late in the 8th Baktun, a large force from Teotihuacan led by warrior-chief Siyaj K'ak "arrived" at Mutul, overthrew and killed the Maya ruler, and installed Yax Nuun Ayin on the throne (378 CE). These agents of the pre-Mexica empire continued to spread its influence in the Petén region. Yax Nuun Ayin was a son of Teotihuacan ruler Spearthrower Owl and married into the Mutul royal family, merging the bloodlines. His son, Siyaj Chan K'awiil II, came to rulership at age eleven, and his mother Lady K'inich acted as regent for several years, assisted by a young warrior-chief named Yax K'uk Mo'. This enterprising noble later became ruler of Oxwitik.

Siyaj Chan K'awiil's heritage was emphasized in the codices that Kan Bahlam studied. The young ruler, who ascended about two katuns later (411 CE), asserted his right to rule through a female lineage, similar to Kan Bahlam's own situation. Three generations before, a royal woman named Une Bahlam, whose origins traced to Teotihuacan, had become ruler of Mutul. She was ousted by a competing lineage and Muwaan Jol became ruler (320 CE). It was his son, Chak Tok Ich'aak, who was killed when the Teotihuacan forces "arrived" at Mutul under the leadership of Siyaj K'ak.

According to Oxwitik archival priests, the Holy Lady Une Bahlam escaped from Mutul and sought refuge in Teotihuacan. This cosmopolitan city with a population exceeding 200,000 was home to people from many regions. It had compounds for different groups, including the Olmecs, Zapotecs, and Mayas. She resided in the Maya compound, married into local nobility and became influential in politics. Her daughter married the Teotihuacan ruler Spearthrower Owl and persuaded him to send forces to restore Une Bahlam's lineage to the Mutul throne. Thus the son of Spearthrower Owl, Yax Nuun Ayin, who was installed by Siyaj K'ak, was also the great-grandson of Une Bahlam.

Kan Bahlam found the parallels in Mutul's history fascinating. The tendrils of Teotihuacan reached to many corners of the Maya world, including Oxwitik, Tulan Tzu, and possibly even Lakam Ha. Yax K'uk Mo' had led conquering forces to unseat the long-established local Oxwitik dynasty and assumed the throne, in a repeat of the earlier Teotihuacan "arrival" at Mutul. He married the ruler's widow, infused the Teotihuacan bloodline and brought its cultural and architectural styles to the city.

Subsequent rulers gave great honors to their founder, while culturally becoming more Mayan.

Most intriguing to Kan Bahlam were hints that Teotihuacan may have also seeded the Lakam Ha dynasty. The first human ruler of B'aakal, K'uk Bahlam, appeared suddenly from an unknown place, was called a "Toktan lord" and acceded as Baktun 8 was drawing to a close (431 CE). This dated Lakam Ha's genesis to the rule of Siyaj Chan K'awiil at Mutul during the time of Teotihuacan's greatest influence in the Petén. Toktan and Tulan had similar meanings as "places of reeds" and Teotihuacan was known as a Tulan. Might his own lineage be connected to the great empire? He recalled that Lakam Ha and Mutul had been allies as far back as anyone could remember. Given their geographic distance, such an alliance seemed unusual. This puzzle provided fodder for his fertile mind, and he contemplated the mysteries of how Gods interacted with humans to bring divine intentions into worldly manifestation.

4

S everal moons earlier, when Kan Bahlam's messenger had arrived at Lakam Ha with his request for funds, his parents were relieved. Pakal was happy to send cacao to fund his son's trip home, and Lalak felt reassured that he had reached the southernmost point of his travels. They still faced many moons of uncertainty before he could be expected to return, due to the distance involved and the delay caused by the rainy season. Lalak moodily watched heavy raindrops plopping from the roof eaves of her new residential chambers, forming rivulets across the patio.

The corridors leading through the new palace were expansive, their width supported by the innovative trusses developed by Yax Chan that permitted wider corbelled arches. Utzil walked slowly, taking in the murals painted on walls and ceilings, admiring the gracefully curved pillars and the unusual tri-lobed windows. Her gait was steady but less springy than before, her hair showing streaks of grey. In the dampness her joints tended to ache; she wished this interminable rain would stop. Reaching the quarters of the K'uhul Ixik, an attendant took her to Lalak's reception chamber, a pleasant room with colorful door and window hangings, plush cotton floor mats, and several tall painted ceramic vases. The thick drapes kept dampness away and warmed the room.

Lalak called for hot cacao laced with chiles as her priestess healer and good friend settled upon a mat beside her. A boy about two years old squatted on a mat nearby, forming small wooden toys into shapes that only his mind understood. Utzil knew that unless his mistress was out on formal duties, Koyi would be at her side. Since the royal consort had rescued him from an abusive merchant household, severely disciplining his widowed father, who drank too much balche, the haunted look had disappeared from his eyes and his bruises had healed. He had attached himself to Lalak as securely as a vine to a tall mahogany tree, feeling safest when in her company.

Lalak had developed the practice recently of walking through many city areas, including residences of merchant and artisan classes, and outlying huts of commoners. Her purpose was to ensure that all levels of society at Lakam Ha benefited from their city's prestige and wealth. All should have dry, comfortable dwellings and adequate nourishing food, clean water sources, good clothing and times of enjoyment. When she found families in distress, she took official actions to improve their conditions. Her reputation as an advocate for the less fortunate spread widely, and she was much loved by the people.

"How fares the jaw?" Utzil asked. "I see the swelling is less. Do you still have much pain?" The day before she had drained an abscessed molar in Lalak's lower jaw. Recurrent abscesses and decayed teeth made Utzil worry about Lalak's ability to chew. The priestess thought she had already lost too much weight, her broad frame angular without enough flesh to fill it out.

"It is better," Lalak replied, patting her puffy cheek gently. "Your remedies are helpful; the poultice of allspice and buttonwood that you applied to the gum much reduced the pain. I am taking the Cha-ca tea three times daily to fight infection, as you prescribed. How my joints ache! This rain is doing them no favor." Lalak extended a hand to show Utzil swollen, reddened finger joints.

"We are getting older, Holy Lady," Utzil said. "My joints are complaining also. I will bring poultices to place on your swollen fingers, and you must soak them in warm water several times daily."

"Better, I shall enter the sweat bath more frequently," Lalak offered. "That moist heat always makes my achy body feel good. It is truly a luxury that Pakal included a pib nah within the palace residential quarters."

"And so many sources of fresh water and toilets," remarked the priestess. "I saw that the eastern structure is nearly complete. Where did he get the idea to make such strangely-shaped windows? Almost like a clover leaf with three lobes. Most exotic looking."

"He saw drawings brought by a visitor from the vast southern lands beyond the narrow isthmus. This design was carried by sea voyagers from across the Chik'in-nab, perhaps from islands lying days beyond the western horizon. I find the shape most pleasing, perhaps I shall weave it into fabric for a huipil." Lalak eyed her swollen knuckles dubiously. "If these hands will allow me."

"What other plans has Pakal for expanding the palace complex?"

"He wants to close in the East Court, so it has buildings on three sides. A long corridor is being designed by Yax Chan to span the northern end of the complex, and perhaps to continue along the western side also. Another building on the west could create a closed-off West Court, too. Although the corridors facing out will have many doorways, only a few will allow admittance to the interior structures and courts. Wide stairways will rise from the plaza the entire length of these corridors. It will give an expansive and welcoming feeling, but also control traffic into the Royal Court Chamber, the Popol Nah and the new east chamber."

"If the western corridor extends all the distance to the new south residential chambers, the Sak Nuk Nah will also be enclosed," observed Utzil.

"Yes, I believe that is Pakal's intention. In a way, I regret making the palace less public, but I understand his reasons. With so many distinguished visitors, he must make a powerful impression. Having these key buildings sitting exposed on the huge plaza creates a sense of vulnerability, and even simplicity that does not serve our city's status now."

Lalak paused and sipped her hot, bitter and spicy drink. Her memories turned toward the Sak Nuk Nah in its early days, to the momentous time of solar eclipse when she and Pakal danced in ecstatic sexual alchemy to give rebirth to the divine portal. Her images of that time were amazingly clear, given her state of altered consciousness. An un-summoned sigh escaped as she reflected that her aging body and achy joints could never reenact this feat. It was true that she and Pakal still enjoyed sexual intimacy, and he was amazingly vigorous, but those peak experiences had passed.

"The palace is truly magnificent," said Utzil. "It is the crown jewel of Pakal's building efforts. Though luxurious, it is also comfortable."

"That is so, and I am glad to be living here. I do yearn to be closer to nature. You know this has been my refuge since childhood. I have asked

Pakal to build another residence, smaller and more private, located in the new complexes being planned along the Sutzha River cascades. There is a special place, one that holds my fondest memories, a flat meadow perfect for a residence. He also loves this meadow next to waterfalls and a pond, and agreed to a home there for us."

"Would you move from the palace?"

"No, we must remain here to fulfill our royal activities. It would be a retreat, where we can go at times to restore ourselves." Lalak smiled at the thought of returning to the magical meadow where Pakal's love was kindled.

"That does sound perfect." Utzil sipped cacao then inquired, "How are your two younger sons?"

"Kan Joy Chitam will undergo transformation into adulthood rites soon," Lalak replied. "It is hard to believe my third son is already a man. Tiwol Chan Mat progresses well in his training, although he would rather be enjoying dancing and socializing at feasts. Not that he is shallow, just one who savors social activities."

"Ever a delightful boy, that youngest one. Are you planning their marriages?"

"This is in process. It is Pakal's thought to seek a wife for Tiwol from the ruling family of Uxte'kuh, to solidify that alliance. The second daughter is very close in age and this match will be negotiated after Tiwol's transformation into adulthood ritual. Pakal's intentions for Kan Joy are to bind a problematic family in Lakam Ha to us with a royal marriage. The Chuuah family has long questioned the legitimacy of Pakal's succession. You may recall that Ek Chuuah led attacks upon our city to unseat the Bahlam dynasty many years ago. His distant cousin Matunha was the prior High Priestess, and she was plotting against us before her death. To circumvent further scheming by that family, Pakal has selected the oldest daughter for Kan Joy's wife. Their bloodlines are appropriate, and with this marriage will flow into the ruling dynasty. A good way to satisfy their ambitions."

"A wise choice. Pakal is a great strategist. Will this happen soon?"

"Shortly after Kan Joy's adulthood rites, negotiations are taking place now."

"What hear you of Kan Bahlam?"

"Ah, my wandering son is finally turning his eyes homeward. Presently he waits in Oxwitik for the rains to stop, and then he will undertake the river journey back. He has not been much concerned with keeping in touch with his family. We received only two messages; you remember the first sent during his stay in Coba." Lalak smiled wryly and added, "The impetus for this message probably came from the Coba emissary who visited here. The second message requested funds to complete his travels, a most practical communication."

"Sending messages over such long distances is difficult, and he had few attendants to spare. Kan Bahlam is prudent, he would shepherd his resources to accomplish his travels," said Utzil.

"I wonder if they will change him. Surely he will have both profound and troublesome experiences, things that mature and broaden one."

The drapes covering the door swayed and Muyal's head peeped through.

"Pardon me, Holy Lady; are you ready to receive the wives of our visiting dignitaries?"

"Very soon, please keep them entertained for a few more moments. We are just finishing our session, bring them in when Utzil leaves," said Lalak. She thanked Utzil for the visit, reassured the healer that she would take remedies faithfully, and bid her good-bye. Her heart was thankful for the lengthy services of the Ix Chel priestess; they had endured times of tragedy and celebrated joys over many years.

5

Lakam Ha was in a mood of celebration when Kan Bahlam returned. Preparations were underway for the marriage ceremony of his brother Kan Joy Chitam and Te' Kuy, oldest daughter of the elite Chuuah family. The safe return of the royal heir and his companions was another cause for rejoicing, giving the people several more days of festivities. Even in the swirl of activities, the royal family found time for long sessions together, hearing about Kan Bahlam's adventures and exclaiming over his presents of jade and marine objects. Pakal held private meetings with his son for debriefing about political situations in distant regions, and concurred with the goal of a marriage alliance with Oxwitik. Chak Chan received praise when he presented Pakal with the codex detailing traditions of the women's island, Cuzamil, and exploits of the Ix Chel priestesses there.

Kan Bahlam was disturbed to see that his mother had aged during the three years of his absence. Though her spirit was vibrant, her body appeared thinner and she moved more slowly. He inquired of Utzil; the priestess-healer reported that chronic joint and bone diseases were wearing Lalak down but posed no immediate threat to her life. That he felt such deep concern for his mother surprised him. Kan Bahlam found encouragement in Utzil's stories of Lalak's interest in lower levels of society and admired her adoption of the mistreated boy Koyi.

After Kan Joy Chitam's spectacular wedding with lavish feasting and days of dancing at the winter solstice, conflicts in the region commanded the men's attention. News arrived by messenger that the rulers of Yokib and Kan had performed a joint ceremony reaffirming their alliance. Six days afterwards, Yokib attacked Wa-Mut because its rulers were not providing enough tribute and support to the Kan overlords. This renewed hostility was occurring too close to home. Pakal called a war council, which decided to launch a raid against Yokib to be carried out quickly. Less than a moon later, Lakam Ha's forces delivered a decisive blow to Yokib, destroying several monuments and taking captives. Kan forces continued to vie with Lakam Ha for dominance of the plains to the northeast, re-installing the boy ruler of Moral who had recently been unseated by Lakam Ha's ally Popo'.

Kan Bahlam joined his father in the raid on Yokib. Once again he fought fiercely, unleashing his aggression on enemy warriors and earning the respect of Lakam Ha leaders. Kan Joy Chitam did not accompany the war party, as he was newly married and not well trained as a warrior. He was becoming known as a court dilettante, whose sharp and witty tongue put many a courtier to shame. Command of the courtly language and using it to disparage others had become his forte. This was a talent that Kan Bahlam disdained, preferring the straightforward ways of warriors, although his mind also held the arcane complexities of astronomy and numerology.

Hostilities continued to simmer with the contested cities of the plains northeast of Lakam Ha. Pakal carried out raids against Wa-Mut and the nearby site Pipá, which maintained their alliances with Kan. Several captives were taken, including two lords from royal families captured in a battle over two successive days. These captives were kept under guard at Lakam Ha and displayed in public processions as proof of the city's prowess against its enemies.

Pakal discussed plans with his chief architect Yax Chan for constructing a mirror image building across the courtyard from the Royal Court chambers. The new structure would be the same length, parallel to the existing one. Both would thus be oriented north-south with stairs providing access into the East Court, flanked by alfarda-style sculptures.

The six piers on the eastern and western sides of the Royal Court building would be repeated in the new one, along with central doorways. The new building was intended to complement the existing one architecturally, and to demarcate the limits of the East Court. The central doorway of the new building would become the principal entrance into the palace. Going through this door, visitors would directly enter the East Court, the largest and most accessible palace courtyard. Standing at the threshold of the East Court, visitors would see a large, elaborately decorated, semi-public space bounded by lavishly decorated façades relating the military victories of the city.

It was meant to impress and intimidate delegates and visitors. Until this point, Pakal had not commissioned sculptures or panels with militaristic themes. That he felt compelled to do so was testimony to the unsettled conditions in the region. Already his stone-carvers had nearly finished the sculptures of captives lining the foundation of the Royal Court building facing onto the courtyard, and were working on glyphs for the hieroglyphic stairway. Six captives from Wa-Mut and Pipá were depicted on the building foundation in poses and garments of subjugation. They were kneeling with arms grasping shoulders in the traditional supplication posture, attired simply with a bar pectoral, plain loincloth with bell ornaments, wristlets with ahau bones attached, and minimal headdresses. Two figures were identified as Ba-ch'ok, heirs of royal families. One wore a zoomorphic headdress and the other a Jaguar God headdress. On the alfardas that flanked the stairs, sculptures of two additional captives were dressed similarly. Both wore simple cloth headdresses, rectangular pectorals, and loincloths that displayed stacks of knotted bars.

All the captive figures had strips of white cloth pulled through each ear perforation that would normally hold elaborate ear flares. Replacing ear jewelry with white cloth strips was widely used among the Mayas to indicate captive status. The identities of all these figures were drummed home three times: in the stairway text, in their own personal captions, and in the glyphic headdresses they wore.

Glyphic narratives of military activities of these times were tied to the earlier attack by Kan that had destroyed Lakam Ha's portal to the Gods. The narratives re-told this momentous event and presented the city's victories during the past several years as proper retaliation, commemorating these dates in sculptures and hieroglyphic stairways of the buildings of the East Court.

Baktun 9, Katun 11, Tun 9, Uinal 10, Kin 12, on the date 6 Eb 10 Uo (March 25, 662 CE)

Baktun 9, Katun 11, Tun 9, Uinal 10, Kin 13, on the date 7 Ben 11 Uo (March 26, 662 CE)

Pakal undertook yet another event to emphasize his intention to impose retribution on cities that joined the Kan alliance against Lakam Ha. One year after the victories against Wa-Mut and Pipá, he publically executed the captured Pipá Ba-ch'ok. This was carried out in an impressive ceremony held in the East Court. Standing on the east steps of the Royal Court, beneath the large stucco heads of Gods on the mansard roof, he oversaw the young lord's decapitation. It was recorded that "he entered the road." This signified setting out on the Xibalba Be, the Dark Road that led to the Underworld journey. Later, the date of this event would be commemorated on the foundation and alfardas of the new building that complemented the Royal Court building, on the opposite side of the East Court.

Baktun 9, Katun 11, Tun 10, Uinal 16, Kin 7, on the date 13 Manik End of Yaxk'in (July 13, 663 CE)

Experiences during this period of regional aggressions brought Kan Bahlam into a pensive state of mind. He was wounded in the left side during one battle. Although the wound was not deep and the spear point glanced off his hip, it would have been fatal if the spear had pierced his lower abdomen. This caused him to reflect upon life and death, especially continuation of his lineage. His feelings toward his family softened. Signs of his mother's deteriorating health saddened him. He became more attentive to his wife, Talol, than he had been before his trip. He sought confirmation that the time had arrived to engender heirs. Calendar priests calculated auspicious dates for the birth of their children and priestess-healers prepared her for conception. Although the couple followed these instructions meticulously, months passed without Talol becoming pregnant. Kan Bahlam underwent more examination by healers, but no evidence of disease could be found.

Kan Joy Chitam's new wife conceived as planned within a few moon cycles, but the pregnancy ended in early miscarriage. After a second miscarriage the next year, Lalak and Pakal became concerned about succession. It was now essential to learn whether Kan Bahlam was capable of fathering a child. Lalak set up an experiment to find the answer, with Pakal's concurrence. She selected a minor noblewoman, widow of a warrior who had produced three healthy sons, and offered a mutually beneficial arrangement. The woman would become a concubine for Kan Bahlam, with the promise of support for herself and her children the rest of their lives. Should pregnancy and birth occur, she would become his second wife so their sons could enter royal succession. If no children resulted after one year, the conclusion would be that Kan Bahlam was sterile. The woman could continue her relationship with him or not, as the two preferred.

The widow agreed and Kan Bahlam followed the mandate of his parents, not altogether objecting, as he was tiring of Talol. Once again the couple followed protocols for conceiving according to the well-established science of Ix Chel healers, but each cycle the widow's moon flow repeated, signaling no pregnancy. When a solar year had passed, the priestesses arrived at the conclusion that Kan Bahlam was incapable of producing offspring. This was most likely an aftermath of his episode of jungle fever.

Lalak and Pakal called a session with Kan Bahlam to discuss the ramifications of this experiment. It pained Lalak to emphasize such an undesirable conclusion to her son, but she believed facing it squarely would be best. She could tell that Pakal was deeply disturbed, noting signs of tension around his eyes.

"The priestesses of Ix Chel have reached accord," Pakal said after greeting his son and settling onto mats. "Much is it my regret, that they concluded the widow's not conceiving in over a year does indicate that you will not be able to produce heirs. This is cause for great concern over the future of our dynasty."

"It is not to place blame upon you," Lalak added quickly as she observed her son's expression darken. "The jungle fever was not something you brought on, but an unfortunate imposition by the Gods. Their ways and motives are often beyond human understanding."

She caught Pakal's eye, warning him to avoid revealing his bargain with the Death Lord. They had discussed this before, and decided any mention would further complicate a difficult situation.

"Indeed," Pakal rejoined. "Even rulers must bow to the will of the Gods. This is not something that sits well with me, or with you I am sure, but we must accept it."

Kan Bahlam shook his head and made the hand gesture for "no."

"I do not accept it," he said forcefully, keeping his tone carefully controlled. "It is completely unreasonable that a young man as strong and virile as I am would be unable to have sons. The priestesses are wrong. They have reached an erroneous conclusion. The widow's womb has dried up from producing too many children. She is unable to conceive more. Why must we accept their verdict?"

His parents were shocked by this stark denial and exchanged glances. Moments of tense silence hung heavily in the chamber.

"So, you question their conclusion." Pakal's voice sounded thin and strained.

"Yes, I hold it in question. It is too soon to decide such a momentous thing," Kan Bahlam replied.

"But, my son, over several years of marriage and another with a concubine, while following procedures known to enhance conception, no pregnancy has resulted," Lalak enjoined as gently as she could.

"That is still not conclusive," retorted Kan Bahlam.

Pakal's face flushed; he felt a surge of anger at his son's hard-headedness.

"Be honest with yourself, Kan Bahlam," he barked. "There is evidence beyond these two women. It is no secret that you spread your favors among many women in our city. Have any of them conceived your child?"

"They all use herbs to prevent pregnancy, that is widespread among our women," Kan Bahlam said heatedly.

"Not even one might have desired a child by the Ba-ch'ok?" Pakal shot back.

Kan Bahlam set his jaw and stared into the distance.

"Dear one, try to accept what appears inevitable," Lalak said softly. "Well do I know how deeply this wounds you. Our hearts also grieve over this."

"No, it cannot be so!" Kan Bahlam sprang to his feel, eyes blazing. He stretched his tall, muscular body its full height, both fists clenched. "I will sire an heir! My potency is not damaged; this is all conjecture, not true evidence. You will see—there will be a son to continue our dynasty!"

He stomped out of the chamber, tossing the door hanging aside noisily.

The royal couple sat silently, each lost in a swirl of emotions.

"He is difficult," Pakal murmured.

"What he is facing is difficult," Lalak said.

"Ah, that is so. The drive to have sons to perpetuate one's bloodline is strong among men, and becomes an imperative among rulers."

"Perhaps he will come to accept his constraint in time."

"Or perhaps not. His will is immense."

"Pakal, soon you must set the succession. You must designate the heirs to follow Kan Bahlam. Otherwise, our polity could be thrown into chaos."

After the contentious meeting with his parents, Kan Bahlam avoided them as much as possible. While Pakal dedicated his new additions to the palace, completed residential complexes across from the palace and bordering the Sutzha River cascades, and planned further structures on the main plaza, Kan Bahlam retreated into his astronomy academy. Surrounded by fellow star-gazers, his fertile mind conjoined streams of knowledge from his own training and what he learned during his Yukatek travels. Cycles upon cycles, patterns within patterns, were taking shape in his inner cosmos. The scholars used the walls of one chamber as a workshop, drawing glyphs and writing numbers with paint upon the plastered walls as they worked out stellar almanacs and numerological sequences. When finished with a set of calculations, they had the walls re-plastered in readiness for the next explorations, copying into codices their relevant conclusions.

"There is an underlying cycle that can connect all others, of this I am certain," Kan Bahlam reflected after long days of calculations failed.

"This may be so," said Mut, "but it certainly is eluding us."

"My head is swimming, I can think no more," moaned Chak Chan.

"This is far beyond my comprehension," complained Yuhk Makab'te. "Why you want me here escapes my understanding. My place is in court, not drifting hopelessly among your stars and incessant numbers."

"Yours is a sharp mind," retorted Kan Bahlam. "A fresh perspective, a grounding energy when we fly too far into cosmic vastness. You will know when we are off course, or when something significant is found."

Four other aspiring astronomers slumped against walls, the picture of defeat.

"You are laggards!" Kan Bahlam strode in front of the deflated lineup, eyes blazing. "All these calculations! Cannot you find something meaningful, some buried pattern? The best minds in Lakam Ha and you act like snot-nosed boys. Where is your fortitude? Where is your vision? We can accomplish this, you must not give up."

Several young men squirmed under this tongue-lashing, but Chak Chan just laughed and clasped his head in both hands. Spending three years as close traveling companion with the heir put him at ease with such outbursts; he knew Kan Bahlam's moods were volatile and could change in a heartbeat.

"Let us call for some strong cacao drinks," Chak Chan said. "This late in the afternoon, our minds fall into somnolence and must have a boost."

"Just so!" Kan Bahlam at once clapped for attendants and ordered the drinks. He and Chak Chan walked outside to stand on the platform, gazing west toward the lowering sun. It was a lovely sight, the expansive main plaza stretching from the three-building educational complex past the palace and temples to the steep hill on which perched the Lak'in-East

Temple. Not the easternmost structure anymore, Kan Bahlam reflected, but still the highest pyramid that caught the first rays of sunrise. The white plaster of the plaza was taking on golden hues and the red-orange buildings glowing as if on fire, creating a magical tableau.

"Ah, this view always takes my breath away," murmured Kan Bahlam.

"It is striking," Chak Chan agreed.

"Can you see the markers where my father is laying out his mortuary pyramid, right next to the foundation being built for my mother's crypt?"

"I believe so, just at the base of the Lak'in stairway?" Chak Chan shaded his eyes against the sunlight.

"Yes. It makes one think of life's fragility." Or perhaps not, Kan Bahlam mused. His father was now sixty-three years and showing no signs of decreased vigor. Was he indeed a God who would live forever?

"To the left of the palace, over there," Kan Bahlam said, waving his arm toward the towering mountain south of the palace, across the Otulum River. "An image of a triple pyramid group in that location keeps coming to me. Strange that we have no hearthstone group in Lakam Ha. Remember how many we saw in Yukatek cities?"

Chak Chan nodded, gazing in the direction of the mountain.

"These will be my legacy," said Kan Bahlam. "A stunning new triple pyramid group that mirrors the hearth of creation, that reconstructs the three cosmic hearthstones in the heart of Lakam Ha. That records in stone our people's origins and history, our dynasty's oneness with the Triad Gods, for all in the future to see. That, and the calendar linking all other calendars, the numerology of the cosmos, the secrets to decode all cycles. This knowledge will be held by only a few, an elite intelligentsia whose power will spread over our region through a language of numbers and symbols. We are the core."

They were interrupted by servants hurrying up the stairs with steaming cups of cacao and snacks. Before turning to re-enter the chamber, Kan Bahlam grasped Chak Chan's shoulder and pierced him with burning eyes.

"In this we must succeed. We will find that underlying cycle. It is my inheritance, the product of my creative power."

Chak Chan knew perfectly what he meant.

6

Tiwol Chan Mat stood back to admire his latest creation, a clay figurine of Itzamnaaj that he had modeled and painted. The figurine was the size of two hand-breadths, seated in cross-legged posture with the left arm flexed, hand reaching out in a receptive gesture, and the right hand curved over his lap. As the paramount sky deity, inventor of writing and the calendar, Itzamnaaj was usually portrayed as an old wise man seated on a sky band. In Tiwol's depiction, the God wore the spangled turban and pectoral ornament typical of scribes, emphasizing his role as the patron of learning and arts. Long quetzal feathers arched from the headdress over his back, and in front foliated elements and flowers protruded, suggesting his connections to the Maize God. Brightly colored paint created a lively image as the figurine seemed in the act of leaning forward, reaching out as if expecting some gift.

The youngest son in the Bahlam dynasty had become enamored of clay sculpting, finding an unexpected talent for creating life-like replicas. His ability to shape fine details of adornment and dress, and reproduce facial expressions accurately drew praise from carvers and painters, scribes and potters. Tiwol had a steady hand for writing intricate Maya glyphs in the flowing cursive style that was greatly admired throughout B'aakal. His sense of color created a sprightly palate with its unique signature. His figurines and painted pottery were in great demand.

It pleased Tiwol to have a work of his own that gained him recognition. His elder brother Kan Bahlam had a growing reputation as an astronomer-scholar, drawing students to his academy from many distant regions. Kan Joy Chitam, four years his senior, was the darling of the Royal Court, much in demand at feasts and celebrations for his amusing though biting oratory skills. And his father, the renowned and deified Pakal, commanded the highest respect and admiration for envisioning the dazzling architecture that made their city unique in the Maya world. Perhaps his own creations were diminutive in comparison, but none would gainsay their exquisite perfection.

Life at Lakam Ha was going well for Tiwol Chan Mat. He was much honored during his transition to adulthood rites the previous year. His circle of close friends included some of the finest artists in the city. Only two moon cycles ago, his father had performed a major ceremony to set the dynastic succession, into which Tiwol was placed. This ceremony made clear the ruler's wishes for inheritance of the throne, taking every contingency into account. As the youngest son, Tiwol had not expected to be mentioned. But Pakal informed him that indeed he would be in line for the throne, and must participate in the ceremony.

In splendid ritual attire, Pakal and his three sons promenaded through the great plaza that was packed with people. Musicians, dancers, and warriors carrying Lakam Ha banners preceded the royal men around the plaza and up the stairs to the throne room in the Sak Nuk Nah. In sacred ceremony with priests chanting to accompaniment by ceramic whistles, gourd rattles, and turtle carapace drums, Pakal sat upon the throne with his sons on mats in front. Seated there, on the top step of the stairs leading to the throne room, they gazed across a sea of faces filling the inner courtyard and spilling down the wide stairs onto the plaza below. It was a heady moment, a time of maximum adulation by the people.

In a ringing voice, Pakal ceremoniously called forth the setting of the succession.

"First there shall be the Ba-ch'ok, my eldest son Kan Bahlam. Should he have sons, they shall follow by age, from oldest to youngest. Should he have no sons, succession shall pass to my second son, Kan Joy Chitam. Should he have sons, they shall follow by age, from oldest to youngest. Should he have no sons, succession shall pass to my youngest son, Tiwol Chan Mat. Succession shall then pass to his sons, and they shall follow by age, from oldest to youngest.

"Thus have I, K'inich Janaab Pakal K'uhul B'aakal Ahau, set the succession for rulership of our city Lakam Ha, and governance of our polity, B'aakal."

No one questioned where succession would go if none of Pakal's sons had male descendants. The three men were young enough and seemed healthy; surely one of them would have a surviving male offspring.

Lalak harbored concern, but recognized that Pakal's tactic was the wisest course. It was best to avoid seeding doubt about the Bahlam dynasty's future. In her heart, she believed that Kan Bahlam would never have children, despite his defiant stance. Kan Joy Chitam and Te' Kuy had lost four pregnancies when Lalak felt compelled to intercede. She performed a ceremony to Ix Zuhuy K'ak, the Goddess who brought fertility into her own life, and requested permission to help Te' Kuy with sexual alchemy. During this ritual trance, the Goddess appeared and granted the request. Lalak undertook training her daughter-in-law, while instructing the Lunar Priestesses to renew training her son in techniques he had already learned, but probably had forgotten. Because of Lalak's diminished vigor, the training was exhausting. She found it difficult to sustain the level of concentration such teaching required, and could not keep up walking through the city, assessing the conditions of the commoners. But her resolve was firmly set, and she persisted over many moons until she sensed that her student had attained adequate mastery.

After this lengthy time of abstinence and building sexual energy, prognostications were cast by Solar Priests and a time for conception set. This pregnancy did take hold, and went to successful completion. Although techniques for conception were used that should guarantee a boy, the baby was a girl. She was healthy and vigorous from the moment of birth, however, and all rejoiced simply to have a living child. Now the child was nearly three years old, and the parents were once again using sexual alchemy for conception. So far, a second success eluded them.

Pakal would not name his granddaughter to dynastic succession, of this Lalak had no doubt. He was convinced that Lakam Ha would not accept a third female succession. There had been enough issues with the Bahlam dynasty continuing through his mother and grandmother. Even co-opting the Chuuah family through Te' Kuy's marriage into the royal lineage, sufficient challengers to royal succession remained among elite families. Pakal's successor would have to be male. To attain this, he might need to rule a very long time, Lalak feared.

There was fresh hope on the horizon, however. Plans were underway to seek a match between Tiwol Chan Mat and the second daughter of the Uxte'kuh ruling family. Pakal would dispatch his Royal Steward Muk Kab to this city, bringing preliminary gifts and beginning the negotiation process. Though rather old for travel, Muk Kab had the status and experience needed to represent the Lakam Ha royal family. His trip would be by litter, a leisurely journey of several moons. Should the preliminary negotiations be successful, a member of the royal family, probably Kan Bahlam, would visit Uxte'kuh to finalize the arrangements.

The prospect of a lovely young bride, for traders reported her attributes in glowing terms, added to Tiwol's contentment. For the present, he was satisfied with the services of Lunar Priestesses. He did not share his elder brother's appetites for women, for which he felt grateful. Life was simpler when devoted to his art, his round of feasting with friends, and his enjoyment of dance and music.

7

N uun Ujol Chaak rejoiced that his exile in Lakam Ha was about to end. Thirteen long years had elapsed since he arrived in the city, years of waiting and politicking to gain Pakal's agreement for a campaign to restore the Mutul ruler to the throne. The time was finally right, the stars in proper alignment and the warriors ready. Spies sent to Imix-ha and Mutul brought information about the patterns of residence and warrior forces for Balaj Chan K'awiil, who divided his time between the two cities he now ruled. Pakal's strategy was to attack at Imix-ha and either capture or expel the ruler, decimate the city's warriors, and set up a puppet Sahal from Lakam Ha. His forces would proceed to Mutul and defeat enemy forces there, restoring Nuun to the throne.

Bahlam Ahau did not join in this campaign, for he was elderly and ill, contending with succession issues at B'aak. Lakam Ha had a large military force, sufficient to mount the campaign, thanks to its population growth. Allied forces from Sak Tz'i and Popo' bolstered the number of troops. Additional warriors had migrated from occupied Mutul over the years to join their preferred ruler in exile.

Pakal went with his forces during the initial phase, but his presence was required in Lakam Ha to conduct katun end ceremonies. He left Kan Bahlam and K'akmo to command the warriors in collaboration with Nuun. The day before the eleventh katun ended, messengers brought word of a resounding defeat of Imix-ha, sending Balaj scurrying into the jungle to find refuge once again at Kan's city, Uxte'tun.

With high spirits, Pakal conducted his third k'altun stone-binding ceremony at the end of Katun 11. At this ritual, the re-opening of the portal was completed, and the religious charter at Lakam Ha fully restored. His prior rituals and his steady fulfillment of the deities' requirements accomplished this over a lengthy time period, nearly sixty years. In ritual language, this slow progression moved from the Gods "possessing the katun" on the first period katun end; to the "naming of the Gods' adornments" on the second period katun end; and now to the "Gods re-seating themselves" on the third period katun end.

The third period katun end date and description of rituals were later carved on the middle tablet in the temple of Pakal's mortuary pyramid, under Kan Bahlam's direction.

Baktun 9, Katun 12, Tun 0, Uinal 0, Kin 0, on the date 10 Ahau 8 Yaxk'in (July 1, 672 CE).

"It is his third k'altun on 10 Ahau 8 Yaxk'in, the twelfth katun.

K'inich Janaab Pakal K'uhul B'aakal Ahau oversaw it. Ten becomes ahau.

The Jeweled Sky Tree matured.

The West ahauob and the East ahauob descended.

They seated themselves, the 9 Chan Yoch'ok'in, 16 Ch'ok'in, 9 Tz'ak Ahau.

It is Janaab Pakal's second taking of the white paper headband on the altar of the Gods. He is the juntan-beloved of the Gods.

He ties on the paper headband on the throne of the three Gods: Hun Ahau, Mah Kinah Ahau and Unen K'awiil, the B'aakal Triad.

He appeases the heart of the God of 10 Ahau 8 Yaxk'in k'altun."

The celestial tree had matured, and this allowed the descent of the Lords of the First Sky, those ancestral deities who had been unreachable after the destruction of the portal. The maturing of the celestial *ikatz* flowing through the tree allowed for renewed communication between cosmological realms. Once again Pakal gave to the Triad Gods their gift bundles, now including their earspoowls and necklaces along with their special hats. They were fully adorned, their ritual acknowledgement completely satisfied. The portal to the Gods and ancestors was firmly re-established. Pakal added a promise for future stability in this renewed relationship with the deities.

"And then he appeases the heart of the successor, the lord of 8 Ahau 8 Uo,

The thirteenth katun..."

The deities would continue to be satisfied at the next katun ending, whether or not Pakal was alive. The ruler's duties to adorn and give gifts to the Gods would still be performed. Pakal had fundamentally reconstructed the conditions through which rulers fulfilled their responsibilities. The text assured that his successors could perform these duties seven generations into the future.

When Kan Bahlam and the warriors of Lakam Ha returned triumphantly, they reported that Nuun had been reseated on the Mutul throne. His loyal followers were rejoicing and the opposition either killed or expelled from the city. Yuhk Makab'te had been appointed as Sahal of

Imix-ha, to oversee the city's administration and keep insurrection under control. For the time being, the upper K'umaxha River region was stable and under Lakam Ha and Mutul control.

8

L alak lay on thick mats placed on the patio of her residence in the Sutzha River complex. Her ever-present shadow Koyi dozed at her feet in the warm sun. The small patio was open on one side to give full view of the waterfall and pond where Lalak and Pakal swam together long ago. The rest of the meadow was covered by buildings, all part of her residence. Birds twittered in the tree canopy, insects buzzed, and monkeys chattered; the jungle sounds all blending with the splashing waterfall. The sun made Lalak drowsy and she drifted between dreams and memories, barely able to distinguish between them. Was there truly a difference? These seemed more real to her than her waking moments.

She could not rise or walk now without assistance. To ease her constant pain, Utzil plied her with pain-numbing teas that made her even less cogent. It did not matter; her council was no longer needed, her work in this life completed. What was the measure of a person's life? What one produced, what one accomplished, one's children, one's regard by others? Surely she had attained plenty of these things, but she wondered if that would leave any impression many years in the future.

She had fulfilled her purpose in coming to Lakam Ha, she had lived up to the burdensome name given by her mother-in-law. Tz'aakb'u Ahau, she who ordered the succession of lords, she who produced the dynasty. Four living sons she had borne Pakal, and several others lost, but with little dynastic result so far. Kan Bahlam would never have children. Kan Joy Chitam and Te' Kuy had not yet brought a living son into the world, although their daughter was delightful. Tiwol Chan Mat's marriage was being negotiated; the results of this union remained to be seen. Unless he produced a male heir, the dynastic succession was looking uncertain.

A deep sigh escaped her lips, causing Koyi to grunt and change positions, but not to awaken. The boy was a heavy sleeper, and seemed to have no interests but being beside her, tending to her needs. That was sufficient, she decided. Although now ten years old, he asked for no training in a skill or art, and he sought no other children's friendship. It seemed uncanny that his entire existence was invested in her. Life had many mysteries, she concluded, far more than her mind could comprehend.

Perhaps Tiwol Chan Mat would save the dynasty. Pakal was making final arrangements for his youngest son's marriage to the Uxte'kuh ruler's daughter. They had waited longer than usual for this match; Tiwol was now twenty-five years old and eager for a wife. Pakal's military campaigns and katun end ceremonies were part of the delay; the other part was the tedious negotiations necessary to obtain consent from the wary ruling family. They had not forgotten her brother Bahlam Ahau's raids on their city, and were driving hard bargains in setting conditions of the alliance. It was almost settled now, but Lalak doubted she would live to see this marriage.

She knew death was approaching, she could feel the life force slipping from her crippled body. Death did not frighten her; she had prepared with the priesthood for this final transition, the moment when her being would change irrevocably into another form of existence. Her soul would be ready to confront the Death Lords of Xibalba, her path through the Dark Road smoothed by proper rituals and offerings, her tomb equipped with everything she needed on this afterlife journey. Pakal had nearly finished building her mortuary pyramid, a modest building abutting the ground he had marked for his own pyramid tomb. The large stone sarcophagus was carved, ready to receive her mortal remains. It was all as it should be.

Lalak's eyelids drooped and she nodded off again, soothed by the warm sunshine on her face and legs. She pulled off the light blanket due to the warmth, and relished a soft breeze caressing her skin. Memories welled of another caress in this place, of Pakal's gentle hands and scintillating embrace, of the love-making when their hearts and bodies magically joined. Half-conscious, she luxuriated in these delightful images, once again a voluptuous young woman with passion and vitality. Surely the dimensions between realities were thin, if she could relive such moments as if they were now happening.

Vaguely through her reverie, she felt a tiny sting on her left shin. Unwilling to awaken, she ignored the sensation and submerged into delicious images that filled her body with ecstasy. On her leg, a wasp perched, turning in circles to examine its handiwork. Curling its tail toward the tiny bite that broke the surface of Lalak's skin, the wasp extruded her ovipositor, a thin stinger, into the nick and deposited several tiny eggs. She danced around celebrating her work, and then buzzed off into the foliage. Lalak did not stir, and Koyi snoozed on undisturbed.

Utzil hurried up the steep steps that ascended from the Sutzha River complex to the main plaza, covering the distance to the palace as quickly as she could. Her knees creaked as she climbed the final stairway of the palace platform, and she breathed hard to regain her composure. It would not do to bring her sad news to Pakal all flustered and breathless. Everyone knew it was coming.

Pakal's attendant admitted her to his chambers without question. As her eyes met those of the ruler, she knew speaking was not necessary, but convention forced the words out.

"Holy Lord, her time has come. It will not be long now, and you wanted to be beside her. Much do I regret bringing you this notice. My heart is heavy."

"This I know, Utzil. You have ever done difficult duties for our family, and I truly admire you for it. Tell my attendant to inform the others. I shall leave immediately to be with her."

Pakal walked slowly, as though the delay might put off the inevitable. Lalak had been by his side for so many years, he could not imagine being without her. Yet he knew her suffering, and watched as illness overwhelmed her once strong body. The fluid that had accumulated from malfunctioning elimination caused her lower legs, abdomen and face to swell. Apparently her mind was also affected, because she often had trouble recognizing people or following their words. Seeing her in such a state pained his heart beyond measure. As hard as it was for him to release her, he knew this transition would free her spirit into the realm of ancestors. She would become a twinkling star in the sky to delight him, beckoning him to join in celestial dance.

He sat beside her as she lay upon her sleeping bench, holding her hand. He was not certain she knew he was there; she appeared unconscious and her breathing was rasping and difficult. Attendants hovered outside the chamber doorway, admitting family members as they appeared. Utzil rejoined her mistress and sat solemnly on a nearby mat. Koyi crouched at the end of the bench, tears rolling down his cheeks. In the exterior courtyard, people were gathering as word spread that the K'uhul Ixik was dying. Soft drumbeats accompanied mournful chanting, the dirge of death for those making the transition.

When there were long pauses in her breath, Pakal thought her spirit had departed, only to be startled by sudden onset of another round of labored breathing. He could tell by the anguished faces of his sons that they also were having difficulty. Kan Bahlam sat with face buried in his hands, perhaps lost in remorse for past offenses or omissions. Muyal, closest attendant and long-time friend to Lalak, who had eased her adjustments to life at Lakam Ha, wept silently. The two daughter-in-laws, main courtiers, and the High Priest and Priestess stood vigil outside the chamber.

At the end of several gasps, Lalak's breathing quieted and her eyes flew open.

"Pakal." Her croaking voice was barely discernible.

He leaned toward her, engaging her eyes that were clear and lucid.

"Here I am, beloved," he whispered.

"Heart of my heart. My love for you will never end."

"Nor mine for you."

"It will be well... do not worry. Look to Tiwol, he will carry the dynasty forward."

Pakal smiled at her commitment that fended off even death.

"So I shall. We have accomplished what was needed, have we not?"

"Ah... it is so." Her eyelids fluttered and she drifted into somnolence.

Pakal felt tears burning behind his own eyelids, his heart torn by this moment of deep communion that reminded him of what he had lost. Memories rushed in, threatening to overwhelm him and he fought for self-control. Tiwol and Kan Joy knelt beside him, arms around his shoulders. Kan Bahlam stood behind, his eyes moist also.

Without opening her eyes, Lalak's airy words floated on her final breath.

"The paddler Gods are here... they draw me into the canoe... I come... the sky is so full of stars..."

The sacred itz that infused life-force departed Lalak's body and her features settled into the mask of death.

Burial rituals for the K'uhul Ixik of B'aakal took several days. Her body was bathed and cleansed, then covered with a paste of cinnabar, red mercuric oxide that was a preservative and symbolized the color of birth, death, and blood. Cinnabar was toxic and the embalmers took care to prevent it from touching other parts of their bodies except the hands, which they washed frequently. She was adorned with expensive jewelry, including a 1,200 piece jade necklace, a diadem of shell and copper discs in a double row upon her head, and numerous pearl and jade beads, obsidian blades, bone needles, and shells placed over her body. Large earspools and wristlets of jade were put in place. A belt with three small limestone axes wrapped her waist. Pakal lovingly dropped a small jade mask of his own face into her left hand. The final adornment was a mask of malachite and jade made of thousands of pieces and shaped to fit her face, with white shells for eyes and round obsidian pupils. A red-colored shroud of highest quality cotton was used to carefully wrap the body in an extended position, ankles close together.

In formal procession, Lalak's wrapped body was carried on an open litter from the Sutzha River residence, across the main plaza to the small mortuary temple. The route was lined by warriors and priests forming a passageway; residents of Lakam Ha and other polity cities filled the plaza creating a sea of humanity that lapped onto pyramid and palace stairways. The High Priest and Priestess led the procession, followed by other priesthood and ahauob, with the royal family immediately in front of the litter. Musicians played drums, long wooden trumpets, and flutes in stately cadence. Behind the litter came royal attendants and servants.

The sarcophagus waited, a huge monolithic tomb made from a single limestone block. Its interior was completely coated with red cinnabar. The sarcophagus would be left open during a moon cycle for people to individually pay their last regards to the Holy Lady. Then it would be sealed with a fitted limestone slab. This heavy lid had a tiny hole drilled through its center, a psychoduct that permitted the interred spirit to send messages to the Middleworld. Other offertory objects waited their ultimate placement, a lidded censer, vases and plates, small bone spindle whorl, and a diminutive figurine carved in finest limestone placed inside a bivalve seashell. This expressed the Maya belief in resurrection of the spirit from the watery Underworld domain.

The small mortuary temple was entered through a narrow corridor that led to a tall-ceilinged gallery made of large limestone blocks. At the southern end of the gallery, three chambers were built. The central vaulted chamber held the sarcophagus, which had been placed inside before final construction, filling the space. A heavy stone lintel supported the upper doorway, and a decorative cornice capped the upper walls of the corridor. The two flanking chambers were for the use of mourners or vision-seekers who would burn copal incense to expand their consciousness. Custom encouraged mourners to dip their hands in paint and leave impressions on the stucco coating of gallery walls to commemorate their homage.

Passing through billowing clouds of incense, a small group filed inside the temple, standing to each side of the gallery as the litter bearers lifted Lalak's body and placed it inside the sarcophagus. Only a few people could gather around the sarcophagus within its chamber; led by the royal family, the elites took turns offering prayers to the red-shrouded form. Pakal lingered at her head, striving for psychic contact, but sensed that her spirit was already well into its Underworld journey. Later, after she navigated past the tricks and threats of the Death Lords, he would find it easier to communicate with her spirit.

And he would communicate with her again. In the midst of his grief, Pakal knew death could not really separate them. He was a shaman-ruler, steeped in the mystical methods of inter-dimensional journeys. In the world of spirit, he would find her and again share the embraces, the blending of hearts and minds that had brought such happiness to their earthly lives. He already knew how he would portray her on the piers of his own pyramid temple. Standing regally and facing the main plaza, she would hold Unen K'awiil as her infant, his serpent foot curling downward toward the earth. From the lineage patron deity's foliated jaws would emerge the ancestral face of K'uk Bahlam, the dynasty founder. For she had indeed put in order the royal succession.

She entered the road, the K'uhul Ixik of B'aakal, the honored and beloved of her people, Tz'aakb'u Ahau. The shy girl Lalak who won the heart of the K'uhul B'aakal Ahau, the great K'inich Janaab Pakal, as well as the hearts of her people.

Baktun 9, Katun 12, Tun 0, Uinal 6, Kin 18, on the date 5 Etznab 6 Kank'in (November 16, 672 CE).

Ten days after Lalak's body was placed in the sarcophagus, the *mukah* events surrounding her initial interment came to conclusion. Companions to give support during her transition to the Underworld were selected. To offer one's life was a high honor, the ultimate dedication to serving the Holy Lady. Koyi volunteered without hesitation; his sole purpose to remain beside his mistress whether in life or death. A young woman from among Lalak's attendants was also selected for the ritual sacrifice, carried out by the High Priest, Ib'ach. Their bodies, once devoid of itz, became ritual artifacts that were deposited beside the sarcophagus along with jade and ceramics. Their spirits were ceremonially ushered into the spirit world to join their mistress.

After the *mukah* events were completed and the time of visitation ended, the doorway into the crypt containing the sarcophagus was sealed. Large limestone blocks were used with mortar applied to close them tightly, and coated with stucco. The two side chambers remained open for future pilgrims to pay homage.

Kan Bahlam tired of mourning long before the city completed its period of rituals and tomb visitations. His restless, creative mind hungered for opportunities to bring into physical form the great works he envisioned. True, his cadre of elite intelligentsia was making progress on their astronumerology projects, and he was meeting with several architects to begin drafting shapes of his triple pyramid group, but things seemed to move so slowly. He had now seen thirty-seven solar years pass, an age at which many heirs had already acceded and ruled their cities for some time. The passage of time weighed heavily upon him and brought unbearable pressure to get something accomplished. Yet he dare not start his construction projects while his father still ruled.

He bolstered himself by endlessly reviewing his plans. With his dedicated followers, he would create a network of the highest elite who would know each other by a secret code language that they named *Zuyua*. They would recruit the right ahauob from polity cities and bring in select members of the priesthood, those who understood the uses of secret knowledge. This power base of intelligentsia would be linked by their special knowledge of calendars, astronomy, and numerology. Their understanding would delve more deeply into cosmic mysteries of time and existence than presently available, even to the most advanced experts.

Already he was observing the power base of elites and priests being whittled away, in no small part due to his father's policies of making religion more accessible. Lesser nobles, merchants, and artisans were starting to think they could stand alongside the upper echelons. They thought they could share the decisions and creations that rightfully were undertaken only by initiates of the highest order. Would commoners be next? This violated his sensibilities and his notions of the correct power structure for this world. His plans, and his select group, would halt this dangerous process. They would bring their people back into proper alignment with the Gods' intentions, with the sacred contract B'aakal lords had with the Triad Deities.

When he became ruler, he would shape the world to match his visions.

If only the old man would die.

Field Journal

Universidad Autónoma de Yucatán
Francesca Nokom Gutierrez
Mérida, Yucatán, México

January 15, 2004

A t last we are closing in on the identity of the Mayan Red Queen of Palenque. When our field season closed in 1994 after our momentous discovery of her tomb, it was like leaving a mystery story just as the suspect was about to be identified. It's hard to believe it took ten years before we had technology to make her bones reveal their secrets. Ten long years during which I finished my doctorate in archeological restoration and went to work in Mexico City.

I'm on leave this semester from my university position, studying with Dr. Vera Tiesler at Universidad Autónoma de Yucatán (UADY) in Mérida. Her team recently made inroads into the Red Queen's identity using strontium isotopes analysis. They examined her tooth enamel and bones to find out where she was born and grew up, and where she spent her final years. Then they made comparison with Pakal's teeth and bones to see if they came from the same locale. If the strontium isotope signatures are the same, then both came from Palenque. In that case, the female skeleton interred in the second richest Maya tomb yet found could be Pakal's grandmother, mother, or wife.

Mariela Moran, research assistant for Dr. Tiesler, caught me up on the team's work. In 1998, Dr. Tiesler was assigned to take a look at Pakal's skeleton where it rested in its sarcophagus, deep inside the Temple of the Inscriptions at Palenque. Looking through the four plug holes made in the sarcophagus, she saw vestiges of insect infestation and bat excrement.

This showed that the skeleton was at risk for more deterioration, and a project was started to preserve the bones. Samples were taken from Pakal's skeleton, which had been coated with the red pigment the Mayas used for royal burials, cinnabar or mercuric oxide. This acts as a preservative and insect retardant but colors the bones red, making later analysis difficult. The Red Queen's skeleton was even more permeated with cinnabar; that's how she got her nickname.

Several universities participated and took samples, doing research on diet by trace elements, identifying dietary components and location using strontium isotope ratios, age estimation through dental evaluation, and new approaches to age determination using bone characteristics. A study of bone DNA, both mitochondrial and nuclear, is still ongoing. For understanding the epigraphic history of the Palenque dynasty, the researchers sought advice from Maya epigraphers Simon Martin and Nikolai Grube.

More research from 2002-2003 studied strontium isotopes from fragments of Pakal's skull, vertebrae, and ribs; as well as skeletal remains of Pakal's burial companions and others from Palenque's core area. These established an isotopes profile for Mayas born and raised at Palenque. Strontium is absorbed from eating plants and animals, and stored in bone and tooth enamel. Since bone is constantly renewing itself, the strontium found in bones reflects the diet in the latter years. Tooth enamel, in contrast, forms during infancy and early childhood and doesn't change much in adulthood. Strontium in teeth reflects the diet of earlier years of life. We assume that most of the ancient Mayan diet came from nearby food sources.

Strontium isotopes ratios typical for Palenque are in the mid-high range, around 0.7085. The lowlands of northern Yucatán are are higher (above 0.7090); regions to the south of Palenque are lower (less than 0.7075), and the volcanic terrain to the far south is even lower (less than 0.7060). Western Veracruz is the only nearby region of similar geology to Palenque. These differences may seem small, but from a geological point of view they are exceptionally large and far in excess of measurement error.

Since 1999, the team of Dr. Tiesler and collaborator Dr. Andrea Cucina has also studied the remains of the Red Queen and her burial companions from Temple XIII. Isotope ratios in tooth enamel and bone samples obtained from the Red Queen were compared with Pakal's newer samples for evidence about both their residential histories, giving important clues about their family ties by determining if they were born and lived in the same locality.

The results from Pakal's bones showed the local Palenque signature with an average strontium isotopes ratio of 0.7084. As long as Pakal did not move to the city as an elderly adult, which we know he did not based on epigraphic data documenting his birth and death, we accept the bone data as verifying that he lived at Palenque. His tooth enamel, reflecting childhood residence, also had the local signature ratio of 0.7086.

The result for the Red Queen's tooth enamel was different: she had a ratio of 0.7081, considerably lower than Pakal's ratio, yet still within the range for regional isotopes signatures. This ratio points to the east-west fringes of the Chiapanec Mountains in western Veracruz, which has similar sedimentary bedrock. She probably spent the first years of life in a near-by city such as Pomoná or Tortuguero. The two companions interred with the Red Queen had tooth enamel values within the Palenque range, indicating that they were local residents.

These strontium isotope studies support the identity of the Red Queen as Pakal's wife, Tz'aakb'u Ahau. While they don't conclusively tell us where she was born, they reduce the likelihood she was born on the coastal plains of Tabasco, as has been suggested. Epigraphically she is identified as "of Toktan," an unidentified site in the region considered the place of dynastic origin.

This brings us closer to identifying the Red Queen. I've been fascinated by this mysterious royal woman ever since I was part of the archeological excavation that discovered her tomb in 1994. My memories of those few months spent in the ruins of Palenque remain vivid, as if they only happened yesterday. I can feel the excitement of first viewing the red-hued skeleton inside its huge sarcophagus, sensing that it might be a woman, the first Mayan queen discovered. Chills creep up my spine and my heart pounds all over again, recalling that fateful day when Arturo Romano, Mexico's leading physical anthropologist, looked into the sarcophagus and without touching the bones declared "It is a woman." Tears well into my eyes, remembering how we hugged and celebrated, especially the women in our team, congratulating Fanny Lopez Jimenez who actually uncovered the hidden substructure in Temple XIII that led to the queen's crypt.

In the ways of patriarchal cultures, the professional credit for discovering the Red Queen's tomb went to Arnoldo Gonzales Cruz, director of the excavation. It makes me sad that Fanny got so little recognition, though her role was huge in discovery and preservation of the find. All the more reason to learn everything we can about the powerful women who ruled and shaped ancient Maya society. The world should know that women have attained such leadership in the past, and are emerging now to resume their key roles in many realms, from science to governance.

Since my specialization is restoration of artifacts, my studies at UADY focus on newer techniques used by the project. I've poured over the report of expert restorer Haydée Orea-Magaña, who had responsibility for restoring Pakal's bones in 1999. The national coordinator of restoration for INAH (Instituto Nacional de Antropología e Historia), her job at Palenque was a real challenge. Pakal's skeleton had generalized fragmentation and deterioration at that time, but they found both his pubic symphyses bones that had been covered by debris and not used for age estimates during the initial evaluation by Romano. Orea-Magaña was able to recover these bones without further damage. Thus the pubic bones became available for examination, a critical resource to determine both sex and age at death. See what a skilled woman can do!

This re-evaluation of Pakal's skeleton in 1999 convincingly resolved the age controversy. When Romano first examined the bones, he concluded that the interred person (they had not deciphered Pakal's name glyphs back in 1952) was a robust adult male in his forties. When epigraphers and archeologists got together for the First and Second Palenque Round Tables in the 1970s, they constructed a "king list" for the Palenque rulers based on interpreting hieroglyphic panels that abounded in the city. The panels gave the birth, accession, and death dates for nearly all the rulers. From this work they concluded that Pakal was eighty years old when he died. From carvings on the sarcophagus in the Temple of the Inscriptions, they matched up Pakal's name glyphs and learned that he was the ruler buried there. Mexican archeologists resisted this new data for some time, sticking to Romano and Alberto Ruz' interpretation that he was forty years old at death.

Using more recent techniques of skeletal evaluation, the accuracy of the epigraphic reading was confirmed—Pakal lived to be eighty years old. Characteristics of the pubic bones were key factors, along with examinations of cranial sutures and ribs showing that he was of advanced age.

Of greatest interest to me, however, is determining Pakal's relationship to the Red Queen. The strontium isotopes studies of their teeth and bones done by Dr. Tiesler's team points toward different places of birth and early years, and supports the idea that the Red Queen was not native to Palenque. That makes it unlikely that she was Pakal's grandmother or mother, both of whom were born and raised in Palenque. By the process of elimination this points toward his wife, Tz'aakb'u Ahau, as the Red Queen.

January 22, 2004

M y stay in Mérida is proving quite pleasant, and a nice change of pace from frenetic Mexico City. It's only a day's drive from my family home in the village of Palenque, near the famous ruins in Chiapas, so I can visit more frequently. This makes my parents happier although they've never fully recovered from my choice of a university career that takes me permanently out of village life. My mother in particular is secretly convinced that I will never marry, which pains her. My father, an amateur archeologist devoted to ancient Palenque, is proud of my accomplishments but misses me.

Being in the colonial city Mérida makes me reflect on the history of my people, both the Mayan and the Spanish sides—and the majority of Mexicans are a mixture as I am, called *mestizos*. Our history always leaves me with conflicted feelings. Being part-Mayan I am anguished by the Spanish destruction of native culture. Although the great cities of stone built during the height of Maya civilization were already abandoned when the Spaniards arrived, much additional damage was inflicted through looting artifacts, burning codices, and the imposition of Christianity. My career is dedicated to archeology and the restoration of Maya culture, so perhaps in some way I can make amends.

Mérida is called *La Ciudad Blanca*, "The White City" because its buildings are mostly white or soft pastel shades. An old colonial city, it was founded over 400 years ago by Spanish conquistador Francesco Montejo as the seat of governance in the Yucatán region. The older central area, *El Centro*, has high-ceiling houses along narrow cobbled streets with tiny sidewalks bordering busy streets; tall doorways and windows are shuttered against noise. Flat fronts with huge doors, windows with thick metal bars, and wrought-iron balconies on second stories are flanked by potted palms and colorful flowering shrubs. Wryly, Mérida residents call it *La Ciudad Gris*, "The Grey City" because fine black film from bus fumes covers every surface. Busses careening down streets built for horse and buggy also puts pedestrians at risk.

Colonial homes are deep and always have a central patio tucked between breezy verandas with a string of rooms, offering a haven of solitude amidst hectic city life; open to the sky, with lovely plants and fountains, tables and chairs for leisurely sitting and hammocks for a nap. Kitchens are at the rear with nearby dining salons. In colonial times, a storage bodega and stable yard was behind the kitchen. In modern times, most colonial haciendas were split into several residences, losing the functional beauty of that more gracious style of living.

"*Mérida es tranquilo,*" residents boast of tranquility as the number of cars and crazy drivers increase daily; but still nothing in like my megapolitan residence, among the largest cities in the world. Crime in Mérida is minimal though its population is about 800,000; one of the safest cities in the world, especially compared to Mexico City. Truly I feel safe, walking the streets at night unafraid. For the six months I'm here, I've rented a room in a remodeled colonial house in El Centro, an easy walk to UADY. Just a block east of my place is the famous Avenida Paseo de Montejo, called the Mexican Champs Elysees. Center meridians divide the street with flowering bougainvillea and oleanders, as gloriettas channel traffic around fountains and impressive monuments. Elegant houses line the avenue, graceful French colonial mansions or hacienda style stuccos that are now mostly banks and restaurants. In former times fine carriages drawn by fancy horses promenaded the wealthy; tourists still take calesa rides drawn by local nags. At the turn of the 20th century, Mérida had the greatest number of millionaires per person in the world. Their wealth came from "green gold," the henequen trade that produced sisal fibers from agave plants making the strongest rope then available. All around the Yucatán you can see remnants of henequen plantations, sadly deteriorated after nylon rope replaced the natural fiber.

Along Paseo de Montejo are the impressive Museum of Anthropology in the "Canton Palace" and a pair of matching three-story buildings known locally as "Casas Gemelas," the Twin Houses. You'll see huge hotels including the Hilton, Hyatt, and Fiesta Americana; Wal-Mart with tasteful minimal signage; north on Prolongation Montejo are U.S. staples McDonalds, Burger King, Sam's Club, and Costco. The street ends at the Grand Plaza, Mérida's ultimate mall.

I prefer to spend time in El Centro, with its magnificent Zócalo (Plaza Principal), old colonial buildings, and cathedrals. Every Mexican city has its Zócalo, but the one in Mérida is special. The initial thing that strikes you is the immense, lofty San Ildefonso Cathedral. The first Catholic Church in Yucatán, built between 1561 and 1598, it has stark Renaissance mannerist-abstract architecture with two soaring bell-towers and a central squared entrance. The interior has a high cupola, vaulted ceilings and grand columns with a twenty-five-foot cross on the altar; a few saint statues and graves in the floor dating back several centuries. It was built on top of an ancient Maya pyramid set on a platform of Ixcan'tiho, an ancient city called "T'ho" by locals. Many stones used in construction of the cathedral and older buildings in El Centro were taken from Maya structures, often employing Maya laborers to replace their sacred temples with the religious icons of their conquerors.

Wide sidewalks border the Zócalo with steps leading to walkways that meet in the round paved center. Every evening local military hold a formal flag lowering ceremony that is popular with tourists and residents. Areas of grassy lawn, flowering trees, and palms add greenery. "Conversation chairs" dot the square, their curved arms meeting in an S-shape so lovers and friends can whisper in each other's ears. Benches and raised borders provide seating and are filled to capacity at noontime and evenings. Hordes of pigeons patter around offering delight to pursuing children. On weekends there are fairs and dances, booths for food and shopping, bands and artists, and the famous Mestizo Dancers in typical Yucatán hacienda-era costumes doing fancy footwork while balancing trays of beer on their heads.

The evening promenade is something to behold. A constant stream weaves between tables set on the verandas, vendors and hawkers voice their wares, and musicians vie for attention. The promenade passes the historic Governor's Palace with Mexican artist Pacheco's riveting depictions of Mayan history; the Bishop's Palace housing museums and shops; the luxurious residence of Francesco Montejo dated 1549 with profusely sculpted façade and giant Spanish halberdiers, feet resting on heads of the vanquished. The imposing Municipal Palace houses the City of Mérida offices, more shops and restaurants, and my favorite bookstore, Librería Dante. This large store offers books in many languages, regional and Mayan history, and a nice collection of archeology and anthropology.

I could say a lot more about Mérida, major tourist destination and jumping off point for tours of the Yucatán Peninsula and numerous Maya ruins. Rich in history, architecture, music, dance, art, and culture; it's well-known for delicious Yucatecan and international cuisine. The peninsula, surrounded on three sides by seas, has glorious beaches, wildlife reserves and wetlands, and an amazing range of seafood. I'm glad to spend some time here again.

Mariela and I frequently come to the ice cream shop facing the Zócalo for an afternoon treat. Though there's a wide array of local fruit-flavored ice cream, Mariela always has guayabana, a delicately fragrant white fruit native to Yucatán, and I have coconut. Nothing beats the smooth richness of Mérida's coconut ice cream! Lazily watching passer-bys, we chat about archeological things. She's interested in my experiences when I was at the dig where the Red Queen's tomb was found during my graduate student days.

"It was amazing," I said. "That date is etched in my mind, May 16, 1994. About a month after Fanny Lopez detected an opening into the substructure of Temple XIII. This unknown substructure contained a gallery with three chambers; in the middle one Arnoldo Gonzalez Cruz found the sarcophagus that held the Red Queen's skeleton. He managed to get the lid lifted two weeks later and that was when we first viewed the red-colored bones: May 31, 1994. We were awestruck; the skeleton was covered with jewels, jade and pearls and shells, and many ceramic burial objects were in the vault. The spindle whorl, plates and vases for food, and female figurines made us think this could be a woman's burial."

"Arnoldo thought it was a male at first, according to his report," said Mariela.

"Right, the skeleton was robust and tall for an ancient Maya, but Arturo Romano Pacheco confirmed that it was female when he examined the skeleton three months later. What a celebration we had then! Fanny believed it was a queen from the beginning; we were all in tears when it turned out she was right."

"Romano, our leading physical anthropologist," Mariela observed. "I heard he only looked at the skeleton, especially the pelvic bones and jaw, not even taking measurements, and knew it was female. Remarkable."

"Truly he was a wonder to watch. I was really lucky to be inside the temple with Romano that day, it was a small group. The suspense was incredible; would this be the first discovery of a royal woman's tomb? After the confirmation, speculation ran rampant in camp about who she was. Arnoldo coined the title 'Red Queen' and it has stuck with her ever since. Obviously she was someone of great importance, since her tomb was placed right next to Pakal's in an adjoining temple."

"The lack of glyphs makes it difficult to determine her identity. Strange, since Pakal's crypt and sarcophagus contained so many."

"Yes, there's much speculation about why; maybe they buried her quickly, maybe they planned to carve glyphs later, maybe women don't get identified as well as men, who knows?"

"Dr. Tiesler's work is so important. Finally we've got scientific evidence for who the Red Queen probably is. You must feel happy about that."

"I am. I'm grateful for this chance to study with your project at UADY and examine the research about the Red Queen. Any idea when the DNA studies will have results?"

"Not really." Mariela made the hand gesture that waved toward a distant place. "Carney Matheson and his group at Lakehead University in Canada are working on it, but they're having problems due to the poor preservation of the bones and the massive cinnabar coating."

"They've got samples from both Pakal and the Red Queen, right?" I asked.

"Yes and three other individuals from Palenque. Successful DNA results would give definitive data about the Red Queen and Pakal's relationship."

"I hope they find a way to get the DNA information from those samples," I sighed. "I really want to know for sure who she is."

Distracted by horns blaring as two cars barely missed colliding at the street corner, we returned to our ice cream. Savoring the last few drops of unctuous coconut nectar, I conjured the Red Queen's face as reconstructed from her facial bones by Dr. Tiesler's team, using forensic technology. It was a severe face, with a large prominent nose between high cheekbones, firm chin and full lips, almond eyes and a high slanting forehead. Severe and strong, intent and focused. What must this powerful woman have been like, when she walked the plazas of Lakam Ha?

January 26, 2004

Yesterday I had a wonderful experience. I walked over to Dante to peruse the archeology/anthropology section, my favorite Saturday pastime. Bending over to look at a book on the lowest shelf, oblivious to everything around me as I often am when engrossed in the Mayas, I was startled when something bumped soundly against my backside. The bump sent me sprawling to the floor in a gawky heap. Before I could gather up my demolished dignity, strong hands grasped my arms and assisted me up while a flow of perfect Castilian Spanish offered profuse apologies. Tilting my head back to see my tall assailant, I was astonished to gaze into sky-blue eyes set under golden eyebrows in a square-jawed ruddy face. A mass of thick golden curls all had their individual ways upon his head and a mat of golden hair peeped through the open neck of his polo shirt.

As northern European-looking as they come, his flawless Spanish held me in thrall.

"Please forgive me, miss, I am nothing but a clumsy idiot, I cannot tell you how sorry I am, my deepest apologies, I am mortified by this inexcusable accident, to knock you over and to your knees, how can I ever be forgiven, what can I do to make you comfortable, please pardon my reprehensible behavior ..."

Unable to contain myself, I started laughing. He was stringing phrases together and using hyperbole in classic Spanish style; if I closed my eyes I would swear he came from Madrid. My laughter stopped the stream of apologies, but his warm hands continued to grip my upper arms causing surges of excitement up my shoulders.

"Excuse me ... are you well? Is something wrong?"

"Ha, uh ... ha-ha ... no, I'm all right ..."

Suppressing laughter with some difficulty, I managed to smile and wipe tears from my eyes.

"I'm fine, truly I am, don't be concerned."

He smiled back but continued to hold my arms securely. It felt incredibly comforting.

"That is wonderful," he said with a smile that lit up his clear eyes and exposed even white teeth. "I am so sorry, what can I do to make amends for my clumsiness?"

"Buy me a cup of coffee."

I astonished myself with this brash reply. I have no clue what made me so forward with this complete stranger. Usually I'm reticent with men and infrequently date; my academic studies and professional career have demanded almost all my attention. This is much to the sorrow of my family, who despair that I will never marry, having attained the over-ripe age of thirty-six with no prospects.

"My pleasure, miss," he jovially replied. "Name your place."

"Let's go to the Italian Coffee Company, it's nearby on Calle 62."

Releasing his grip on my upper arms, he made a flourishing bow and offered his elbow.

"Allow me," he said as I slipped my arm inside his elbow. "Shall we go?"

With my hand tucked securely, I matched his long strides with extra steps as he led the way out of Dante and we navigated the crowded sidewalk. The Italian Coffee Company was a Mérida hot spot, especially popular with artistic and intellectual types who lingered over steaming cups of espresso and cappuccino. We covered the half-block to the cafe quickly and found a table tucked in the back with a modicum of privacy. As usual, the cafe was lively and conversation echoed off the plaster walls. After our cappuccinos arrived, we smiled at each other somewhat awkwardly and admired the perfect floral designs in foamed milk covering the coffee's surface.

"Allow me to introduce myself," he said. "I'm Charlie Courtney, lately of London but presently working at UADY as a visiting professor. Most of the time I have a bit more tact when meeting someone new."

"My name is Francesca Gutierrez," I replied. "What a coincidence! I'm also working at UADY this semester, doing special study in bio-archeology with Dr. Tiesler. I work in Mexico City at UNAM where I'm an assistant professor in archeological restoration."

"Pleased to meet you, Dr. Francesca Gutierrez. Quite a coincidence, both of us at UADY, but then that's why we ... ah, bumped into each other, if I may be so bold as to say, in the archeology section at Dante."

This brought a smile to my lips. I liked his sense of humor. So far, I liked everything about him, a sobering thing for me.

"Enchanted to make your acquaintance, Dr. Courtney," I said with exaggerated formality. "You are obviously British, how did you come to speak such perfect *peninsulare* Spanish?"

In the archeology field, we all know that *peninsulare* refers to Spaniards who were born on the Spanish peninsula. Historically, it was used to distinguish the pure-blooded Spaniards from those born in Yucatán who were often mixed with Mayas.

"My field is linguistics. Languages come easily to me; I studied and resided in Madrid for several years. My specialty is Mesoamerican dialects, both ancient and modern. That's why I'm teaching at UADY."

"How many languages do you speak?"

"Oh, about fourteen or fifteen, I forget. Do you speak English?"

"Yes, passably well. All educated Mexicans speak English. But to my dying shame, I don't speak Yukatek, or any Mayan dialect. That's quite sad, since my family is part-Mayan."

"I thought I detected a tad of native in your features ... that adds quite a touch of charm, if I may say. Where is your family from?"

"My parents live in Palenque town, in Chiapas. We've been there a few generations. My Maya grandmother comes from Tumbala, a tiny village way out in the forests."

"Chol Maya. They were the group that came from the Chiapatecan highlands to settle in the fertile plains north of Palenque. Perhaps their ancestors lived in ancient Lakam Ha."

"I've often thought so. Put a Maya headdress on my grandmother and she looks as if she stepped off a carved panel on one of Lakam Ha's temples. Quite a nose!"

We both laughed and sipped our cappuccinos.

"Your nose is rather small," Charlie observed. "Must be from your Spanish side. Where did you get those blue eyes?"

"Funny you should ask. I've posed that question to my grandmother many times, and she hints at some big secret but won't tell me, at least until I'm ... uh, uh ... I'm married, that's what she says," I quickly added lamely. Without wanting it, I felt a blush coloring my cheeks.

"So you're not married. Well, neither am I, and we're both of an age, I might suggest, where conjugality is expected." Charlie's blue eyes were twinkling.

I was insanely glad to hear that he was not married. What had gotten into me?

"Tell me about your grandmother, and your parents, and growing up in Palenque town. Tell me about how you became a professor and what work you've done. Tell me about yourself."

His warm sincerity completely disarmed me, his transparent eyes exposing a kind and friendly soul. I felt as though we had known each other a long time. I poured out my story to the most attentive listener I'd ever met. We ordered more coffee but only took tiny sips; the afternoon whiled away and the Italian Coffee Company saw turnover of many customers. When we could sit no more, he invited me to stroll the Zócalo and watch the flag-lowering ceremony. After that it seemed natural to have dinner at a restaurant along Calle 60 where we found tables set out in the street. On weekends, Calles 60 and 62 are closed off to traffic for a couple of blocks near the Zócalo, and all the restaurants set up street dining. Over wine and Yucatecan food, we talked endlessly, weaving together topics such as archeological interests and family background.

I learned that Charlie was born and grew up in London, his father a businessman and his mother a seamstress. Somewhere far in his ancestry were minor lords and ladies; many Brits have a touch of nobility given the propensity of their lords to take mistresses and womanize. Not that the Mexicans take a back seat in those amusements! Probably 80 percent of Mexico's population is mestizo, mixed Mayan and Spanish. The early hacienda owners always had Mayan house servants and mistresses; some even raised their mixed-breed children as family members. After a few generations it was hard to find Mexicans with pure blood, thus the designation of peninsulares to set the real blue-bloods apart. A disproportionate number of political leaders were peninsulares for many years, but our numerous revolutions managed to put more mestizos in power.

Charlie showed a propensity for languages at an early age, having a Portuguese housekeeper. London is a melting pot for world cultures; he learned smatterings of Hindi and Chinese and quickly mastered German, French, and Italian. After finishing college with a major in romance languages, he spent five years in Spain working as a translator and language teacher. He became fascinated with ancient dialects, journeyed to Egypt and Turkey, but eventually found that Mesoamerican languages were his passion. He studied Na-Dené and Algic-Algonquian in the United States, and then migrated south to tackle archaic Mayan and Aztec. Research and teaching in this area naturally became his specialty.

We didn't talk much about our romantic involvements. For my part, there were few and none became serious. He mentioned a girlfriend or two, but was never engaged. When the evening drew to a close, he walked me home. It was delicious, feeling his warm presence beside me as guitar music wafted from plazas, horse-drawn calesas clopped along stone paving and streetlights cast a golden glow. Saying goodnight, he bent down and brushed his lips across my cheek. It seemed so natural.

February 6, 2004

An urgent phone call from my parents summoned me to Palenque town. My grandmother suffered another stroke and she is failing. Abuelita Juanita already had a couple of minor strokes, but this one is severe. She is paralyzed on one side and can barely speak. The doctor does not give her much time. Although saddened, I am not surprised; she must be well into her nineties and has lived a long and full life. I left Mérida at once, settled in for the eight-hour bus ride and arrived late last night.

Juanita lay corpse-like in her bed in the house where I grew up. She has lived with us for so long that my early childhood memories hold many images of her room. It has changed little over the years, with its spare furnishings and colorful striped bedspread. I've watched her become very old, but her appearance now was startling. The skin of her face was darker brown than I recalled and pulled tightly over high cheekbones, her mountainous nose peaked sharply and her thin lips sunk in over bare gums. I suppose it was pointless to insert her false teeth now. Neck, arms and legs were slim as willow poles and the tiniest of bodies barely raised its covers. Hair white as kal, lime powder, was neatly braided around her head. My mother was taking good care of her.

She was so still that I feared she was already dead. I touched her right hand, it felt cold but the fingers moved slightly against mine. The stroke had affected her left side. Fighting tears, for seeing her this way breaks my heart; I murmured her name and some rambling words about being there beside her. After some moments, her eyelids fluttered and her mouth tried to move, but it sagged on the left. She seemed unable to turn her head, so I leaned over and put my face close to hers. The right eye opened fully but the left lid drooped. I was again astonished by the contrast of sky-blue eyes to a dark brown face, made even more dramatic by the crown of white hair. She tried to say something, her voice a whisper, but all I could understand was my name.

Several days passed as I caught up on things with my parents, visited my brother and sister and their families, and took walks around town for diversion. The doctor and the priest came daily; we were marking time until my grandmother's soul departed. Memories of times with her flooded my awareness; her humor and her sternness, the never-ending stories she told, the way she baited me about my blue eyes, and cryptic messages she gave me about my heritage, initiations and lightning in the blood. Perhaps now her promise would never be fulfilled. She was dying and I was approaching midlife still unmarried. The secret story of how I got my blue eyes might never be revealed.

One morning my mother María rushed into the patio where I was having morning coffee in the dappled sunlight.

"Francesca, come quickly! Juanita is awake and her mind seems clear. She wants to talk to you."

I hurried to my grandmother's room to find her propped up on pillows, looking almost her normal self. Settling into the chair placed next to her bed, I grasped her good hand and kissed her on the forehead.

"I'm so happy to see you more like yourself," I said.

"Arrgh! This is not who I am ... this is a shell of me ... soon I shall spring away from it." Her voice was slurred and the words came out slowly, but I could understand without difficulty.

"Listen carefully, Francesca," she continued. "These things I can only say once, for not much ... time remains."

"Yes, abuelita, I am listening."

"Take the key ... on the chain around my neck. It opens the box underneath my bed. Inside the box ... is a book ... I have kept for you, kept for many years. The book passed through my family ... for generations. It is ... a language I do not understand. It tells of things, the things that I ... wanted to tell you ... when you married ..."

Her voice trailed off as her eyelids slowly closed. I sat and waited, my body electrified by her revelation. Would she speak again, and tell me what she knew? Her breath became ragged and noisy; I worried that she might actually be passing. Squeezing her hand, I kept calling her name. Finally, the eyelids flickered open again.

"Abuelita, can you tell me? Tell me something about it?"

"A great lineage ... so far back ... she came from far away, but they rescued her, took her in, saved her life ... it caused difficulties ... tainted the family ..."

"Yes, yes, go on!"

But Juanita's strength failed and she sank into unconsciousness. She never became lucid again and her soul separated from her body that night. I stayed at her side most of the time, and close to midnight when alone with her, I removed the chain and key from her neck. Slipping it into a pocket, I knelt by the bed and looked underneath to see a small cedar box, about shoebox size, with a lock in place. I retrieved it, glancing surreptitiously around, and snuck it to my own room without being seen. For some reason, I understood that Juanita wanted only me to know about it and examine its contents.

The next several days were taken up with Juanita's funeral and wake, receiving visitors and attending the requiem mass our priest, Father Julio Mendez, conducted in the main Catholic Church. The day before my return to Mérida, I managed to get time alone to open the box. Sitting on my childhood bed in the room I shared with my sister, I inserted key into lock with both trepidation and anticipation. The lock resisted, I jiggled the key until it caught and the protesting lock responded. Inside was a rectangular object coated with a rubbery white substance. It felt smooth to touch and had a few cracks here and there. Turning the object around, I detected seams and carefully pried them open. Some flakes broke off from the rubbery substance as I unwrapped the covering that appeared to be cloth. It emitted a pungent odor that had distinctly herbal qualities.

My expertise in restoration quickly kicked in. The wrapping fabric was permeated with insect-repellant herbs to prevent *bichos,* wood and paper eating insects, from getting inside. The white outside coating appeared to be a form of latex, probably taken from rubber trees to give additional insect protection and make the package waterproof. These were antiquated methods that tropics-dwelling people would use. My excitement grew exponentially.

Fingers trembling, I slowly unwrapped the herb-permeated cloth to find an old, leather-bound book. Its cover was faded maroon without lettering, a typical leather cover used in Spanish colonial times. Opening the book, I saw the pages were discolored by time and felt fragile, but they were intact, without evidence of water or insect damage. A date was written in Arabic numerals on the first page, 1886, but thereafter I could not read a word. The letters were in the Arabic alphabet but the words made no sense at all. Sounding them out, I suspected this was some ancient Mayan dialect, but written in Spanish letters.

This is a job for Charlie, I thought at once. It must be a form of archaic Mayan, and his linguistic skills are exactly what I need.

I flipped through the pages, not finding any different style of writing. Tucked at the back of the book was a separate single page with the look and feel of bark paper. It was charred around all four edges, as though it had been burned, and covered with Mayan glyphs in the flowing Palenque style, almost like calligraphy.

Now my heart was pounding! This could be a page from an original ancient Mayan codex! I would certainly need help from an epigrapher to decipher what it contained.

One other object was inside the cedar box. It was a single jade stone, square-shaped and carved with an ancient Maya symbol. It looked like a glyph, but not one I could immediately identify. I'm not much of an epigrapher; reading the glyphs requires specialized training. The jade stone had a small hole at the top center, so I deduced it must have been worn as a pendant or as part of a necklace, using the hole to pass the string through.

After re-wrapping the book and returning it and the jade stone to the box, I sequestered my mysterious treasure inside my luggage. I felt a little guilty about not sharing Juanita's legacy with my family, but felt sure of her intention that it was for me alone. With my archeological training, I'm the only one who has any real chance of unraveling what the book says, and understanding its significance.

February 24, 2004

"I'll be gobsmacked! You've got a real find here."

Charlie's enthusiasm about the old leather book bolstered my confidence. In his able hands, we might manage to make sense of the strange language.

"I'll need several references from my office," he said. "This is definitely written in the late colonial period alphabet, but these are not Spanish words, as you gleaned. I think you're onto it; probably these are Mayan words phonetically translated into period Spanish. At least we know the time frame for writing the journal; its date of 1886 gives a point of focus."

"And the codex-style page? Know a good local epigrapher?"

"A capitol one. And he's a good friend, will keep things under wraps until we're ready to let on about your cache. This is the Dog's Bollocks!"

"Pardon me?" I just could not follow Charlie's British slang.

"Meaning, just great. Sorry, it happens when I get excited."

I smiled. He was even cuter when excited. We agreed on a work session that evening when he had his references in hand. Later, ensconced at my dining table with thick tomes spread around us, Charlie began construing the mysterious letter.

"Spanish uses the Latin alphabet, spread across Europe during the Roman Empire and derived from Cumaean Greek as modified by the Etruscans, the ancient Roman precursors. The orthographic rules of Old Spanish were reformed many times, such as during the 16th century when the voiceless palatal sound 'ʃ' was merged with the breathy 'j'—sounds like 'ho' to English speakers—even though it was written as 'x.' When Cervantes wrote *Don Quixote*, he spelled it the old way, and we still see this spelling used in English. But since 1815, modern Spanish now spells it with a 'j' as in *Don Quijote*."

Charlie was a quintessential professor and could not help expounding. I listened attentively since much of this was new to me.

"The Spanish Royal Academy kept old spellings with 'ç' for 'z' and 'ze' for 'ce' until around 1860 to 1880 when they standardized to the current spellings. So *zelo* became *celo* and *fuerça* became *fuerza*. After the reform of 1815, an especially interesting change sequence took place when one publication replaced 'xe' and 'xi' with 'ge' and 'gi' but another used 'je' and 'ji' sounds. By 1832, the latter sounds were firmly established, so what was once *muger* became the present *mujer*. This word for woman originally derived from Latin *mulier*. So the language is complex and changing."

"Can you tell which version of old Spanish the book uses?"

"Well, it definitely uses some early 19th century changes, such as spelling woman as *mujer*, but there are odd discrepancies. See here. This word for 'also' is spelled *tambien* without an accent mark. I needn't tell you that today it's written *también*. Here, there's another example. Look at *accion*, now we write the word for 'action' using the accent, *acción*. Words today written with accent marks appeared more often without them up until around 1880. The book's date of 1886 puts it after this change was common."

"Hmmm. If the book was written by a Mayan living in an outlying village, wouldn't it be likely that he was not up to date on changes in Spanish orthography?"

"Good point. Dissemination of orthographic changes, especially from the mainland to the New World, would take time. Whoever wrote the book had learned an intermediate form of Spanish, with some 19th century revisions but not all. If he learned Spanish as a boy, studying with the village priest using the 1832 orthography, he would have been in his forties when writing the book. That makes sense. Gives me guidance on how to translate the Spanish letters into phonetic Mayan."

Charlie labored into the night as I plied him with coffee, cursing now and again with such British expletives as "bugger" and "that threw me a spanner!" Around midnight he finished translating as much as he could of the twenty pages covered with Spanish lettered Mayan words.

"The fellow seems something of a Chilam Bahlam," he said. "This is voiced in the obtuse prophetic style of those village 'Jaguar Spokesmen.' It's a chronicle of time and things happening, I suppose, near his village, which is never identified. Maybe he couldn't spell very well; many words are just not intelligible. Or, he could be wrapping his communication in metaphor, much of which is lost to us. But here it is, the best I can do for now."

Running a hand through his toppling curls, he asked for some water and read the translation to me.

"Two Lord. The sky stones were set.

"Thirteen Lord. The mat was put in order.

"Eleven Lord ... something descended, can't read it.

"Nine Lord.

"Seven Lord.

"Five Lord.

"Three Lord.

"One Lord... don't know what all these Lords are about."

Charlie glanced up at me, perplexed.

"He's making a record of time, using the count of scores of stones, which are Katuns. It's a chronology using a Katun Count," I offered.

"Bingo! Here it continues," he replied.

"Twelve Lord, the jaguars aligned and ... something unreadable ... from K'awill.

"Ten Lord. They built homes on the mountain. There they had many waters. On the plains were fields of maize.

"Eight Lord. The stones were raised, the Gods were praised. It grew, their city.

"Six Lord.

"Four Lord. They were beloved of their Gods, the three Gods."

Turning over his written page, Charlie shook his head.

"Seems the pattern repeats itself, starting over with Two Lord, then Thirteen Lord, Eleven Lord, Nine Lord and so forth. Isn't that a particular calendar count?"

"Yes, let me see." I squeezed my eyes, concentrating hard to remember all the various Mayan calendars. "It's the K'altun Count, what they call the Wheel of the Katun. A picture was drawn by Diego de Landa taken from records of the Xiu Mayas in Yucatán. They count the Katuns backwards in a clockwise motion, dropping by two so you get: 13-11-9-7-5-3-1-12-10-8-6-4-2, then back to 13. The Wheel consists of 13 cycles of 20 years each, for a total of 260 years. Each Katun is named for its numeric lord, thus Bolon Ahau or Nine Lord, for example."

"Right! The Chilam Bahlam is relating what happened during each Katun, or at least those when something important took place."

"But we've got no starting Katun date," I observed. "How do we know when this count began, or what city it describes?"

"Ah ... can we count how many Wheels of 260 years are listed here?"

"Brilliant! Let's go."

We kept track of how many times the Katun Count started over at Two Lord, finding five and a half repetitions. Multiplying that by 260 years, we got 1,430 years; when subtracted from the date in the book, 1886, we arrived at 456 CE. A significant date, very close to the accession date carved for the first ruler of Palenque, K'uk Bahlam I who ascended to the throne in 431 CE and is credited with founding the royal lineage of B'aakal.

When I pointed this out to Charlie, his eyes lit up. How they sparkle like blue crystal when he is delighted.

"Palenque, of course! There are lots of other clues pointing toward it. See how often the book makes reference to a city of many waters, of large stone structures on a mountain. That's right along with the ancient Mayan name for Palenque, Lakam Ha, the place of great or many waters. I think you're on to it."

"It makes sense; my grandmother's village is close to Palenque. The Chilam Bahlam was writing about the great ancient city in his vicinity. What else does he say that might shed light on whatever mystery she kept secret all her life?"

"Mmmm ... mostly just tagging the Katun Lords and a few words about rulers' exploits and crop fluctuations. They had some bad event around 600 CE and went away from the city around 900 CE for reasons he doesn't address. Once we're past the third Katun Count, things get dicey and there are many words I can't decipher. Seems some people retreated into the forests and eked out a living foraging and hunting. They continued to plant maize fields, lots of references to ceremonies for the Maize God and several to Chaak the Rain God when times were dry. Around the time the Spaniards came, the Chilam Bahlam makes the usual pessimistic prophecies, here are some examples.

"Within the count of stones the foreigners arrive, they violently seize land.

"Prepare yourselves to bear ... can't make out word, something like burden of misery?

"Katun 5 is established, harsh is its face, harsh its tidings, there is affliction.

"They bring the pestilence, the red vomit ... the pox ...

"Katun 1 ... the rope descends, the cord descends... fulfillment of the word of the True God, the dog is its tidings, the vulture is its tidings.

"These were the eaters of their food, the destroyers of their crops.

"It is Katun 13 Ahau, blood shall descend from tree and stone ... Heaven and Earth shall burn ... something unreadable, then says our two-day men, because of lewdness.

"Something ... the sons of malevolence. At the end of our blindness and shame our sons ... I think it says will be regenerated from carnal sin. There is no lucky day for us."

"It sounds a lot like the Chilam Bahlam of Chumayel," I observed. "Pretty grim."

"Well, there is something quite different near the end, and very interesting," Charlie rejoined. "It says, roughly translated, that the woman arrived, she had suffered much, she was taken in by, I can't tell exactly by whom. It created some kind of problem with the village priest who seemed to want her thrown out. If I'm reading this right, it hints at something unusual in the village, some kind of scandal. Related to this woman, who appears to be a foreigner."

"Can you glean anything more about her or the situation?"

"No. The writing ends there. I hope when my friend deciphers the glyphs we'll learn more. We might have to do a tad of field research to figure this out."

March 21, 2004

It took us nearly a month to arrange time off for the field research that Charlie suggested. I took him to Palenque town, and to visit the ruins of the ancient city, Lakam Ha. He has been to the Palenque archeological site before, but this time is special because we're getting admitted to Temple XIX, currently being restored and not open for tourists. My friend and restoration colleague Sonia Cardenas is working there, part of the Group of the Cross Project, Proyecto Grupo de las Cruces that began excavating in 1997. The project is directed by Mexican archeologist Alfonso Morales, a University of Texas at Austin graduate who was born in Palenque town, like me. He's been an inspiration to me and encouraged me in my studies. I was able to work with him one season; Sonia and I were there when the team made a significant discovery in July 1998.

An exploration probe made in the upper level of Temple XIX revealed a chamber below. It contained a central pilaster with a beautifully carved stone panel and a damaged polychrome stucco relief, most of its pieces scattered over the floor. Deeper within the chamber was an altar-like platform or throne sculpted with figures and hieroglyphic text incised in the celebrated calligraphic style of Palenque. The building's exterior had fragments of a balustrade, called *alfarda,* from the upper stairway with inscriptions. Removal and restoration work was immediately undertaken to prevent deterioration; Sonia and I were part of this effort. It took several months to complete the work; the originals were taken to the Palenque site museum for climate protection and sometime later reproductions were put in place near Temple XIX. Harvard University epigraphist David Stuart did interpretation of the glyphs, identifying the main figures as Palenque rulers K'inich Ahkal Mo' Nab III and Upakal K'inich, grandson and great-grandson of K'inich Janaab Pakal I. The temple was dated to the mid-700s.

Whenever I enter the shaded walkway and climb the modern stairs leading to Palenque's main plaza, I am filled with anticipation laced with awe. This most elegant of ancient Maya cities has captivated my heart and fired my imagination. I am especially intrigued with the royal women in Pakal's lineage, the four Mayan queens who are candidates for interment in Temple XIII. Walking across the wide grassy area, recalling that it once was a paved plaza shining white in the hot tropical sun, I remember the excitement Sonia and I shared during that season in 1994 when we were part of the team that discovered the Red Queen's tomb.

Charlie and I met Sonia at the entrance to Temple XIII, which holds the queen's tomb. We climbed the stairs, joining her at the palm-thatched roof protecting the opening into the low structure. When I introduced her to Charlie, she must have read something in my voice, because one eyebrow lifted slightly. When I'd seen her last, at my grandmother's funeral, I didn't mention him. We had very little time to visit in the whirl of activity, but I did mention the old leather bound book I had inherited. Hastily I added that Charlie was my linguist friend from UADY who was helping me decipher the book.

Reverently we passed through a narrow entryway, not a natural door but made by the archeologists for access, and stepped into the substructure's corbelled arch chamber with three inside doors. The two on the sides were closed; the middle one had been partially removed so visitors could look into the Red Queen's crypt that held her sarcophagus. Metal bars were set over the opening to prevent entrance. Electric lights strung along the ceiling gave a pale yellow glow to the time-darkened stones of the interior crypt that was almost completely filled by the huge sarcophagus. The lid had been removed and the queen's bones taken to INAH headquarters in Mexico City. I hoped some day they would be returned to Palenque, as were Pakal's bones.

Inside walls of the sarcophagus were deep red, coated with cinnabar. The queen's skeleton was also permeated with cinnabar, making scientific analysis difficult. We three stood gazing inside, alone with the silent sentinel of past greatness. By getting to the archeological site early, we avoided the crush of tourists who arrived daily. I paid whispered regards to the resting place of this great woman, and then turned to Sonia.

"Dr. Tiesler's latest strontium isotopes analysis strongly points toward a non-local origin for the Red Queen," I said softly. "She came from a site with similar geology, but not Palenque. Pakal and her two companions all showed the Palenque isotope signature. That just about eliminates his mother and grandmother. We're thinking it's his wife, Tz'aakb'u Ahau."

"Makes sense," Sonia replied. "Very unlikely the daughter-in-law; she came on the scene after Temple XIII was built."

"More confirmation for the wife comes from Dr. Tiesler's facial reconstructions. Forensic techniques were used to model a face on the Red Queen's skull, following clues given by facial bone shapes. Comparing the results with relief carvings of the three later queens, the face most resembled Tz'aakb'u Ahau."

"Fascinating! I'd love to see those, email them to me when you're back."

I nodded. Charlie seemed pensive, keeping his thoughts to himself.

"The strangest thing," I added, "was the cocoon of a wasp containing a larva found in her left shin bone. Don't you wonder how that happened?"

Both my companions emitted "uh-hum" sounds but kept staring into the empty sarcophagus. It mesmerized us; we didn't stir until we heard tourists' voices outside.

Leaving the row of temples dominated by Pakal's Temple of the Inscriptions, we followed Sonia along a path leading through lush jungle foliage and up a hill that skirted the Cross Group. A guard at the roped off section saluted Sonia and waved us on. We passed Temple XXI, where discoveries made in 2002 are shedding more light on the Temple XIX texts, passed the tall temple-capped mound of Temple XX and climbed onto the platform leading to our goal. Much work had been done clearing the platform of trees and shrubbery, creating a flat approach to Temple XIX. The two-level structure was not tall, and a wooden stair with railings gave easy access to its upper level. Near the base were reconstructions of the most important discoveries, the breath-taking stucco panel with blue and red pigments, the elegant stone panel, the alfarda and throne panels. We admired these while Sonia and I reminisced about our efforts piecing together the thousands of remnants to recompose the stucco panel.

We climbed the stairs for a look inside the restored temple, reading posters that gave an account of the discoveries. I called to mind how this building would have looked in its prime; painted red-orange with gleaming white stairs, panels and latticed roofcomb colored green, blue, yellow, and white. The long rectangle with its two-tiered platform once was lovely and symmetrical, and faced toward the imposing Temple of the Cross. There was certainly a communication in this placement; K'inich Ahkal Mo' Nab expressed his lineage and descent through this *en face* with the main temple of his predecessor Kan Bahlam II.

The temples speak to us, the sacred geometry of buildings and ritual space express their profound messages.

To complete our experience, Sonia had arranged a visit to the tomb of Pakal, deep inside the Temple of the Inscriptions. Not everyone could do this now; you had to obtain a permit by giving authorities at Palenque a written justification for your visit. Being among the archeological team, Sonia had easily obtained this permit and got our appointment. We climbed around the side of the tall pyramid, following a footpath and stairs, showed the guard our permit, and entered the awe-inspiring top chambers with their famous inscribed tablets that record the history of Pakal's dynasty from its mythological beginnings. I am deeply moved by these graceful calligraphic glyphs, thinking of those talented scribes who long ago carved them.

We descended the steep, narrow stairway leading down eighty feet, with one switchback, to arrive in the chamber facing Pakal's immense crypt. Metal bars keep visitors out, but you can see well into the vaulted chamber. The magnificently carved sarcophagus lid delights and confuses the eye; it is so intricate with every inch carved in symbols that surround Pakal's body as it drops into the maw of an earth monster. Or, as some propose, escapes the jaws of death to become resurrected as the Maize God, with the Wakah Chan Te' rising from his mid-section. It would take hours to discuss the layers of meaning on the sarcophagus lid; perhaps someday I'll take that on. From our angle, we could not see the carved ancestor figures on the sarcophagus sides, but the wall panels were visible though faded.

Standing in front of Pakal's tomb, sensing his presence inside, I felt a whirring sensation coursing through me. It pulsated in my bloodstream, making my fingers tingle and filling my ears with buzzing. My legs felt weak and I leaned against Charlie, who quickly put his arms around me for support. I remembered the time before when the same sensation happened in exactly this location, and my grandmother hinted at "lightning in the blood." Sonia noticed my faintness and, attributing it to the oppressive heat and humidity deep inside the pyramid, signaled for us to climb back up.

After the fresher though still warm and moist outside air revived me, Sonia took us to the archeological camp dining room for a cold drink. Sipping our Coca-Cola—the Mexican national drink—that rejuvenated us with caffeine and sugar, we talked about the leather bound book. Charlie told Sonia what he had been able to translate, and the cryptic Chilam Bahlam quality of the writing. She agreed that it sounded like a great mystery and held something tantalizing about my grandmother's history. In recounting the background to Sonia, a few details returned to my memory. Our family's priest in Palenque had mentioned rumors he had heard from old village priests serving Tumbala.

"That's where you can pick up the trail," Sonia said. "Regional parishes keep records for the small outpost priests who attend the villages, as many don't even have their own church. Maybe you can uncover something about Tumbala from the Palenque church archives."

"Bob's your uncle! That's where we should begin. Perfect idea, thanks Sonia," Charlie said.

Sonia looked puzzled so I told her his expression meant "that's great!"

"We're on our way there when we leave," I added. "Maybe we can see Father Mendez tomorrow."

March 22, 2004

My parents like Charlie. I think they would like any man I brought home who appeared to be a reasonable prospect. They have long given up hoping I would marry a village man; my years in Mexico City at the university have squashed that possibility. It pleases my father, Luis, that Charlie is a professor with a bright future; even better that his field is related to the ancient Mayas. That's my father's passion also; he is very proud of our local yet famous archeological site and often acts as an unofficial tour guide for friends. My mother María worries, I am sure, that I will end up living in England, a country so far away that she can hardly imagine it. Not that Charlie and I have talked seriously about our future together; we are both cautious. We've just begun exploring the romance potential.

I told them that we are doing field research on early Spanish records and Mayan dialects, one of Charlie's current projects. The stories my grandmother told me about growing up in Tumbala have sparked his interest, so he is pursuing data related to languages in this region. It sounds plausible and linguistics is so removed from their experiences that they don't question our activities. A few phone calls set up a meeting with Father Julio Mendez, the rector of the Catholic parish of Palenque and regional prelate. He has been ranking priest of my family's church since I was a child.

Father Julio had aged in the past ten years, his white hair giving him a distinguished look. I recalled that he was open-minded for a priest and more tolerant than most. When I explained that we were attempting to trace an unusual event in my grandmother's village that happened many years ago, he surprised me by remembering our last conversation about her.

"Juanita Nokom, always an enigma to me. When you visited me and we talked about her, when was that, at least ten years ago, yes? You asked about secrets she held from her village past, but I knew no details. Some big scandal that the village still gossips about, so I hear. Did she ever tell you what it was?"

"No, unfortunately. I take responsibility, since I've lived far away and didn't visit as often as I should. When she became very ill last month, she tried to tell me but was unable to get the words out. She did leave me an old leather bound book that I believe came from her village. It's written in Spanish letters phonetically spelling out Mayan words. My colleague Charlie Courtney is helping interpret what it says, but nothing seems to relate to my grandmother. It's a chronicle of events and book of prophecy, written by the village Chilam Bahlam. At the end, there are a few curious phrases about a foreign woman who came to the village. We thought we might explore your parish archives, trace back Juanita's family tree and look for anything unusual."

"As a linguist," Charlie added, "I can probably detect variations in names that might indicate foreign roots. We want to see if there is any connection between the Nokom family and this foreign woman who came to the village; we assume it's Tumbala though the book never says the location."

"The book does have one date, 1886, and we assume that's when it was written. It gives a point of reference," I said.

"I see," said Father Julio. "Yes, the archives may be useful in your search. We have records kept by many village priests in which they recorded baptisms, marriages, and funerals. I believe there are some from Tumbala. You are welcome to examine them."

He brought us to the church library, several dark and musty chambers tucked behind the kitchen and storage rooms of the large church complex. After an hour searching, he helped us locate several volumes from Tumbala and the closest other villages in the jungles surrounding Palenque. We opened our notebooks, poised our pens and began the long, tedious reading of names, dates, and occasions that were perhaps the only things remaining of many villager lives in years past.

We looked for dates around when my grandmother would have been born, which I estimated as 1914 since my parents thought she was in her 90s when she died. Eyes straining in the dim light, we scrutinized tattered volumes of yellowing pages covered with long lists of Tumbala villager church events.

March 25, 1901: baptism of Olivo Pech Chan, born to Lilia Chan Keb and Edwardo Pech Chi, both of Tumbala, male infant born March 16, 1901.

March 30, 1901: marriage of Camila Ku May to Javier Couoh Ek, both of Tumbala.

April 4, 1901: baptism of Emiliana Xeceb Kuk, born to Yachel Kuk Tun of Nututun and Mateo Xeceb Aké of Tumbala, female infant born March 26, 1901.

April 12, 1901: confirmation of Luz Tzuc Moo, age 12 years, daughter of Itzel Moo Dzul and Ramón Tzuc Poot, both of Tumbala.

April 12, 1901: confirmation of Xuxa Uc Keb, age 12 years, son of Valentina Keb Tzen of Tumbala and Diego Uc Kan of Yahalon.

April 14, 1901: funeral of Marcelo Kahum Chi of Tumbala, age 48 years, survived by his wife Adel Ek Bacab, two daughters Isabella and Emiliana and son Antonio, died April 10, 1901.

"Typical naming patterns, using Spanish first names and Mayan surnames," Charlie observed. "This was common following widespread conversion of Mayas to Catholicism during the 16th and 17th centuries. Note how the Spanish name format is used, father's last name comes first, then mother's last name. That can be confusing to English speakers, with our practice of mother's last name preceding the father's. When we bother to include the mother's name, which frequently just gets omitted. Bloody patriarchs, we northern tribes!"

"Huh! Do you imagine the southern Europeans are any less patriarchal just because we include the mother's surname? I'll show you machismo, just look at the typical Mexican male," I retorted with some heat.

"Is that why you've avoided them?" He had a wicked twinkle in his eyes. I blushed and bent over my tome so he wouldn't see.

"Back to work," I commanded.

Hours passed as we plowed through volumes working our way up to 1914. Charlie's sudden yelp almost lifted me out of my chair.

"Smashing! Call me jammy!"

"What on earth?"

"Oh, sorry, I mean I just got lucky and found something terrific. Here it is; your grandmother's baptism."

He pointed to the middle of the open page in his mildewed book and read aloud.

November 11, 1913: baptism of Juanita Nokom Aké, born to Itzel Aké Kanul and Kayum Nokom May, both of Tumbala, female infant born on November 7, 1913.

"Let me see!"

I grabbed the book and focused on the undulating cobwebs of thin, wavering handwriting. It was difficult to make out, but finally I saw the words that Charlie had just read.

"Wow! This is great! You've found it; we have a thread to follow."

Overcome with enthusiasm, I turned to Charlie's close-by face and kissed his cheek. He seized the moment to cup my chin and give me a real kiss on the lips. We lingered for a long moment, enjoying our closeness and our victory.

"Keep going," I urged. "We're on to it now."

The Tumbala records of 1925 listed Juanita's confirmation. I knew she was married in Palenque, recalling the date as 1935. We didn't need to search for this; our task was to go back tracing the line of her parents and grandparents in Tumbala. We figured that we needed to follow her genealogy for three generations to get into the time frame of the 1880s, giving about twenty years per generation. Another couple of hours and we found the marriage record of her parents.

June 21, 1893: marriage of Itzel Aké Kanul to Kayum Nokom May, both of Tumbala.

Next we needed to search for documentation about *their* parents, looking for the surnames Aké, Kanul, Nokom, and May. These are common Mayan names, and our task became exponentially more difficult. How would we determine which of the numerous villagers with those surnames were my grandmother's ancestors? Without a genealogical chart, or some type of family record, we were left guessing.

"I'm knackered," Charlie sighed.

I'd heard this slang enough to know he was really tired. Glancing at my watch, I was surprised that it was 4:30 pm. We had been at this most of the day, even forgetting about lunch.

"Let's call it a day," I said. "Are you as hungry as I am? There's a decent restaurant just down the street, and I could really use a cold beer."

We thanked Father Julio for his help, told him about our success so far, and obtained permission to return to the search tomorrow. Several cold Coronas and a meal of Yucatecan delicacies such as pollo asado made of chicken roasted in red achiote sauce, and the mouth-watering black bean paste you can only get regionally, put us in a more hopeful frame of mind.

The next morning Charlie came up with a brilliant idea. We were looking for something out of the ordinary, some deviation from the repetitive pattern of combined Mayan and Spanish names. We would check each listing of the four surnames, but only make note of those combined with an unusual first name, going back to the mid-1800s.

Another day of tedious work unfolded. We reminded ourselves to take a lunch break, and returned to our task as the afternoon wore on. Page after page our bleary eyes saw only the expected names, until I caught a blip in the pattern.

"Charlie! Look here, something's different."

I showed him a notation made in the firm, rounded script of a no-nonsense priest.

September 27, 1874: baptism of Ximina Nokom Naach, born to Ele Naach and Francesco Nokom Tzuk of Tumbala, female infant born September 22, 1874.

He stared at the page and glanced up, looking puzzled.

"The mother's name!" I exclaimed. "I've never seen this name before, see how unusual it is, just 'Ele Naach' without the second surname. What do you think?"

"Might be a fluke, er, something good happening by chance," he said on further examination. "You're right, that's a different pattern. No second surname, and 'Ele' is certainly not a usual first name in either language."

Tapping his finger on the line, he wrinkled his forehead in concentration.

"That surname, the mother's only surname ... Naach, not a common one. Something tickles my brain cells, think you dolt!" Squeezing his eyes, he made funny faces and I had a hard time not laughing, but I didn't want to break his train of thought.

"Naach!" he suddenly exclaimed, eyes shining and mat of golden curls dancing. "It's the Mayan word for 'far,' not a surname. I'm gobsmacked! The priest used a word to indicate this woman was from far away, a foreigner.

He didn't know her last name, or she wouldn't tell him. Franci, that's our foreign woman!"

I sat in stunned silence. I'd nearly given up hope that we would find anything of use.

"So this must be a reference to the foreign woman in Juanita's family who is linked to the scandal in her village."

"Exactly! And with her husband's surname Nokom, we can almost be sure this is the family lineage. Your grandmother even insisted you take her birth name as your primary surname. Francesca Nokom Gutierrez. She switched the pattern, an honoring of this lineage."

"I'm amazed my parents went along with it, since it drops out my mother's surname altogether and places my father's surname in second position. Of course, I used his surname in primary position for my professional life, makes things easier in Spanish-dominated society. Juanita must have been an irresistible force."

"From looking at her pictures, I'd say she was a knock-out. With force of personality to match her looks," Charlie observed.

"*Exactamente!* Well, we have a birth date of 1874 for my grandmother's grandmother. Where to from here?"

"Try to find the parents of Ele? No, that's not possible if she was a foreigner and they didn't even know her last name. Drat, I think we just hit a wall."

We went to Father Julio and explained our dilemma. Charlie asked if going to the Palenque town offices would be useful, but the priest advised these would have nothing related to Tumbala in the late 1800s. He considered us lucky to have found what we did in the church archives.

"I believe you will need to pursue a route I once advised against," Father Julio said. "That is to visit Tumbala and try to find an elder who remembers the stories of past times. It might be necessary to seek out the village shaman; I'm certain Tumbala still has one although he keeps hidden from church eyes."

"All right, we'll go to Tumbala," Charlie said. "Can you advise us how to get there?"

"At the Palenque marketplace, villagers frequently come to sell their fruit and crafts. You might find one from Tumbala willing to drive you to the village in his truck. Automobiles cannot navigate that rutted mud road, you would need a Jeep and I don't think one is available here. The market is open every day except Sunday."

"I know where it is," I said.

"Then we're off to Tumbala," Charlie concluded. "We'll find that shaman and learn Juanita's secrets about her ancestor Ele."

Sneak Peek into Book 4 of the Mists of Palenque Series

The Prophetic Mayan Queen: K'inuuw Mat of Palenque
Mists of Palenque Series Book 4

B orn into a maternal lineage devoted to the Goddess Ix Chel, young K'inuuw Mat connects deeply with her tradition during a pilgrimage to Cuzamil Island for menarche rites. Although K'inuuw wants to serve the Goddess, instead her marriage is arranged for political purposes to Tiwol Chan Mat, the fourth son of famous Palenque (Lakam Ha) ruler Janaab Pakal. Through a vision she realizes that her destiny is to continue the Lakam Ha dynasty by bearing an heir to continue Pakal's lineage, and helping preserve Maya culture for the distant future. She embraces the path the Goddess has given her, only to find she is irresistibly attracted to her husband's older brother, future ruler Kan Bahlam II. The magnetic force of their attraction propels them into forbidden embraces, until Kan Bahlam designs a bold plan that would solve his inability to produce a son—if he can gain his brother's cooperation. Set in the splendor of Lakam Ha's artistic and scientific zenith, royal family conflicts and ambitions play out in a tapestry of brilliant calendar creations, esoteric astronomical knowledge, vibrant art and sculpture, and advances in sciences that will astound people centuries later. As K'inuuw Mat contends with volcanic emotions, she must answer the Goddess' mandate to find ways to save Maya wisdom and cultural achievements as their civilization begins the decline and eventual collapse her prophetic vision foresees.

Contemporary archeologist Francesca and her partner Charlie, a British linguist, venture into Chiapas jungles to a remote Maya village, seeking to unravel her grandmother's secrets. The hostile village shaman holds the key, but resists sharing with outsiders the scandal that leads to ancient Palenque lineages. Only by re-claiming her own shamanic heritage can Francesca learn the truth of who she is, and bring her dynasty into the present.

The Prophetic Mayan Queen: K'inuuw Mat of Palenque

Mists of Palenque Series Book 4

K'inuuw Mat—I
Baktun 9 Katun 11 Tun 12
Baktun 9 Katun 11 Tun 13
(664—665 CE)

1

The prow of the sea canoe sliced through choppy waves, sending foamy spray along its length. As the beach receded, the sea turned from turquoise to deep blue, dotted by small whitecaps. On the far eastern horizon, a dark expanse of land formed an island, a low mound surrounded by glittering waters. Overhead the cries of sea birds merged with the rhythmic slap of oars against the waves. Eight muscular men pulled at the oars, four on each side. The sea canoe was the length of six men and the width of two, and carried twenty-five women and girls. Wind whipped their dark hair that was tied in topknots or wound in long braids. All wore white garments, the ceremonial color of pilgrimage. Most of the passengers crouched inside the hull, grasping ropes to stay put as the canoe tossed over turbulent waves. The passage from the mainland to the island was treacherous, swept by unpredictable currents that could cast a canoe far from its destination.

The sun peeped out between billowing white clouds. It had moved halfway across the sky since the sea canoe launched forth to make its way among deceptive currents. From time to time, four additional men traded places to relieve paddlers, rotating after a short period of rest. To complete the journey during daylight, they had to paddle relentlessly, struggling against wind and currents. Women offered them water from long-necked gourds, but no food was taken during the journey. Some passengers dozed fitfully and a few retched over the canoe sides, seasick from the constant pitching and dipping. One passenger, however, stood braced against the prow as far forward as she was allowed. Face tilted to receive salty spray, hands clinging to ropes and feet widely apart for balance; she swayed with the canoe's motion. Strands of dark hair had pulled loose and whipped in the wind. Soundless songs escaped from her lips, simple chants to the Goddess she had learned from earliest childhood. She felt as though she was coming home.

K'inuuw Mat had waited all her life for this journey to Cuzamil. Now she had reached twelve solar years; about to blossom into womanhood. Small pink breast buds rubbed against her simple white shift, called a *huipil* by her people. A few hairs sprouted under armpits and over her pubis. Her mother said she would soon be graced with the first moon blood, a sacred gift from the Goddess that gave women the power to create life. Her mother Chelte' was taking her to the island for the puberty pilgrimage. It would be especially powerful to have her initial moon blood on the Goddess' special island. With the flow of this sacred *itz*, liquid of life and precious fluid of the deities, she would dedicate herself to serving Ix Chel.

A large wave burst against the prow and drenched her, but she only laughed and shook water out of her hair. The forward paddlers exchanged smiles, nodding in appreciation of her adventuresome spirit. K'inuuw Mat blinked as salty water stung her eyes, keeping her focus on the gradually enlarging mound of land where she could begin to distinguish treetops.

The sea journey to the island of Cuzamil, abode of the Great Mother Goddess Ix Chel, required most of a day. Only a very few men, members of a hereditary lineage dedicated to serving the Goddess, could navigate the secret currents. Any who tried paddling canoes to Cuzamil without knowing these currents were repeatedly swept back to the mainland, or propelled into the deep seas where huge waves could crush them. The Cuzamil paddler lineage lived on the mainland by a small bay that provided shelter for their canoes, in a village called Paalmul. The paddlers' wives provided housing and meals, offered freely to honor the women and girls who came on pilgrimage to the island of Ix Chel. In the coastal Maya lands bordering the Great East Sea, the K'ak-nab, women had a long tradition of making pilgrimage to the Goddess' island at least twice during their lives: at the time when their moon cycles started and again when these ceased. Many women also sought the Ix Chel priestesses' healing skills, especially for problems with childbearing and infertility. For a child to be born on Cuzamil was considered a special blessing.

K'inuuw Mat remembered many things her mother told her about Cuzamil. It was the larger of two islands off the coast of the Yukatek peninsula, both dedicated to Ix Chel. Cuzamil was the main pilgrimage site, with a sizeable village and several temples. Some temples sat on pyramids of modest height; others took different shapes or were inside caves. One shrine had a long wall of seven high stone towers in the central ceremonial district. Every year, flocks of swallows called *cuzam* returned to nest in these towers, giving the island its name Cuzamil, Place of Swallows (Swifts). The city had complexes where the priestesses offered their healing work, residences for villagers and visitors, workshops and marketplaces, and a royal complex where the ruling family lived.

Cuzamil was ruled by a female lineage; the ruler also served as High Priestess of Ix Chel. Before K'inuuw Mat's mother was born, the ruler decreed that only women could live permanently on the island. Children of both sexes could stay there with their mothers, but once the boys reached puberty they were sent back to their family's city for male training. On the northern tip of the island, a trading village called Chayha had long existed. It engaged in lucrative trade in salt, honey and marine products, holding a monopoly on sea mollusks whose shells were ground into powder for intense purple or blue dyes. These were highly prized for dyeing fabric worn by elites throughout the Maya world. No permanent stone structures were allowed in the village, and its wood and thatch-roofed palapas needed frequent replacement. It was separated from the rest of the island by a mangrove swamp with dense tangled roots and swampy regions, making travel over land from the village impossible. Men could reside in Chayha on a temporary basis. None were permitted to make it their permanent home; they needed to leave periodically to ply their trade routes along the coast.

The royal family resided in Chel Nah, Place of Large Rainbows, and largest city on Cuzamil. They arranged marriages for their daughters to nobles on the mainland, often with the stipulation that the first daughter born of this union would be returned to the island to serve the Goddess. Rulership was not strictly hereditary; the Ix Chel priestesses held council to determine who would next ascend to the throne.

When K'inuuw Mat asked her mother why men were excluded, she was told that prophecies warned the priestesses of perilous times to come when men would attempt to dominate the Maya world, even trying to take over Ix Chel's domain. These men would strive to place a male ruler upon the throne. While many men were sincerely devoted to the Goddess and served her faithfully, those who would attempt the takeover had selfish motives. They coveted the lucrative trade of Cuzamil Island, and intended to appropriate its wealth. To forestall this from happening, the island was turned into a sanctuary for only women and children, so it could continue to fulfill its sacred mission.

Cuzamil had served since distant times as a sanctuary for women. It welcomed those women whom society rejected and despised: abandoned childless women, orphaned girls, women who preferred the love of other women, cripples and the deformed, and those whose soul journeyed in other dimensions. On the island, childless women were given the responsibility of raising orphans, a compassionate practice that benefitted all. Selling orphaned children into slavery was a common Maya practice, so the island was their hope for a meaningful life. Childless women, often rejected by husbands and families, would suffer in poverty and servitude without this sanctuary.

Women came to the island on pilgrimage to honor Ix Chel and her priestesses, and to make requests of the Goddess. They asked for a happy marriage, prosperous life, fertility and health for themselves and their daughters. They might remain there to study midwifery and women's care, the weaving of sacred patterns, and the mysteries of the Goddess. They could learn divination by water scrying and crystal gazing, astronomy and calendar lore. Those who showed aptitude would be trained in the demanding art of prophecy. A famous oracle lived on the island; her prophecies were sought by many women throughout the Maya world.

Everything about Cuzamil was enthralling to K'inuuw Mat. For generations her maternal lineage had been devoted to the Goddess Ix Chel. Her mother was born in Altun Ha, a city near the coast south of the Wukhalal

Lagoon, the renowned waters of seven colors. The girl could picture its many-shaded waters clearly from her mother's descriptions, transitioning from deep blue to turquoise, then gradually fading to shades of green and ending in milky white at the shore. Now the sea below the canoe was dark blue, but in the distance it became lighter, what she imagined the turquoise of the lagoon might be.

K'inuuw Mat anticipated her first moon blood eagerly. She would follow her family's tradition by saving a few bark paper strips holding this rare substance, placed in a hollow gourd with a tight cap. She would use it for an important future request. When she wanted something very much, she would burn the strips in a censer with sacred copal resin, saying invocations to the Goddess. There was no offering more precious to Ix Chel than blood from a maiden's first menses. To collect this offering on the island of the Goddess made it immensely potent. The Goddess could not refuse a request so empowered.

Another family tradition had her insides in a dance of delight. Whenever possible, at least one woman per generation was dedicated to serving the Goddess. It was a special honor to be selected, for it meant you would become a Priestess of Ix Chel and live on Cuzamil. She could not imagine a better life! Spending her days doing rituals, taking part in seasonal ceremonies, learning the skill for which she was best suited, and applying that skill to serve the needs of others. Priestesses supervised acolytes, carefully assessing each girl's unique gifts, then giving the Charge of the Goddess: You will be a healer, you a midwife, an artist or stoneworker, or a dancer and song-maker. Yet others would become weavers or musicians or herbalists, teachers or preparers of food. Of all the charges a girl might be given, the one that she most desired was that of a seer.

Had her mother not hinted of such abilities? Since earliest childhood, K'inuuw Mat recalled being able to sense things that others could not. She always seemed to know where the first ripe plums hung in the orchards, and under which bush the delectable wild grapes were concealed. Even before the Uo frogs began their rain song, she could smell the Goddess' sky itz preparing to refresh the dry earth. Her friends refused to play hide and seek games with her, because she always knew their hiding places. She had even foreseen her grandmother's death, an ability that pained and frightened her. To be given the charge of a seer caused her some trepidation; she knew it involved both joy and sadness. But an urge beyond all reason pushed upward in her young mind. She felt the beckoning to open her awareness to messages from the cosmos, the sky and earth deities, even the Lords of the Underworld.

What form that calling might take, she did not know. She had heard about women who were visionaries, who made prophecies, who could foresee things in the future, and even who became oracles for a particular God or Goddess. Coming to Cuzamil would give her understanding of these things. She was eager to learn, to meet women who served as seers, and to explore her own aptitude. In particular, she was excited to meet her mother's sister Yatik, an Ix Chel priestess, who was skilled in the art of scrying with both water and crystal. Her mother told many stories about Yatik's uncanny abilities to read what the stars reflected in gazing pools, and what mysteries were revealed in the veins and inclusions of crystals.

Most of all, she was thrilled to be able to watch the famous Oracle of Cuzamil in action. The Oracle was a priestess selected by her peers, and approved by the High Priestess, to actually receive into her own body the Goddess Ix Chel. Through using a secret recipe of mind-altering substances, the Oracle would vacate her body and offer it as a vessel for the Goddess. It required great strength and extensive training to survive the rigors of this process, and rumor said that some priestesses died of its effects. During the time that the Oracle was the Goddess' vessel, people could ask any question and receive a true answer. They came from near and far, the wives and daughters of rulers and commoners, seeking knowledge to guide their lives. Their gifts to the Oracle were another source of Cuzamil's wealth.

The canoe slammed against an undertow current rushing around the island's northwest edge, tipping sideways in the cross-currents. The paddlers made quick adjustments to set the canoe upright and continue their course around the point, but not before wails from the exhausted passengers pierced through the wind. K'inuuw Mat braced herself and managed to remain on her feet, gaining more nods of respect from the men. She glanced toward her mother, who was cradling her older sister's head against a shoulder, arms securely around the distraught girl. Sak T'ul looked awful; her contorted face a sickly yellow, eyes squeezed shut. She huddled against her mother's chest, knees pulled up into fetal position. Her entire being was a statement of misery.

It is good that she was not chosen to serve Ix Chel, K'inuuw Mat thought to herself. *She has no stamina. And besides, she is betrothed to the son of our Nakom—Warrior Chief. The life of a noble wife will suit her better; she will marry upon our return from Cuzamil.*

K'inuuw Mat was almost certain that she would be the one chosen for the Goddess' service during this pilgrimage. It was her utmost yearning, and she knew that her mother had discussed it with her father.

I am a worthy offering to Ix Chel, she asserted. *I am strong and smart. I will do whatever the Goddess requires of me. No reward is greater than living on her island.*

A sudden pang pierced her heart. Living on the island and serving the Goddess meant that she would never see her home again, her father and brother, cousins and friends in Uxte'kuh. Their modest-sized city sat in the middle of the broad plains that stretched north from the K'umaxha River to the Great North Sea, the Nab'nah. It was a pleasant place with gentle hills, waving grasses and clusters of forests. The fertile soil provided crops and several creeks fed clear waters to their fields and basins. As second daughter of the ruler, her life there was one of ease and abundance. Was she ready to leave the security of her comforting home?

A flood of conflicting emotions surged through her, breaking her concentration and causing her to fall to her knees when the canoe hit the next big wave. Sharp pain from bruised knees cleared her mind, and she arose resolutely to fix her gaze upon the approaching island. Whatever the Goddess chose for her, then that would be her dedicated path in life. She did not have to decide now. The Goddess would guide her way.

The paddlers followed the island's contour around the point, passing along beaches lined with palm trees. Leaving the rough currents of the channel, they pointed the prow toward a white crescent of sandy beach that cradled a calm lagoon. It was the harbor of sanctuary, a safe landing place for pilgrims arriving to honor the Goddess. When the canoe stopped tossing, sighs of relief were heard from many passengers. Sak T'ul raised her head from her mother's chest, opened teary eyes and gasped a few words.

"Are we there? Is the canoe ride over?"

"Yes, my heart," whispered Chelte' into her daughter's ear. "Only a few more moments."

K'inuuw Mat kept her gaze fixed on the beach, now able to discern several palapas shaded by trees and three long sea canoes pulled up on the beach. Several women came from the palapas to meet them as the forward paddlers jumped into the water to pull the canoe onto the beach. They helped the passengers climb out of the canoe and gather their belongings. As older women stretched cramping legs and mothers held tight to daughter's hands, K'inuuw Mat leapt ahead and ran up the beach, her toes digging into the warm sand. She turned at the tree line to watch her mother and sister, who were moving slowly and casting long shadows as the sun dipped toward the western horizon. She had never been on an island before, and the sensation of being surrounded by a vast expanse of water was exhilarating.

Ix Chel priestesses in blue and white robes greeted the pilgrims, offering gourds of water and honey maize cakes. They guided the travelers to an area where they could relieve themselves after their long sea passage, and explained that the walk to Chel Nah was short and easy. They would travel on a wide white road, a sakbe, built of stones covered with smooth plaster that stood well above ground level. The men who served as paddlers would remain in the beach palapas overnight, and then in the morning convey departing pilgrims on the return trip from the island. The priestesses provided the paddlers with food, drink, and bathing supplies.

In the gathering dusk, the weary pilgrims set foot on the sakbe for the last phase of their journey to the Place of Large Rainbows, city of the Goddess Ix Chel—Lady Rainbow. Twitters and squawks of birds settling onto night perches mixed with the loud humming of insects and the shrill screeches of monkeys in the jungle canopy. Palms, shrubs, and low trees lined the sakbe, many with red and yellow flowers. The smell of rich humus mingled with fragrances of allspice berries and sweet nectar exuded by thousands of tiny white Chakah flowers. Stingless bees collected this nectar to make a high-quality, pale honey for which Cuzamil was famous.

Chelte' called K'inuuw Mat to her side, reaching to squeeze her daughter's hand, and smiling despite her fatigue. In the twilight she could still see the sparkle in the younger girl's eyes. Sak T'ul trudged behind, head lowered and feet dragging.

"We are here at last. Can you feel the Goddess' presence?" Chelte' asked.

"Yes, Mother. She is everywhere. My heart is singing. This place feels so familiar, as though we are in our true home."

2

"Sister! Greetings in the name of the Goddess. It has been too long since we beheld each other. Your daughters are two budding flowers. Come, enter in peace and love." Yatik spread her arms to embrace Chelte' and the two girls.

After embracing her aunt, whose resemblance to her mother was striking, K'inuuw Mat glanced around the palapa. Two small torches set in sconces on the doorway frame spread soft, wavering light around the interior. Shaped as a large oval, the dwelling had a hard-packed dirt floor and walls constructed of thin poles filled in with plaster. The roof was made of dried palm fronds tied to a wooden frame that left an open strip all around the top of the walls. How different this simple dwelling was than the stone-and-stucco home of her family in Uxte'kuh. She wondered if rain blew in through the opening below the roof. Several sleeping pallets were spread against the far wall, and sitting mats surrounded a central altar holding a clay image of Ix Chel, several offering bundles, flowers, and a small censer. Hanging from the walls were various household implements, including a broom, woven baskets, and strands of rope holding garments and mantles.

"You will all stay with me during your visit," said Yatik. "The other priestesses who live with me are staying elsewhere, so we can have private time for visiting."

"Of this we are deeply appreciative, Sister," replied Chelte'. "Indeed, it has been many tuns since I last came to Cuzamil."

"Was it not shortly after the birth of your youngest?"

"So it was. I made pilgrimage to offer gratitude to Ix Chel for giving me three healthy children and a life of abundance. Blessed be the Goddess. And here is my younger daughter, K'inuuw Mat, now almost a young woman. We planned this trip so her first moon flow will happen on the Island of the Goddess."

"Excellent!"

K'inuuw Mat blushed and bowed respectfully, clasping her left shoulder with her right hand. Sak T'ul looked annoyed and pulled at her mother's skirt; she felt slighted because as first daughter, she should have been introduced first.

"Here is my older daughter, Sak T'ul," Chelte' hastened to add. "She has reached sixteen solar years, and is betrothed to one of our city's leading nobles. Their marriage will take place after we return."

Sak T'ul made the bow of respect to her aunt, and then they settled onto mats as Yatik called for the evening meal. Next to the large palapas of the priestesses were smaller ones, made in the same style, in which their attendants lived. Cooking palapas were set near the periphery of the complex, with walls left unsealed so smoke and heat could dissipate. Each priestess had attendants, women of common status who committed their lives to Ix Chel. Two women in simple white and blue huipils brought wicker trays filled with an assortment of savory items: gourd bowls with a steaming stew made of peccary, squash, tomatoes, and beans; ceramic plates containing fresh papaya, mamey, mangos, and plums; and flat maize bread used to scoop up the stew. For seasoning, red chiles gave spiciness, golden annatto added astringency, and an assortment of herbs such as basil, oregano, epazote, and coriander contributed depth and subtlety. After setting the trays on the floor between the pilgrims, the two women returned with cups of kob'al, a drink made of ground maize mixed with water and fruit juice.

K'inuuw Mat realized that she was starving as soon the succulent aromas reached her nose. Her sister reached greedily for a bowl of stew, but their mother grasped her arm.

"Let us give thanks to the Goddess first," Chelte' whispered.

Yatik was already reciting the food blessing with closed eyes. K'inuuw Mat felt glad that she had not reached for food along with her sister. Eyes closed, she joined the chant which she had learned from her mother.

"Ix Chel, Mother of All Creation,
Giver of life and sustenance,
For those of your creatures whose flesh feeds our flesh,
For those of your plants whose leaves and fruits nourish us,
We offer our gratitude; we honor their ch'ulel, their soul-essence.
All comes from you, all returns to you.
Thus it is. Highest praise to you, Great Goddess."

Satiated by the delicious meal, the two girls were tucked into sleeping pallets by their mother, who then rejoined her sister for further talk. Soon Sak T'ul fell asleep, her regular breathing blending with chirps and hums of night insects. Although K'inuuw Mat's stomach was full, her mind was still alert. Lying with her back to the women, she pretended to be asleep while she listened to the conversation.

"When is the next speaking of the Oracle?" asked Chelte'.

"On the full moon at fall equinox," replied Yatik. "Ab'uk Cen is growing old; she does not speak as often as before. Now she speaks only at the four major sun positions, the equinoxes and solstices. Some grumble because her services are not more available. Women often must wait several moons to seek the Oracle's answers, and this causes complaints."

"This is not fitting. Followers of Ix Chel should realize that what happens is in the Goddess' timing, not their own. They must learn the virtue of patience."

"Would that all the Goddess' followers were as wise as you, dear Sister. Wives of rulers and daughters of ahauob think the world revolves around their desires."

"All are equal in the eyes of Ix Chel! They deserve no better treatment simply because their blood is elite."

"This we know, those of us who are truly devoted to the Goddess and what she teaches. Commoner and noble, slave and servant, man and woman, human and animal, all have the same innate worth to the Creator and Destroyer of All. But, very few are able to live by these principles. This is the great flaw of humanity: that we fail to remember the divine *itz* of all existence, and come to believe we are better than others. Even here, in the very heart of the Goddess' domain, this forgetting happens."

"That is sad to hear," murmured Chelte'.

"Ah, so it is. Let us speak of your pilgrimage. Do you seek an audience with the Oracle?"

"Yes, I wish to hear her pronouncement about the path of my daughter, K'inuuw Mat. It has been considered by her father and me, that she might be dedicated to serving the Goddess."

K'inuuw Mat's eyes widened and she caught her breath. She desperately wanted to know what the decision would be.

"My own thoughts had traveled to this consideration," said Yatik. "It would be a fine continuation of our family tradition. Does she show aptitude for such service?"

"She appears to have the potential for being a seer," Chelte' replied, and described some of her daughter's uncanny abilities to foresee events and discern things others could not. "Would you teach her scrying, and further test these abilities? I am certain she would be thrilled to study with you."

Yatik nodded in agreement. She was one of the leading priestesses of scrying, and was pleased to be asked.

"This I will undertake immediately," she said. "Since you must wait another two moon cycles until the Oracle speaks, there will be time to evaluate your daughter's talents. Although there are many ways of being a seer, scrying is a most useful tool for those who become adepts."

Tears moistened K'inuuw Mat's eyes. Her heart beat a glorious little pattern of happiness; its greatest hope was about to be fulfilled. That is, if the Oracle pronounced this as her destiny. Her ears perked again as her mother asked more about the Oracle.

"What will happen when Ab'uk Cen can no longer fulfill the Oracle's duties?"

"We will enter the difficult process of selecting a successor to the Oracle," Yatik said while making the hand sign for trouble. "I have been part of this once before, when I had just arrived as an acolyte. It was a rude initiation into the unseemly politics of power among women. My ideals became somewhat frayed, to express myself politely. You recall how much we revered all the Ix Chel priestesses when we were growing up in Altun Ha? We could not imagine anything but sincere dedication and the highest morals among them. In that cloud of blissful anticipation, I expected my life on Cuzamil to be filled with only serenity and comradeship, as we all found happiness serving the Goddess. So soon was I disillusioned, my youthful ideals shattered. Selecting the new Oracle was an ugly process."

"Tell me about it, dear Sister. Much am I saddened over your suffering. Why did you not mention this before?"

"Ah, for many reasons ... such things are usually best kept to oneself. But, since my niece might be dedicated to the Goddess, I am guided now to tell you. There are competing lineages upon Cuzamil, women from elite families who cannot put away the quest for power. Perhaps it is bred into the fiber of their being. These women seek prominent positions within our simple society; they reach for status through becoming the ruler, or the Oracle, or the Head Priestess of one guild or another. Since all noble priestesses have a voice in these selections, and even the views of commoners and artisans are heeded by the High Council, much is done to influence them. Everything from making arguments in support of a candidate, to bribes of goods or favors, to outright threats have been used. Giving reasons why one woman would make a better Oracle than another is understandable; but threats and bribes violate the Goddess' own teachings."

"Just so! She instructs her followers to be ethical in all things, and to consider the greater good when taking actions. It sounds very similar to what happens when royal succession is challenged in our cities. I can understand your disappointment."

"Perhaps the worst thing is the evil words spoken against each other during these contests for power. This pains my heart above all. Festering wounds in the soul can persist that sustain long-lasting enmities. These divisions mar the unity that I imagined on this island. At the least, women have not taken to using physical force to further their ambitions." Yatik gave a wry smile and shook her head. "If certain men attain their goals to dominate Cuzamil, this tactic may yet come to us."

"Let us pray to the Goddess that such a time never comes to pass."

Both women raised their hands in the supplication gesture and whispered a fervent prayer. K'inuuw Mat was bewildered; she could not imagine that women who had dedicated their lives to the Goddess would do such selfish and destructive things. Could her aunt be wrong? Perhaps she misunderstood the other women's intentions. There did seem an edge of bitterness in Yatik's voice.

"Do not misunderstand me, Sister," Yatik murmured after their prayer was finished. "I love my life here, I am ever close to the Goddess, and many among us live in harmony and sisterhood. These conflicted times come and go. In the opportunity to overcome enmities, the Goddess gives us a path for growth."

K'inuuw Mat was startled; had her aunt read her thoughts? She must remember that many priestesses had intuitive abilities. She would not be so different here. Her mother whispered something that she could not hear, and then silence prevailed for what seemed a long time. Eyelids heavy, the girl began to drift toward sleep. She roused enough to catch a few more phrases when the women's conversation continued.

"When Ahau K'in, the Lord Sun, raises his face in the dawn, the newly arrived pilgrims will undergo purification," said Yatik. "After this ceremony, you will be received and welcomed by the ruler of Chel Nah, she who is also our High Priestess, K'ak Sihom. Her leadership has brought us a long period of harmony. She has earned my great respect; you will find her impressive."

"So have I heard," Chelte' replied. "Much do I anticipate meeting her, and presenting my daughters for her blessings."

As the women discussed aspects of the ceremony and reception, their voices blended into the humming and chirping nighttime choir and eased K'inuuw Mat into sleep.

In the grey pre-dawn light, a line of pilgrims followed Ix Chel priestesses along a sakbe leading into the center of Chel Nah. They walked in silence, white mantles wrapped closely around their naked bodies, hair loose and streaming down. At a juncture of the plastered roadways, the lead priestess veered to the right and continued to a plaza facing a small flat-roofed building, its stucco façade painted sky-toned Maya blue with black lines in flowing designs. They entered through a single doorway into a rectangular chamber, where images of Ix Chel were painted on the walls. As an Earth and Moon Goddess, she represented the three phases of a woman's life: maiden, mother, and grandmother.

As the maiden, Ix Chel was portrayed as a young woman kneeling before a backstrap loom, weaving in the traditional Maya fashion. Bare to the waist, she wore a colorful woven skirt with a twisted waistband that hung between her thighs. In her right hand, she held a smooth tapered stick used to create the warp and woof on the loom, which was tied to a sacred ceiba tree. She wore a coiled snake headdress to signify her powers of healing and intuitive knowledge, her skills at medicine and midwifery, and her ability to control earthly forces. The glyph for *sak*, Mayan word for white, appeared in her headdress to indicate her presence in visible phases of the waxing moon. A blue-green jade necklace and earspools associated her with waters, where rainbows often appeared. From this came her title, Lady Rainbow.

As the mother, Ix Chel appeared seated inside a crescent moon, holding a rabbit. She wore a short latticed bead skirt, her headdress full of maize foliation to signify her merger with the Young Maize God— Yum K'ax. Both the rabbit and maize imagery announced her powers of fertility, and associated her with sexual desire, motherhood, earth, crops, abundance, and fecundity. The symbol for sacred breath hung below her nose, signifying that she had the power to breathe life into creation. As her left arm cradled the rabbit, her right arm extended out, with the hand making the bestowing gesture. In this potent form, the Goddess exuded sexuality and reproductive prowess. She was the mother of all Maya people, and took many lovers to create the various Maya groups. She controlled all aspects of reproduction, determined the face and gender of children, women's moon cycles, pregnancy and childbirth. As mother, Ix Chel did not wear the coiled snake headdress of healer, because she was too busy as wife and mother to attend to healing needs. The headdress did contain weaving symbols, indicating domestic responsibilities and her powers to weave the fabric of people's lives. With qualities of both moon and earth Goddesses, her title was Ixik Kab—Lady Earth.

As grandmother, Ix Chel was depicted with both benevolent and destructive aspects. The larger image on the wall showed an old woman wearing the coiled snake headdress, bare to the waist with a long woven skirt that had patterns along the waist and lower fringed border. A twisted waist band hung in front, nearly to her feet. She wore a jade necklace, earspools, and wrist bands, and poured water from a womb-shaped clay pot onto the earth. These symbolized her dispensing blessings and healing onto the world, preparing soils for planting, restoring waters of lakes and streams, and managing menstrual bleeding and childbearing fluids. She again attended to healing needs and dispensed intuitive wisdom, functioning as the aged healer, diviner and midwife, who also eased people through the dying process and absorbed their bodies into her great body, the Earth.

A smaller image below the benevolent grandmother depicted her destructive aspects. Here she had a monstrous appearance with sharp claws and a long skirt covered with crossed bones. Jaguar spotted eyes and clawed hands and feet conveyed the power of the jungle's most dangerous predator, the taker of lives. The coiled snake headdress, jade jewelry, and water motifs in her skirt continued her shamanic and life force associations, now with an ominous portent. From the upturned clay pot she poured huge amounts of water, sending forth storms, floods, and hurricanes. A large sky serpent hovered above her head, disgorging more deluge from its mouth. In Maya mythology, the creator deities destroyed their second attempt at human creation, the mud people, by an immense deluge that flooded the lands and dissolved the people.

The grandmother was also a moon goddess, called Ix Chak Chel— Lady Red Rainbow. The Mayan word *chak* could mean either red or great, associating her with the full moon before heavy rains that had a red glow. Goddess of the waning moon, she was connected with frightening solar eclipses, because these were more frequent when the new moon appeared.

Small altars were stationed below each of the three images of Ix Chel. Priestesses gave the pilgrims granules of copal to drop into burning censers on each alter, while reciting prayers to each aspect of the Giver and Taker of Life. K'inuuw Mat offered her copal granules reverently, transfixed by the vivid images of the Goddess. She crossed both arms over her chest and bowed deeply, giving the salute of highest respect in front of each image, while murmuring prayers she had memorized in early childhood. The slowly moving line prevented her from staying as long as she wanted with each Goddess aspect. Moving from the last images of the grandmother, the line passed through a side doorway that opened on a small alcove shrouded by trees and vines. A few steps brought them across the alcove and into a cave entrance.

The smells of wet stones and bat guano filled K'inuuw Mat's nose as she stepped carefully along the damp stone passageway, gradually descending into the cave. Its ceiling was high enough to walk upright, and the walls stood an arm's length away on each side. Only the sounds of water dripping and bare feet splashing reached her ears. She glanced ahead at her sister's back, craning her neck to make sure her mother was still in front. Reassured, she attuned her senses to the mysterious cave energies and focused on placing her feet carefully.

Caves and all watery places were sacred to the Goddess. Pilgrimage circuits on the island were centered on caves and sunken water holes, called *t'zonot*. The Yukatek lands, of which Cuzamil Island was an offshoot, had no ground level rivers. Set upon a limestone plateau, the Yukatek had a web of underground rivers traversing all through its regions. Openings occurred when the ground over a portion of the rivers eroded and collapsed, forming the *t'zonot* or water hole. Some *t'zonotob* were close to the surface, while others could be extremely deep. They were an important source of water in this dry tropical landscape. On Cuzamil, shrines were built at the entrances to caves and water holes, and the white causeways that connected them defined the paths followed during pilgrimages. Rites at these shrines drew upon the energies of water, earth, the moon, and the rising sun, since the island was located at the far eastern limit of the Maya lands. The focus of the rituals included fertility, healing, renewal, women's mysteries, and the wellbeing of humans and the cosmos.

The group of pilgrims reached a t'zonot at the bottom of the cave. A tiny opening in the ceiling far above allowed a thin shaft of light to penetrate the gloom. Since the sun was still low in the east, only a dim glow entered the cavern. Clusters of roots hung from the ceiling, reaching toward the water below. Long fingers of stone protruded where constant dripping formed calcifications over many years. The priestesses guided the pilgrims to stand at the water's edge and drop their mantles. Using small hand-held censers, the priestesses waved feather fans to blow fragrant copal smoke around the heads, bodies, and feet of the pilgrims. Copal was the resinous blood of a sacred tree, used by the Mayas since time immemorial for purification. Its dried sap formed granules, highly prized and ceremonially harvested for ritual use. As they cleansed the pilgrims, the priestesses chanted in low monotones.

"Holy Goddess, Our Mother and Protector, receive into your waters these women and girls. They have come to your sacred island to pay homage, to make offerings, to seek your wisdom. Make them pure; remove all impediments, so they may be worthy to come before you. This we ask, Beloved Mother, because we know you love us."

With gestures, the priestesses indicated that the pilgrims should enter the water. K'inuuw Mat stepped in quickly, anticipating the cold and blowing out through her mouth to prevent shuddering. She had learned this technique from her mother; it eased her body into harmony with the chilly waters. In a few steps, she was submerged to her neck. The water was sweet, clear and cool. Its stillness contrasted with the rushing streams and swirling rivers of her home on the plains. She turned to watch her mother, who was encouraging her sister to advance further into the pool. Sak T'ul was being cowardly as usual, arms wrapped tightly around her shoulders and shivering mightily.

What a timid mouse! K'inuuw Mat thought. Tossing her head, she submerged completely and swam a few strokes. The cool water cleansed her skin, hair, and soul. She reveled in the Goddess' life-giving, sacred fluid.

Accept me, Holy Mother. I was meant for this. Purify and strengthen me. I am yours.

After the sunlight made a bright beam that reflected on the pool's surface, the pilgrims were called out of the water and wrapped in their mantles. Skin tingling and hair dripping, they followed the priestesses out of the cave, and returned to their dwellings to prepare for the ruler's reception.

Later that morning, the steady beat of drums summoned the pilgrims. Wearing newly made white shifts without adornment, their hair braided and tied with rainbow colored ribbons they walked on bare feet over the smooth plaster sakbeob leading past the flat-roofed temple with Ix Chel murals, and entered the city center. The causeway continued under an archway, wide enough for four women to walk through, its white surface painted with an arcing rainbow. Beyond the archway was the central temple complex, a large plaza paved with stone and stucco, bordered by modest-height pyramids. Three tiers of stairs led up the north and south pyramids; the eastern one was tallest and had five tiers. On top of this pyramid was a square palapa-type structure, four thick poles at each corner supporting a thatched roof, with open sides. In the center was the throne of the Cuzamil ruler.

The throne was made of stone carved in the shape of a large marine bufo toad. Fat, bulging legs supported the throne; the frog's flattened face formed the front with huge poison glands swelling behind prominent round eyes, bumpy skin, and a curved, smiling mouth. A panel below the frog face was decorated with water swirls, fish and lilies. Ceramic incense burners shaped as mythical creatures with animal and human features stood knee-high lining the stairway. Clouds of pungent copal smoke poured through their mouths, eyes, and ears. A line of priestesses in blue and white robes stretched along the base of the pyramid, their headdresses waving in a rainbow blend of assorted bird feathers. The plaza was filled with many women and children, who gathered to behold their ruler greeting the new group of pilgrims now passing across the plaza.

Repeated blasts from large conch shells sounded from the four directions, announcing the appearance of the ruler. Musicians blew high trills on clay whistles, clacked wooden sticks and shook gourd rattles as the Ruler of Cuzamil, Ix Chel High Priestess K'ak Sihom stepped onto the plaza, entering around the northeastern edge of the tall pyramid. She presented an impressive figure, richly adorned with jade and pearl jewelry, wearing a fine blue and white woven huipil and shoulder cape covered with glittering shells. On her head was an impossibly tall headdress of multicolored feathers, with rare blue quetzal tail feathers soaring above. Voices from the crowd rose in salutation. Drums and rattles kept rhythm as the ruler's stately figure walked along the pyramid and then climbed the stairs, followed by her main officials. At the top, she turned and raised both arms in the blessing gesture to the crowd below. Again, their voices soared in acknowledgement.

Turning slowly, K'ak Sihom sat upon the throne and signaled her steward to bring the pilgrims forth. As the small group climbed upward, priestesses below sang lilting songs of the Goddess' love for all her children. Their pure, sweet tones brought tears to K'inuuw Mat's eyes, and she surreptitiously wiped them with hair ribbons. This was a moment she had long anticipated: her first meeting with the revered Cuzamil ruler.

Each pilgrim was introduced to the ruler by the steward, who asked their name and city. In contrast to court protocol in other Maya cities, no gifts for the ruler were expected. The tradition on Cuzamil was for visitors to bring gifts and offerings only to Ix Chel, and place these at various shrines according to their particular quest. K'ak Sihom greeted each pilgrim warmly, taking hold of both hands while inquiring about the purpose of this visit. She exchanged a few words of information or encouragement, and wished the pilgrim well in fulfilling her quest.

Mothers kept young children at their sides when they approached the ruler; girls who had already begun their moon cycles could approach on their own as emerging women. When Yatik had discussed this with Chelte' and the girls, Sak T'ul immediately demurred, saying she preferred to stay beside her mother. K'inuuw Mat was not surprised. If *she* were having moon cycles, she would certainly have enough courage to approach the ruler alone.

Now standing before the elegant form of K'ak Sihom, whose penetrating eyes seemed to bore into one's soul, K'inuuw Mat felt awestruck by the immense magnetism that the ruler emanated. Instinctively, she grasped both her shoulders and made the bow of highest respect. As she looked up from her bow, the ruler's eyes met hers. A spark passed between them that the girl felt stabbing deep inside her bowels, making her knees weak. A quiver of fear passed up her spine. What did this High Priestess already know about her? And why did it frighten her?

A slight curl moved the corner of K'ak Sihom's chiseled lips. Her eyes became hooded and she shifted them to look at Chelte' and Sak T'ul, smiling broadly and inquiring about their purpose for visiting the island. K'inuuw Mat kept her eyes downcast and listened as her mother explained.

"For myself, I come to give thanks again to the Goddess, who has given me healthy children and an abundant life. For my older daughter Sak T'ul, we seek the Goddess' blessings on her marriage, to bring her fertility and happiness. For my younger daughter, we request that the Goddess give us guidance for her path in life. K'inuuw Mat is drawn to serve Ix Chel, in accord with my family tradition, although we live in far western lands that do not follow the Goddess."

"You are wife of the Uxte'kuh ruler, is that correct?" asked K'ak Sihom.

"Yes, Holy Lady," replied Chelte'.

"As daughter of a ruler, there might be reasons for making a marriage alliance for K'inuuw Mat that serves her city," observed K'ak Sihom. "Has this been discussed in your family? Does your husband concur with her serving the Goddess?"

"This we have discussed. My husband remains open to both possibilities. I believe that what happens during our pilgrimage, what guidance we receive, will be of utmost importance in this decision."

"Indeed, so shall it be. Do you stay long enough to hear the Oracle speak?"

"Yes, we intend to remain for some time, waiting for K'inuuw Mat to begin her moon flow. The Oracle speaks next when Ahau K'in reaches the midpoint of his travels southward, I have been told. That is not far off."

"You are correctly informed. It is good that you bring your question to the Oracle. You are to be commended for seeking Ix Chel's guidance in this matter. The ways of the deities are often beyond our human capacity for understanding. What may seem obvious to us as the proper choice may not be so, in divine vision. Receive my blessings upon all aspects this quest, for yourself and your daughters. May the Goddess grant what you request."

Chelte' bowed and thanked the ruler, turning to walk away. K'inuuw Mat remained motionless, her feet unable to move; they felt heavy as huge stones. Glancing back with a puzzled look, Chelte' grasped her daughter's hand and pulled gently. K'inuuw Mat stumbled as her numb feet failed to step evenly. Both her mother and sister grasped her arms to keep her upright. Through a haze she heard her name called, and looked back.

"K'inuuw Mat!" The imperious voice of the ruler pierced the girl's ears. "Listen well to the words of the Oracle."

Startled, Chelte' looked up toward the ruler, but K'ak Sihom was already greeting the next pilgrim. Sensing her daughter's disorientation, she kept an arm around her as they descended the stairs, and wondered what had transpired to cause such upset in the usually confident girl.

3

K'inuuw Mat and Yatik knelt in front of a wide, low-brimmed clay bowl filled with water. On the other side, Olal, an acolyte who was studying scrying with Yatik, sat cross-legged with eyes closed in deep concentration. The surface of the clear water was completely smooth, protected by the nearby buildings surrounding the small patio of Yatik's workshop. The priestess held a small gourd full of flat oval-shaped rocks, offering them to K'inuuw Mat.

"Select one of these scrying stones," Yatik said softly. "These stones have been activated through prescribed rituals. It is best to use experienced stones in the beginning. Once you become familiar with this technique, you must find your own collection."

The girl placed a hand above the stones, palm open to sense which stone would call to her. A tingling sensation in her fingertips led toward a reddish-brown streaked stone, and she picked it up from the rest. Following instructions Yatik had recently given, she blew several breaths over the stone and recited the scrying chant.

"From the depths, from the dark,
In the mystery of the unseen,
On the surface of these waters,
Show me that which I ask.
In the name of the Goddess,
She, the Knower of All."

Eyes closed, K'inuuw Mat breathed again on the stone and said her own prayer inwardly: *Ix Chel, guide my vision, open my inner sight. All is done in your service.*

Extending her arm over the bowl, she gently slipped the stone into the water and watched as it settled to the bottom. Rings of ripples spread quickly across the water's surface, rebounded from the rim and crossed each other, creating a tiny jumble that soon dissipated. When the surface was again smooth, K'inuuw Mat stared fixedly at it, clearing her mind of all thoughts. She watched and waited for an image to appear. Her task was to read in the scrying water the image of the animal that the acolyte Olal held in mind.

At first the water only reflected clouds passing above and a corner of one building. Trying not to blink, K'inuuw Mat kept staring and intensified her focus.

Animal of the jungle, animal of the fields, animal of the plains, whoever you are, come to me now, she called mentally.

Slowly, tantalizing shapes began forming on the water's surface. She could not make out a distinct feature that might reveal which animal was starting to appear. Breathing in deeply, she closed both eyes and intensified her intention. On the exhalation, she expanded her awareness and opened herself to receive.

Both eyelids flew up and she fixed her gaze upon the water. There, almost as clearly as if she was seeing it on a jungle path, was the face of a gray fox. Its dark nose quivered, sniffing for a scent; its sharp eyes with pale brows stared at her below large cupped ears. The image remained for a brief time on the surface, and then dissolved.

"A gray fox!" she exclaimed.

Olal, the acolyte holding the animal image in mind smiled and clapped her hands together.

"It is so!" she said. "You have seen truly."

Yatik squeezed her new student's arm and nodded.

"You have done well, to be successful on your first attempt at scrying. Your mother is right; you must have the seer's gift. Let us do another practice."

As the morning went by, K'inuuw Mat made repeated attempts at scrying the image of an animal, bird, or marine creature which Olal held in mind, and was mostly successful. Yatik ended the session when time for the midday meal approached, adding that the next level of scrying would involve plants. This was more difficult, because plant images had fewer distinctions than those of animals. After that, they would proceed to identifying locations, such as cities or rivers, and implements with symbolic meanings. Once a good command of the art was attained working with an acolyte who held the image in mind, they would move to the next skill level. This required working alone, posing a question and scrying for an image that would give the answer.

K'inuuw Mat and Olal walked together to the acolyte dining palapa. Olal was two years older and had the square face and short body of Yukatek Mayas, making her just taller than her companion from the highlands. The southern highland Mayas had long, narrow faces and slender bodies, their skin tones lighter brown and noses sharper than those of the northern plateau. Although their dialects were different, most ahauob learned several during childhood, and all Mayas of the period shared a common courtly language used by scribes and carved on monuments.

"It appears that Yatik is pleased with your first scrying session," said Olal. "Plan you to train as a priestess of scrying?"

"I am not certain," replied K'inuuw Mat. "My hope is to learn the seer arts, and through this find the path the Goddess has chosen for me."

"Will you be dedicated to her service?"

"This is my most fervent wish, although it seems that the Oracle must confirm it."

"Let us make offerings that it be so. I can take you to a special place where I feel Ix Chel's presence strongly. It is a hidden cove on the eastern shore of the island. There you will find many flat stones to collect your own for scrying. You might also find a sastun. Or, more accurately, a sastun might find you, if you are meant to have one."

"What is a sastun?"

"It is a crystal or clear stone, about the size of your hand, which is used for divining," said Olal. "Most healers have their sastun, and use it to scan the body and emanations of those seeking healings. I am surprised that you do not know of it."

"I have not been much interested in the healing path. Perhaps the healers of my home regions do not use such stones."

"All priestesses of Ix Chel must know some healing arts, even if this is not our primary path. You never know when such skills will be needed. Certainly you will receive training in herbs and remedies while you are here. The path of the midwife is more specialized; one must feel the call to follow it. The training is rigorous. Personally, I am not drawn to this, but I have found much fascination in herbal studies. It will be fun to test you with plant images; there are many that I can call to mind."

"You will try to trick me!"

"Not so, only to stretch your talents. You will do well, do not worry. Let us hasten or the best food will be gone."

The two girls took longer strides as they turned into the patio of the dining palapa.

Several days later, Olal took K'inuuw Mat to the hidden cove. They followed a causeway from the center of Chel Nah that went some distance eastward, ending at a large plaza facing a rectangular shrine set upon a round substructure. Olal explained that this shrine was the place of sunrise rituals. Two columns stood at each end of the round building, marking the farthest point of the rising sun during winter and summer solstices. The round substructure was a *pib nah*, a sweat bath used for purification before the solstice ceremonies. These were major events on Cuzamil, filled with potent itz and attended by everyone.

Lush jungle foliage and vine-draped trees crowded in at the edges of the plaza. Olal headed to a place that looked no different from everywhere else to K'inuuw Mat's eye. Waving her companion to follow, Olal slipped into an obscure opening between waving palmettos and wild papaya bushes. Quickly K'inuuw Mat stepped down from the plaza before the bushes closed over the entrance, and found she was on a dimly lit, narrow path shrouded by dense, moist jungle. Stillness descended, an expectant hush, as the girls' footsteps squished softly. They were startled when a pack of spider monkeys began chattering angrily at the disturbance. Squawks of green parrots and honks of toucans filtered through the trees.

"Watch for snakes," whispered Olal.

K'inuuw Mat treaded gingerly and kept her arms close at her sides, as she had learned to do when traveling jungle paths. Her feet had little protection in their woven strap sandals, and she looked apprehensively at every dark stick on the ground or green branch hanging across the path.

"If we sing chants to the Goddess, she will keep us safe," she whispered to Olal.

"That is a good thought," Olal replied.

Their voices joined in soft chanting, each taking turns leading. They were certain that the Goddess must have heard them, for soon they arrived safely at the cove. It was a magical place. Tumbled masses of black volcanic rock formed a cup-shaped basin with a small beach at its base. The pale golden sand sparkled with thousands of tiny shells, from pure white to rosy red. Gentle waves lapped the shore; the light turquoise of shallow cove waters gradually deepening to blue as they merged into the ocean. The crash of waves against rocky outcroppings sounded in the distance.

"Oh, how beautiful!" breathed K'inuuw Mat.

"Ummm, every time here is special," Olal murmured.

They removed their sandals and walked on warm sand, toes curling into its softness. Back and forth from one side to the other, they danced and cavorted on the small beach, arms swinging freely and feet kicking up sand. After several passes, they collapsed breathlessly and rolled, laughing and throwing sand on each other. Thoroughly sand-covered, they pulled off their huipils and splashed into the cove, walking out until it deepened and forced them to swim. Colorful fish with white and coral stripes, iridescent blues and tawny gold spots dodged around their legs. A few small sea turtles hastily paddled out to open waters.

"Over here!" called Olal. "Here are many flat stones."

K'inuuw Mat swam to join her companion, who crouched near the beach pointing behind a cluster of lava rocks. Spread around the edges she saw rocks of many shapes and colors. Kneeling, she carefully passed her palm over the rocks, waiting for a signal. Whispering a prayer for Ix Chel's guidance, she began selecting those stones that signaled her palm with a subtle sense of warmth or a tingle. After selecting seven flat stones, she set them aside and went for her pouch beside the discarded huipil. Still naked, she placed the stones in the pouch and strung it over her neck, returning to the water. She swam with the stones, feeling their weight pulling against her neck. Returning to shore, she took each stone out and reverently washed it in the gentle waves. She examined each, imprinting its color and design on her mind. She would practice with each rock to learn its particular conjuring patterns, and then use each accordingly in her scrying.

The girls combed the beach searching for interesting shells. K'inuuw Mat wanted to find gifts for her mother and Ix Chel. She discovered an elegant conch tip, cut by waves and sand abrasion into a perfect flat spiral, its glowing pink hues shading into pearlescent edges. This would make a magnificent pendant for her mother's neck. For Ix Chel, she found three perfectly shaped scallop shells. After cleaning these gifts and putting them into her pouch, she guiltily remembered her sister. She should find a present for Sak T'ul, for her wedding. A little more searching led to a sea star of purest white, its round rim the size of her palm. The perfect star that formed the shell's interior held the promise of Sky God blessings. Her sister would appreciate this as a wedding pendant.

Before leaving, both girls replaced their huipils and joined in prayers of gratitude to Ix Chel. K'inuuw Mat thanked Olal profusely, embracing her warmly. Olal returned thanks for the opportunity to be of service to a follower of the Goddess. Filled with happiness and refreshed by the sacred waters of the sea, they returned buoyantly, albeit carefully, along the path to the city.

4

"Mother, my breasts are very sore," said K'inuuw Mat.

"Ah, it is a sign that your moon flow will begin soon," Chelte' replied, giving her daughter a hug. "We must get everything ready."

They had been on the island nearly long enough to watch the moon complete two cycles. Lady Uc was starting to diminish in size, the edge fading from her glorious silvery globe. The next time she became full would be near the fall equinox, and the Oracle would speak.

Chelte' rummaged in bags she had brought with her, pulling out three small pouches. She took them to her daughter's sleeping pallet, where the girl sat cross-legged. Opening the first pouch, she withdrew a small yellow gourd decorated with conjuring symbols. It had a tight-fitting lid, which she twisted off to show the strips of bark paper inside.

"The earliest drops of first moon blood hold the greatest *itz,* although the entire flow is full of power," Chelte' said. "As soon as the blood appears, soak all the strips. This may take some time, because first flow is often slight and erratic. When the strips are dry, put them in the bowl and keep it on your home altar. Be most selective in using this sacred offering, burning the strips ceremonially while making your heart's deepest requests."

"And the Goddess cannot refuse these requests!" exclaimed K'inuuw Mat.

"Exactly so," her mother replied. "That is why you must be careful of what you ask."

From the next pouch Chelte' removed wadded cotton along with a loincloth to hold it in place. She showed her daughter how to secure the wadded portion in position to catch the blood, held up with a band around the waist. There were several cotton wads and an extra loincloth in the pouch. She remarked that the fine green moss found on trunks and branches of mahogany and oak trees made a nice substitute for cotton, and was often used when women were traveling. All of the cotton wads from the first moon flow were placed in a special bowl full of water kept for that purpose. The blood-tinged water was poured onto the city's maize fields as a blessing to keep the soil fertile.

The third pouch held offerings for Ix Chel. Chelte' had placed jade and obsidian beads from home inside, along with the finest quality cacao beans from K'inuuw Mat's father. The girl was to add her own gifts as her moon time approached. She eagerly brought out the pouch of shells she had gathered at the hidden cove, and removed the three lovely sea scallops, their interiors glowing in rose-hued mother of pearl. Each was perfectly shaped without the slightest defect, and they were graduated in size. She explained that from smallest to largest, they represented the three phases of a woman's life. Chelte' nodded approval and gave assurances that Ix Chel would be pleased.

Each day K'inuuw Mat watched for drops of blood, aware of intermittent belly cramps. Her emotional sensitivity increased, and she became teary-eyed easily. After her trainings, now focused on herbal healing, she spent time alone at the jungle's edge singing songs to nature and its wonders. After a particularly sweet song, during which butterflies danced around her head, she stood up from the stone on which she had been sitting, and felt wetness between her thighs. Dabbing a finger to check, she saw red-streaked mucus on the fingertip.

It had happened! Her first moon flow had begun.

But, she was a distance from her palapa, without the gourd of bark paper strips. Glancing around, she saw a green mango leaf that was just the right size and shape. Picking the leaf, she tore a strip from the hem of her huipil and wrapped it to hold the leaf in place. The leaf felt scratchy and she walked straddle-legged, feeling a little foolish. It was vitally important to catch the first flow, however, so she slowly waddled back to her dwelling. Once there, she carefully removed the mango leaf and soaked up the small pool of blood with a bark strip from her gourd. She placed another strip to catch more blood, and lay to rest on her pallet, hoping to ease the cramps.

When the others returned to the palapa and she informed them, excited congratulations and comments about the menarche ceremonies flew around. A first moon flow ceremony was held during each new moon at Chel Nah, which served as a rite of passage into womanhood. All the girls beginning their flow since the previous new moon would take part, receiving public acknowledgement and being ritually ushered into their new status as vessels of the Goddess. They were now young women, who were able to bring forth new life in their wombs. The Ruler and High Priestess, K'ak Sihom, would officiate at this transformation ritual. It denoted that the participants were now transformed from one phase of life to another; from the state of child to that of maiden. Transformation rituals were held by the Mayas for each important life phase. The final rite was a transition ritual, performed after death to demarcate moving from life in the Middleworld to spirit in the Underworld.

Before the public ceremony, Chelte' and Yatik held one just for their family. The women led the two girls close to the forest's edge, where a young ceiba tree stood. The ceiba tree was sacred to the Mayas; it was the Wakah Chan Te', the Jeweled Sky Tree that connected the three dimensions. Its large roots reached into the Underworld, its trunk stood straight and strong in the Middleworld, and its branches soared into the Upperworld. The trunk of the young ceiba was covered with thick thorns, which protected it from assault. When the tree matured, it became immense with a trunk as thick as half a man's height, and branches disappearing into the forest canopy. Then it no longer needed thorns. Root buttresses emerging from the trunk base could be higher than a man. Among the tallest trees in the forest, the ceiba's branches were laden with mossy clusters and lovely orchids. In early spring it dropped its narrow green leaves and replaced them with bouquets of whitish pink flowers, whose blossoms opened after the Sun Lord slipped from sight into the Underworld. At night, bats drank flower nectar and ate pollen, and in the morning many songbirds, hummingbirds, and brown jays flocked to the branches along with bees, wasps and beetles.

In addition to giving nourishment to many creatures with its flowers, the ceiba provided a luxurious item to humans from its fruit. After attaining the age of seven to ten years, the ceiba produced fruit, as many as four thousand slender oval-shaped fruits the length of a hand. The fruits appeared in clusters on branches that only grew at the top of the tree. The husks were gray and rough, but when they opened the inside was lined with a bed of lustrous, silky white fibers. Soft and slippery, the fibers were used to stuff bedding and pillows. They cushioned the heads and bodies of the people, soothing them into relaxation and sleep. The fruit of the ceiba was another gift of the deities who looked after the Mayas. The ancient Mayan word for ceiba was *yáaxché*, meaning "first tree."

The family knelt at the base of the young ceiba; the tree was already the height of three men, its trunk well-covered with pointed thorns. They bowed with their arms across their chests. Yatik led a prayer to honor the ceiba tree, and then Chelte' instructed K'inuuw Mat to remove her loincloth and squat over the ground close to the trunk of the tree. The girl was to remain squatting until several drops of moon blood fell onto the ground. Chelte' made the pronouncement that now the divine woman's essence flowed onto the ground. The ch'ulel of K'inuuw Mat, her soul energies, became one with the ceiba tree, the earth, and the Great Mother Goddess. Then Chelte' joined the others, singing the traditional song to welcome a girl into maidenhood.

"In her company, the drops of blood and her,
The blood of the lineage, of the creation, and the night are untied.
Her strength is tied up in the company of her,
The drops of blood and her, the blood of the lineage."

*"Bin Inca ix hun pucub kik ix hun,
Pucub olom u colba chab u coolba akab tit.
Kax u kinam icnal ix hun pucub,*

Kik ix hun pucub olom."

Taking a carved bone staff, Yatik worked the ground until it had absorbed the drops of K'inuuw Mat's blood. Replacing her loincloth, K'inuuw Mat stood and repeated the song, her voice lilting as she sang the time-honored words that proclaimed the ritual power of women's menstrual blood. The term *kik* meant menstrual blood, and the term *olom* signified both lineage and coagulated blood. Used together, they united the powerful symbols of blood and lineage, the power to bring forth life and to continue family lineages.

The others hugged her when she finished singing, showering her face with kisses and stroking her hair.

"By giving your first moon blood, you are now merged with the Goddess, the Earth, and the sacred ceiba tree. May Ix Chel protect you and bless your womb, the sacred vessel of life. All honor to Ix Chel, our mother and our guide." Yatik raised her hands in the blessing sign as she pronounced the words that denoted becoming a maiden.

5

At the first sliver of the new moon, the public menarche ceremony took place. It began just before sunrise, when the thin crescent hung over the eastern horizon. Everything signified newness, fresh beginnings, and the dawning of a new life phase. Thirteen girls participated; a significant number that symbolized a circle and the endless spirit domain. For the Mayas, thirteen represented the major articulations of the human body, the wandering stars of the solar system, the cycles of the moon, the number coefficients of the days, and subdivisions of the day. This number was the basis for the sacred Tzolk'in calendar, with its $13 \times 20 = 260$ computations, which integrated into most of their other calendars.

Yatik considered it most auspicious that thirteen girls would undergo transformation into maidenhood rituals. K'inuuw Mat gathered with the other girls, all wearing fine white huipils, with rainbow-colored ribbons streaming from headdresses of white shells and feathers. They stood in a line in front of the large temple in the main square, waiting for the High

Priestess to appear. Shivering in the pre-dawn chill, K'inuuw Mat worried about facing K'ak Sihom again. Her last encounter had left her shaken, and she feared another such episode. As the voices of priestesses trilled the sunrise chant, the regal figure of K'ak Sihom appeared at the top of the temple stairs, and she slowly descended to the line of girls below.

The High Priestess walked slowly along the line, taking a bundle of herbs from an assistant and dipping it into sea water, then sprinkling each girl. Another priestess came behind, wafting copal incense around the girls' heads, bodies, and feet. The priestess chorus chanted the traditional coming to maidenhood song. K'inuuw Mat tensed her body against flinching as the cold drops of water struck her, and glanced up at K'ak Sihom. The ruler did not meet her eyes, however, gazing above her head with a distant look, appearing to be in a trance. Walking behind the line of girls, she repeated the sprinkling of their backs, followed by the incense cleansing. Once this was completed, the ruler returned to the stairway and walked halfway up. There she turned and lifted her arms, giving the hand sign for blessing with palms open to the girls below. She made a short speech of welcome to the status of maiden, congratulated them upon becoming vessels for the lives given by Ix Chel, and invoked fertility to their wombs.

The plaza was filled with observers who came to bear witness to this change of status. After the ruler finished speaking, the observers raised their voices in acknowledgement, while tossing flowers upon the new maidens who proceeded across the plaza onto the sakbe leading to the small flat-roofed Ix Chel shrine. Once inside the sky-toned building with flowing black designs, the maidens placed their offerings on the altar of Ix Chel portrayed as the maiden. When K'inuuw Mat's turn came, she knelt and reverently placed her scallop shells, jade and obsidian jewels, and cacao beans before the young Goddess. She murmured her thanks and prayed fervently that the Goddess accept her offerings, and take her into service on the island.

6

K'inuuw Mat could barely contain her excitement as the time of the full moon arrived. This was the full moon of the fall equinox, and the Oracle would speak. She would accompany her mother and sister to a session with the Oracle, at which her mother would ask about her daughters' futures. A quiver of trepidation arose; would the Oracle confirm a life of serving the Goddess? She wanted to find out as much as she could about the Oracle. For this, she queried her aunt.

"Tell me about the esteemed Ab'uk Cen," she entreated. "How does she prepare to serve as Oracle for the Goddess? What things does she say, and how does she speak?"

"Your interest in the Oracle is commendable. She lives a most secluded life," Yatik explained. "When a priestess is chosen for this vast responsibility, she knows that her life is forever changed. She lives alone, attended by specialized priestesses who prepare her food, maintain her quarters, and communicate with the outside world. Everything the Oracle needs is provided. But, she revokes family connections and personal desires. Her complete focus is upon staying in a high spiritual state, and following prescribed regimens for making prophecies as the Oracle."

"How does she appear when she makes prophecies?"

"Inside the Oracle's temple, which adjoins her residence, is a large wooden statue of Ix Chel. It is hollow inside, and large enough to hold a person. The Oracle sits inside the statue and speaks through its open mouth. You cannot see the Oracle, for she is not her priestess self; she has become the Goddess. Therefore, we are to look only upon the image of the Goddess, not upon a human face. There are other priestesses in the chamber, who remain in the shadows, and tend the incense burners and snakes. Only the supplicant asking a question of the Oracle can enter the chamber, so her quest is kept private. Of course, when it is a mother with her daughters, as in your situation, all three of you enter together."

"There are snakes free in the chamber?"

Yatik laughed and replied, "Yes, these are special snakes. They have been tamed and trained; they convey subtle perceptions to the Oracle. Snakes are among the animal uayob, the familiars of Ix Chel along with felines, butterflies, hummingbirds, and rabbits. The snakes have extra sensitivities beyond those of humans, and they impart information to the Oracle that may be unknown even to the supplicant. Although the Oracle's snakes are poisonous, they will not harm you. Usually they remain inside the statue."

K'inuuw Mat hoped that the snakes would do this during her visit. She had heard about the Oracle taking substances to alter her consciousness, and was curious.

"What does the Oracle do to prepare herself to become the Goddess?"

"Ah, this is a complicated process, but I will tell you, since your goal is to become a priestess of Ix Chel," Yatik said. "It is complicated and dangerous. The preparation must be undertaken very precisely. The substances that the Oracle uses are highly toxic, and must be exactly prepared or they can kill her. The life of the Oracle is in the hands of her medicinal priestesses who mix these ingredients. These women also give over their lives, remaining inside the Oracle's chambers except when they must collect more herbs and substances. They tend a garden within an interior courtyard, where plants and toads are kept. It is a solitary life, and they are carefully chosen.

"When the time for making prophecy comes, the Oracle undertakes ritual preparations. First, the body of Ab'uk Cen must be rigorously purified in a special *pib nah*. This steam bath is located inside her chambers, and it is scrubbed with water infused with crushed sour orange flowers. This imparts a fresh citrus odor that repels malevolent forces. Censers of clay with faces of protector deities stand beside the door, burning dried herbs that include basil, cedar, Pay-che and vervain to clear away evil magic and spirits. The Oracle fasts for two days before, and is cleansed with copal smoke before she enters the pib nah. She removes her robe and enters naked, lying upon a stone bench while attendants pour sour orange flower water over the heated rocks. The flower-filled steam gives another level of body purification through sweat, and protection from of evil spirits.

"Once this process is completed, the Oracle is taken to a small room hidden deep inside her chambers. Only her most trusted attendants know the location of this room. It is the place where substances are administered that will separate the Oracle's awareness from her body."

Yatik paused, gauging whether to reveal more. K'inuuw Mat appeared totally absorbed in the description, her eyes wide with eagerness. *Perhaps such knowledge would serve her well in her path*, the aunt thought.

"Three priestesses do the final preparation," Yatik continued. "They are the ones who prepare the ingredients for each stage. First, the eldest priestess, who represents the grandmother, gives the Oracle a small clay pipe to smoke. It holds rare blue-leafed tobacco grown only on Cuzamil, dried and crushed while secret chants are sung to enhance its potency. The Oracle takes four puffs while facing each of the four corners of the world upheld by the four Pahuatuns, inhaling deeply. The tobacco smoke causes her to begin distancing from her body, feeling a floating sensation.

"Next, the middle-age priestess, who represents the mother, massages the Oracle's body with a mixture of crushed morning glory seeds and cohune palm oil, rendered over a fire of cedar wood and copal. Both cedar and copal are cleansing agents; morning glory seeds change one's consciousness and open the path to disembodiment. Palm oil gives off smoky, dark aromas of fertile earth. Every part of the body is massaged, including all the openings of the head and bottom. As this mixture takes effect, the Oracle floats in semi-consciousness, and needs assistance walking. At this point, before the final stage, she is dressed in flowing white robes embroidered with Ix Chel's sacred colors: blue, red, purple.

"The last stage is an enema administered by the youngest priestess, representing the maiden. She uses a long-neck gourd with a small tip, cut and smoothed at the end. The enema solution contains a mixture of poison from the glands on the bufo toad's neck, fermented juice from maguey, and a concentrated solution made with Datura flowers. The milky substance from glands of older toads is hard to control, so it must be obtained while the toad is young, but mature. Then, it must be measured very carefully. The juice extracted from thick maguey stalks is combined with honey and fermented until a powerful alcoholic brew is produced. Datura, which is known as *tah k'u*, "with god," invokes the capacity for envisioning. Many use it to seek the vision serpent. All three substances are toxic, and together their power is immense.

"So you see this is an exacting formula. If not made correctly, the Oracle can die. Even when carefully made, with the Oracle's weight and age taken into consideration, the enema mixture causes sickness for several days after use. It does have cumulative effects, weakening the Oracle over time. Ab'uk Cen has served as Oracle for more years than most, I am told. She is growing weaker, however, and must step down soon."

"Might this be her last prophesying?" asked K'inuuw Mat, genuinely concerned.

"It is possible. You are fortunate to benefit from her long experience. You may trust the prophecy she gives for you."

"What happens once the Oracle is given the enema?"

"This becomes the final severance of the Oracle's human presence. There are frightening physical changes, in which she sees flashing lights and grotesque creatures, feels intense pressure within her body, and her heart races. She becomes nauseated; sometimes she will vomit several times. Her limbs shake and tremble; soon she has seizures which throw her out of her body. Once her body becomes still, it is an empty and purified vessel for the Goddess. This stillness signals the attendants that she is ready. They carry her into the wooden statue, place her in a wooden frame with seat and back to support her body, and tie her wrists, waist, and ankles to prevent slipping off. They release the two snakes from baskets inside the statue, light the censers to diffuse copal smoke through the statue's eyes and mouth, and then stand behind until needed. A different priestess acts as the Oracle's steward to summon supplicants for an audience.

"There. That is more than I have ever told any acolyte before."

"How can the Oracle speak, when she has taken so many substances?"

"She speaks through the power of the Goddess. It is beyond human capacities. You will see soon for yourself."

7

A stream of pilgrims began filling the plaza early in the morning. At the north edge was the entrance to the sakbe leading to the Oracle's shrine. A solitary arch framed the sakbe; tall censers emitting copal smoke stood near each pillar. Ix Chel priestesses waited beside the arch with large baskets to receive pilgrim's offerings, an expression of gratitude for this opportunity to question the Oracle. Each day that the Oracle did prophecy, the priestesses allowed 100 pilgrims to pass under the arch and continue on the sakbe that led straight north, ending with a second arch that opened onto the Oracle's plaza. There the pilgrims waited until called into the Oracle's shrine. It was traditional for the Oracle to continue daily sessions until all pilgrims were received. Given Ab'uk Cen's fragile health, however, this year it was uncertain how many days she could continue.

An air of tension mingled with anticipation as pilgrims jostled each other trying to get through the arch. The sky reflected uncertainty; brisk winds blew from the north and storm clouds gathered on the horizon. Palm fronds and tall branches tossed and hissed in the wind that whipped the pilgrim's hair, headdresses, and huipils. Wealthy noble women regretted their fancy feathers that threatened to fly off their headbands, and their layered jewelry that clinked and jangled excessively. Children milling around the plaza earned shells and beans by rescuing escaped feathers.

Chelte' and her daughters had dressed simply and kept heads bare, except for braiding rainbow colored ribbons in their hair. She believed her family's wealth was better expressed in gifts to the Oracle, which were recorded by the priestesses. An early start and light snack at home allowed them to arrive among the first in the plaza, and they stood near the head of the line. Conches blew to announce the beginning session, and soon

Chelte' and the girls handed their gift bundles of cacao, jade, and weaving to the priestesses. Crossing through the arch, they were cleansed with copal smoke and basil-infused water by other priestesses, and then walked the sakbe in silence.

K'inuuw Mat kept her eyes downcast and concentrated on repeating mental prayers to Ix Chel. She desperately wanted the Oracle to prophesy her dedication to serving the Goddess. Chelte' watched the horizon and puzzled about the ominous appearing clouds and wind. Storms were not uncommon in the islands, and this was the stormy season. A flicker of uneasiness made her whisper a quick prayer that all would go well with their Oracle prophecies. Sak T'ul used her mother's body to shield her from the wind and cast fearful glances up the sakbe. She was not looking forward to meeting the Oracle.

At the second arch, another cadre of priestesses held smoking censers emitting copal and cedar smoke, the final purification. Entering the small plaza, Chelte' and the girls sat in order of arrival on lines of mats where pilgrims waited to be summoned. The Oracle's shrine was situated on the north border of the plaza, set on a base rising four stone tiers to a tall temple made of wood with thatched roof. The temple walls were enclosed, constructed of large tree trunks joined solidly, smoothed and painted in sea and snake motifs. A wooden door was guarded by two priestesses, who opened it just enough to allow the summoned pilgrim to enter and exit. Incense smoke wafted through the opening between the thatched roof and upper walls. A chorus of priestesses seated on the stairs kept up monotone chanting accompanied by soft rattles and drumbeats.

When her mother was signaled to come forward, K'inuuw Mat's heart skipped a beat. She jumped to her feet and followed behind the lagging Sak T'ul, hardly able to keep from pushing her sister. The large door swung silently open, and the triad entered a dimly lit chamber filled with smoke. Immediately the towering wooden statue of Ix Chel commanded attention. The standing figure soared to the height of three people, feet firmly planted apart and arms held in the "creation or break sign" gesture that signified emergence or renewal events. With elbows bent 90 degrees held close to the waist, the left land flexed upward with fingers aligned to the sky, and the right hand flexed downward with fingers aligned to the earth. It was an immensely significant hand sign, used for all creation or birth events— whether of universes, planets, people, or creatures. It represented daybreak, breaking through to new levels, breaking away from constraints.

The Goddess commands us to rebirth into new identities, thought K'inuuw Mat, transfixed by the arresting image.

A priestess stood at either side of the statue. The pungent, woody scent of copal was strong and smoke burned eyes and nostrils. Other aromas combined in an intoxicating mixture of sweet flowers and acrid minerals. Sak T'ul appeared to be almost swooning and clung to her mother's arm. K'inuuw Mat breathed the fumes fearlessly and felt her awareness beginning to change. She looked carefully around the chamber to commit details to memory, but found nothing else inside except the statue and priestesses. The inner walls were unadorned and the stone floor was bare.

"Speak, pilgrim. Ask what you will of the Ix Chel Oracle," intoned one priestess.

Chelte' bowed with crossed arms, and the girls followed suit.

"Esteemed and honored Oracle, this one before you is Chelte' of Altun Ha, wife of the Uxte'kuh ruler." Chelte' said reverently. "For myself I have no questions. My purpose is to give thanks to Ix Chel for her blessings, for an abundant and comfortable life, and for my three children. Please accept my undying gratitude and unceasing devotion."

New curls of smoke emanated from the statue's mouth and nose, and an eerie voice replied, seeming to come from nowhere and everywhere.

"Pleased am I to accept your gratitude, Chelte' of Altun Ha. Your family is well known to me, true servants of my work. May you abide in my future blessings. So it is."

Chelte' bowed, pushed Sak T'ul in front of the statue, and spoke again: "For my eldest daughter, Sak T'ul, I seek your prophecy for her upcoming marriage, her fertility and happiness in our city. She is shy and requested that I ask for her."

After another release of smoke, the Oracle's voice wafted through the thick air.

"The fate of this one hovers on jungle vines,
wherein the balance of wisdom and audacity are tested.
Aptly balanced, she lives a life of ease, abundance, and blessed fertility.
But failed, her life is short. Destiny lies not in her hands.
Those close to her take care. Great happiness can be hers."

Sak T'ul was crying, her body shaking as the Oracle ended the prophecy. Chelte' wrapped both arms around her daughter to keep her from crumpling to the floor. In her mind, Chelte' repeated the Oracle's words to memorize them for future analysis. She nodded to K'inuuw Mat to pose her question.

Although shaken, K'inuuw Mat mustered her courage and stepped in front of the statue. Gazing upward at the implacable face, crowned with a coiled serpent headdress and wearing huge earspools, the girl breathed deeply and felt the edges of her awareness dissolving. Quickly she posed her question, afraid she might lose consciousness soon.

"Oh great and glorious Goddess, standing before you is the new maiden K'inuuw Mat of Uxte'kuh, second daughter of Chelte', one who comes to your sacred island for first moon rites. My deepest desire is to remain here and dedicate my life to your service. May I receive your prophecy for the purpose and direction of my life."

It appeared to K'inuuw Mat that an unusual amount of new smoke poured out of the statue's mouth and nose. As the spirals drifted down, they circled around her body almost making her cough. She felt something cold and smooth against her leg, and then a squeezing sensation caused her to gasp. Looking down, she saw a long black snake slithering up her right leg. Its wedge-shaped head alerted her that this was a poisonous viper, and a bolt of terror shot through her. The snake halted its ascent, drew its head upward and fixated beady eyes upon her face, forked tongue rapidly quivering.

She glanced wide-eyed at the nearest priestess, but the woman simply stared into space, appearing not to notice. The statue was half-hidden by smoke and her mother not visible behind her. Remembering her aunt's description of the Oracle's snakes, she withdrew her awareness and dropped into her center, willing a state of calmness. Mentally she communicated to the snake: *You are welcome here, servant of Ix Chel. You come in peace and I receive you in gratitude.*

The snake waved its head several times, flicked its tongue and slowly slithered down from her leg. She watched it disappear through a hole in the base of the statue. The Oracle's voice startled her.

"A seer you are and well command your fears.

The gift of prophecy resides within you; use it in service of others.

Deep is your tie to Ix Chel, but not to be realized here.

A destiny beyond your own awaits. A people's legacy depends on you.

In the high court of royalty shall your life unfold.

Rulers shall seek your wisdom; leaders your guidance.

Through you shall dynasties abide."

K'inuuw Mat stood in stunned silence. The Oracle's prophecy was emblazoned in her mind, but she refused to accept it. Surely this was not correct! How could her destiny be other than serving the Goddess on Cuzamil?

She managed a slight bow when prompted by Chelte', who led her daughters, both in tears, out of the Oracle's shrine.

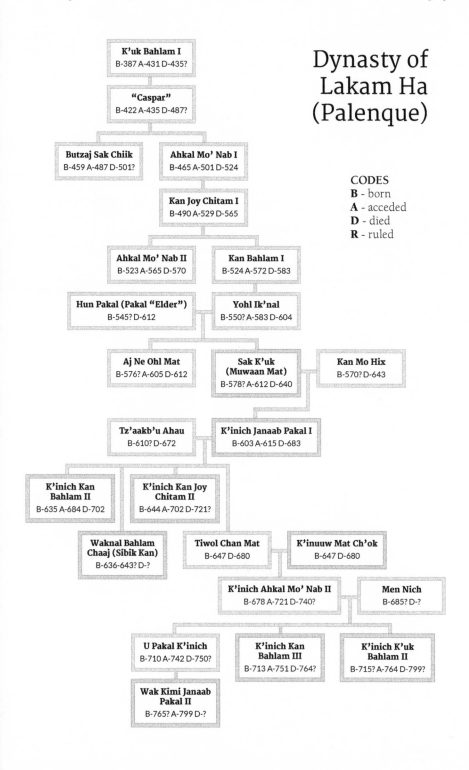

Dynasty of Lakam Ha (Palenque)

CODES
B - born
A - acceded
D - died
R - ruled

K'uk Bahlam I
B-387 A-431 D-435?

"Caspar"
B-422 A-435 D-487?

Butzaj Sak Chiik
B-459 A-487 D-501?

Ahkal Mo' Nab I
B-465 A-501 D-524

Kan Joy Chitam I
B-490 A-529 D-565

Ahkal Mo' Nab II
B-523 A-565 D-570

Kan Bahlam I
B-524 A-572 D-583

Hun Pakal (Pakal "Elder")
B-545? D-612

Yohl Ik'nal
B-550? A-583 D-604

Aj Ne Ohl Mat
B-576? A-605 D-612

Sak K'uk (Muwaan Mat)
B-578? A-612 D-640

Kan Mo Hix
B-570? D-643

Tz'aakb'u Ahau
B-610? D-672

K'inich Janaab Pakal I
B-603 A-615 D-683

K'inich Kan Bahlam II
B-635 A-684 D-702

K'inich Kan Joy Chitam II
B-644 A-702 D-721?

Waknal Bahlam Chaaj (Sibik Kan)
B-636-643? D-?

Tiwol Chan Mat
B-647 D-680

K'inuuw Mat Ch'ok
B-647 D-680

K'inich Ahkal Mo' Nab II
B-678 A-721 D-740?

Men Nich
B-685? D-?

U Pakal K'inich
B-710 A-742 D-750?

K'inich Kan Bahlam III
B-713 A-751 D-764?

K'inich K'uk Bahlam II
B-715? A-764 D-799?

Wak Kimi Janaab Pakal II
B-765? A-799 D-?

Alliances Among Maya Cities

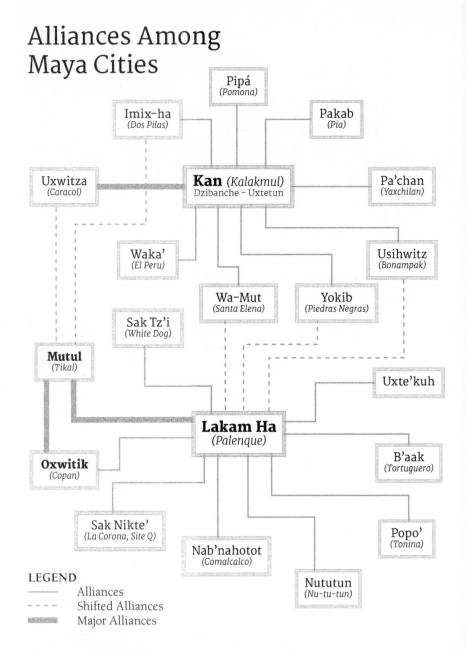

Pipá
(Pomona)

Imix-ha
(Dos Pilas)

Pakab
(Pia)

Uxwitza
(Caracol)

Kan (Kalakmul)
Dzibanche – Uxtetun

Pa'chan
(Yaxchilan)

Waka'
(El Peru)

Usihwitz
(Bonampak)

Wa-Mut
(Santa Elena)

Yokib
(Piedras Negras)

Sak Tz'i
(White Dog)

Mutul
(Tikal)

Uxte'kuh

Lakam Ha
(Palenque)

Oxwitik
(Copan)

B'aak
(Tortuguero)

Sak Nikte'
(La Corona, Site Q)

Popo'
(Tonina)

Nab'nahotot
(Comalcalco)

Nututun
(Nu-tu-tun)

LEGEND
——— Alliances
- - - - Shifted Alliances
▬▬▬▬ Major Alliances

Long Count Maya Calendar

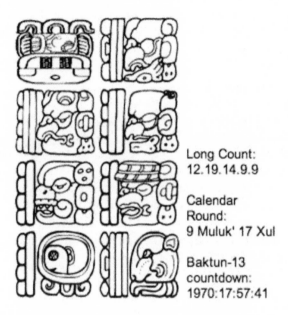

Long Count:
12.19.14.9.9

Calendar
Round:
9 Muluk' 17 Xul

Baktun-13
countdown:
1970:17:57:41

Although considered a vigesimal (20 base) system, the Maya used modifications in two places for calendric and numerological reasons. In Classic times the counts went from 0 to 19 in all but the 2nd position, in which they went from 0 to 17. Postclassic adaptations changed the counts to begin with 1, making them 1 to 20 and 1 to 18.

Mayan Name	Count		Solar Years	Tun
Baktun	0-19	144000 kin = 20 Katun = 1 Baktun	394.25	400
Katun	0-19	7200 kin = 20 Tun = 1 Katun	19.71	20
Tun	0-19	360 kin = 18 Uinal = 1 Tun	0.985	1
Uinal	0-17	20 kin = 20 Kin = 1 Uinal		
Kin	0-19	1 kin = 1 Kin		

After 19 Kin occur, the Uinal count goes up by 1 on the next day; after 17 Uinal the Tun count goes up by 1 on the next day, after 19 Tun

the Katun count goes up by 1 the next day, and after 19 Katun the Baktun count goes up by 1 the next day.

Thus, we see this progression in the Long Count:
11.19.19.17.19 + 1 kin (day) = 12.0.0.0.0

Increasingly larger units of time beyond the Baktun are: Piktun, Kalabtun, Kinchiltun, and Alautun. These were usually noted by placing 13 in the counts larger than Baktun, indicating 13 to a multiple of the 20th power:
13.13.13.13.13.0.0.0.0

When a 13 Baktun is reached, this signifies the end of a Great Cycle of 1,872,000 kins (days) or 5200 tuns (5125.2567 solar years). But this does not signify the end of the Maya calendar. Larger baktun units occur on stela with numbers above 13, indicating that this count went up to 19 before converting into the next higher unit in the 6th position. When the 5th position (Baktun) reaches 19, on the following day the 6th position (Pictun) becomes 1 and the 5th position becomes 0. This results in a Long Count such as that projected by glyphs at Palenque to a Gregorian date of 4772 AD (GMT correlation), written as 1.0.0.0.0.0.

About the Author

Leonide (**Lennie**) **Martin**: Retired California State University professor, former Family Nurse Practitioner, Author and Maya researcher, Research Member Maya Exploration Center.

My books bring ancient Maya culture and civilization to life in stories about both real historical Mayans and fictional characters. I've studied Maya archeology, anthropology, and history from the scientific and indigenous viewpoints. While living for five years in in Mérida, Yucatan, Mexico, I apprenticed with Maya Elder Hunbatz Men, becoming a Solar Initiate and Maya Fire Women in the Itzá Maya tradition. I've studied with other indigenous teachers in Guatemala, including Maya Priestess-Daykeeper Aum Rak Sapper. The ancient Mayas created the most highly advanced civilization in the Western hemisphere, and my work is dedicated to their wisdom, spirituality, scientific, and cultural accomplishments through compelling historical novels.

My interest in ancient Mayan women led to writing the Mayan Queens' series called *Mists of Palenque*. This 4-book series tells the stories of powerful women who shaped the destinies of their people as rulers themselves, or wives of rulers. These remarkable Mayan women are unknown to most people. Using extensive research and field study, I aspire to depict ancient Palenque authentically and make these amazing Mayan Queens accessible to a wide readership.

My writing has won awards from Writer's Digest for short fiction, and *The Visionary Mayan Queen: Yohl Ik'nal of Palenque (Mists of Palenque Series Book 1)* received the Writer's Digest 2nd Annual Self-Published eBook award in 2015. *The Mayan Red Queen: Tz'aakb'u Ahau of Palenque (Mists of Palenque Series Book 3)* received a Silver Medal in Dan Poynter's Global eBook Awards for 2016.

For more information about my writing and the Mayas, visit:
Website: **www.mistsofpalenque.com**
Blog: **http://leonidemartinblog.wordpress.com/**
Facebook: **https://www.facebook.com/leonide.martin**

Author Notes

T his book, third in my *Mists of Palenque Series* about four great Mayan Queens, has been both intimidating and exhilarating to write. Intimidating because the main male character, K'inich Janaab Pakal, is the most famous Mayan ruler and there is a copious amount of archeological and epigraphic information about him and his legendary accomplishments. His wife Tz'aakb'u Ahau, the main female character, is the well known "Red Queen," although documentation about her actual life is scanty. Another well-documented ruler enters the story here, their son K'inich Kan Bahlam II; an amazingly brilliant and creative man who became ruler after Pakal. With advances in epigraphy that allow experts to interpret over 80% of Maya hieroglyphs, and recent discoveries through excavations of later temples built by Pakal's successors, I had to digest a huge amount of data and fit what is factually known into the story line.

It was exhilarating because the data provided so many opportunities to take facts and weave them into the development of characters and fleshing out events in their lives. When taking on these opportunities, the author's creative imagination can blossom. As I said in previous author notes, *history is interpretation*. Thus, historical fiction is interpretation with a flourish! Here are a few of those key interpretations that offer my take on the lives of these famous Mayas.

In the hieroglyphic records about Pakal's reign, there is a gap of eighteen years between his accession at age twelve and his celebration of the tenth katun at age thirty. A few references are found for the next nineteen years, but the detailed narrative carved on the Temple of the Inscriptions really takes off at the eleventh katun celebration, thirty-seven years after Pakal took power. Then we see progress in his re-building the portal to the Gods and ancestors that was destroyed by the enemy Kan dynasty of Kalakmul. The portal is completely resurrected twenty years later at the twelfth katun celebration. In all, it took Pakal some sixty years to re-establish the religious charter of Palenque. What was happening in his life during those early years? Why did resurrecting the portal take so long, and how did he do it?

Enter his wife, Tz'aakb'u Ahau, whom I name "Lalak" in the story. It's amply clear that Tz'aakb'u Ahau was her ceremonial, official queen name.

No one would name a young girl "The Orderer of Royal Succession" or "The Accumulator of Lords" as her name translates. There is scientific evidence through strontium isotopes and DNA analysis of her bones and teeth that she was not born in Palenque, but came from a nearby city with similar geography. She bore Pakal four sons, three of whom survived to adulthood; but the first was not born until they had been married for nine years. Who was she, where did she come from, and why did they wait almost a decade to have a child? From these curious facts, I created Lalak from neighboring city Tortuguero, a shy and homely girl brought to a sophisticated, complex court by Pakal's mother, Sak K'uk, to become the producer of heirs. Thus, the story has Lalak experiencing several miscarriages during the early years of her marriage, and struggling to find her place at court and in Pakal's heart. Winning his love is especially challenging since he is in love with a local beauty banished by his mother to a distant city.

The relationship between Pakal and Lalak is central to the story. Their journey is to discover each other's innermost gems, to overcome preconceptions, to meet challenges in a turbulent political landscape. During this time Pakal comes into his own as a major creative genius, building most of Palenque that is admired by visitors today. And, the glyphs proclaim that he did restore the portal, bringing stability and prosperity to his city far into the future.

How does one reconstruct a mystical portal to the Upperworld, a channel for communication with Gods and ancestors? This puzzled me for some time, and it certainly is not explained in the cryptic carvings. I asked myself, what force would be potent enough to resurrect a spiritual pathway between earth and the heavens, and the answer came to me—the most powerful creative energy upon the earth, the procreative and ecstatic power of sexuality.

This led to Lalak's training in sex magic, more accurately known as sexual alchemy. With her abilities in sexual alchemy at the core of resurrecting the portal, she became an immense asset to Pakal and this transformed their relationship. My intention was to describe the sexual scenes with reserve and taste, avoiding explicit words and using poetic or allegorical approaches, yet conveying the intensity and eroticism of these magical moments. I hope I have succeeded.

The character of their son Kan Bahlam deserves some comment. He accedes to the throne after Pakal's death, which takes place in Book 4. Pakal is eighty at death, and Kan Bahlam is forty-nine when he becomes ruler a year later. However, he apparently had no heirs; for his brother K'inich Kan Joy Chitam II is his successor. These facts raised two questions in my mind. Why did Kan Bahlam have no children, and what did he do for forty-nine years while waiting to become ruler? He was another creative genius, the builder of the Cross Group, creator of the 819-day calendar and a mysterious code language called Zuyua. Maya experts suggest he probably traveled widely during those years, studying and learning in other Maya centers.

To create a provocative character, in my story Kan Bahlam is a self-involved man of gargantuan appetites. His licentious sexuality, unusual among Maya elite, creates tensions in his family. A febrile illness as a young adult leaves him possibly sterile. With knowledge that he might not have children, Kan Bahlam throws himself into creative realms to leave his mark on the world. He develops an "academy" of astronomers, calendar experts, artists, and architects to carry out his projects during the years before his accession. However, he refuses to give up hope of fathering an heir. This theme plays out in the subsequent book, during the last years of Pakal's reign and after Kan Bahlam becomes ruler.

Mayan culture had cooperative aspects and Palenque engaged in less warfare than many other cities. Palenque became a prominent regional center and vortex of creativity and artistry, hosting visitors from distant places. There is evidence of widespread trade networks, leading to visitors from North and South American native groups who came to trade and study. Some suggest hints of Asian design in some Palenque structures. A complex web of alliances and enmities existed among Petén cities, reaching as far south as Copan and north onto the Tabascan plains. Decades of conflict between Palenque's enemy Kalakmul and ally Tikal drew Palenque into battles and political strategies, as it tried to maintain fragile equilibrium in its polity. Disagreements among Maya experts around these events forced me to choose an interpretation; I elected to interpret the 659 CE "arrival" event of Nuun Ujol Chaak as Palenque giving refuge to the ousted Tikal ruler. Palenque had long-standing ties to Tikal, possibly through the "entrada" of Teotihuacan forces three centuries earlier and the great central Mexico empire seeding local royal lineages. There is archeological evidence that the Teotihuacan bloodline merged with the ruling lineage of Tikal; perhaps it also sent a shoot to establish a lineage at Palenque.

The Mayas were profoundly engaged with spirituality through vital and immediate relationships with their deities. Mayan rulers and priests were mystics and shamans. They envisioned and experienced other realities, interacted with otherworldly creatures, communicated with and even became the earthly manifestation of the Gods. Historical fiction about their experiences, in my view, must include these extraordinary events, which are part of Mayan history and cosmovision. What modern readers might consider fantasy was actually reality to ancient Mayas.

As previously stated, my interpretation of dynastic succession at Palenque is based on the work of Peter Mathews and Gerardo Aldana. Different successions were proposed by David Stuart, Linda Schele and David Friedel, Simon Martin, and Nicolai Grube. For my focus on the women rulers, succession makes more sense by placing Yohl Ik'nal as the daughter of Kan Bahlam I, Hun Pakal as her husband, Aj Ne Ohl Mat as her son, and Sak K'uk as her daughter and the mother of K'inich Janaab Pakal. After Pakal, succession is clearly established. Other early family trees are suggested by some Mayanists.

Book 1 in the *Mists of Palenque* series tells the story of Yohl Ik'nal, who ruled in her own right for twenty-two years, the first woman ruler of Lakam Ha. Her visionary abilities enabled her to predict and deflect enemy attack. She expanded construction in the city and brought a time of peace and prosperity to the people.

Book 2 is about Sak K'uk, whose times were steeped in turmoil after Lakam Ha suffered a terrible defeat by Kalakmul (Kan) in 611 CE. She became the earthly presence of the Goddess Muwaan Mat, guided the city through chaos, and held the throne until her son Pakal acceded at age twelve. No doubt she acted as regent for several more years.

Book 3 tells the story of Pakal and his wife, Tz'aakb'u Ahau the "Red Queen." It's essentially a profound love story where two disparate people overcome preconceptions to find each other's soul essence, and together restore the spiritual charter of the city.

Book 4 is about their children; the fourth son Tiwol Chan Mat and the woman he marries named K'inuuw Mat, a devotee of Goddess Ix Chel. She realizes her destiny to continue the lineage through their son K'inich Ahkal Mo' Nab III, but faces royal family intrigues and contends with a forbidden passion with Kan Bahlam, the first son.

Notes on Orthography (Pronunciation)

O rthography involves how to spell and pronounce Mayan words in another language such as English or Spanish. The initial approach used English-based alphabets with a romance language sound for vowels:

Hun – Hoon	Ne – Nay	Xoc – Shoke	Ix – Eesh
Ik – Eek	Yohl – Yole	Mat – Maat	May – Maie
Sak – Sahk	Ahau – Ah-how	Yum – Yoom	Ek – Ehk

Consonants of note are:

H – Him	J – Jar	X – "sh"
T – Tz or Dz	Ch – Child	

Mayan glottalized sounds are indicated by an apostrophe, and pronounced with a break in sound made in the back of the throat:

B'aakal	K'uk	Ik'nal	Ka'an	Tz'ak

Later the Spanish pronunciations took precedence. The orthography standardized by the Academia de Lenguas Mayas de Guatemala is used by most current Mayanists. The major difference is how H and J sound:

H – practically silent, only a soft aspiration as in hombre (ombray)

J – soft "h" as in house or Jose (Hosay)

There is some thought among linguists that the ancient Maya had different sounds for "h" and "j," leading to more dilemma. Many places, roads, people's names and other vocabulary have been pronounced for years in the old system. The Guatemala approach is less used in Mexico, and many words in my book are taken from Yucatek Mayan. So, I've decided to keep the Hun spelling rather than Jun for the soft "h." But for Pakal, I've resorted to Janaab rather than Hanab, the older spelling. I have an intuition that his name was meant by the ancient Mayas to have the harder "j" of English; this gives a more powerful sound.

For the Mayan word Lord – Ahau – I use the older spelling. You will see it written Ahaw and Ajaw in different publications. For English speakers,

Ahau leads to natural pronunciation of the soft "h" and encourages a longer ending sound with the "u" rather than "w."

Scholarly tradition uses the word Maya to modify most nouns, such as Maya people and Maya sites, except when referring to language and writing, when Mayan is used instead. Ordinary usage is flexible, however, with Mayan used more broadly as in Mayan civilization or Mayan astronomy. I follow this latter approach in my writing.

Names of ancient Maya cities posed challenges. Spanish explorers or international archeologists assigned most of the commonly used names. Many original city names have been deciphered, however, and I use these whenever they exist. Some cities have conflicting names, so I chose the one that made sense to me. The rivers were even more problematic. Many river names are my own creation, using Mayan words that best describe their characteristics. I provide a list of contemporary names for cities and rivers along with the Mayan names used in the story.

Acknowledgements

T wo-and-a-half centuries of Maya exploration and research underlie this story. Since the mid-seventeenth century, numerous expeditions penetrated the jungles, swamps and savannahs of southern Mexico, Guatemala, Belize, and Honduras in search of fabled cities of stone. Over the years, archeology and anthropology grew as scientific disciplines and began to reveal the history of the Maya people who once populated these magnificent structures. Recent advances in epigraphy, linguistics, ethnology, art history, and iconography have added depth and breadth to our understanding of their rich and complex culture. To all the experts in these fields, whose work has given me a foundation for creating characters and events, I owe untold gratitude. Many of these researchers were acknowledged in the first two books of this series. Several deserve particular recognition in shaping my conceptions of locale and ideas for characters and plot of The Red Queen.

Gerardo Aldana's brilliant interpretations of events leading to the reign of Pakal were my guiding lights for the story. (Aldana: *The Apotheosis of Janaab' Pakal*, 2007) Making his own translation of glyphs on the tablets of the Temple of Inscriptions, he deduced the process of ritual progression in which Pakal brought the Jeweled Sky Tree to maturity and reopened the portal of communication between earthly rulers and Sky Gods. This sixty-year process was Pakal's mission and destiny. Key plot elements were built around this process, including my creation of Lalak's role using sexual alchemy. Aldana's piecing together of conflicts and alliances among cities led to my creating Pakal's marriage and military alliances with B'aak, and the rescue and sanctuary offered to Mutul's ruler. Aldana also describes amazing calendric accomplishments exemplified in the 819-day count, and the Zuyua construct used to maintain elite prestige that will have a large role in the next book. Aldana's reading of glyphic texts inspired the major themes surrounding accession of Sak K'uk and Muwaan Mat, told in the second book of this series.

David Stuart is closely identified with Palenque, where he first visited as a toddler with his father, archeologist George Stuart. As a youth, David Stuart copied glyphs at Cobá and worked with Linda Schele interpreting drawings of the Cross Group tablets at Palenque. He became a leading epigrapher and made major advances in cracking the Maya hieroglyphic code. The Stuart's detailed work on Palenque's history provided an invaluable foundation for seeing the city and its rulers in a broad context. (Stuart & Stuart: *Palenque, Eternal City of the Maya*, 2008) David Stuart's exquisite renditions and interpretations of inscriptions from Temple XIX tablets enriched my understanding of later rulers and guide the setting for the sequel to Pakal's rule. (Stuart, D: *The Inscriptions from Temple XIX at Palenque*, 2005)

Edwin Barnhart oversaw the masterful Palenque Mapping Project, uncovering numerous hidden structures west of the Great Plaza and demonstrating that Palenque was a very large city. His detailed maps guided me time and again to conceptualize spatial locations within the city. Without these fabulous references, I could not describe the visual layout of plazas, palace complexes and temple-pyramids. He generously gave me permission to use and adapt his maps so readers can also get a visual image of the City of Great Waters as it spread between rivers across a narrow ridge of the Chiapas Mountains.

Adriana Malvido told the story of discovering the Red Queen's tomb from the perspective of a journalist. (Malvido: *La Reina Roja*, 2005) She was assigned to cover the work of Arnoldo Gonzalez Cruz and his INAH team during the spring of 1994, when they excavated the first Mayan queen's sarcophagus. The small opening in the stairway of Temple XIII was spotted by Fanny Lopez Jimenez, and she first observed the passage leading to an unknown substructure that held the queen's crypt. Arturo Romano Pacheco, the famed Mexican physical anthropologist, determined that the bones were those of a woman.

Further understanding of whose bones resided in the Red Queen's sarcophagus needed to wait for advances in bioarcheology. Studies using strontium isotope analysis of bones and skeletal DNA were reported by Vera Tiesler and Andrea Cucina. (Tiesler & Cucina: *Janaab' Pakal of Palenque: Reconstructing the Life and Death of a Maya Ruler*, 2006) These studies showed that Pakal and the Red Queen were born in different regions and did not share genetic DNA. The data eliminated Pakal's mother and grandmother, making the obvious candidate his wife, Tz'aakb'u Ahau. This upholds my story in which she is buried in the Temple XIII crypt, adjacent to Pakal's own mortuary pyramid.

Dennis Tedlock translated the *Popol Vuh*, giving us a poetic rendition of Maya creation mythology. His lyrical translations of several other ancient and colonial Maya documents provided examples of how to construct ceremonial language for scenes in my story. (Tedlock: *2000 Years of Mayan*

Literature, 2010) As I read the words of actual Maya scribes, in both Classic Cholan and phonetic English translation, it resonated deeply with some ancient cellular memory. This was the template I used for cadence, sentence structure and imagery when writing ceremonial and ritual language.

Prudence Rice provided fresh and instructive interpretations of Maya social and political organization, including the *may* cycle in which ceremonial and political leadership passed cooperatively among cities. (Rice, *Maya Political Science*, 2004) Her ideas about Maya warfare influenced my perspective that aggressive actions were primarily raids to take captives or destroy monuments, making a statement about power or delivering retribution for affronts. The ambitions of Kan to expand territorial control violated principles of the *may* cycle. The Classic Mayas did not engage in incessant warfare, although their conflicts seemed to escalate as their civilization faced stresses from resource depletion. Theories about the "Maya collapse" that occurred around 900 CE will play an important role in the fourth, and final, book of this series.

Patricia Morris Cardona and Daniel J. Cardona share my passion for the Mayas. Their book *Female Sex Magic: The Secret Path to Healing, Love, Longevity, and Enlightenment* (2014) gave invaluable background in theory and techniques of sexual alchemy. These profound insights into the power of human generativity were of great assistance in writing the scenes for rebuilding the portal to the Gods.

The richness of my experiences with indigenous Mayas goes beyond description. I could not write about the ancient Maya without the insights gained in ceremony and study with mentors Hunbatz Men and Aum Rak Sapper, who initiated me into Maya spirituality and the examples of ancient rituals provided by Tata Pedro Cruz, Don Alejandro Cirilio Oxlaj, Don Pedro Pablo, and members of the Grand Maya Itzá Council of Priests and Elders. With Miguel Angel Vergara, I experienced mystical aspects of Maya spirituality and the deep connections with other ancient cultures.

Thanks to my beta readers Lisa Jorgensen, Lynn Albright, and Tina Schweikert for perusing the first version and providing invaluable feedback. A special note of appreciation is due to Tina Schweikert, whose eagle-eyed editing helped me correct numerous grammatical and spelling errors. Endless accolades and big hugs to my husband David Gortner, intrepid web researcher who ferreted out esoteric facts and elusive images, slaved away redesigning maps, made insightful suggestions, and encouraged me to create a story both engaging and authentic.

Other Works By Author

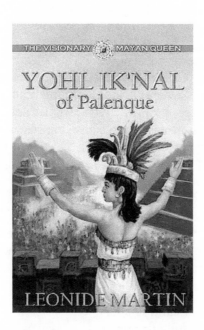

The Visionary Mayan Queen: Yohl Ik'nal of Palenque
Mists of Palenque Series Book 1

Amazon Kindle Top 100 Books -- Amazon #1 in Historical Fiction and Historical Fiction Romance - Ancient Worlds

In misty tropical jungles 1500 years ago, a royal Mayan girl with visionary powers – Yohl Ik'nal – was destined to become the first Mayan woman ruler. Last of her royal lineage, her accession would fulfill her father's ambitions. Yohl Ik'nal put aside personal desires and the comfortable world of palace women to prepare as royal heir. Love for her father steeled her will and sharpened her skills. As she underwent intensive training for rulership, powerful forces allied to overthrow the dynasty and plotted with enemy cities to attack.

As the first Queen of Palenque, she built temples to honor her father and her Gods, protected her city and brought prosperity to the people. Her visionary powers foresaw enemy attack and prevented defeat. In the midst of betrayal and revenge, through court intrigues and power struggles, she guided her people wisely and found a love that sustained her. As a seer, she knew times of turmoil were coming and succession to the throne was far from certain. Could she prepare her headstrong daughter for rulership or help her weak son become a charismatic leader? Her actions could lead to ruin or bring her city to greatness.

Centuries later Francesca, part-Mayan archeologist, helps her team at Palenque excavate the royal burial of a crimson skeleton, possibly the first Mayan queen's tomb ever discovered. She never anticipated how it would impact her life and unravel a web of ancient bonds.

Praise from Reviewers and Readers:

"A story that is fully imagined yet as real as the ancient past that it gives voice to once again... The characters here are fully realized, vivid and alive, and often do surprising things... The reader is able to understand the truth of these people's lives and struggles while also welcomed in to a conception of the world that is bigger than anything they might have expected or experienced before."

~ Writer's Digest 2nd Annual Self-Published eBook Awards (2015)

"... storytelling that leaves you breathless and amazed at the life Yohl Ik'nal leads as she uses her visionary ability ... in an era of uncertainty. It's about royalty and leadership, about family and strength, determination and faith."

~ The Bookreader Review

"Spellbinding, exciting and beautifully paints a picture (of) the world of the ancient royal Mayan Queens."

~ S. Malbeouf

"A page turner ... draws the reader in with the drama of the era... One can smell the incense, feel the tension, share the spirituality, experience the battles, and live the lives of the characters."

~ H. and N. Rath

"... vibrant storytelling, strong dialogue and authentic characters ... that ring true to the Mayan culture... stunning job of keeping this story fast-paced, compelling, emotional and engaging to the very end."

~ S. Gallardo

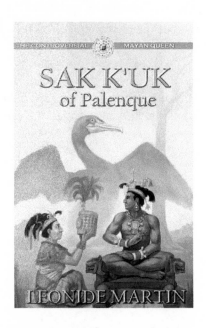

The Controversial Mayan Queen: Sak K'uk of Palenque
Mists of Palenque Series Book 2

Amazon Kindle Top 100 Books -- Amazon #1 in Historical Fiction and Historical Fiction Romance - Ancient Worlds

Strong-willed Sak K'uk, daughter of Yohl Ik'nal, assumes rulership of Lakam Ha after her brother is killed in the devastating attack by arch-enemy Kan, which leaves her people in chaos. She faces dissident nobles and spiritual crisis caused by destruction of the sacred portal to the Gods. Undertaking a perilous Underworld journey, she invokes the power of Primordial Goddess Muwaan Mat to help her accede to the throne and hold it for her son, Janaab Pakal, until he is old enough to become ruler. His destiny is to restore the portal and bring Lakiam Ha to greatness. Their intense trials together forge a special bond that proves both a blessing and a curse.

In modern times archeologist Francesca continues her quest to uncover the identity of the crimson skeleton found by her team in a rich burial at Palenque. Further examination of the bones confirms that the skeleton was a royal and important woman, dubbed The Red Queen. Francesca is also perplexed by her grandmother's cryptic message to discover her true self by listening to the lightning in her blood.

Praise from Reviewers and Readers:

"Martin's writing and characterization are both excellent ... she writes with loving detail about ... Mayan life ... The story is a seamless blend of history and mythology ... Sak K'uk believes that Pakal is meant to be the next ruler ... (but) Ek Chuuah, who was injured and exiled ... will stop at nothing to harm the royal family, even to the point of devising a plan to desecrate one of their holiest shrines... can't wait to read the third book in the series."

~ The Seattle Book Review, Jo Niederhoff (2017)

"The Controversial Mayan Queen... is well-done, entertaining, and revealing... profile of a Mayan leader simultaneously struggling with family life and the future of her people... the emotionally charged and complex relationship between Sak K'uk and her son... lends it an extra dimension that is unexpectedly and compellingly engrossing."

~ The Midwest Book Review, Diane Donovan, Senior Reviewer (2017)

"The author has great skills at world building and crafting a story that will keep the reader engaged and entertained from cover to cover. Great author voice and writing style... an entertaining mix."

~ Writer's Digest (2016)

"Beautifully written account of the Mayans, their culture, and how one woman held them together! This book gives the reader an inside view of this ancient culture and the reader just can't help but learn something from it! I guarantee if you like ancient history told in story form as I do, you won't be able to put this book down!"

~ D (Amazon reviewer)

"... this second book in the Mists of Palenque series... weaves a fascinating tale of the transition in the leadership of Lakam Ha after the reign of Yohl Ik'nal... reveals the interplay of events that allow the prophecies to be realized... The tale is a superb one and I highly recommend it for other readers."

~ Peter H. Berasi

"I have visited Palenque and other Mayan ruins, and Leonide Martin makes these cities come vividly alive for me... incredibly engaging scenes, her description is masterful... research is thorough ... made me feel like I was walking through the world of the ancient Maya ... I'm especially thrilled that the royal women of the Mayan culture are the focus of the series... fantastic supplemental reading in any class on ancient Mexico or Guatemala."

~ M.M. Drew

"If you are a history buff - or if you are not - you will enjoy this well researched and well written book... will open a window into pre-Columbian Central America and allow you to understand the habits, the beliefs, the culture and the values of the Maya... "wrapped" in a story that is interesting and intriguing. This book is going into my "read again" list... You won't go wrong buying this book. Settle down and enjoy it."

~ A. Pabon

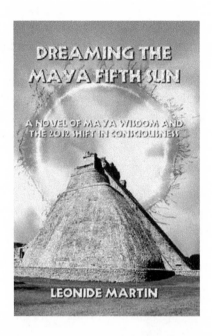

Dreaming the Maya Fifth Sun: A Novel of Maya Wisdom and the 2012 Shift in Consciousness

The lives of two women, one modern and one an ancient Maya priestess, weave together as the end of the Mayan calendar approaches in 2012. ER nurse Jana Sinclair's recurring dream compels her journey to jungle-shrouded Mayan ruins where she discovers links with ancient priestess Yalucha, who was mandated to hide her people's esoteric wisdom from the Spaniards. Jana's reluctant husband is swept into strange experiences and opposes Jana's quest. Risking everything, Jana follows her inner guidance and returns to Mexico to unravel her dream. In the Maya lands, dark shamanic forces attempt to deter her and threaten her life.

Ten centuries earlier, Yalucha's life unfolds as a healer at Tikal where she faces heartbreak when her beloved, from an enemy city, is captured. Later in another incarnation at Uxmal, she again encounters him but circumstances thwart their relationship. She journeys to Chichén Itzá to join other priests and priestesses in a ritual profoundly important to future times.

As the calendar counts down to December 21, 2012, Jana answers the call across centuries to re-enact the mystical ritual that will birth the new era, confronting shamanic powers and her husband's ultimatum—and activates forces for healing that reach into the past as well as the future.

Fans of historical fiction with adventure and romance will love this story of an ancient Maya Priestess and contemporary woman who unravel secret bonds to fulfill the Maya prophecy that can make the difference for the planet's future.

Praise from Reviewers and Readers

"Travel through time and space to ancient Maya realms ... details are accurate, giving insight into Maya magic and mysticism and bringing their message of the new era to come."

~ Aum-Rak Sapper, Maya Priestess and Daykeeper

"Few people have listened to this call and made pilgrimage to ancient Maya centers, but many will follow ... to serve the planet in the Fifth Solar Cycle."

~ Hunbatz Men, Itza Maya Elder, Daykeeper and Shaman

"...power-house historical novel ...unlocks (Mayan) civilization... This well documented book is spellbinding, romantic, thought provoking and gives an insightful look into the spiritual side of ancient Mayas...a must read!"

~ J. Grimsrud, Maya travel guide

CPSIA information can be obtained
at www.ICGtesting.com
Printed in the USA
BVHW03s0446100318
510213BV00002B/5/P